A CURSE OF FLAME AND ASH

Books by Kaitlyn L. Hill

A Dark Duet Series
A Witch's Cottage: Part I
Bloodstone: Part II

A CURSE OF FLAME AND ASH

A REALM OF CHAOS BOOK ONE

KAITLYN L. HILL

First Published by Tainted Fate Publishing House 2024

First edition

ISBN: HB: 978-1-7388899-2-1; PB: 978-1-7388899-3-8; eBook: 978-1-7388899-4-5

Cover art by K.D. Ritchie – Story Wrappers

Editing by Jade Church

Blurb by Jessie Cunniffe – Book Blurb Magic

Map illustration by Rena Violet – Covers by Violet

To find out more about the author and their books visit www.kaitlynlhill.ca and sign up for her newsletter.

Content Warning

This book is +18 with mature content. This book is strongly not recommended for minors. Dark themes and explicit sexual content are very prevalent in this series. Please consider all triggering content before reading.

non-consensual sex | rape | foul language | stockholm syndrome | abuse (physical, sexual, verbal, emotional) | domestic and family violence | explicit sexual scenes | detailed bloodshed/gore | alcoholism | drug abuse | anxiety and panic attacks | attempted murder | attempted rape | incest | misogyny | attempted suicide | thoughts of suicide | torture | death

For those who found their light in the darkest of moments.

Pronunciation Guide

Aberevin: AIB-rev-in

Agrafina: ag-ra-FEE-na

Aideen: ay-DEEN

Ammar al-Nazir: aa-MAAR al-NA-zeer

Andraste: aan-DRAS-tay

Aramis: air-A-miss

Basilius: ba-sil-EE-us

Cara: KAR-a

Conláed: KON-lee

Düghall: DOO-gawl

Elowyn: ell-O-win

Ellaria: ella-REE-a

Fairban: FAIR-ban

Haldwin: hal-d-WIN

hiisi: HEE-see

Iniga: ih-n-EE-g-uh

Iris: EYE-rus

keiju: KAY-ew

Keniris: ken-I-ris

Kenna: KEN-a

Linnaea: li-NAI-aw

Molvys: MOL-vis

Niafell: NEE-a-fell

Orla: OR-la

Oulixeus: uh-LEK-sis

Penre: PEN-ray

Rhyddean: reye-DEEN

Rune: roon

Solandis: so-LAN-dis

Sévérine: sev-err-EEN

Playlist

Heart of Darkness by Secession Studios, Greg Dombrowski

To Build A Home (feat. Patrick Watson) by The Cinematic Orchestra

Where is my Mind? by Yoav, Emily Browning

Paint it Black by Hidden Citizens, Rånya

Big Bad Wolf by Roses and Revolutions

Onward & Upward by Tommee Profitt, Fleurie

Love The Way You Lie by Eminen, Rhianna

Black Widow by Martin Phipps

Happy Together by Filter

Nocturne No. III by Yanson

Madness by Ruelle

Scars by Boy Epic

Climb by ADONA

Even If It's A Lie - Demo by Matt Maltese

Lucifer's Waltz by Secession Studios

Valiant by Phantasia Music

Can't Help Falling in Love - Instrumental by Vesislava

Talk by Hozier

Mombasa by 2CELLOS

Make Me Believe by The EverLove

Experience by Ludovico Einaudi, Daniel Hope, I Virtuosi Italiani

Paradise Circus by Massive Attack

Madeline by Kiki Rockwell

My Darkest Hour by Jimmy Svensson

Waves by Dean Lewis

Would That I - Hozier

I Found by Amber Run

Don't Save Me by Chxrlotte

Unholy by Ground Zero Academy Orchestra

I'm Coming For It by UNSECRET, Sam Tinnesz, GREYLEE

Control by Halsey

Unstoppable by Sia

Who Is She? By I Monster

Hunger by Ross Copperman

I'm Yours by Isabel LaRosa

Girls Like You by Vitamin String Quartet

Vendetta by UNSECRET, Krigarè

Safe & Sound (feat. Joy Williams and John Paul White) by Taylor Swift

In Flames by Digital Daggers

Bad Dream - Ruelle

No Time To Die by Sybrid, Brittney Bouchard

Never Surrender by Liv Ash

Between the Bars by Elliot Smith

The Worst In Me by Bad Omens

Sober by TOOL

Lost Without You by Freya Ridings

Darkside by Neoni

Soldier by Tommee Profitt

Run Run Rebel by Hidden Citizens, ESSA

Take It All by Ruelle

City of the Dead by Eurielle

Tonight by R3YAN, BLVKES

Dancing in a Daydream by Roses & Revolutions, Weathers

Way Down We Go - KALEO

How Villains Are Made by Madalen Duke

Water Court
Soul Court
Light Court
Aegir Sea
Air Court
Earth Court
Dark Court
Fire Court
Abaeuin Court
Turban Court
Peace Court
Rhyddean Court
Eternal Sea
Niafell
Veil
N
S

CHAPTER 1

Girls don't gamble. At least, men in Rhyddean believed so and I revelled in proving them wrong. The glittering prize of coins, illegal Fae jewels, and a peculiar dagger held my attention as crude remarks swirled around me. Their jokes increased in vulgarity the longer I ignored them, my full breasts now the primary source of their material.

Go ahead, make your remarks. The more they jeered, the less they noticed my assessing gaze. Little did they know that their tells were obvious, but arrogance was a common trait among men. They didn't need to evaluate others' emotions and determine the best way to interact in every given situation.

The resentment I held for men possessing that freedom and power bubbled through me, mixing with my distrust for how they used women in their schemes all hid behind my neutral features. I reached for my cup and gulped the remaining alcohol, savouring the way it flowed through my veins and burned away the emotions I avoided on a daily basis, wishing to banish them forever.

Two fiddlers riled up the crowd who clapped in tune, encouraging a confident dancer—Cara, my closest friend.

Sparks of excitement surged through my veins as my eyes fell upon the dagger once more. These hands were never meant to wield a weapon, but it called to me all the same. Its presence had drawn me to the game in the first place. Its quillon, expanding like branches, rested on the illegal jewels while the jagged blade nestled between coins, making my mouth water, craving to possess it, as if being reunited with a past lover.

The hooded man against the wall wagered the unique weapon. A single sconce above him created an eerie light around his hood, a halo hiding his face in shadow like an angel of death—one of the fabled demons from the Veil. But his presence radiated serenity. A chaotic serenity—but serenity, nonetheless.

The entire round proved easy. Too easy. The man with round jowls brushed his nose every time he lied. The man to his left laughed a little too hard when the dealer drew a desirable card. My breasts created a remarkable distraction for the onion-scented man next to me, who lost all notion of what occurred in the game. Squeezing my arms against my sides probably didn't help as I was wearing one of Cara's smaller dresses that unequivocally displayed the curvature of my chest.

The hooded man against the wall was harder to read, but I figured him out eventually too. Ever so slightly, his index finger would slide against the edge of his cards. Such a minor movement that no one would recognise it if not searching for it. Even I almost missed it. I caught it by the scratch of cracked skin running along the rough card paper—it should have been indecipherable, but I'd always had a good ear.

I had them beat. I *always* had them beat.

The table erupted into a fury as I tossed my winning cards face up upon the glinting treasure. Even the hooded man, remaining relatively passive throughout the game, let out a frustrated grunt and threw his cards to the wooden table, sticky with booze.

With a wide grin, I embraced the loot and drew it to my chest, never tiring of the feeling that accompanied victory. The rush that overcame me once I identified each of their tells, knowing they'd never discover mine, and the final sensation of teeny, tiny electric impulses surging through my body as I claimed my winnings.

"Sorry, boys. You were all only playing for second." I winked at the round-faced man. He gripped my wrist as the coins and jewels clinked against each other in the leather satchel, jerking me across the table.

"What are you playing at, little girl?" He scowled and panic clutched my throat, as if trying to swallow my voice. I talked big and Cara had taught me a bit about fighting, but I'd never actually experienced a genuine struggle outside of our lessons.

He stared down at me with plain, beady brown eyes, his thin lips drooping. He was only slightly taller than me, with a square frame built like a bombard, chasing away my brashness.

"Nothing," I snapped, faking a calm exterior to hide the fear prickling the back of my neck. His hold on me tightened, and he wrenched my arm toward him. Sinking my teeth into my lower lip to suppress a cry, I took a slow and deep inhale when the hooded man pushed the bully away.

"She won fair and square, Damien. It's not her fault she's more clever than you," his smooth, almost familiar voice chided the mercenary. I gave him a thankful look, but still couldn't make out his face beneath the shadows of his hood. "I knew you had 'em. Shit, I'm six shots in and I had 'em. What gave me away?" he asked, fairly steadily for consuming so much liquor, but disappointment threaded through his voice while handing over his dagger.

"That's for me to know and for you to figure out." I grinned, my confidence returning as I strapped the sheath of his dagger around my waist. *My* dagger. Even beneath his hood, I knew he smiled back at me.

"Have we met before?" Squaring my shoulders to him, I squinted my eyes, attempting to uncover his secrets.

"Perhaps in a dream." He nodded, similar to a bow, and strode out of the dark tavern. I watched after him, curious what he'd meant, as a boisterous cheer erupted from the dance floor and I caught a glimpse of Cara's wheat-coloured hair twirling.

Spotting me at the same time, she abandoned the dance as I made my way over to an empty bar stool.

"You won." Cara slid in next to me, eyeing my new weapon and stuffed satchel.

"Did you doubt me?"

"Never."

"This round's on me." I grinned and waved two fingers at the barkeep, Remy.

"Foster's going to be upset that you're gambling and drinking," Cara warned and I snorted at the mention of her older brother, my only other friend.

"So? How else does he expect me to afford my new life? Why does he even have to know?" I needed to get the fuck out of here. I needed to go find a life of my own and live it.

Oulixeus, my uncle, would be furious if I ran away. His wrath and obsession would follow me to the ends of this realm and into the Veil, using all of his connections to find me and if he succeeded... A shiver raced down my spine, imagining the punishment he'd unleash upon me.

It's what had convinced me to ask Cara for help. I hated to ask. She did more than enough for me already, but I had no connections, no papers, and no idea where to flee. She'd excitedly agreed with one stipulation—I had to learn how to fight if I were to be a single woman living alone.

I wanted her to join me. Cara needed to find a life of her own too, but she refused to leave her grandparents behind and they were too old to travel. Even with Foster taking care of them, she wouldn't dare to leave.

In five days, I'd ride away with everything I needed. Cara refused to divulge precisely *how* she did it, but she'd obtained the appropriate papers required to own property. And her friend, Nolan, a merchant from Aberevin, would sneak me from the castle hidden in his wagon and take me to his village.

I'd be prepared for my new life, having snuck to Cara's grandparents' so often over the years. Grandpapi, as he insisted I call him, taught me to grow crops and care for livestock. Whereas, Grandmama taught me how to garden, cook, and brew herbal remedies. Authentic herbalists were rare, and that's how I'd earn a living on my own.

Yet, the most crucial art they'd imparted was winemaking. In solitude, my thoughts roamed untethered, unsettling my very core. The realms my mind explored in the absence of alcohol... Not even the promise of freedom could salvage me from those shadowy depths.

Sipping the dry, full-bodied wine from my chalice, I pushed the worry away and instead focused on what tonight's winnings offered me—a cottage with land and livestock, with enough to leave behind for my surrogate family to ease the burden of taxes.

Cara nudged my elbow and tilted her head toward the two men sitting nearby.

"It's true!" A scraggly, bearded man hiccupped while slurping from behind his tankard.

"Bullshit! If we lost the war, our lands would be swarming with Fae!" his comrade insisted.

"Roman told me himself, King Evander's best Spellcaster blew up the Fae king!"

"Ah, Roman's a lunatic. Though the thought of the Fae king's son ruling sure has me sittin' uncomfortable."

"Aramis? He's more diabolical than his father! My friend saw him on the frontline once, said his entire body was engulfed in flames, ripping hearts and spinal cords straight through men's chests instead of fighting honourably with a sword."

"Let's hope he's dead, too."

The scraggly bearded man stumbled into me as they walked away, nodding an apology before staggering off.

Cara and I looked at each other. I laughed, shaking my head at their drunken nonsense, while her brows narrowed, taking their conversation more seriously.

"Men." I rolled my eyes, grabbing the chalice Remy had finished refilling, and surveyed the tavern's joviality. Patrons danced and drank in the infectious mirth, but something else felt off... Threatening. Damien, the mercenary from the game of cards, sat with his eyes boring into me, the source of the sensation pinching my neck.

"Ready to leave after this one?" Cara shifted on her stool as Damien's glare tightened my throat, tangling my words in a web of unease.

"Yeah, I'm ready."

Gravel crunched beneath our feet as we walked along the road lined with tall, lush bushes separating us from fields reeking of fresh manure stretched beyond as far as the eye could see. We reached the halfway point between the castle and village, neither in sight as the moonlight illuminated our path.

I smiled at Cara and the way the stars shone in her honey-brown eyes. As much as I tried to enjoy the prospect of freedom, I couldn't stop thinking about when we'd part ways and say goodbye. Inching towards her with each step, I wrapped my arm around her waist and pulled her into me. She bounced her hip off of mine and we swayed with each other along the gravelled road.

"Don't forget about me, okay," I told her.

"You? I could never forget about you," she promised. "You're too much of a pain in my ass, Princess." Resting her head on my shoulder, we squeezed each other tight before letting go and continuing a steadier walk back to the castle.

"Do you think it's true?" she asked, the night failing to conceal the concern etched across her face.

"Do I think what's true?"

"What those men at the bar had said about the war being over?"

"No. I agree with his friend. If the Fae had won, we'd all be enslaved by now. You know how it is. These rumours resurface every few years." I squeezed Cara's hand to comfort her.

"It feels different this time. I've heard murmurs in the castle—"

"Shh." I cut Cara off. A deathly silence surfaced, but my unnatural hearing, as my mother called it, detected something. Leaves rustled in the depths of the tall shrubs surrounding our path. Branches swayed as the leaves' murmuring amplified. A cold, damp air settled around us.

"I hear it too," Cara whispered as I squinted into the foliage. The moon's light cast a sliver of light into the shrubbery, illuminating the outline of a head. I parted my lips to tell Cara to run when my entire body was lifted into the air and pinned to the ground.

Pieces of gravel pierced my skin as a large, leather-armoured body lay on top of me. With a shriek, I attempted to push the man off, overhearing Cara shout in the midst of her own struggle.

The body on top of me laughed.

"Think you're so clever, don't you, little girl?" The enraged voice was familiar.

"Get... off!" I grunted, shoving my palms into his chest as he chuckled again.

"Stupid little girl. Win that dagger and don't even know how to use it, eh? It's okay. I'll show you." The stench of poorly distilled booze wafted from his lips and I grimaced as I looked up into eyes I recognised. Damien. The mercenary just couldn't let my win at the card table go.

My pulse thumped along the side of my throat, begging me to run, to punch, to do something, but I froze. A man, thrice as large as me, pinned me to the ground with his hands wrapped around my wrists, next to my head. My hips flailed, but he didn't move.

"Push up!" Cara's voice distantly instructed. I couldn't see her, but instantly, I recalled a specific manoeuvre she'd taught me. I dug the heels of my feet into the gravel and pushed my hips into Damien's groin. His entire body fell forward and his forehead smacked against the ground, as I twisted my head to the side to avoid being squished by his massive torso. I readied to wrap my arms around his waist to reduce his mobility, but I moved too slowly. Damien caught on to my strategy and rushed a hand to my face, holding me firmly against the ground.

Pebbles scratched my cheek as I squirmed beneath him and clenched my teeth around one of his fingers near my mouth. Biting until a warm liquid ran over my tongue.

CRACK!

My jaw slacked, releasing the digit, and my skull throbbed from where his fist met my head. Tears stung beneath my eyelids as the entire world spun around me. Another fist collided with my face, snapping my head to the opposite side.

More blood seeped onto my tongue, but this time, it belonged to me. My lip stung from where it split open and a haze clouded my vision.

The attacker straddled me as he explored my dress, his weight restricting my lungs from expanding. Pudgy hands dipping between my breasts and pulling the material to the side, exposing a nipple to the brisk night. I shifted my hips again, hoping to bump him over me again, but the pounding in my head and eardrums disorientated me. His hands pushed further down to my waist.

"No." The plea quietly left my mouth and the daze slightly broke. Blinking rapidly, my sight continued to clear and reveal Damien's sick grin.

"She's beautiful." He unsheathed the dagger strapped to my waist, the moonlight glinting off its intricate shape. "I wonder how sharp she is."

The man held the blade to my throat, and my body involuntarily froze, seized by paralysis. Whimpers caught in my throat, wanting to surface but unable to scream.

Hot blood ran down my throat, and my skin burned where the blade pierced deeper into my neck. This was it. I would die here in the gravel all because of a man with too much pride to lose to a girl.

I prepared myself for the pain, for the dagger to slice through my vocal cords and stunt my ability to scream, shout, cry, or even whimper. It would be worse than anything my parents or uncle had previously inflicted upon me.

His free hand continued to tear through my dress, reaching under my linen skirt and sliding a hand up my thigh, wanting to take more than just my life.

There were no feelings for me to suppress because my body refused to respond in any sort of way. Even my mind shut down, ready to transport me away from the assault upon me. His fingers continued up as the blade slipped further into my skin. Slicing deep and long.

A tear escaped my locked eyelids when the burn of the blade lessened and his vile fingers inching closer to my centre stopped. His hand hesitated on the scar marking my left inner thigh.

He shuffled off of me and I gasped for air.

"We gotta get outta here. Now!"

Rolling over, I witnessed two men lying on the ground. One knelt over, clutching his head and crying. The other lay in a fetal position, cupping his groin. A third man backed away from Cara, and with a hint of excitement in her eyes, she spat blood onto the ground and raised her fists to her face.

"Scared?" she taunted.

"Fuck you!" He grunted and helped his friends off of the ground.

"Think you could handle it?" Cara laughed as the four men ran away. The dagger lay next to me, my blood coating the once-shining blade. Two more drops splattered from my neck next to it, the dirt greedily absorbing it.

I brought my hand to my neck and traced the length of the wound, encouraging more hot liquid to dribble onto the blood-stained ground. A heated anger swirled with a newfound tenacity. I should be dead and that thought eclipsed through me, reaffirming the time to leave Rhyddean neared. To stop cowering and leave before anyone else robbed me of the chance to live freely.

More movement in the bushes caught my attention and I leaned forward, trying to see into the shadows between the branches, but darkness encompassed whatever lurked in the depths.

Cara knelt next to me, but my focus didn't break. "I'm so sorry, Elle! I tried to come to you, but... what are you looking at?" We both gazed into the shadows. I thought I heard the steady pulse of a heart, but saw nothing.

"Nothing." I deserted the concern, attributing it to shock producing hallucinations. But as Cara took my hand, I could've sworn I heard the swishing of a cloak

CHAPTER 2

Heavy drops of rain splattered on the ground, thudding against the soil and leaving red welts on my skin. I held my skirts and ran as fast as I could, away from the heart-wrenching wailing.

Branches caught my dress, ripping away pieces of silk. One grabbed my hair, and I skidded to the muddying ground, hissing as strands ripped.

Trees grew taller and further apart and mist floated between trunks. I didn't know where I ran, but I had to run away. Stopping, I wrapped myself in my arms and spun. Round, round, round.

I collapsed to the ground and stretched out my arms, my fingers spread in the dirt. But as I lifted my hand, I didn't see mud. A burgundy liquid coated my palm—blood. Tears trickled down my cheeks as something dragged across the ground toward me, whirling the leaves into a frenzy...

Lurching over my knees, my chest heaved as air fell from the room. A hand reached towards mine, but I pulled away.

"It was a nightmare." Words sweet as honey called to me, and strands of warm wheat-coloured hair surrounded a comforting face. Cara—but blood seeped from the corners of her eyes, staining her round cheeks, and a haze blurred my peripherals.

I pulled back as a scream caught in my throat.

"Elle, it's okay, you're with me."

"The blood—" My hands cupped Cara's face, and I desperately tried to wipe the blood away, but more spilled from her eyes.

"Blood?" Stopping the sweep of my thumbs and forcing me to steady, the red I believed to be staining her ivory skin disappeared with each flutter of my eyelids. She wore a simple grey linen nightgown and a matching one fit snugly around my soft curves, a patchwork blanket stitched with bright yellow flowers spread across the both of us.

The wooden frame of the bed creaked as Cara shifted closer to comfort me. We didn't lay in my bed, surrounded by cold stone walls, and I recalled sneaking into Cara's grandparents' cottage to dress my wound last night.

"Was it the same dream as before?"

Yes, but... Something had changed. There had never been blood before.

Studying my friend's eyes, I decided not to share those bits with her. She worried enough.

"Yeah." I faked a smile and leaned on the lumpy pillow. Nothing stood out as luxurious here, but it felt more comfortable than the tower I'd called home since my seventh birthday, when my parents had locked me inside, far away from the rest of my sisters.

A small single bed sat under a window framed by burlap curtains, recycled from vegetable sacks. A three-drawer dresser stood hardly a foot away from where Cara lay, and two trunks stacked inches away from me hid the portion of last night's winnings that I intended to leave. Cara and her grandparents wouldn't accept the money, so I'd wait to reveal its location when saying my last goodbyes.

"Let me check your cut." She removed the linen tied around my neck and her astonishment became evident in her hushed exclamation.

"What?"

"The cut! It's—Elle, it's almost gone!" Wide eyes carved her face into an expression of disbelief.

"What?" I grabbed my neck. No sting, puffy flesh, nor blood. I outstretched my arm, and Cara passed me the simple hand mirror from the dresser. Sure enough, it looked more like a paper cut than a near-death wound. Only a thin scab sat over the cut.

"I knew Grandmama's ointment worked well, but damn. Maybe she is a witch?" Cara gaped as I continued to study the cut, along with the other marks on my body.

A slight yellow discolouration marked my skin where there should've been deep indigo and maroon bruises, and while my muscles were tender, I swallowed and spoke easier than when we'd first arrived at the cottage. My wounds always healed quicker than most, but these had healed unnaturally fast.

"Yeah, maybe," I whispered, returning the mirror to her and sneaking back under the quilt as a chilling unease washed over me, contemplating the rapidly fading bruises.

Cara stood, and cold air swept under the quilt to kiss my skin. I groaned, not ready to meet the brisk dawn air yet. Changing in the tiny gap between the bed and dresser, Cara tilted her head. "Why do you think those men left so abruptly last night?"

Pulling the patched fabric over my head, I hid my face and quivering lungs from her.

The mercenary felt *it* while exploring my thighs, excited to put me in my place. The scar I'd received on my sixteenth birthday, the night Oulixeus claimed me as his own by branding the letter *O* to my inner thigh. No one spoke of it, but everyone, including my parents, knew I belonged to Oulixeus.

I loved him long before that night. He'd shown me kindness when no one else did after falling out of my parents' favour. He visited me, brought me presents, allowed me to sneak into the library and gardens, and ensured the maintenance of my chamber.

As I matured into a young teenager, our relationship grew sensual, and I fell in love with him. But like a flash of lightning, he changed from loving to manipulative and cruel. Maybe a sick part of me still loved him, or maybe I just clung to the hope he'd shift back to the man I remembered.

"Do you think it's because I was kicking their asses?" Cara tried lightening the mood.

"Yeah." A laugh slipped through my lips as I firmly reined in my thoughts. Cara could never know about the mark. It wasn't her burden to bear.

"Speaking of which, we should train today. It'll be good to know what it's like to fight while injured, too. I want fighting to become so second nature, you don't freeze." Cara ripped the cosy blanket from me and threw a clean dress at me.

"Remind me to thank Grandpapi for teaching you to fight." I rose to my knees and pulled the night shift over my head as the spring air marred my skin with goose flesh.

"Oh, he never taught me."

"He didn't?" Cara's grandfather was a retired soldier, so I'd always assumed she learned everything from him. "Then who—"

The bedroom door burst open and my shoulders jumped as I clutched the dress in my hands tighter to hide my exposed body. Foster stood in the frame, his chest rapidly rising and falling. His tousled sorrel hair cascaded over his forehead and dark circles laid beneath his eyes, the same soft-brown as Cara's.

"Foster! What the—"

"Shit," Foster mumbled as his eyes landed on me and my naked body behind the material in my hands. Discomfort painted his cheeks a bright shade of crimson.

"Sorry." He whipped around, back facing us, as he continued speaking. "We need to hurry."

"You can't just burst into my room," Cara scolded her brother as she helped me into the dress, tugging the hem down once I slipped into it.

"It's safe, Foster. I'm clothed," I said as I adjusted the laces in the back.

Foster met my gaze, seriousness burning through him. "Oulixeus is looking for you. The war's over."

Cara and I shared a startled glance, our simultaneous questions chasing Foster into the kitchen.

For over two hundred years, the Fae fought to regain control over the mortal courts, claiming to want nothing more than to unite Niafell into a single realm and build our strength against any foreign threat. But mortals refused to believe the Fae's supposedly pure intentions, recalling the Fae's brutal enslavement of mortals centuries before.

Dawn's light crept into the cottage, but Grandmama and Grandpapi remained sleeping as we slipped into our boots and cloaks. Reaching for the brass handle, a phantom voice sharply murmured in my mind. *Take me. My dagger.*

Caution flickered across my thoughts, warning me of the shadowed whisper. Objects don't speak. But I couldn't afford to dwell on it. Not now. I swiftly belted the sheath around my waist and grabbed the satchel, holding half of my winnings.

We stepped into Ravenwood Forest, a large wood sprawling from the west to the north of the castle, to hide from any prying eyes. Most refrained from venturing into it. Even though the mortals banned Fae centuries ago, many claimed evil magical creatures still roamed the trees.

"Oulixeus knows you're not in the castle and he's looking for you." Foster provided a bit more detail as Cara sent him daggers of frustration through her eyes.

But his intel didn't make sense to me. "Oulixeus? No, he's on the battlefront for another two months."

"The war is over, Elle. Oulixeus returned a few hours ago, already drinking."

He'd be visiting me then, and if he found me gone... Tremors rippled through my legs as phantom pains stung all over my body.

"And the war, did we—" I stopped hearing Cara as Foster briefly stopped and reached his hand out to me, a sign I moved too slowly for his anxious state. Exhaling away the fear building inside of me, I took his hand and allowed him to guide me through the mossy woods.

Birds chirped in the tree canopy, oblivious to the news Foster reported. "We lost. We lost and the Fae are riding to Rhyddean. That's all I managed to hear before rushing to find you two." He looked back at me, eyes grazing the now paper-cut thin slice on my neck. "What happened?"

"Nothing."

Foster studied our faces before continuing to help me navigate the forest floor, dodging small moss-covered rocks embedded into the ground. Dew collected on the hem of my cloak as Foster squeezed my slender hand, as if to reassure me he wouldn't have judged the truth. I sent a *thank you* pulse back to him.

The rising sun bathed the forest-edge in a caressing golden glow, though brooding clouds promised to snatch away the day's embrace.

Across the wildflower field lurked Elmswood Castle, enclosed by a stout wall crafted from brownish-red stones. The ancient castle, built by Toivo, the God of Truth, featured a newer wall erected by Rhyddean's first mortal king, intended to ward off magical creatures. My tower jutted from the southwest corner. Did he know they'd also be used to keep princesses inside?

"The wall's guarded." Cara turned to Foster, an eyebrow lifted. Blocking the rising sun's rays with a hand, I squinted to see multiple guards pacing.

With little threat to the north, guards seldomly monitored this section of the wall with a hole buried beneath lilac bushes, making it ideal to sneak in and out.

"Shit."

Cara sighed. "You could leave right now, Elle."

"To Aberevin?"

She shrugged her shoulders. "If we find a horse for you and if you avoid the main roads—"

"Cara, I haven't ridden a horse in fourteen years."

"How will she navigate a land she doesn't even know?" Foster chimed in, and I scowled at the thought. I studied maps of Rhyddean and the other mortal courts until I memorised them, but I had never actually been out there. As much as it pained me to admit it, memorising maps and using them to navigate were two different things.

"And my papers are in my chambers." I sighed, extending my arm to the tower.

"Okay, not a great plan." Cara took my hand and guided me back into the woods. "Guess we're going through the front gate."

We back-tracked a little way before Cara and I stepped into the wildflower field again, but Foster stood firm in the shadows.

"You're not coming?"

"No. If you're caught, you'd be in more trouble having a man with you. Plus, I have no plans to be on your uncle's hit list," he noted. I didn't want that either, so I sent him a grateful smile and stepped out into the field.

"Hey, Elle!" a whisper-shout called out from behind me. I turned to watch Foster lift a pretend hood over his head. "Don't get caught."

Heeding his advice, I slipped the hood of my cloak over my hair.

CHAPTER 3

The fairytales got it wrong. Elaborate costumes and glamour enchantments weren't necessary to disguise oneself successfully. Simply lowering your status sufficed. Two chambermaids dressed in cheap woollen dresses and cloaks did not threaten the men guarding the front gate, so they waved us through without question.

Castle servants bustled about the grounds and corridors and paid us no mind, too preoccupied with their own work. The few nobles we passed viewed us the way they saw fit—invisible.

Cara helped me into a sage green dress with a tulle skirt in the laundry room, a hand-me-down from one of my younger sisters, and found a matching silk scarf that she tied around my neck to hide the wound and resized my dagger's sheath to fit around my right thigh. The new accessory emitted an assurance that I'd be safe as long as it remained within arm's reach.

Hearing Geraldine, the Housekeeper, approaching as she barked orders at other chambermaids, Cara pushed me into one of the unused servant corridors where I hurried to my tower chamber to face Oulixeus' wrath. He saw through my lies and I never understood how. I trained my face to remain neutral in high stake situations, learning how to breathe in a way to keep my heart rate at a regular beat without fidgeting.

The heavy latch clunked as I lifted it and pushed into the door. It used to require all of my strength to open the massive wooden door, but after two months of training with Cara, I'd slowly built strength. Peeking through the crack, I surveyed the room to discover it was vacant.

The weight forcing my lungs to take tight breaths lifted and my shoulders relaxed until I glimpsed the neatly folded parchment resting on the modest table beneath the window.

Shards of porcelain from a vase Oulixeus had once gifted me were scattered across the tattered area rug and I closed the door and tiptoed around them, my silk slippers whispering against the coarse wool. Lightning flashed in the distance and large drops of rain drummed against the glass, pelleting from grim clouds shunning the day's earlier light.

As I neared the unmarked note, an unruly gust of wind whistled through a cracked windowpane, brushing a chill along my skin and lifting my skirts. The clean edges of the paper scratched against each other as I opened it, immediately recognizing Oulixeus's refined cursive, a light stain beneath the words.

Stay put. You'll be seeing me later.

The paper, reeking of whiskey, held a promise of wrath. The scent burned my nostrils before my mouth salivated, the panic building within me begging for alcohol to numb it away.

Tossing the parchment into the hearth, I watched as the dying embers glowed to life, and paper's edges blackened, a small flame burning it. The ashes swirled amongst the soot like dandelion pappus floating around the wildflower field. I tried not to think of that day often, my mind hiding the worst of the memories from me, but I vividly remembered the streaks of blood on my sister, Linnaea's, stunned face, and my mother violently shaking me, screaming, "You did this!"

I didn't know what I did, but the darkness inside me I now kept at bay had clearly enticed me to do something terrible. My parents couldn't allow a child holding such darkness to succeed their throne. So, they locked me away, only to be seen at the odd public event to prevent rumours. To legitimately disinherit me, they continued to bear children until my mother birthed my little brother, Octavian. A *proper* male heir.

Five days, I reminded myself, kneeling to the floor and falling into a rhythm as I plucked sharp pieces of porcelain from the carpet. Less than a week from freedom and my plans unravelled instantly. How could I break free from not only trained soldiers, but from the approaching Fae? Biting my lower lip, I rocked on my toes, reevaluating my options.

Running without Cara's friend wasn't an option. I didn't know the land, and relying on the main roads with the Fae travelling here... It created too many unknown possibilities.

I needed more information about the Fae's arrival. When would they arrive? How many travelled this way? Were Fae soldiers being stationed in every mortal court? Were they coming to stay or kill us? And what about my family? Despite our strained ties, I couldn't bear the thought of harm befalling on my sisters and brother. They didn't deserve that.

Standing and dropping the shards into a wicker basket, I swiped my hands together, preparing for an unpredictable night with Oulixeus.

You'll be seeing me later. Those haunting words held a promise he never broke. Not once. I remained in my room all day considering the level of Oulixeus' anger, and what excuses to share with him. Not like I was allowed free reign of the castle, anyway.

Sitting in front of the window, thunder rumbled in the distance. Storms here lasted days, complimenting my melancholy, but a few sunny days afterwards brought a restored hope with the uncommon light.

Dancing yellow orbs held my attention as anxiety coursed through me. Fireflies. They danced in the woods and wildflower meadows surrounding the castle, frolicking in the rain like playful, rebellious children instead of avoiding it. Tree branches and spring flowers glimmered in their gentle light, casting a mystic aura onto the world around them.

BANG! My shoulders jumped to my ears, and a palm landed on my chest. Within seconds, my tense muscles relaxed, realising an unlit brass candlestick on the table had fallen to the floor. It was late, and I was on edge from waiting all afternoon and evening for Oulixeus.

I wanted to strip into my nightgown and relieve myself from the claustrophobic sensation of the tight silk bodice. Formal dresses were never comfortable, and I wished to be in something lighter and flowy, like muslin. But I wore it because I never knew what version of Oulixeus awaited me.

He might be the sweet man who I once loved, or the venomous snake he became. The additional layers of fabric between us made everything less real, though sometimes it didn't matter. He'd do it himself, remove my clothing, making me fully vulnerable to him.

CLANG! Again, my shoulders leapt. Before the wooden door fully creaked open, the sharp scent of whiskey reached me. Ice cubes clinked against crystal, and Oulixeus took a sloppy sip before discarding the glass on the fireplace mantle.

"Where were you?" A stringent venom injected the timbre of his voice. A voice that hadn't tormented me for three months. I needed him to be calmer to reveal the answers I sought about the Fae's arrival and their purpose here.

Focusing on the fireflies to keep my composure, I maintained a meek tone. "The library—"

"*Don't* lie to me. I've spent the entire day in meetings. Where. Were. You?" Oulixeus grabbed the nape of my neck with icy fingers and kneaded my muscles. An act meant to be loving, but by him—an act of dominance. The pressure tensed the muscles along my neck, to the base of my skull, and throbbed my temples. "You didn't stay in your room like a good girl, did you? You didn't even stay in the castle. Do you not want to be with me anymore?"

Blood shot through my veins to desperately subside the pain increasing by the gripping knead, heating my skin.

"I haven't wanted to be with you for a very long time." My rising frustration prevailed over my strategy to remain calm. Summoning enough strength to escape his grip, I faced him. The embers of the dying fire highlighted the angry tick along his jaw and reflected the ire sloshing between the earthy, burnt sienna tones in his eyes. His anger should've warned me to remain quiet, but an unexpected boldness overpowered me. "You can't control me."

"Control you? I *saved* you!" He spoke through gritted teeth. Cruel, that's what he'd be tonight.

I wanted to increase the distance between us. Beginning to stand, he clenched my shoulder and aggressively pushed me back into the chair. Strong fingers dug into my flesh as I protested, "You're hurting me."

"You have no idea what kind of pain I saved you from today," Oulixeus snapped like a viper. Refusing to retreat, I held his stare.

"How could anything be any worse than *you*?" I quivered at the challenge.

"Someone sharpened her teeth since I've been gone." He snorted. "Don't lie to me. Don't lie to yourself, Ellie. I love you. The *only* one who ever will love you. And I'm only rough on you when you make me. If you'd just learn to *listen* to me, *obey* me."

An involuntary wicked laugh slipped from my lips. The way he rationalised his actions astonished me. Oulixeus snatched my throat, quick like the viper hiding within him. Choking, I started to fall, but his tight grip kept me in place as the chair tumbled onto the stone floor.

He sneered. "You want to know what's worse than me, Princess? We lost the war and Aramis, our new *king*, is who you should fear. He'll fuck any woman he pleases. If he's unsatisfied or she objects, she doesn't continue to live.

If she's lucky, he'll slit her throat. But if she's unlucky... Let's just say he'll spend days torturing and mutilating her 'til there's nothing left. And because of me, you'll be safe from it."

I coughed again, struggling to swallow. His hold on me loosened, and he brushed a light kiss along my skin. A tingle shot through me. He always lavished me with delicate kisses after horrid moments, chasing them away. His lips as tender as a raindrop rolling along a delicate rose petal, though tainted by poison.

"You don't believe me, and you don't have to. You'll see just how vicious those beasts are. How they slowly burn their victims with fire magic and string them up for all to see."

My lips quivered.

"Are you afraid?"

"Yes." Though I didn't know whom I feared most, the Fae or Oulixeus—maybe both, equally.

"You should be. The minute we officially surrendered, Aramis slashed his blade down your father's prized general, dug his hands into the wound and split the general's ribcage like a starving man ripping apart a chicken carcass. He ordered his army to resume the slaughter as he ripped our soldiers apart with his bare hands, leaving barely any of us left. Our new ruler will not be a benevolent one," Oulixeus predicted as the image of bloodied hands consumed my mind.

"Is he coming here?"

"He'll be here within the week, and when his beasts' greedy eyes fall upon you, you'll be begging for my safety." My heart pounded as the pad of his thumb stroked my neck, catching on the scarf as his lips followed the path his hand had taken. *Five days.*

"That's not so bad. I guess he didn't have to die after all," Oulixeus whispered, kissing the fast healing wound on my neck as my eyes widened. *He knew.*

"You killed—"

"I'll kill anyone who touches you. You're safe with *me.*" He abandoned his hold on my neck and moved to the tattered armchair near the hearth. A ragged exhale escaped my bruised throat as Oulixeus rubbed his forehead.

"Safe? You call being stuck in this castle an outcast and with you safe?" I spat, my temper flaring.

"You won't be an outcast for much longer. I'm seeing to it."

"What's that supposed to mean?" My brows furrowed.

"It's none of your concern." Frustration coated his words, but I pushed him. Unable to contain myself and going too far.

"But—"

"Where's the dagger?" My uncle interrupted, and I feared if I didn't speak the right words, his anger would flurry into an obsessive rage.

"I don't have it." *It's in the nightstand.*

"Ellie." My nostrils flared at the nickname only he used, despising how he used it to speak down to me while comforting me. "Don't play games with me. I'm not mad about you sneaking off with your friend and living your secret life with her family."

Fuck.

"I just want the dagger, Ellie." He sighed, dropping his elbow to the armchair. "You have no idea what kind of weapon it is."

Lie to him, the dagger whispered, urging me to keep it away from my uncle. "I left it on the road."

Oulixeus chuckled and paced over to me, wrapping his fingers around my chin and kissed me, lips pressing notes of buttery caramel and rich vanilla into my mouth.

I didn't want this anymore. A sick masochistic control shaped his desire for me, not love or respect. He didn't wish to be equals. To avoid escalating his wrath, I allowed the kissing and touching, but stood lifeless in his hands.

"Look at you. You've certainly changed since I've been gone. Braver. More vocal... Stupider." His smile dropped. "You may be good at bluffing, beautiful, but you can't lie to me. Now, be a good girl and give me the dagger."

I furrowed my brows, refusing to surrender the one thing offering me security.

"I'll ask one more time, Ellie, before I rip this room apart," Oulixeus warned. "Where. Is. The dagger?" A vicious scowl marked his strong features. He truly would rip this room apart. A tangy, sharp fury emanated from him, overcoming the odour of alcohol.

Oulixeus laughed. Not a humorous laugh, but something sinister. He shook his head and stalked toward the armoire. Ripping the doors open, I jumped as they banged against the stone wall. He tore dresses and cloaks from their hangers, hurling them to the floor.

Nothing.

He could destroy the entire room and everything in it. I wouldn't care. But my gut warned me not to allow the dagger to slip into his possession. Oulixeus yanked the dresser drawers out, upending them, and sending garments tumbling atop the discarded dresses and cloaks.

Nothing.

Whipping his head to me, his lips drew into a thin line.

Pushing past me, he swiped everything off the table in front of the window and flipped it over, searching underneath. Again, nothing. He gripped my hair, forcing my head back to meet his wrath. Standing nearly half a foot taller, he looked down at me, studying me and searching for any clue I may accidentally spill in my fearful state, but I forced myself to remain neutral.

It's just like a card game, I reassured myself.

"Where is it?" he demanded, but I refused to give in. "Did he lie to me, Ellie? Did my mercenary lie when he said you won the dagger in a card game? That when he recognised you, he let you go instead of taking the dagger and your life? Did you make me kill him for no reason?"

"I never asked you to kill anyone." I bit the snake back.

"And you'll never have to." His angry shouting dropped to a compassionate whisper, softening his eyes. "It's what you do when in love." He inhaled the rose scent of my hair and tantalised me with fingertips tracing my spine and lips caressing my jawline. Fuck, I hated him. He was erratic. Torturing and abusing me one second and tender the next.

And he knew it tampered with my mind.

"You love me, Ellie. You want me. You crave my attention." He kissed my chin. "My kiss." His lips hovered along the fabric around my neck. "My touch." His thumb glided across my jaw. "My cock." He pressed his pelvis into my stomach, and a moan slipped through my lips, betraying me as old emotions resurfaced. Emotions I thought I'd successfully discarded.

Unable to resist any longer, I pressed my lips into his, giving his lush bottom lip a quick nip, and simultaneously digging my nails into his hair.

He's manipulating you. The dagger insisted, and I ignored whatever magical properties the dagger seemed to possess.

My fingers played with the laces of his breeches, the firmness of him pressing further into me stoked the coals within. My zealousness made me fumble and struggle to remove his pants. Oulixeus blew out a light chuckle and took my hands to steady me.

Looking through my lashes, I saw it. His compassion. Tenderness rippled through the whiskey irises of his eyes. No sign of malice, only affection rested upon his face. My gaze darted across him, dedicated to memorising him at this moment, as the man I fell in love with years before.

We untied the laces together before Oulixeus wrapped my fingers around his emerald green shirt, directing me to remove it. Pieces of ebony hair caught on the collar as I pulled it over his head.

Continuing to lead me, he hooked my thumbs inside his breeches, and jointly, we pulled them down. Finally, my eyes left his face and looked at his sturdy frame. The light from the hearth cast a hazy glow across his broad chest, defining the muscles across his abdomen. A thin trail of black hair appeared as his breeches fell. Beginning at the base of his navel, the trail continued further and further down until...

His firm length finally released. A rush of air moved through my lungs, not realising I held my breath.

You'll regret this. The dagger urged.

No. No. No... I implored. These contrary emotions were more than I could bear. One side of me agreed with the dagger. It, too, reminded me he was nothing more than manipulative and capricious. But this side of him. Oh, gods, *this* side of him!

With a tug, the scarf around my neck spooled to the stone. My turn. He fiddled with the silk laces of my bodice. The looser they became, the more the fire within me blazed. Pausing, he peered deep inside of me, recognizing everything I hid from myself.

There *he* was. The gentle, sweet, caring man I knew as a young girl. He placed a hand above my breast and my heart pounded against it. Flashing a quick mischievous grin, he resumed work on undressing me.

Let him go. The dagger encouraged me.

Fuck off. I wanted this, and I deserved to enjoy him. His torment and cruelty were worth it. Worth this ecstasy. And if I could listen and obey, maybe we could be happy— like he said.

My eyes shifted to the nightstand where the dagger hid to reaffirm the belief. Oulixeus slightly pulled back, and a darkness clouded his eyes, the malice taking over. *No, no, no.* Desperately searching for something sweet in his features, I failed, finding only masochism.

"I knew one way or another you'd tell me where the dagger is. I'll take it after I'm finished with you." Returning to kissing me, I stood motionless, dumbstruck.

The fingers caressing my skin transformed into thin, slithering snakes. Sweet kisses morphed into unspoken commands. He'd tricked me.

See. The dagger voiced and tears surfaced, welling under my lower lid.

Kill him, it suggested. And as if a bolt of lightning from the storm outside had shattered the veil of ignorance, a newfound understanding illuminated in my thoughts like dawn breaking over a long, treacherous night. Oulixeus would continue to betray my trust time and time again. This wasn't the first time, and it wouldn't be the last. So I agreed.

I allowed Oulixeus to lay me across the duvet, and shifted closer to the nightstand as he slowly drew the tulle skirt up my legs. Sensing my one chance, I rolled onto my side. My nails grazed the brass knob when he grabbed hold of my hips and pulled me toward him. "Don't you dare change your mind, beautiful."

Making a second attempt to retrieve the dagger, I decided against subtlety. Fury took control. My foot slammed into his chest, and he tumbled backward to the foot of the bed. The nightstand wobbled as the drawer slid half an inch. Dipping my fingers inside, the cold metal of the hilt sparked hope until Oulixeus caught my waist, turned me around, and pulled me into his chest.

"I wasn't in the mood for rough tonight. But if that's what you want, Ellie, then that's what you'll get," he declared.

Adrenaline pounding through me, I gripped my hands on his shoulders and struck my knee to his abdomen. He let out a loud groan. These weren't Cara's fighting techniques. No. Basic instinct emerged.

Before I could make a third attempt, Oulixeus confined me in his arms. Struggling to free myself, I bit his shoulder, teeth sinking into his skin, and a hint of whiskey tinged the blood drawn. He groaned again, but this time, a chuckle accompanied it.

He let go for a brief moment before searing pain radiated from my stomach. All the air left my body. I leaned over, gasping from the pain as he reached for me again. Gripping my hair and pulling my head back, he forced me to rise until our faces met. The skin along my head burned as his fist seized my curls. Tears glistened on my lower lid. Refusing to look at him, I stared at the canopy hanging from the bed.

Sneering, he wrapped his free hand around my neckline. I grunted a protest, but he pulled my hair more.

Fighting a losing battle, I looked out the window in a desperate plea to escape. If not physically, then mentally. My sight latched onto the fireflies from earlier. Their dancing slowed to a hover. One of my tears finally betrayed me and rolled over my cheek, hot with embarrassment and rage.

"Ellie, you're safe." And he truly believed it. A sharp tug and my bodice fell to my navel. This wasn't what safety should feel like. His hand cupped my breast. Sinister fingers pinched my nipple, forcing it to harden and my body arched into him with a contradictory moan.

"Yes." A brazen rumble emanated from his throat. "That's a good girl."

Kissing my neck, he reached below to rummage through my skirts. Finding my thigh, his fingertips snaked across my skin. Shivers crawled along me as I involuntarily craved his familiar touch again. The gentle, sweet touch from moments ago—not this.

Recognizing my eventual surrender, Oulixeus let go of my hair and laid me on the bed. I kept my gaze on the fireflies, disgusted with myself. They hardly danced now, like they wanted to help but didn't know how to.

With my skirts hiked around my waist and my chest exposed, I waited. Waited for the inevitable. A combination of alcohol and arousal had his chest heaving. My fists balled around the duvet in anticipation of what came, my fight dying.

My stomach churned as he entered me, and I bit my lip to suppress the despairing gasp caught in my throat as he loosened a groan of ecstasy in my ear. After a fleeting pause, his pace quickened, and I forced my lids shut. *I'm not here—I'm not here—*

Instead of seeing him on top of me, I saw a canopy of trees. Light speckled through the chartreuse leaves and onto my skin. The sunlight a pulsating heat, turning his hot breath into a summer breeze through the woods.

Instead of panting in my ear, I heard water trickling in a nearby stream. Birds flitted above me and others splashed their feathers in the icy cold water.

Instead of feeling him inside of me, I felt the feathery touch of grass and moss against my skin.

I had never been there before. Not physically. But mentally, I transported myself there whenever agonising pain threatened to push me too far. Whenever my shame overpowered my desire.

Teeny tiny wildflowers of all colours grew between the moss and grass. The flowers created a civilization of their own. Some wore little bell-shaped hats. Others stood tall and proud, showing off their petals, and some hid in the shade. My mind fixated on a group of white flowers, their petals bunched together, forming a spiral shape and the centre still green from the newest petals. Reaching for the flower, a smile tugged on my lips. Smooth liquid velvet. Slowing my racing heart, I went to pick one when a thunderous gasp exploded.

Snapping out of my fantasy, Oulixeus leaned his head back into the air, pressing himself deep into me, and his cock jerked.

Once his groan finished, he fell into me, burying his face into my hair. Tangling his fingers between my curls, he stayed inside of me as his panting slowed.

"I love you," he whispered in my ear and kissed my neck. His lips travelled to my tear-stained cheek as his thumb attempted to wipe away the tears on the other. Muffling another uncertain moan of pleasure or distress, he tucked his head between my breasts and slid himself out of me to dress.

He approached the nightstand and unsheathed the dagger, twirling it in his hands. The steel reflected the light of the dying fire, begging me to not let Oulixeus take it. But I couldn't move.

"Go to sleep. It's going to be a busy week." He leaned in, kissing my forehead. Kindness or dominance? "You know, even if he lied about the dagger, I would've killed him just for touching you."

As the latch thumped close, I rolled to my side and tugged my knees into my chest. Once his footsteps faded into the distance, I sobbed. Holding nothing back.

CHAPTER 4

*F*lowers were beneath me. The other blooms towered over, and threatening storm clouds swirled above.

A song hummed far away as I sat up and surveyed the sea of yellow and ivory. Something sang to me, and my eyes fell upon the forest. It was Ravenwood Forest. We weren't allowed in there. Monsters haunted it. But the singing coaxed me forward, growing louder and louder until—

I jolted, my heart pounding beneath a winded chest, as beads of sweat dripped from my forehead.

The bedframe groaned from a moving body next to me and I instantly struck out.

"Elle! Wait, it's me. Breathe! You had a dream, breathe..." Soothing, gentle hands wrapped around my arms and I instantly relaxed as I recognised her sweet scent, blue light from the night sky cascading through the window, tinting her freckled face.

Cara.

I collapsed into her and wept all over again. I'd allowed Oulixeus' manipulation to succeed, and I lost the dagger. For some reason, it was the last that felt the most defeating, like a piece of me had been ripped away. "I know. You're okay now." Long, smooth strokes along my hair sent comforting pulses through me.

Cara held me and let me sob into her shoulder for hours. She didn't say a word or show any sort of impatience or judgement. She laid with me, held me, and allowed me to feel whatever I needed to.

Once my crying faded into whimpers, the pitter-patter of rain on the windowsill became the sole sound.

Eventually, Cara grabbed a nightgown from the floor. The room remained in shambles but, without a word, she guided me through the abrasive fabric. Covering my chest, she knelt on the floor and pulled the silk and tulle dress off, examining the red marks on my soft abdomen. They'd bruise in a few hours. Her brow twitched as the nightgown bundled around my waist and continued to fall to my knees. Spreading a wool throw over my legs, she threw the dress onto the dying embers in the hearth, knowing I'd never wear it again.

"When did you come in?" I whispered, watching her stoke the newly born flames. The attendants never added more wood throughout the night, as they did for members of my family and the other nobles residing in the castle. The fire would die until Cara had time to bring more wood.

"Shortly after midnight. Your uncle stumbled into the kitchen with his friends, bragging, and showing off the dagger." Commiserative eyes met mine.

She crawled into bed, spreading the feather-filled duvet over our bodies, trapping us in a consoling warmth. Folding my legs into my chest and resting my cheek on the covers, I looked at my friend.

"I learned a few things. The Fae will arrive within the week, and their king is coming. But... things happened before I could ask more." I was too embarrassed to explain it was my fault I didn't extract more information from Oulixeus. That my anger stoked his cruelty, instead of calmly talking him down. I didn't know how to control myself enough to manipulate others like he did.

"There's time. We'll figure it out. The Fae are returning for the first time in over a thousand years. How much can your parents keep secret from the court?"

Nodding my head, I stared blankly at the chamber door behind Cara. She sighed and her hand clutched mine. For a chambermaid, she had supple hands with immaculate fingernails. "Sometimes letting it happen is how we survive."

"I'd rather be dead than continue to be a captive in this castle." My voice held firm through the statement.

"Don't say that. Please don't say that." The rising flames from the hearth reflected the beads of anguish rimming our eyes as she pulled me closer. This couldn't be the only way to survive. There had to be something more.

"Our plan can still work. We'll free you." She looked out of the window before scooting closer to me. "Let's rest. The sun's rising." The indigo night skies faded into a deep royal blue, and along the horizon of trees, a dash of cadmium orange burned through. Rolling over, I winced at my aching body.

"I'll put one of Grandmama's ointments in the places he hit you, it should help with reducing any bruising. And I'll make a contraceptive tea for breakfast."

Facing each other and resting our hands under our cheeks, I mouthed to her silently—*I love you,* and Cara smiled.

Love you too.

CHAPTER 5

Trapped beneath Cara, I bucked my hips to the ceiling with force and snapped my head to the side. As predicted, Cara's body toppled over me as I wrapped my arms around her torso and wiggled up to meet her face. The new position allowed me space to trap Cara's arm around my own, knock her off balance, and flip her over.

Straddling her hips, I struck my elbow toward her face as quickly as a whip, stopping inches from her chin.

"Good, you're getting quicker."

My face lit at her praise, and my mind stepped into a state of ease as I slowly mastered the defensive move, making the panic of this week settle.

Oulixeus had predicted correctly, and the week flew by. The castle bustled with mayhem, gossip spread like wildfire, and we expected the Fae to arrive two days after my planned escape. Although my uncle's presence posed a risk, Cara and I agreed that it remained my best chance to leave.

So I followed the new routine established for me. A walk through the gardens in the mornings, dress fittings before lunch, and afternoons spent with my sisters' governess ensuring my education and dance skills remained sufficient.

A note in Oulixeus' handwriting had appeared on my table after the first day—*You're welcome.* He had done as he'd promised and influenced my new schedule, convinced he'd done me an enormous courtesy by adding a bit of freedom and stimulation to my caged life. It hardly resembled freedom, not when he still made the rules and his guards watched my every move.

"Next time, I want you to throw a jab and hook instead of using your elbow. Those punches seem to be your strength and if you're being attacked, play into those."

"Okay." Standing, I panted while helping Cara up. We trained in the early morning before my schedule started, determined to perfect the defensive move I failed during our assault on the road, refusing to be alone and helpless in Aberevin.

"I told you, running would increase your endurance," Cara lectured.

"Yeah, yeah." She laughed while I waved her off, recalling the time she made me run through the forest. I loathed how it exhausted my lungs and legs and refused to try again.

"Are you ready for today?" Cara threw a towel at me, and I dabbed the sweat running down my forehead. Nolan would arrive this afternoon, and I'd slip into his empty wagon once he unloaded his shipment. It felt surreal to be this close to everything I'd been dreaming about. Freedom. A life of my own.

"As ready as I'll ever be." I walked into the bathing chamber and sunk into the copper bathtub. The scorching water Cara brought up earlier had cooled to a tepid temperature, reflecting the state of calm I currently felt.

"Coffee's brewing," my friend called from the bedchamber and a weak smile spread across my cheeks. I'd miss Cara and her family. They did their best to show my tarnished heart what real love looked like, but they couldn't offer me safety here in Rhyddean. I remained unconvinced I'd ever find safety, not while Oulixeus lived.

"Here." Cara entered, offering a mug.

"Thanks." I brought the hot, nutty liquid to my lips, and it quieted my mixed emotions. "I'm having a difficult time relaxing."

"Oh, let's try this." Cara pulled a small vial from her apron, popped the cork, and dribbled a concoction into the water. An infusion of sweet cranberry, verbena, and rose drifted into my senses and assisted the caffeine I drank.

I'd be lost without Grandmama's creations. They hid my wounds, helped me avoid unwanted pregnancies, and brought a bit of joy to my life.

"I'm going to finish packing your bag. Knowing you, you probably forgot all the essentials," she teased and stuck out her tongue. I chortled and splashed water at her retreating form.

Inhaling another whiff of the soothing fragrance before dunking my head under the water, the silky water enveloped my skin, moisturising every inch of me. But the bedchamber's latch had my body tensing as I emerged. The seamstress had finished her work yesterday, and it was too early for tutoring. I leaned over the edge of the copper tub to hear better.

"Your Highness," Cara answered, her voice tinged with a startle. "You shouldn't be here. Princess Elowyn is not decent."

"It's fine," came a male voice, and my heart raced, a sense of unease caused my fingers to tighten on the bath's edge. As footsteps neared, I hurried to stand, water sloshing around my calves and cresting over the sides of the tub. I scrambled over the edge and snatched the towel resting on a nearby wooden stool.

"Good morning, beautiful." Oulixeus beamed at the sight of me wrapping the linen around my dripping body. Four days had passed since we'd last seen each other, and the torment from that night reminded me not to trust his tender look.

"What do you want?" I forced a stoic face and tightened my grip on the towel, its hem tickled my thigh, barely low enough to cover me. His gaze intensified as it left my stare, drawing along the length of my neck to pause at my breasts pressed together, creating a deep crevice.

Irises filled with whiskey proceeded to trail along the curvature of my hips, and settled on the towel's hem, devouring the sight of me and making my insides squirm.

Licking his lips, he flirted, "You." My face heated. "But unfortunately, we don't have time... yet. The Fae travelled quicker than expected. Their scouts are already here. The royals and the rest of their army will be here soon." He returned and marched out into my room, expecting me to follow.

Cara rushed in with a robe, helping to thread my arms through the sleeves and tying the belt around my waist tightly, trying to protect me from his prying eyes. Cara's gesture sparked a reflexive grin. Slipping on leather slippers lined with wool, I entered the other room feeling a bit more secure.

"These will do nicely." He inspected the new clothing. A particular gown, the shade of currant berry wine, caught his attention and his grin grew menacing. "I'm not certain if you should wear this at the welcome feast tomorrow or if I want this reserved for me exclusively." He slid a thumb along the plunging neckline and knots formed in my stomach.

You'll never see it on me.

"Today you'll wear this."

The colour reminded me of the lemon cake served at my last real birthday party. Loose and flowing fabric cut to display my breasts like the others. Oulixeus chose all the dresses, like he wanted to show me off.

As he continued to inspect the wardrobe he'd paid for, a shuffle caught my attention. I subtly peered at Cara, cautiously tucking my small leather travel bag under a pillow. My heart sped as Oulixeus turned while the bag's strap was still visible.

"I-I've never worn gowns so... revealing." I grabbed his hand and turned his focus back to me, hoping to distract him long enough to give Cara time to hide my supplies. She took the dress from him and laid it on the bed, strategically covering the evidence of my escape and, following protocol, stood by with her head bowed and hands folded over each other.

"You don't like them?"

"No, I don't. Their style will just be another catalyst to provoke my parents." I crossed my arms as he sauntered to me and wrapped an arm around my waist, pulling me uncomfortably close. My breath hitched.

"They're no longer in charge of you. At least not for much longer."

I pushed my hands against his chest to regain some control, but stumbled in the process. Cara balled her hands into fists and bit the inside of her cheek while Oulixeus' jaw twitched at the obvious rejection in front of another.

"Get dressed. Your presence will be requested once they arrive. No morning walk today." He left the room, closing the door so forcefully it bounced back open.

"Oh my gods, are you okay?" Cara rushed over and looked me over before hurrying to close the door properly.

"Yes, I'm fine," I said, Oulixeus' controlling nature had only strengthened my desire to run away.

"Good, because you need to leave now."

I paused, considering Cara's words. "Has Nolan arrived yet?"

"No, but I think it'll be difficult to sneak you into his wagon with Fae roaming the grounds. And what if they decide to search everyone leaving the castle?"

I nodded in agreement—too many unknowns. Being so far away from the Fae border and the battlefront, my parents didn't concern themselves with searching familiar merchants, but the Fae may want to display their new authority over us.

"It's still reckless for me to travel alone, though."

"You won't. Take the route we use to sneak out and run into Ravenwood, keep straight until you meet the stream and follow it east to a small waterfall. Wait for Nolan there. I'll tell him where you are," Cara firmly instructed as my mind blurred, piecing the information together rapidly, attempting to find holes and threats.

"My guards—"

"I'll take care of them. When those doors open, I want you to run. Fast. No matter what you hear behind you, don't stop. Just get out of here." Cara untied my robe and started dressing me in the yellow dress Oulixeus pulled out for me as I absently stared at the floor.

"This isn't very practical..." I frowned at the flimsy material Cara wrapped me in.

My friend sighed, "Nothing you own is practical."

"And the guards on the wall—"

Cara tightened the laces before grabbing my cloak. "I'll find a distraction."

"But if someone sees me, if Oulixeus finds me..." The thought twisted my gut.

"Elle," Cara grabbed my shoulders and stared straight into my eyes, her honey irises crystallising into a fortified battle shield. "It's not ideal, I know, but if you want out, this is our moment to try."

My heart hammered against my rib cage, clamouring for freedom. I nodded and Cara thrust my small travel bag filled with coins, jewels, and my papers into my hands.

"Okay, repeat the plan to me."

I recited it perfectly, and we pressed a kiss to each other's cheeks, knowing we may never see each other again. A rushed goodbye, leaving an empty pit within me.

Cara silently lifted the normally creaky latch, and we spotted my guards, Patrick and Eric, at the end of the hall. Tiptoeing toward them, Cara swept her leg low and brought Patrick to the floor. His large head thudded and blood marked the carpet. Her next set of movements unfolded swiftly. Wrapping her arms around Eric, she swung herself onto his back and pulled him into a chokehold.

"*Now!*" Cara hoarsely cried while putting all her strength into choking Eric.

I ran. Fleeing so swiftly, I gripped the wall at the end of the corridor to turn sharply and steadily. A broad central staircase in the tower featured stone columns on every floor, and as I hurried across the balcony, I halted, hearing the clinking of armour ascending the stairs.

Fuck.

Slipping behind a column, I sucked in my stomach and held my arms rigid, clutching my bag as the guards made it to the top. If they turned right, I'd be discovered within moments.

Please turn left. Please turn left.

And they did—relief didn't last long, though, when they marched toward my chamber. Toward Cara.

Fuck. Fuck. Fuck.

She'd instructed me to leave her behind, no matter what. Did she subdue Eric? Could she handle two more? The night of the attack, she successfully fought three men at once. My confliction hindered me.

"Hey," a guard shouted, pieces of armour clanging as they hurried toward the commotion. It pained me, but Cara had insisted. *No matter what you hear behind you, don't stop.* I trusted in her capabilities to defend herself. If I went back to help, and made things worse, then Cara had sacrificed herself for nothing.

Lunging for the stairs, I rushed. Steadying my lungs proved more challenging than forcing my steps to stay silent. Surely the entire castle would hear my huffing, as I snuck into an ancient passage hiding on the second floor. It led me straight through the kitchen and into the stables where I crouched along the wooden partitions, sneaking past the horses crunching on their hay and clomping their hoofs. Aside from the quiet horses, the stable appeared empty.

Creeping toward the doors, I peered into the stable yard just as a woman screamed at two large men wearing unfamiliar leather armour, highlighted in the sun like gold. The woman crawled away from them, her nails digging into the dirt as she trembled.

The men stalked toward her and her fear became my own, until I saw Oulixeus' face in place of the guards. I needed to help her.

"Oh, come on. I've never been with a human female before." One of them whined as they both continued to approach the woman with terror painted on her face. *Human female.* These weren't men at all.

The hair on my neck rose as the other Fae turned his head to the side and chuckled. "Aramis has fun playing with them."

His ear arched to a point, his jaw as straight and sharp as a blade, cheekbones high and narrow. These were predators. These were Fae.

Mortals were no longer safe in the courts we'd won centuries before. Digging the ball of my foot into the dirt and preparing to sprint into the yard, my heart thudded hard when an arm reached around my waist and pulled me back. A hand covered my mouth and carried me into an empty horse stall and I swatted my hands, hitting any part of my captor I could as I tried to squirm free. Pushing me into a mound of straw at the back of the stable, the arm let go of my waist, but the hand remained over my mouth. Snapping around, I recognized my abductor's sorrel hair and gentle features.

Foster.

I fell into his arms as he lifted a finger to his lips. "What are you doing?"

"Escaping," I whispered.

"Now?" He ran a hand down his face and sighed. The straw next to us suddenly thumped.

"It's her last chance." Cara. *Oh, thank the gods!* We embraced one another.

"How?" A bruise had already formed along the side of her face and her lip had a cut, but she was here, safe, and I allowed the relief I felt wash over.

"Another time, Elle," she said as she let go of me.

"That woman, we have to help her." I pointed to the yard, afraid she'd be assaulted before any of us could stop it.

"No time, Elle. There is literally no time left. The Fae are here. They're *here.* The longer you stay, the more there will be, and the harder it'll be to sneak past them." Cara rationalised with me, her way of begging me to let it go.

"They don't seem to notice us!" I argued. Maybe they didn't possess heightened senses after all.

"They're preoccupied," Foster chimed in, souring my stomach because mortal predators behaved the same—nothing else existed while preoccupied with their prey.

"I can't leave knowing they raped and murdered her." We argued with hushed voices. Cara bit the inside of her cheek, but she understood more than most why this mattered to me. She tended too many of my own bruises.

"Fine. I'll deal with it. Foster, get her out." Cara gave in, her eyes flickering to my throat.

"No. No, no, no. This is insane. Cara, you can't take on two Fae. Elle, this isn't the plan. What do you think your parents will do if you're caught? What will *Oulixeus* do?" Foster shook his head wildly, fear strumming through his honey-brown eyes, identical to Cara's.

"Foster, I'm running with or without your assistance. I'd rather *try* than do nothing."

His face softened at my tenacity. "What's the new plan?" He relinquished with a hand drawing across his face.

"Just help me to the garden."

"Is anyone else involved?" He sighed, clearly already hating this plan.

"Just Nolan."

"How far do you think he can travel with his wagon before Oulixeus realises she's gone?" Foster weighed the problems with the abrupt change in plans, always our voice of reason.

"He'll be so distracted with the Fae that it'll take him a few hours before he discovers she's gone, and by then I'll have it figured out." Cara affirmed, tugging at my heartstrings. My life lacked abundant experiences, yet I recognised the rarity of our friendship and her loyalty. They both pulled me from darkness, comforted my demons, and provided the hope I needed to stay alive. I didn't know if I deserved this type of love, but I would be forever grateful.

"Fine." He shook his head, reddish-blonde hair catching on his lashes.

Cara embraced me and I squeezed her tight, memorising the familiar scent of cloves and grapefruit that often comforted me after nightmares.

"Let's go," Foster interrupted. Opening his palm, I took it and he pulled me away from my best friend. We shared one more look before he had me through the hidden door in the back of the stables, leading to the garden.

Cara's voice shouted at the Fae in the distance. If any mortal woman could succeed, it'd be Cara.

"You know where you're going?" Foster asked as we crept through the garden, hidden behind giant trees. I nodded and replayed Cara's instructions, my heart quickening the closer we reached the lilac bushes covering our secret exit.

Staring at the hole, my entire life flashed before me. Feeling loved as a young child before my banishment to the tower, my overwhelmingly confusing relationship with Oulixeus, all the times I almost allowed the darkness to consume me, and the family I found in the midst of it all. I turned to Foster and draped my arms across his shoulders and he enfolded me in his, holding me firmly but lovingly.

He parted his lips but changed his mind about whatever he wanted to say. Instead, he pulled from the embrace and swept the branches blocking the hole. "Elle, go."

Sucking back the tears, I crouched in the soft garden dirt and crawled through to the other side before running with all my might to the woods.

I refused to stop running, even with the trees hiding me. Even when branches ripped threads from my cloak and grabbed my hair, causing me to trip onto my knees. Nerves in my wrists pinched as they caught my full weight, moist dirt digging under my fingernails.

The further I ran, the more familiar this became. The trees grew taller, trunks thicker, and spread further apart. But sunbeams floated between the empty spaces instead of the mist from my dreams. Freedom, as fresh as the rain soaked into the forest floor, rested on the horizon, and the notion forced the panic to dissipate.

Following Cara's instructions, I easily discovered the rushing waterfall. Blood carrying adrenaline through my veins slowed and weak legs guided me into the clearing around the waterfall. *I made it.*

A man kneeled at the river, splashing water onto his long golden hair and face. My brow rose as I contemplated the chances Cara or Foster already found Nolan and told him to meet me here. Driving a wagon, he could potentially arrive sooner than me.

I stepped closer to him and searched the clearing to discover three massive horses, but no wagon. "Nolan?"

He stood and slowly turned at my greeting, displaying golden armour. My stomach sank and my legs halted, noting the intricate flames etched on the breastplate and gauntlets.

I muffled a gasp as a burning heat wrapped around my left hand, a pulsating throb originating in my ring finger, and drawing to my elbow.

He cocked his head and parted his lips. Thick, lush lips, and a smoky voice rolled from them. "Why, hello there." He advanced a step, wearing a smirk. Golden locks, wet from the water, curled around copper skin. Dimples cradled by high cheekbones and a square-cut jaw, as if chiselled from marble, served as both a warning of his fearsome nature and a source of inexplicable fascination. His emerald eyes, reflecting sunbeams like swirling flames, beckoned me forward despite my instincts urging to flee. Running a hand through damp hair, they appeared—pointed Fae ears.

I stumbled backward and the hands of another found me. Firm umber hands clasped my dainty biceps and I twisted to look over my shoulder as my stomach plummeted. Another Fae. His amber eyes glinted like jewels and studied me, as if anticipating any move I may consider making. His stern expression highlighted the diamond-shape of his face, pointing to a pronounced dimple in his chin, and with that look, I instantly recognized he didn't play games. He watched the golden-haired Fae in front of us, awaiting instructions.

"Don't be afraid," the golden-haired one insisted, coming closer to run a finger along my cheek.

"She's quite beautiful." A third Fae spoke, stepping into the clearing. He wore similar armour to the other, but only the edges were gilded in gold, not the full suit. I angled my face away from the fingers gliding along my face, snarling. "And feisty. I like that."

"What are you doing in the woods all alone?" The stern Fae holding me spoke smooth and slow, but with a force that made my trembling difficult to hide. My shoulders thrashed back and forth, attempting to break loose, and he held me tighter with little effort.

"None of your business!" I snapped my teeth at the green-eyed Fae, his dimples deepening, amused by my reactions. The burning sensation in my arm increased. It had to be some kind of magic. "You're hurting me!"

"Let her go, Molvys." Following orders, the one called Molvys freed me.

The third Fae from across the clearing sauntered over, his sandy hair shining in the sunlight peeking between spring leaves. "What's she going to do? Run?" He laughed and I contemplated it, but I knew they'd be quicker.

Evaluating me, the emerald-eyed Fae asked, "What's your name?"

"What are you going to do with it?" I retorted, and a spark lit in the flames swirling in his irises.

"Conláed is right. You really are beautiful." He circled me the way a predator stalks its prey, and I stayed hyper-aware of his movements. The angle of his head. Where his boots squished liquid from the moss. And the closer he came, the more my arm burned.

"What are you doing?" I dared to ask.

"I'm looking at you." He stood directly in front of me again, removing all the space between us and forcing me to tilt my head up towards him. He stood taller than anybody I'd ever met. My arm continued to burn, but another sensation seared deep within me. A hum rang in my ears, drowning the rumble of the waterfall and the conversation between the other two Fae, as a heat flushed over my cheeks. He reached for my left hand, but I stepped away.

"I know who you are," he announced.

"Oh?" My brow arched.

"We've all heard rumours of the beauty possessed by the Rhyddean princesses. Seeing as I've never seen a mortal as beautiful as you, you must be one of them." He reached for my hand again and I tucked it behind my waist.

"You're speculating." Slowly backing away toward their horses tied to a tree, I tried to keep one eye on the distance between my escape and me, and the other on the Fae who watched me with something like amusement.

"I've also heard Princess Orla is a golden beauty. She'd fit right in with the Fire Fae, I'm sure. Most of us share blonde hair." The other two snickered from a distance. He stalked forward at every step I took backward. "The daughter, Princess Linnaea, is said to be a sensuous beauty like her mother."

"I wouldn't know." A little closer. I didn't know how to ride, but I needed to take the chance.

"And then there's the mysterious daughter. The eldest. Some call her the shut-in. Rumours claim she's the most beautiful out of all seven daughters." His chin tilted as I snorted.

"You know what they say about rumours," I said in an attempt to distract him.

"No. Enlighten me. What do they say about rumours?" he urged.

"They're—" Sturdy horse muscles met the top of my shoulders. "They're spread by fools." Carefully and subtly, my hands explored the horse for reins, a saddle, anything to grip. But the massive beast stood too high.

He took another step toward me and tugged on one of my loose curls. "Only a fool wouldn't believe how beautiful she is. But I'm not surprised. Your beauty is more exquisite, elegant, ethereal compared to what these mortals are used to. So, this means one thing." His smoky voice caressed my senses. "You're Princess Elowyn."

A shiver trailed across my spine hearing my name roll off his lips and I slightly arched toward him, almost like he'd called my body to him. But something else spoke to me, too.

Stepping closer, he reached for my hand as I withdrew the dagger hiding beneath my skirts, and pressed the tip into his firm chest.

"My, my. You are full of surprises. Are you going to stab me in the heart, Princess?" His lips curled into a grin full of excitement and intrigue.

"Don't mock me." I added pressure to the tip of the jagged blade, and it pierced the skin beneath his shirt, soaking up the blood. My hand shook at the foreign sensation of piercing a weapon into another living being.

And before I could understand the feeling, he snatched both of my hands, disarming me. "Let go!" His friends approached and laughed as they enjoyed watching me struggle.

"Okay, okay, Aramis. You had your fun." Conláed chuckled and patted my captor on the back, picking up the blade.

"Aramis?" The most vicious Fae in mortal written history?

Fuck. Fuck. Fuck!

"Come on, Princess." He lifted me halfway onto the horse and I kneed him in the throat. The unsuspected action gave me a quick opportunity to try to get out of this mess. He dropped me to the ground, and I crawled away, gripping the spongy moss to help me stand. I pushed up to run, only for my wrist to be snatched by Conláed.

"As much as we all love to play cat and mouse, we don't have time for that, Princess." He winked and pulled me into his clutches. Fuming, I spat in his face and he laughed as he wiped it away.

"We seriously don't have time for this. Bind her," Molvys suggested while Aramis pulled a rope from a saddlebag, already one step ahead of him. I twisted and pulled from Conláed, desperate to be free.

Fuck, fuck, fuck.

Aramis wrapped the thick, rough rope around my wrists, tightening it with a single flick that burned against my skin. I winced, and to my surprise, Aramis bent a knee and kissed each wrist, his mouth lightly touching my skin. The surging pain in my left arm slowed to a gentle simmer.

He pulled the rope down and wrapped it around my ankles. "There." He tugged on it mockingly. "No escaping us now, Princess." I glared at him as Conláed let me go and mounted his horse, Molvys already atop his.

A breath escaped me as Aramis hauled me over his shoulder and walked me to his horse, throwing me atop.

"Just let me go!" Maybe pleading would work since all other ideas failed to present themselves. "You have no need of me. My family hates me. I'm the shut-in, just as you said. They don't want me—*you* don't want me. Let me go and I won't be a nuisance to anyone!"

The giant, murderous Fae king climbed onto the horse and leaned close enough for his lips to brush my ear and his hand slid against my thigh, returning my blade to its sheath. "What gives you the impression I don't want you?"

CHAPTER 6

Gaping at the sight in front of me, I leaned back into Aramis' chest plate and the fabric of my dress stuck to my sweating back as I pressed further against the metal.

"It's a beautiful sight, isn't it?" Aramis whispered into my ear, and the shift of the court's power became a reality, crawling along my skin.

Aramis' army, doubling what we'd had left, spread across the field in front of Elmswood Castle. Servants erected white canvas tents as their army stood in perfect formation, illustrating their strength. Every Fae soldier wore matching silver armour etched with flames. Some had edges gilded in gold, similar to Conláed's, but only Aramis wore true golden armour. Crimson banners flew high above them, a fiery orange flame behind a shield and sword embroidery.

The Fae army parted, allowing us to approach the outer-wall of the castle. The front gate propped open and what remained of the Rhyddean army stood in full armour, lined perfectly on the gravelled ward and glinting in the sun. It baffled me how they could stand the heat wrapped in metal—the knights even wore their bear-shaped helmets.

Comparing our two armies, it's amazing that we resisted surrendering this long. And this was only a fraction of their army—

Elmswood always appeared so prodigious and magnificent with its many towers and wings constructed of reddish-brown stone, but it shrunk in the Fae's presence.

Aramis jokingly shouted, "Found something of yours!"

Something.

My family stood on the lower stone steps leading to the castle's giant oak doors, the Rhyddean courtiers lining the steps behind them. Beads of sweat dripped along everyone's temples, and noblewomen created a minuscule breeze with silk fans that shielded their complaints.

Six posts were staked into the gravel near the steps, and I wondered what purpose they served.

As Aramis dismounted the huge black stallion in a graceful movement, Oulixeus stole my attention, glowering at me while his ebony hair reflected in the sun, showing dozens of colours in each strand. In the dark corridors of the castle, I never noted his complexion. But here, in the bright midday sun, he tanned quite dark for a Rhyddeanne. His time on the frontline most likely contributed to the darker hue. The sunshine accentuated the muscles barely hiding beneath the black military jacket and framed his square shoulders that narrowed to a trim, masculine waist.

Handsome and cruel.

Giant hands securely gripped my hips and guided me to the ground. I stumbled as my feet met the earth, but he held me until I recovered my balance.

"What is this?" My uncle's voice boomed as he stepped forward. Aramis knelt in front of me to untie my binds.

"Mind your place, Oulixeus." My father, King Evander, frowned, the stress lines in his forehead deepening. Oulixeus threw him a glare.

A quiet chuckle reached my ears, and I looked down at Aramis kneeling before me, one of his dimples deepening.

"One of your princesses lost her way in the woods. We rescued her for you," Aramis continued as he loosened the jute and I ripped my hands away, losing my balance again. Conláed caught me and I jumped, not having heard him approach.

Taking advantage of my surprise, Aramis took my hands and gently kissed my left wrist where the fire magic continued to burn. My arm looked perfectly normal, but something roared within. Confused and slightly frightened, I pulled out of his gentle grip.

"Thank you," my mother, Queen Sévérine, offered, reaching her arm out to me. Meeting my parents' gazes, I recognized the fuming anger they concealed. Mother held a talent for arranging an impartial expression, her porcelain complexion adding a certain regality to it. But her pursed lips, clenched jaw, and steady stare showed the cracks in the stone, revealing her animosity.

Father's flaring nostrils and reddening face made him easier to read.

I hesitated to take Mother's hand, recalling how her touch felt over the past fourteen years—angry, fearful, and disgusted with me. Suddenly, Oulixeus' hand appeared next to hers. I bit my lower lip as my throat tightened with the guilt pulsing through me, because Oulixeus felt safer than my own mother, even as a furious energy snaked around me as he scowled. Oulixeus knew. He knew why I'd *lost my way* in the woods.

Pulling me next to him, my younger sisters, standing to my right, giggled, except for Linnaea. I followed her gaze to Aramis, who sauntered up to our father.

"So, where are they?" Aramis tucked his hands behind his back and tilted his head to the side. Father swallowed as he lifted an arm into the air and feet shuffled across the gravel, chains clanking with the steps.

Four Rhyddean soldiers led six people toward the posts near the steps. The soldiers took the chains cuffed to their wrists and hung them on thick nails pounded into the stakes. Four women and two men stood on balls of their feet, arms forced to the sky. They each wore ivory robes, the sleeves and hems lined with silver—our Spellcasters—mortals gifted magic by Toivo, the God of Truth.

Possessing the Gift was rare, and fewer and fewer were being discovered every year. Those born Gifted trained their whole lives to become Spellcasters, lethal warriors in both combat and magic. Any to run away or refuse their duty were named witches and persecuted.

"That's all of them?" Aramis cocked a brow and evaluated my father from head to toe.

Father shifted on his feet and coughed twice. "Yes, the rest died at the battlefront."

"Good. Burn them." Aramis' countenance exuded an eerie stillness.

Without a specific direction, Molvys and Conláed marched over to the Spellcasters and ignited their fists in flames. The courtiers behind me gasped as one shrieked, and my sisters leaned away, the older ones squishing the younger ones' heads into their sides. My little brother, Octavian, held onto Mother's hand and hid behind her black skirts.

The two Fae called forth their magic so easily. No incantation or sacrifice needed like a Spellcaster or witch, they just... did it. One being having so much power... an icy-cold sensation shot through my veins, opposing the magical heat still thrumming in my left arm.

A dimple creased Aramis' cheek as his friends' fire magic surged toward the Spellcasters, and the helpless victims cried out. "If you find others, you will burn them,"

Aramis causally ordered my father, and bile in my stomach rose into my throat as the Spellcasters' caught flame, their skin quickly turning a bright red.

As their ivory robes burnt to a crisp, a man howled as the flames engulfed him, while a woman bit her lip and clenched her eyes shut. The woman's chest heaved as she desperately held onto her last bit of courage, the flames wrapping around her waist.

The second man and another woman stared deeply into each other's tear-stained eyes, but as the pain became too unbearable, the man tucked his chin into his chest. His chained hands above his head banged into the post, and low screams filtered through his mouth.

Blisters opened on their skin and eventually they fainted from what had to be agonising pain.

My hand instinctively snatched Oulixeus' as a woman cried out for her mother. The acidic reek of their burning flesh and hair wafted over to us and my knees buckled. Oulixeus gripped my hand, which helped to ground me. Leaning in, he whispered, "You should be *very* afraid."

CHAPTER 7

Be strong, I chanted internally as Mother's glower rained upon me. *Don't break. Don't falter. Don't let them see you cower.* I stared at the hardwood floor as silence swirled through the drawing room, searching for a place to escape. Father sat on the plush cushioned bay window seat observing the world behind the floor-to-ceiling glass, indifferent to the rest of us. And Oulixeus leaned against a wall, one foot propped against it.

"If a king and queen's daughter runs away, how do you think that reflects upon the reigning family?" She stood across from me, her almost-black hair flowing over her impeccable posture and blending into the ebony fabric of her dress. Mother's complexion was so pale, the contrast of her clothing and hair made her appear ghost-like. Demonic.

I met her black eyes and straightened my spine. "It makes *you* look weak." And as she began spewing insults,

I squinted in her direction, refusing to regret my unexpected moment of empowerment. The darkness within my soul churned, casting a foreboding shadow. Fog blurred the edges of my vision and a high pitch ring echoed her voice. My knuckles faded to white as my hands curled into fists. Latching onto the pinching pain, feeding off of it, I imagined Mother forced against the wall opposite me. Yanked by an invisible power and pinned by it. One side of my mouth curled into a malevolent grin at the horror I'd carve into her flawless face.

I laughed sinisterly as the tendrils of the fog curled around my mother. Tears rimmed her eyes. Recognising I possessed the control now, it was my turn to inflict harm. To cause pain. A furious wind blew from my mouth, encouraging pieces of my mother to fleck away, wisping into ash.

"This is *funny* to you?" Mother's hand slapped me from the deranged daydream, clearing the fog after a few blinks, and the sharp sting heated my cheek.

"What were you thinking?" Her fist clutched my hair and pulled. "You stupid, entitled little bitch!"

I bit down against the pain, and a bead of blood formed where my teeth ripped the delicate flesh. I fell to the floor when follicles loosened from my scalp, but I refused to give her the satisfaction of hearing my cry.

Be strong. Don't break. Don't falter. Don't let them see you cower.

"Now, now, Séverine, relax. The Fae clearly frightened her." Oulixeus pushed off the wall and stalked over, clenching Mother's wrist in a silent command to relinquish, and she did after a moment of hesitation. Oulixeus helped me stand while my mother glared.

"You *stupid* girl," Mother repeated, shaking her head. "Do you understand what is at stake here? Allow me to reiterate." She brought her face close to mine, eyes almost as dark as the Veil. Notes of neroli and jasmine, her usual perfume, filled the small gap between our noses. We reached the same height and shared similar body compositions, but I became a little rabbit quivering before a hungry bear when she exhibited this level of anger. She could be terrifying. "We look weak, we die. We insult them, we die. We fuck up, we *die*."

Be strong. Don't break. Don't falter. Don't let them see you cower.

"I don't want you anywhere near those creatures! You'll ruin—"

"Enough." Father ambled over.

"But she..."

"I said, *enough*, Séverine." He took Mother's arm and led her to the door. "Oulixeus, deal with her. We have a meeting with Aramis."

Oulixeus surveyed me from head to toe. Plotting all the insidious things he wanted to inflict on me. The sadistic prick enjoyed hurting me. If coerced to be terrifyingly truthful, sometimes I enjoyed it, too. But that thought remained buried in the dark depths of my inner soul. The part that I hated, that frightened me.

"Oh, and Oulixeus," Father called. "Not her face. She's to be at the feast tomorrow to keep rumours at bay." Closing the door, they left.

Immediately, Oulixeus pushed me into a wall. Pressing his full weight against me, he claimed my lips with a force so strong and sudden it shocked me. Attempting to drive him off, he pressed in harder.

"Stop it! What if someone comes in?" But the risk sent exhilaration through me.

"I don't care." Fisting my dirt-covered skirts, his desperate kisses moved from my mouth to my neck. Shifting the way he leaned against me, his cock pressed against my thigh. Hard.

"Stop."

Urging again, he strengthened his kisses. This was punishment enough. Stimulated by a man I hated. A man who shouldn't touch me. But the foreign sensation that seared deep within me while Aramis taunted me in the woods begged for a release, and Oulixeus would be that outlet.

"Seeing you with him pissed me off, Ellie. Knowing you ran away really fucking pissed me off. But seeing you bound, well, I liked that." He moaned against my ear, needing this as much as I did.

"I want you," I admitted, more to myself than him. The shame that continuously suppressed my feelings finally unravelled. I didn't care. Not at this moment.

"Good." A cruel smile formed as he lifted me into the air and my legs wrapped around his waist. Carrying me to the ornate walnut writing desk, he swept papers and decor to the floor, turned me around, and I knelt on the desk facing the wall.

His leather belt ripped through the buckle while he hiked my skirts. The tip of him felt smooth and slightly wet against my skin. Gripping my hip with one hand, he easily delved into me, already wet for him. My head leaned back, moaning euphorically.

Seconds later, a loud slap followed by a sting on my backside caused me to whimper. I glimpsed over my shoulder to see Oulixeus gripping his belt, readying to hit me again. He powerfully thrust into me the same moment the belt made contact with my skin and I bit my lip to silence my moan.

"You can't leave me." He leaned over, his chest flush with my back, and his mouth against my ear. The hem of his silk shirt brushed along my skin. Shuddering as another blow from the belt met me, my skin tingled with an intoxicating ache.

"You need me." He sucked on my earlobe and the hits roughened. The opposing sensations were lascivious.

"Please," I begged, not knowing what I wanted. More or less? He pulled out of me and flipped me onto my back. In one swift motion, Oulixeus tugged the back of his collar and ripped his shirt off. I folded my legs around his torso, a silent plea to not leave me as he pulled off the lemony dress concealing my body.

We fucked recklessly. In an unlocked room where anyone could interrupt, on my mother's desk. The indiscretion fulfilled the heat burning inside of me, stroking the dark energy lying within me.

I reached out to explore his body, but he captured both wrists and pressed them behind my head. With his free hand, he guided himself back into me. But before I could moan my desire, his hand moved from his cock to my throat. Coiling his fingers tightly and restricting my airflow, he continued to pound into me. Stars clouded my vision and his panting increased. The room spun. I wanted him to stop. This was too aggressive. The darkness within me morphed into a panic.

"Yes." He moved faster. Seeking air, I gagged on nothing. My hips bucked forward. He moaned louder. Yearning for freedom, I twisted my wrists. His grip needed to loosen, but his vigour didn't cease.

Answering my plea, he finally let go of my hands and relief rushed through me. A false relief. His hand met the other around my throat and clamped tightly. I hit and pushed and dug my nails into his forearms. My body withered, gagging on nothing.

My vision cleared enough to witness Oulixeus gloating. "If you don't like this..." He thrust deeper into me. "Then be a good girl and don't disobey me."

Another gag left my throat with nothing left to cling to. Oulixeus melted. Groaning with pleasure, he loosened his coiling hands but kept them around my neck, scarcely allowing me enough space to draw in the air I desperately needed. He slumped over and kissed me.

"Run away from me again, Ellie, and you'll see just how angry I can get," he said, his words etched with dominance, before rising and watching me regain my breath. He loomed above me and I concluded then, observing the determent twisting in his eyes, I would never leave this place. Not alive.

They're no longer in charge of you. He didn't share his agenda, but I was in more danger than ever before. I'd provoked him. Showed him I can and *will* attempt to break free. He experienced what losing me felt like. And he couldn't bear it.

This whole time, he wasn't a snake. Something else dwelled within.

I fucked up.

I awoke a dragon.

Unable to sleep, I stared at the night sky. Rhyddean saw so many storms and periods of rain the twinkling stars were seldom viewable. When they did shine, Cara and I snuck out to the lake to stargaze. Not tonight, though. I hadn't seen her since we'd parted ways in the stable yard. Where was she?

Oulixeus' guards escorted me back to my chambers after he finished punishing me and took the money and papers I needed to start my new life. Normally, Cara would've heard whispers about the incident and found an excuse to be in my chambers, but she didn't come. And no one came to bring me dinner, so I couldn't even ask. Nerves twisted in my gut as I imagined the worst—the Fae killed her.

The air continued to swelter with heat and, unaccustomed to it, sweat dripped under my thick hair and slid along my shoulders.

I sulked over to the empty hearth and picked up the wrought iron fire poker, falling into a low squat. Poking the cold embers, pieces of ash flaked to the fireplace's soot floor. Calm and quiet—contrasting my troubled mind.

Tap, tap. The chamber's wooden door creaked open, and I tightened my grasp on the poker. With nothing left to lose, I readied myself to strike Oulixeus.

"Hey," Foster whispered and I dropped the poker and threw myself into his arms.

"How did you—"

"I pretended to be an attendant," he explained, and I noted the small wooden tray of food in his arms.

"Where's Cara?" I asked, unwilling to make small talk. He shook his head.

"I don't know. She wasn't in the stableyard, and neither were those Fae or the woman. The stable master had us busy, but I looked out for her and didn't see her. I asked around too and nothing." Foster ran a hand over his distraught face like he could wipe it away.

"Did she escape? Ran to your grandparents?" Before Foster arrived, all remnants of hope were abandoning me. But now, a tiny bit sparked. He shrugged and sat on the bed's edge. I joined him.

"I'll go there to check as soon as I can. I wanted to check on you first. Make sure you're okay. Just... don't do anything to piss them off. Keep your head low until we find Cara. We'll figure this out." He declared. He believed it. I didn't have the heart to tell him my hope diminished. "Do you need anything?" The stars reflected the softness in his eyes, sweet as honey. He leaned in close. Closer than usual. His thumb swirled on the top of my hand.

"Wine?" I laughed, ready to drown my sorrows. Live the rest of my imprisonment in a daze. His thumb stopped, and he leaned away. Releasing a heavy sigh, he let go of my hand and rose.

"I have to go. I'll let you know what I find out about Cara." He paused at the door. "Elle, you don't need wine to get through life. One day you'll find see that."

He left, and I choked down my doubtful laugh. We had a plan to take me somewhere safe, and it humoured the gods to see a mortal attempting to change her fate. They allowed me to get so close, just to yank it away for their own amusement. What else would explain the sudden loss of the war? Aramis coming here instead of the other three mortal courts. Coincidence?

And what was worse than having a glimpse of freedom ripped from me—putting Cara, and potentially her whole family, in harm's way. I needed to find her. Foster had already asked the castle staff who knew Cara. What could I do? Ask my parents?

I sarcastically laughed, imagining it until a clearer option surfaced—Oulixeus. He was furious with me, but I stood a better chance at recovering answers from him than anyone else at this court.

Laying on my bed, I winced at the soreness between my thighs as I slowly crawled beneath the duvet and rubbed my tender throat. Oulixeus always left his marks on me. As I settled in, staring at the blank space where Cara often lay, the tears finally poured as I imagined one day leaving deeper marks on him.

CHAPTER 8

Ridiculous. Utterly ridiculous. Bare, exposed, and vulnerable. The currant berry dress Oulixeus *requested* I wear to the feast had a non-existent neckline reaching far past my sternum. Fabric tickled the edge of my nipples, barely covering them, but despite the lack of material, the boning managed to lift and push my breasts upward and together.

The silk skirts of the gown swelled so wide that it forced Patrick and Eric to stand over two feet away. The dress was meant to send a message—Oulixeus owned me. Controlled me. A statement he sent to me, the court, and the Fae.

For once the corridors were bathed with light, every sconce ablaze. The castle hadn't shone so brilliantly since my youth. Aromatic, mouthwatering scents from the kitchen and great hall permeated the hallways—butter, sage, roasted mushrooms, and sizzling meats, all tantalising my senses. It had been two days since my last meal, presumably part of my punishment for running away.

Lively music and chatter frolicked through the corridors. Regardless of my anger and embarrassment, a part of me felt excited. The first feast between mortals and Fae in centuries, and I'd received permission to attend.

Turning right, Eric stopped me, grabbing my shoulder. "Your uncle wishes to see you first." He lifted his arm, motioning me to walk in the opposite direction. Patrick's eyes narrowed and trailed over my exposed flesh, lips curling into a perverse grin, plunging me into a sea of discomfort.

"Am I to lead the way to this mysterious location, Eric? And get your filthy hands off of me." I commanded, faking the courage I so desperately needed. Eric snickered and led the way and Patrick's grin took on a cruder edge as he followed, making me wonder if Oulixeus shared details about me with them.

Turn after turn, they led me to an unfamiliar wing of the castle. Cobwebs clung to the unlit corners, and layers of dust hinted at its abandonment. Eventually, we arrived at a narrow staircase leading downward, and they stopped. Anxiety churned the acid in my stomach.

"Go," Eric prodded my shoulder. I shot him a glare but complied. The tight staircase compressed my oversized dress, and I gathered the skirts to avoid falling. My escorts remained behind—thank the gods.

Descending into darkness, I stepped cautiously until my sight adjusted. Minutes passed before I reached the bottom of the stairs and found a black studded door. The latch lifted effortlessly, as if someone regularly visited the hidden chamber.

The room was like night itself. Every surface, from the walls to the floors, was carved from black marble, reflecting a muted radiance emanating from flickering white flames in the centre. Impossibly thick columns stretched toward an invisible ceiling, rendering the chamber otherworldly—almost divine. Each step I took rang with a chilling click through the colossal chamber.

Cases of artefacts, jewels, weapons, books, and more lay scattered through the room in no particular pattern. An unravelled, ancient scroll written in the Old Tongue seized my attention, depicting a formidable, scaly beast with flames spewing from its maw, sporting razor-sharp teeth and wings spanning its body's length. A dragon—dismissed as a myth to frighten children and tether them to their homes.

A shiver crawled up my arm, raising hairs and tensing my muscles. I wasn't alone. Something eerie watched me—certainly not Oulixeus.

Summoning courage, I glanced to my right, finding only cases filled with ancient armour. I turned to my left, where in the darkness, two red eyes gleamed. They bore into me, and my palm flinched to my chest. I dared a second look to recognize them as two rubies set into a white owl sculpture.

"I'm going insane." I rolled my eyes, but the prickling sensation intensified, racing up my arm. My hair stood on end, and my muscles begged me to flee as the air thickened, like an impending storm.

BANG, BANG, BANG.

My eyes darted between the cases, searching for the source of the insistent pounding. Against my better judgement, I cautiously followed the sound of multiple hands striking glass. My dress swayed, muffling the clacking of my heels as I reached the end of the makeshift aisle. The frenetic banging on the glass escalated, prompting me to peek around a corner.

A glass case containing armour trembled, as if invisible hands attempted to shatter it. The bust rocked back and forth, the armour clinking ominously until suddenly it ceased, only to resume further down the aisle. The eerie, unseen presence compelled me forward.

"Fuck," I muttered under my breath, and bit my lip. The pounding shifted to another case before I reached it, guiding me through the artefacts as if it wished to reveal something.

The presence led me to a plain wooden pedestal displaying nothing but a thick layer of dust. A thinner layer in a rectangular shape rested in the centre.

Find me. Find me. Find me. Something chanted over and over with a voice so silky, I felt like it would slip through my fingers, gone forever if I didn't hold on to it tightly. But as I neared the pedestal, its silkiness morphed into a stark hiss. I lifted a hand to touch the ancient stone and a cloying voice filled the chamber.

"There she is." Shoulders hiking to my ears, I snatched my hand back and turned to find Oulixeus.

He fit into this place well. Black hair slicked back, white flames glinted off his military jacket's ornate golden embroidery, portraying him as cruelly handsome.

"Where are we?" I asked, dismissing the thought.

"You look absolutely delectable." He ignored me and his gaze trailed from my lips to the non-existent neckline.

"Why are we here?" I refused to encourage him.

"Always so quick to business, Ellie." He lifted my chin and slid his thumb along my jaw, reminding me of Aramis. "That won't do," he brought his lips to my ear and whispered. I expected a kiss, but it didn't come. Instead, he guided me to the other side of the black chamber.

"You're in the Vault. All the family heirlooms, Toivo's treasures, and other valuables are kept here. Our court is wealthier than most recognize. Evander insists it's best to keep it hidden, but I believe wealth is power." He explained and stopped in front of an opened case.

Laying upon hunter-green velvet pillows sat a sparkling necklace. A thin chain made of petite white diamonds, the two strands met halfway down to form a slightly larger chain, and an onyx the size of an egg dangled at the end. The rarest jewel in Niafell.

Oulixeus smiled at my gaping expression. Plucking the necklace from its bed of velvet, he clasped it around my neck. It complimented the gown perfectly. Almost like the seamstress designed the gown to showcase the necklace.

Lost for words, my hand fell over the diamonds, feeling the cold gems against my skin to validate their existence. The onyx and diamonds purred to me, creating a deathly sense of calm. The unusual energy thrived inside.

"It's nice to see I finally did something right." Oulixeus found his way through my skirts and wrapped his arms around my waist. He rested his chin on my shoulder and breathed me in. For a fleeting moment, he encapsulated me in security, making me feel safe, free, and wanted.

I covered his hands with mine, inhaling the scent of oranges and bergamot, the way he did when shielding me from Mother's wrath, and picked flowers during our walks through the field. But it all changed after my sixteenth birthday. Before he'd...

"Oulixeus?"

"Mhm." He kissed the top of my shoulder.

"What are you planning?" My voice cooled to ice. His arms tightened, attempting to restore the serene moment. Refusing to return the gesture, he kissed me once more before letting go.

"It's none of your concern." He returned to the case and collected the matching earrings.

"I want to know," I protested.

"You'll know everything soon enough." He held an earring to the side of my face, evaluating the ensemble before completing it. "The important thing is that you're *safe*."

"Tell me what your plan is." The cold bite in my voice diminished his sweet demeanour, and his jaw tightened as he carefully inserted the earrings into my lobes and pushed a loose curl away.

"Let's make a deal," he proposed, and my brow arched. Oulixeus ensured every agreement favoured him. He only took. Even when he pleasured me, he did so for selfish reasons.

"What sort of deal?" I treaded dangerous ground, like quicksand ready to swallow you if you panicked without knowing how to escape. Using precise words, I aimed to gather the information I needed. However, my fear sometimes clouded my perceptiveness, leading to rash actions and bigger issues—like friends disappearing...

"You're going to be my escort tonight. You dance with *me*. Sit next to *me*. Hold *my* hand. And at the end of the night, I'll walk you back to your chamber and explain everything I have planned for *our* future." His repulsive grin resurfaced, yet, somehow, it painted him charming in this light.

"But everyone will see, it's—"

"I don't give a fuck about anyone else," he spit his words venomously.

"It's immoral. And illegal and what future?" My head swirled in bewilderment, unable to grasp his intentions.

"This isn't immoral, Ellie, trust me. I'll tell you everything tonight *if* you accept my offer." Comprehension failed me. He'd nearly killed me to prove his control. But his bargain restored a bit of my own power.

"Tell me where Cara is and I'll do it." Nothing suggested he knew anything about her disappearance, but I needed to try. Maybe one of his spies held information. He tilted his head and narrowed his eyes. My boldness amused him. He lifted his arm, a signal for me to take it.

"I'll let you know where your little friend is, my love. You'll learn everything tonight after the feast." The new nickname created a repulsion within me, but an energy forced it away. Forced it to transform into something... amorous.

"I'm all yours."

Approaching the black studded door, the hairs on the back of my neck rose and the invisible hand's voice returned.

Find me. Find me. Find me.

"Oulixeus?" I felt confident he didn't hear the voice or pounding from earlier, like the presence reserved its message for the darkness igniting inside of me.

"Yes?"

"The pedestal where you found me. What used to be there?" I asked.

His brows rose, and he turned his head to me. "We lost something very important a long time ago, and I'm going to get it back."

CHAPTER 9

Tangled between the inside layers of my gown, I kicked my feet in a struggle to be unnoticeable. Studying the hemline gliding across the tiled floor, Oulixeus coughed. He stood proud and handsome, staring straight ahead. However, he accompanied a fumbling mess. I followed his gaze to my parents and stood straighter.

Twelve ornate gilded chairs lined an extended table sitting atop a stone platform. My parents sat in the centre with Aramis.

Glowering through thick, greying brows, Father crinkled his forehead at Oulixeus and then at me. His outrage tracked from my face to the audacious dress, while Mother's face paled and the wine goblet she held vibrated.

I firmly believed they knew *exactly* what Oulixeus did to me, and they seemed quite content to allow it behind closed doors. But for Oulixeus to flaunt it in front of the entire court—rebellion curled my lips into a smile, thinking of how the gossip would spread and embarrass them.

"See, you like being with me," Oulixeus noted my reaction. Other mortal nobles assessed our familiarity—ladies whispered behind fans and silk gloves. Lords sent approving and envious nods to Oulixeus. He secured his grip on my hand, making me feel untouchable.

As we approached the head table, the burn in my left arm resumed. My eyes fell on our new ruler, Aramis. His golden hair, now dry and neatly brushed, cascaded gently to his shoulders over a dark red jacket, reminiscent of merlot. Leaning on the table, he trailed a finger along the rim of his goblet, staring at me.

Dark flames glinted within his emerald eyes, his brows slanted and the nascent dimples sent a curious twist through my stomach.

I tripped, and Oulixeus caught me. "Are you alright?" His voice brimmed with... concern? Genuine concern. I tore my fixation away from Aramis to confirm Oulixeus' empathy, and I found it—a subtle touch of compassion.

"Yeah," I quietly muttered. He smiled and kissed my fingertips with butterfly-soft lips. As Oulixeus and I ascended the platform, my sister, Orla, gaped—never able to conceal a damned thing.

We sat in the two empty chairs between Linnaea and the Fae king. Oulixeus took my hand and placed it in his lap before summoning a servant for wine. As the boy turned to leave, Oulixeus coughed.

"Hers too," he calmly but cooly instructed, nodding at my empty goblet. Flustered, the boy glanced at my father, aware of the ban on alcohol I typically had in place. Oulixeus' impatient sigh made the boy nervous enough to relent. He poured the dark red wine into my goblet, and Oulixeus gave me a quick squeeze as my heart sped. Not from him, but from the excitement of finally drinking wine again. "As my *wife*, there'll be fewer restrictions," he leaned over to whisper. I brought the goblet to my lips and took a long, steady sip. *Wife?* What? The mortal court sitting at the long plank tables spread across the floor glared at us. I maintained an expressionless demeanour, pretending to sit at a card game. This, after all, amounted to nothing more than a strategic play. A game to learn about Cara's whereabouts and Oulixeus' plan. A plan that apparently involved marrying me.

Gulping the dry wine, a relief spread through me, accompanying the soothing tranquillity of the onyx stone set in my new necklace. I was doing this for Cara. To find her. I threaded my fingers through Oulixeus', the way young lovers did during Spring Equinox, and his lip curled slightly as he spoke with Aramis.

Orla leaned straight across our sister and hoarsely asked, "What is going on?" Unimpressed, Linnaea's jaw dropped open as Orla's body forced hers deep into the cushioned chair. I had always wondered if my sisters noticed the way our uncle treated me. The discreet touching and staring at dinners, the only one to dance with me at feasts, and sneaking into my chamber.

"Nothing." I bluntly dismissed Orla and Linnaea pushed her away. Orla continued to glance at my hand entwined with our uncle's. Linnaea peeked too. I tried to ignore them, but discriminating leers met me. Judging my breasts on display, my uncle's attention, my forbidden wine, and the exquisite jewels draping my neck and ears.

This time I didn't sip, but chugged the whole goblet.

"You're not supposed to be drinking wine." Orla shoved Linnaea back into her seat again.

"It's fine, Orla. Leave your sister alone," Oulixeus scolded her. He leaned his forehead against my temple to add, "They're all jealous." He kissed the top of my shoulder. The onyx pulsed another calming sensation into me. Did it possess some kind of magic, too? Oulixeus pulled our hands further into his lap. Against his hard length, distracting me and making me forget why I hated him. *Fuck.*

Oulixeus struggled to keep his hands off me—a part of his message. He owned me. A public message to accompany the secretive *O* branded on my thigh. Oulixeus finished kissing my neck when he noticed food being placed in front of us. Throughout dinner, he made pleasant conversation with the Fae king and allowed me some space.

I concentrated on the plate before me. Braised lamb, an assortment of roasted vegetables, caramelized onions, and a thick gravy covering it all. Despite wanting to devour the food after days of starving, I took minuscule bites and kept my elbows tucked tightly to my ribs. Playing the role of Oulixeus' *good girl* to find Cara.

Observing the room, it seemed most mortal's fear of the Fae decreased as they feasted with each other.

Orla covered her mouth to swallow a bite of asparagus. "Jolene told me they're referred to as *males* and *females* because they're not hu-*mans*. You know?"

She continued to make small talk while Linnaea poked at the food in front of her, barely touched. Oulixeus conversed with the king throughout the rest of dinner, and every so often leaned over to whisper something in my ear.

"Are you enjoying yourself?"

"Do you need anything?"

"See how they look at you? You're meant for a greater life. I'm not going to be keeping you locked away in a tower. As long as you behave yourself."

"You are absolutely stunning."

"I love you."

Uncertain if it was the wine numbing my rationale, the onyx with a serene influence, or seeing my parents' mortified reactions, but I started to relish it all. Even Oulixeus' attentiveness and the idea of publicly being his.

Dinner finished, and servants pushed the tables and benches against the walls, revealing the dance floor. An orchestra perched in the mezzanine and played a combination of slow and quick waltzes. Nobles, human and Fae alike, found partners and the dancing commenced.

"Will you dance with me?" Oulixeus courteously asked as I sipped more wine. Caught by surprise, my mouth opened and the dark red liquid dribbled over my lip onto my chin. Without time to process my embarrassment, Oulixeus leaned in to kiss me and licked away the wine.

As someone gasped at his daring act, a thrilling desire sparked within me. Witnessing Oulixeus' mischievous smile, I knew he, too, loved the scandalous attention he drew. As we made our way to the dance floor, a fierce Fae male blocked our way.

"So, this is her. The one that almost got away." Not only did he stand tall, but also colossal. Unlike the lean-muscled Fae males I had encountered, he possessed a robust, neckless build.

Oulixeus laughed. "Oh, I assure you, General, she wasn't running away. Ellie, this is General Keniris. General, Princess Elowyn."

Playing the role of *good girl*, I tilted my head forward and lowered my eyes to the ground. "It's a pleasure to meet you, General."

"The pleasure is all mine, Princess." The massive Fae planted his lips on my knuckles, and my uncle placed a domineering hand on the small of my back.

"We have a lot to discuss, Prince Oulixeus. Our mutual friend is growing restless." The General warned. Shifting my gaze to Oulixeus, he chuckled and examined who stood near. What schemes did he plan?

"Patience, General. I promised my love a dance. Please excuse us."

The General tipped his head, unaffected by an uncle and niece behaving immorally close, and my uncle swept me to the dance floor.

Dance after dance, I couldn't deny that I enjoyed myself. Oulixeus lifted his arm, and we spun in sync with the others. Finishing my fifth spin, I laughed and tripped into his embrace.

Over his shoulder, Aramis monitored me carefully, with a grin wide enough to show those dimples and ignoring my father who spoke. My left hand twitched, but Oulixeus squeezed it.

"I adore your smile," Oulixeus spoke in hushed tones, but my attention remained on the Fae prince. "You're so beautiful when you're happy. You've been unhappy for too long, my love." His touch caressed me, and his scent of oranges and bergamot filled my nose, but I didn't see him. I saw only Aramis, like it was his smoky voice saying those words, touching me.

My heart quickened as his imaginary breath blew softly into my ear. My toes curled, and a moan left my lips as the heat ignited deep inside of me. The twitch in my left hand transformed into a throbbing ache. Another moan escaped. A flush crawled across my chest and into my cheeks. Across the room, Aramis bit his bottom lip as he watched my movements.

"I've waited for this for so long, Elowyn. For you to be mine. For you to… *accept* me. I love you." The heat of the breath cascading the column of my neck became my undoing. My eyes rolled into the back of my head as a muffled whimper left my mouth.

My eyes opened. *Wait.* Aramis disappeared, my view replaced by the staircase crowded with feasters. Oulixeus stated, "Soon you'll have everything you ever dreamed of."

I pushed him away. "What do you mean?" The flush on my cheeks faded into anger. The onyx attempted to soothe me, but a darkness overpowered it.

In the centre of the dance floor, we stopped, and no longer stood in each other's embrace. Oulixeus ran his fingers through his slicked-back hair. "We had a bargain, Ellie. I'll explain everything tonight."

Growing impatient, I whipped around and marched to the privy. Stares of curiosity and judgement found me from all corners of the room, replacing my earlier sense of rebelliousness with shame—embarrassment.

Linnaea followed me, slamming the door and locking it before anyone else entered. The chamber stretched out, with multiple toilets on one side, separated by partitions and small doors. Washbasins with mirrors mounted on the opposite side, and I whirled around to see her fury.

"What are you doing?"

I raised an eyebrow at her sudden interest in me and evaluated her. Linnaea stood slightly taller than me and very thin, her collarbones protruding beneath the extravagant crown jewels she donned. Mocha braids adorned her head in an intricate design and her dress hugged her narrow waist, the obnoxious skirt feigning wide hips. She looked like a queen.

"I don't know what you're talking about." I felt too exhausted to play games.

"You're letting him parade you around like some common whore—" Linnaea's voice rose, and I went rigid, her words slapping me across the face.

"I don't *let* him do anything."

Linnaea faltered, watching me with something close to pity on her face. "So, you're just fine with him using you like this?"

"What? No—" A gentle warmth spread near the onyx laying above my breasts. "What does that mean?"

"Nothing," she muttered, and I moved to block her way but stepped back when I saw the sheen of tears in her downturned sapphire eyes. Gripping a rail thin arm, she squeezed her fingertips into her skin until red marks formed. "I made a mistake."

"Look, I'm sorry. There's a lot on my mind." I sighed, walking over to a basin to lean on. I felt tired, emotionally tired. The smooth wood cooled my skin, trying to wake me up.

"Me too, Elle. I don't think they told you, but—" Before Linnaea could finish, a harsh knock rapped on the door. We stared at each other, hoping the person would go away. I wanted to hear what Linnaea would say. I knew she spoke of our parents and Oulixeus withholding information from me, and if Linnaea shared it with me, I might gain the upper hand on Oulixeus.

"Open this door, *now!*" Our mother's voice barked from the other side. I dropped my head into my hands and pressed the balls of my palms into my eyes, creating a million stars. My left hand still burned, but it had stopped throbbing. The privy door squeaked open, breaking my brief moment of stillness.

"Get out," Mother ordered Linnaea before turning her attention to me. "What are you doing?"

"Can I have a moment? It's going to take me more than a minute to pee in this dress," I remarked. Tonight became unsalvageable. If they wanted to punish me again, fine.

"Seeing as how your tits are on display, I'd imagine it'd be pretty easy to get in and out of that horrendous thing." She marched over and pinched the skin of my tricep. "What are you and your uncle playing at? Are you trying to have your father and I killed?" she seethed.

And it struck me, like lightning striking the earth. Did Oulixeus want my parents dead? To what end? My jaw dropped and she let go, seeing my surprise. Ever so gently, she lifted her hands to my hair. Naturally, I flinched, but the glimmer of shame in her black eyes caused me to reconsider.

She took the braid draping my shoulder, removed two pins from her own hair, and fashioned the braid around my head. Fluffing out the pleats, it slightly covered my ears and made me appear more elegant and mature. My face softened at the rare display of maternal love.

"Get back out there. You've made enough of a scene for tonight." Her moment of kindness ended within seconds. She made her way over to grab my arm, but I left the room before she could touch me.

Oulixeus stood in a crowd of mortal men and Fae males, exuding confidence. As I approached, he wrapped an arm around my waist and drew me as close as the dress allowed. He waved over a servant who carried a tray of sparkling wine, and we each took a flute.

They spoke of the military, politics, and whatever else those trained in war cared about. Uninterested, I surveyed the room. Intoxication overtook mortals and Fae. Conversation increased, dancing became sloppy, and wooing obvious. Spying Orla flirting with two Fae males, I choked on the sparkling wine.

"Are you alright?" Oulixeus attentively rubbed my back. I nodded, and he rejoined the conversation with his audience. A week before, not a single mortal had welcomed the thought of Fae entering our court. Tonight, they were enamoured. Did our new rulers enchant us with magic? Rumours had spread about how Fae held the power to glamour mortals. A magic used to manipulate what mortals saw and felt.

The room spun into a chaotic vortex of colours and indistinct figures and clamouring voices faded. Amidst the blur, Father occupied the centre, speaking with others but scrutinising me. I chortled and pressed further into Oulixeus.

Fuck. I had to stop drinking, but I guzzled the liquid left in the flute. They held a unique kind of liquor. Flavours sweeter than honey and sin burst on my tongue. I held the flute at eye level to see a drop of turquoise blue liquid on the bottom.

"What is—"

Oulixeus snatched the flute from me, and the group gaped. Some restrained their laughter as my body rocked backward and Oulixeus caught me.

"It's time for you to retire, my love," he berated. One of the noblemen standing by grinned.

"Ha! He knows what that means." A braying laugh burst from me, and I pointed at the nobleman. General Keniris stood in our circle and turned his head to hide his amusement.

Oulixeus chuckled again. "Excuse me, gentlemen. I need to make sure she doesn't lose her way." I winked at the grinning nobleman, and Oulixeus dug his fingers into my back.

"I know you're having fun, Ellie, and I got carried away yesterday, but tone it down," he lectured. He nodded his head at the people we walked past.

"Me? You want *me* to tone it down? What about you with the hand holding and kissing and whispering sweet nothings in my ear?" I mocked him. He curled his fingers into my lower back.

"I'm not drunk," he retorted.

I rolled my eyes at the laughable notion. The one time he's not drunk, and he's throwing it in my face. Maybe we *were* perfect for each other, two hypocrites. Oulixeus led me across the dance floor to the staircase when the music stopped. The careless dancers surrounding us halted in the middle of their waltz and the conversations amongst the crowds fell to a hush. Everyone looked toward the raised head table where my father stood with a glass of the turquoise liquid.

"My wife and I are honoured to welcome our new sovereign on behalf of all the mortal courts," his voice bellowed through the hall.

Seeing Aramis at the head table, staring at me again, I leaned into Oulixeus and asked, "What's happening?"

His hold tightened. "I'm not certain," he replied, watching intently.

"It is regrettable how many mortal and Fae lives were lost due to this war." Father continued and Oulixeus snorted. "It is time we move forward, and welcome Niafell into an era of peace, unity, and prosperity with Aramis as our high king!"

The crowd erupted into a roaring cheer. *High king.* My brain tried to organise the information through the alcohol. "High King Aramis has appointed me and my dear wife, Queen Sévérine, to rule the Court of Rhyddean *and* the other mortal courts in his stead to form one united mortal court."

"What does that mean?" I leaned into Oulixeus and whispered, my brows knitting together.

"It means I'm going to get everything I want." A cruel smirk formed across my uncle's face.

"To cement the treaty, I propose a marriage!" Father announced.

The Fae were monsters. They'd proved it the moment they arrived by burning the Spellcasters alive, attacking the woman in the stable yard, taunting me in the woods, and clearly bewitching all of us tonight. Gods save whoever my parents chose for this marriage—because it would surely be a death sentence.

Father walked over to Aramis and grasped his shoulder cheerfully. The Fae high king gave a thunderous pat on my father's back the way close friends do.

"Your Highness, please accept the betrothal of my daughter, Linnaea." Father gestured toward my pale sister. The entire court and Fae guests turned toward her, but she searched the crowd until she found me. I held her horrified gaze.

How could they send her to the Fae court to marry that monster? They loved Linnaea. Their pride and joy. Mother and Father invested impressive amounts of money on her education and refused to marry her off until the most worthy of suitors came forth. Rumours of her marrying the Prince of Penre started spreading just a few months ago.

Why her and not *me*? The daughter they feared and distrusted? They threw me into a tower and nearly discarded the key—why not sacrifice me to the lions? I felt ashamed for not being able to protect my younger sister, regardless of the distance between us.

"No." Aramis stood from the head table and Linnaea's head snapped to watch him as with one graceful leap, he landed on the tiled floor on the other side.

He faced me and grinned, adjusting his jacket. Flames ignited in his eyes, devouring me as if only I existed. A scarlet heat crept into my cheeks, and the room spun.

"Elowyn." The Fae high king said and my eyes widened as whispers broke amongst the crowd. Oulixeus' nails dug through the fabric of my dress and pinched my skin as my throat tightened and a rapid pulse shot from the stone hanging from it.

"I'd much prefer your daughter, Princess Elowyn," Aramis continued with barely a glance at my father as he rolled his tongue along his lower lip.

Linnaea remained still, staring vacantly at me. I could still protect her. In the spotlight, I straightened my posture and raised my chin. I needed to overcome my fear now. For the first seven years of my life, my parents had groomed me to inherit Rhyddean's throne. Even though they stripped it from me, the opportunity to prove my worth presented itself. I wouldn't be afraid of the Fae monster in front of me—at least I wouldn't let them see my fear.

Taking a step forward, the accumulated alcohol swooshed through my head, and I quickly paused to compose myself before walking forward.

One foot in front of the other. Slowly. My skirts hid my wobbling legs, but a toddler walked straighter than me. My right knee buckled, and I paused to catch myself from falling. Aramis beheld me with encouraging eyes, his chin slighting tipped forward. I used those eyes to focus and walk straight.

The great hall descended into silence. The clapping of my heeled shoes became the sole noise.

A shadow enveloped us, and the room stopped spinning. Instantly, it became easier to focus on Aramis. The judgemental nobles, my glowering parents, and furious uncle disappeared.

Meeting him, he gently folded my fingers between large, powerful hands. Heat pulsed from him, sending a wave of comfort through me. Did he create the heat from magic? Fire magic?

Aramis brought his full, lush lips to the top of my hand, and a surprising surge of desire curled in the pit of my stomach.

The crowd finally broke the silence and clapped. Awkwardly at first, but it grew to a steady beat.

I intended to find Linnaea or my parents, but my instinct guided me elsewhere, eyes landing on Oulixeus. He stood across the hall directly in front of me, hands balled into fists, nostrils flaring, and rage thrumming along his jaw.

I walked from one unwanted marriage proposal directly into another.

CHAPTER 10

The corridor spun and swirled. Walls bled into carpeted floors. Flickering flames on sconces blurred. Passing noblemen chuckled and their escorts gasped. Unbeknownst to me, my heels disappeared. Acid formed in my oesophagus. *Fuck.*

I braced against a wall with both hands and leaned forward. Another gag. Spotting a vase displayed on a console table, I stumbled over and vomited into the ancient porcelain.

Fucking fairy wine.

Following the applause, Aramis had handed me a flute of the turquoise liquid and the foreign alcohol disarranged the world. Creating an illusion to stumble through, a Spellcaster's maze.

Finally reaching my chambers, I gripped my forehead.

Tonight had to be some sort of dream. Too bizarre to be reality. The Fae high king proposed to me. *Me.* I refused to be passed from abusive man to abusive... male, but I felt helpless to stop it. Cara spent two months training me to defend myself and to throw a punch, but I was no match against the skilled warriors who sought after me.

The door swung open. Whirling around to identify the intruder, the entire room morphed into a spiralling mess. One side of my brain flew to the other with no warning, causing me to fall into a sea of skirts.

"Ellie!" Oulixeus shut the door and rushed to my aid. The dress swallowed me and my legs weakened. He joined the waves of rich berries, pulling me close. I anchored my hands to the arm stretched across my chest. A hopeless effort to stop the spinning. Varied emotions flooded me. Fear. Excitement. Anger. Relief. Desperation. Adrenaline. Mostly confusion. All expelled through sobs.

"It'll be okay," Oulixeus promised.

"How?"

Nothing felt okay. A heinous beast proposed to me, mortals lost the war, my escape failed, and worst of all—Cara went missing because of *me* and *my* stubbornness.

Oulixeus' grip tightened, and the familiar sensations he used to trigger pulsed through my veins—safety and love. If I could convince Oulixeus to break the engagement, and keep me here, then at least I could somehow help Foster find Cara.

He unsheathed a dagger at his waist and wrapped my fingers around its hilt. "You're going to the Fae Court. You're going to kill Aramis and come home to me."

The familiar chaotic quillon glinted in the fire's light. *My* dagger.

"I can't—"

"Yes, you can. You have no idea just how unique you are." Oulixeus' eyes reached into uncomfortable depths of my soul. "Allow him to get close to you, and when you have his trust, sink this blade into his chest."

"Please don't let me go." I resorted to begging and resented myself for it. The remnants of wine dispelled every ounce of pride from me. I buried my face into his chest, the detailing scratching my cheeks. Only Oulixeus loved me enough to save me from the Fae.

He framed my face with his hands and kissed me frenziedly. Instead of pulling away, I welcomed him. Returning his kiss beseechingly, my mouth opened. Our tongues met, and I tangled my fingers through his hair. He rolled me onto my back and into the delicate silk of my skirts.

The thrill I felt earlier returned hungrily. Oulixeus trailed rough kisses from my lips, along the diamond necklace, and finally to the exposed curves of my breasts. I released a shallow gasp of pleasure.

The dress hindered my desperate attempt to wrap my legs around his waist. Aware of my desire, Oulixeus ripped through the laces of my bodice. My impatience encouraged him to hurry.

"You're mine." His voice blew against my ear as he loosened my bodice to tug my breasts free, taking a one in his mouth.

"More," a breathy plea. He grinned while flicking the tip of his tongue along my taut nipple and stripped the rest of the gown off, leaving only the onyx. Craving more, Oulixeus slid his hand to my aching core, stroking my clit. I panted, "please... don't... let me go..."

"Never." He drew circles around the bundle of nerves. He had never touched me so sensually before. A different finger stroked my entry as he hovered his mouth over mine, taunting me, and fiercely watching my reaction as he gradually slid a finger inside.

My spine arched. Eyes fluttered. Mouth opened to a silent moan. He had never done *that* before.

"Yes," he groaned, relishing the euphoric tremors he created. Pushing deeper into me, his stroking forced me into delirium, begging for release. Understanding the noises I made, Oulixeus continued to hit the sensuous spot again and again, faster and harder, greedy for my response.

"Good girl," he whispered. Muscles spasming. Nails scratching along his skin. My spine curved further. One final movement, deeper and stronger, and I unravelled with ecstasy.

We sprawled on ripples of silk as he slid the glistening wet finger he used to fuck me into his mouth.

"Let me stay," I pleaded and rested on his chest. Kissing the top of my head, he looped the curls of my hair around his finger and allowed them to fall.

Evading my plea, Oulixeus silently removed his strained breeches. He slowly and gently slid into me. He'd never shown me such gentle pleasure before.

The way his length dragged along my inside made me clench and spasm. How did he make me so exhilarated? My nails sunk into his back. Smiling, he lifted a hand to my neck, calling forth each previously torturous moment with him.

"No." I pushed his hand away. With a frustrated grunt, he lowered it next to my head and pushed into me hard. I pleaded silently. *Stay with me. Don't go back to before. Stay sweet and loving.* His other hand gripped my wrist a little too tight.

Attempting to keep him gentle, I leaned up and whispered, "I love you." And in a way, I meant it. Maybe.

You shouldn't. The dagger scolded me for my recklessness. But my heart fought for love. Any kind of love.

He pulled back to study my face and, satisfied with what he discovered, he fiercely thrust into me. Riding me with a purpose. A purpose to reciprocate the words he's waited to hear for five years, maybe more.

I wouldn't come again. He moved too fast, so I allowed him this moment, wrapping my legs around his waist and bucking my hips into him.

"Gods," he leaned his head into the air and moaned. The effect I had on him filled me with fervour, so I did it again. His abdomen quivered. And the third time, he came, cock spasming before he fell and breathed heavily into my ear.

The onyx jewel around my neck shot an approving pulse through me. The same sensation it had released whenever I did something to make Oulixeus happy tonight.

He rolled to his side and caressed between my thighs, feeling his come drip from my centre. "I'll have a tea made for you."

"You never offered before."

"If you ride to the Blood Fortress carrying *my* child, not the high king's, there will be trouble. And you're going to succeed. You're going to succeed and come home to me. *Then* we'll have children." He pulled on his breeches.

"Succeed in killing him? Won't that restart the war? How will I make it back here alive? I doubt the Fae will allow the woman who killed their high king to live."

Oulixeus sighed. "We'll speak more about this tomorrow, when you've sobered."

"No, Oulixeus, I won't. I'm so sick of this." The onyx cooled and shot a piercing stab into my chest, as if fighting against something stronger residing in me.

"What are you talking about?" He stood over me.

"You men. You're all the same. Using women as your little pawns. You don't care about me. Not truly."

"Don't be ridiculous, you're not a pawn. You're going to be my *wife*. Just not yet. We hit a crossroads. We'll overcome this."

"I have no say in anything. Nobody asked me if I wanted to be the queen of Rhyddean. They thrust it upon me and then ripped it away. You all forced me to play quiet, doting, outcast princess. And I did. For fourteen years." My voice grew with my rage. Oulixeus continued peering down at me, his mouth twitching. "I played your *whore* tonight, with the empty promise of being told what in the Veil is going on and where Cara is! Where is she, by the way?" His eyes squinted as I continued to scream at him. "I was a fool to believe you'd keep me from marrying Aramis. You made me believe that if I played the part, you'd keep me safe! But you lied." Defeated, I threw my arms in the air and let them land on either side of me. Tears rolled down my face.

"Are you done?" he asked, voice cold and smooth as ice. I silently held his stare through tears. "Good." He stalked behind and grabbed my arm to lift me. Gripping my chin and pressing his cheek into mine, he hissed, "Don't you *ever* compare me to others. I am *nothing* like them. I am so much more than they ever will be."

"You're nothing more than an egotistical snake." I spat on the floor. He would never change. He would always be the man who beat me, manipulated me, and controlled me. I couldn't trust my heart.

Ever so slowly, he stalked back around to face me. A familiar sting hit my face. He struck me. Throwing me back to the ground, a stabbing pierced my gut as he drove his boot into my side. I cried out in overwhelming pain.

Something glinted in the moonlight. The dagger. As Oulixeus paced the room, threading his fingers through his hair, I reached over. This was it. I was done. Gone being controlled and kept as his pet. Being a pawn in men's political games.

Kneeling, I angled the dagger parallel to my forearm. The pain would be agonising but brief. Shorter than a life of abuse by Oulixeus or Aramis. I pinched my eyes closed. Holding my breath. Ready to give in. Ready for darkness to consume me. To welcome the darkest depths of the Veil.

The tip pierced into my forearm. A hint of iron and desperation filled my senses. Blood beaded and trickled along my skin. About to slash deeper and quicker, my hand locked. Opening my eyes to see Oulixeus gripping and pulling the dagger from me.

"Please," I begged. "I can't do this anymore!"

"No," he grunted, struggling to release the dagger from my hopeless grasp. A sudden rush of air filled the room. Startled, I accidentally dropped the dagger. A tall and thick figure rushed in and grabbed Oulixeus by the neck and thrust him against the wall.

My sight adjusted to the fresh stream of light pouring into the room. Aramis. And he didn't just push Oulixeus against the wall, he held him off the floor.

My uncle's eyes widened, and he gripped Aramis's forearm, trying to push the powerful Fae off, but Aramis squeezed Oulixeus' throat so tight, his legs kicked out. His face faded to purple and his lips turned blue.

"I'm going to kill you," Aramis casually stated. Oulixeus attempted to plead, but produced only short gasps instead. The Fae's hand tightened. "Do you prefer I crush your neck? Right here, right now. Or I could melt the flesh from your face."

Red and orange flames appeared from his other fist, creating a light bright enough to illuminate their full bodies and scorching hot flames. Oulixeus' legs kicked violently and amusement stretched Aramis' grin.

"Ah, yes. I think I'll enjoy seeing your skin blister and burn." The dangerous Fae announced, raising the conjured flame inches from Oulixeus' face. My uncle pressed his head into the wall, teeth gritting and eyes shut, flesh already reddening.

"Wait," I whispered as Aramis readied to extinguish my tormentor. His smile dropped, and he snapped his head to me.

"Take off the stone."

"What?"

"Take. It. Off." Aramis growled, low and insistent, but reassurance lay within its depth.

I pinched the clasp behind my neck, and the comforting warmth I experienced all evening vanished as the beautiful necklace clattered against the stone.

"That stone's magic has been influencing you all evening. Now, how would *you* like him to die?" His smirk reappeared.

My eyes shot to Oulixeus. Did he know the onyx contained magic? My anger fumed from deep within me. He would never stop trying to control me. The scheming manipulator deserved to die a gruesome death, like the ones Aramis proposed. But a voice within me hesitated. Maybe remnants of the stone's magic, but my gut refused to allow Oulixeus' death.

"Please don't kill him." I didn't plead desperately. I only made a straightforward request.

Aramis tilted his head. "Why not?"

"It's... complicated."

"It doesn't have to be," Aramis said softly, but I shook my head, refusing to relent. "Fine."

Expelling a bored sigh, his flames vanished as he dropped Oulixeus, who collapsed to his knees, coughing. Aramis strode over to me, removing his jacket to cover my naked body. Forgetting I remained bare, I flushed as he clasped the buttons.

"Don't..." Oulixeus coughed. "Touch her!"

Guiding me to the armchair, Aramis sneered, "Don't touch my betrothed?" He paused to assist me. "Get out," he ordered my uncle.

Oulixeus rose, leaning against the wall. He insisted I marry Aramis and kill him to accomplish his unexplained scheme, but was clearly not prepared to surrender his control over me tonight. Oulixeus' desperate eyes found me, and our balance shifted. The control relinquished to me, causing him to panic. My hands involuntarily trembled.

"I said, get out." Aramis' order grew colder. More threatening. More... primal. Testosterone circulated through the air like an electric charge. Part of me wanted Oulixeus to stay. To fight Aramis. To cling to the familiar, the hope of who he used to be, but tonight cemented his true character. So desperate to control me, Oulixeus used *magic* in hopes of making me compliant and obedient. Rationalising ceased to be an option, and my hopefulness died, so I looked away.

I flinched as the door slammed. Aramis sat on the floor and leaned against the stone frame of the hearth. Knees bent, forearms resting on top. Each muscle rippling through his body loosened. "Are you okay?" he asked after a prolonged, drained exhale.

Was I okay? Was *he* okay? I stared at him, unblinking. Attempting to process the past week. The spinning room made it impossible to focus.

Instead of answering, I asked my own question. "How did you know the onyx was influencing me?"

"It's rare for onyx to possess magic, so it was a... hunch." Aramis turned his attention to me and cocked his head at my grimace. "Are you sure you don't want me to kill him?"

Who talked that way? A Fae born and bred to kill, I guess.

"How did you find my chambers?" I asked. He smirked, amused.

"You wouldn't believe me if I told you." He chuckled, leaning his head back against the stone. "Do you have any whiskey? I could use a nightcap."

"They don't let me drink."

"You are certainly drunk tonight." The corner of his lip curved to create a dimple. "No matter. The mortals have shit booze, anyway."

"I still want to know how you found me. Was it... magic?"

With a deep chuckle melting into a sigh, he said bluntly, "I smelled you."

"You...? That doesn't make sense," I blurted, too inebriated or exhausted to care about decorum.

"Fae have heightened senses. Scents are strong to us. Food, foul water, sickness in animals, a mortal or Fae's unique scent, even responses in the body."

"So, you found me by—"

"Smelling your arousal. You have a delicious scent, by the way. Like fresh morning dew and ripe summer strawberries." His voice rumbled like soft thunder through a smirk. I tucked my feet beneath my body and shrugged further into the oversized jacket. "Don't worry, Princess. I won't do anything inappropriate." He stood in a single graceful movement. "Not yet, anyway."

"You may leave," I instructed. I wanted him out. Men. Males. Whatever. They were all the same. Both disgusting control freaks.

He placed his hands on the chair, trapping me. Our noses inches apart. My heart quickened. Deeply inhaling, he flashed those predatory teeth. Canines sharp and elongated.

His eyes closed, and his nose twitched like a predator catching the scent of his prey. Euphoria spread across his features, savouring each note he detected. "Delicious."

"I said, you may leave." My face hardened. He paused before dropping his smile and pushing away.

"If I leave that with you, will you try to kill yourself again?" He nodded to the dagger on the floor.

"You knew?" The way he'd attacked Oulixeus, I'd assumed he'd misunderstood the situation.

"I can smell desperation just as much as desire, Princess." My face grew hot. He lifted the dagger and felt it in his hands, gauging the weight of the weapon. His eyebrows rose, impressed by it.

I'm yours. The dagger called to me.

"I'd like to keep it."

"Then it's yours." He placed it gently on the table.

Yes. The dagger sang.

Aramis walked to the door and opened it before pausing when I found myself asking, "Are you different?"

He turned back to me. A brow raised. "From how they all described you?"

He seemed different. Those intriguing, raging eyes hid something. A truth he suppressed. But why? Was it the monster he struggled to restrain?

Bowing his head low and biting his lower lip, he shook his head. "No. Don't make that mistake, Princess. I'm *exactly* the monster they claim." Without looking at me, he left and the burning sensation returned to my arm. A reminder. I belonged to a new master.

CHAPTER II

"How are you feeling today?" Conláed asked, escorting me to my mother's drawing room. Aramis had posted his two most trusted guards to watch over me after making me his betrothed last night. Molvys and Conláed, the two who helped capture me, took shifts standing outside my chamber door throughout the rest of the evening and this morning.

They had little to report to Aramis, unless he cared to know the hours I spent heaving. Honestly, I felt worse than shit. My head pounded, my left arm still burned from the inside out, and my parents had gifted me to the Fae—not to mention I still needed to find Foster and see if he'd checked the cottage for Cara.

"I'm fine." A lie.

"I don't believe you, Princess. I attended the feast last night, too. You drank nearly as much as me, and you're a third of my size." He snickered, and I rolled my eyes. "You're certainly feistier than we predicted."

Than we predicted. I stopped, spun around, and curiously tilted my head. Aramis and his friends had spoken of me. "Why is Aramis so interested in me?"

"He prefers partners with the strength to sustain his vigour." Conláed shrugged a shoulder and laughed.

"I don't like you." I imagined piercing the dagger strapped to my thigh through his throat.

"We'll change that." He winked, mischief glinting through his brown eyes as we continued our path.

My mother, Linnaea, Orla, and one of our other sisters, Solandis, sat scattered throughout the drawing room when we arrived, each absorbed in a hobby. Linnaea read against the bay window, head leaning against the glass. Orla embroidered, bouncing her frustration through a leg, and Solandis played the piano. Her talent impressed all the mortal courts. A pang of envy flowed through me. I wasn't allowed hobbies. Unless excessive drinking and gambling qualified.

Mother wrote at her desk and pink crawled across my chest as I recalled myself kneeling there while Oulixeus thrust into me. Fury slowly replaced shame as visions of his hands coiling around my throat like a deadly python entered my mind.

"You're late," Mother stated, fixated on her work. I slammed the door in Conláed's smirking face.

"Solandis, play louder." Mother left her paper and stood. "Linny, Elowyn." The cheerful, upbeat melody Solandis played grew in sound. Her delicately long fingers gently plucked each key as Linny and I obediently followed Mother to a hidden door she opened next to the fireplace. Orla tiptoed to lock the main door as the three of us climbed a slim stairwell leading to a dark, wood-panelled room. Fire flickered in a stone fireplace framed by two imposing bookcases lined with ancient tomes. Two leather couches faced each other in the centre, my father sat on one as Oulixeus rose from the other to pour himself a whiskey.

His hair was dishevelled, dark blue circles rimmed his eyes, and he still wore his clothes from the feast. Bruises shaped like fingers wrapped around his throat and old instinct urged me to run to him, but a new one encouraged a smile. He threw back the whiskey and poured another glass.

"Sit," Mother instructed, taking a seat next to Father. Sitting on the couch opposite my parents, I slung my slippered feet onto the coffee table between us, a single folded paper resting to the side. Linnaea stayed near the door, wrapped in her arms as if trying to protect herself from the impending lecture.

"You must be thrilled," I scoffed, slouching into the hard cushions, discarding decorum—why should I care anymore? They probably didn't choose me to begin with to avoid offending him, because gifting your shut-in daughter would definitely send a message. Luckily for my parents, the monstrous Fae wanted me and Linnaea.

"Why would we be thrilled?" Mother's voice stayed cold and surprisingly steady, considering her judgemental stare at my feet on the table.

"You'll finally be rid of me without causing scandal. It's why I'm still here and alive, isn't it? You didn't want to marry me off to anyone, as they would see it as an insult. You didn't want to kill me because of the rumours it would spread. There's no place to ship me off to that someone wouldn't discover. But now, our new ruler actually *wants* the daughter you couldn't get rid of. Convenient for you."

I fluffed the skirt of my dress and smoothed the fine wrinkles forming on my lap, staring at my hands throughout the entirety of my speech. Brave enough to speak it, though not brave enough to meet their eyes.

"You assume wrong. We chose Linnaea for a purpose. The change isn't ideal, but we can't risk offending Aramis. Our plan should still work. You aren't completely useless to us. I had a gut feeling continuing your education after Octavian's birth was necessary." Her voice dripped with sugared malice, each word a cunningly concealed barb wrapped in a veneer of false sweetness.

One, two, three. Inhaling the insult.

One, two, three. Exhaling my anger.

"Hmm, you don't have anything clever to say?" Mother baited, and I took another cleansing breath as Linnaea's hesitant fingers traced patterns on her arm.

Be strong. Don't break. Don't falter. Don't let them see you cower.

My father placed a hand on her lap, a subtle indication to cool her rising temper, and said, "An interesting opportunity has arisen from our disastrous loss in this war. Beneath this castle is the Vault where we store the treasures Toivo left behind."

Stories described Toivo as one of the most powerful gods. He gifted the Fae of his land Mind Magic and later gifted mortals with magic to defend themselves against the Fae, the origin of the Gifted. Ultimately, it allowed mortals to take this land and form the four mortal courts.

"The Book of Toivo is one of those items and someone stole it generations ago. Evander's namesake responsible for the loss—" Oulixeus cut in with a subtle insult, and it dawned on me, the pedestal used to display the Book.

"A book?" I raised a brow, crossing my arms over my chest. Mother frowned at my poor posture, but I had bigger things to fear—Cara's whereabouts and Aramis.

Ignoring both Oulixeus and me, Father continued, "A spell book possessing an incantation to destroy the Fae and the magic of this realm once and for all. Your uncle's source insists it's located in the heart of the Fire Court, at the Blood Fortress."

"We originally meant this task for Linnaea. She's clever and resourceful, but he chose you, so you will be Aramis' bride and find the Book. Once located, you will bring it home to us," Mother finished Father's thoughts and my sister shifted uncomfortably on her feet.

The leather squeaked as I shifted, contemplating their ambitious task and my recruitment. I'd longed for freedom from their dominance for years, but not this. I remained under their influence and would be under Aramis' command, scrutinised at every step—a situation not much different from my current life. Maybe it made me more suited for this task despite my parent's opinions.

"And how am I supposed to locate this book? What does it look like? Does the informant know where it's kept? I need details."

My father's eyes flashed with surprise, not expecting me to be so perceptive. Leaning forward, he slid the lone piece of parchment on the table toward my skirts, and I dropped my feet to the floor. The ancient paper scraped against my delicate skin, and tiny bits of the edges flaked to the floor.

Unfolding it carefully, I squinted, trying to understand what I stared at. Lines formed squares and rectangles of different shapes, with the largest rectangle at the top and eight circles drawn in the centre, almost like pillars in a room.

"What is this?" I dropped it from my hands, letting it float to the table as if it held little consequence for me.

"A partial blueprint of the Blood Fortress. Oulixeus' informant believes the Book is located in that area of the fortress."

"If Fae kings are anything like mortal kings, what makes you think I'll be free to roam the fortress?" A subtle jab of my own.

Mother raised a brow and maliciously smiled. "Oh, I have faith you'll be more successful at enticing the high king to share valuable information than your sister would have been."

One, two, three. Inhaling the insult. Did they presume I sought Oulixeus out?

One, two, three. Exhaling anger. I dared to glance at my uncle, shooting more whiskey.

"What are you insinuating, Mother?" I continued to breathe deeply into my belly to keep myself from exploding on her.

"Seduce him. Make him fall in love with you, make him trust you. Tell him how deeply grateful and honoured you are to be his bride, the first mortal high queen, and I'm sure he'll have no reason to keep you locked away." Her proposition had me curling my hands into fists, knuckles turning white, attempting to suppress my growing fury. Again, Linnaea shuffled her weight, and an invisible hand squeezed my gut as I imagined my sister being told to seduce Aramis.

"Oulixeus' spies never discovered a precise location. It is a rather ambitious task, but this is a once-in-a-lifetime opportunity to finally level the playing field. Our Spellcasters were never enough," Father interjected.

Their plan was undeniably ambitious and foolish. Whether Aramis' bride turned out to be Linnaea or me, all eyes would fixate on the new mortal high queen, driven by either suspicion or curiosity. Aside from the court's obsession, guards and ladies would be in my constant presence.

Even if I seduced Aramis and gained his trust enough to roam the fortress of my own volition, would I ever be truly alone? Would I spend my nights sneaking out of Aramis' bed to find the Book? Would Aramis allow me to leave his bed... alive?

"No," I stated, rising to leave. "I'm not doing this." It was a suicide mission.

"For once, do as you're told." Mother clenched her teeth, fighting to maintain her authority over me.

"I *always* do as I'm told!" The growing fury rumbled more ferociously than I'd felt in a long time, but I couldn't place the familiar surge of power. "You've stripped everything from me. My future, my freedom, my humanity! I deserve a say in my own fate."

Mother stood and struck me across the face. My cheek burned as blood trickled from a cut her ring created and I glowered at her, clenching my jaw. I hated this. The entire situation and them.

The edges of my vision blurred into obscurity, though one figure remained sharply defined—my mother, her gaze as icy and unyielding as stone. Her stance grew more rigid, almost like an attempt to undertake the burgeoning power within me.

The dagger sang.

Do it. It's time.

Glass rattled in the distance as a piercing ringing formed in my ears. Darkness narrowed in on my mother. And there it emerged. Fear. She allowed herself to fear, and I couldn't tell if I liked it or felt sorry for her. The ringing intensified, nearly deafening when it halted and immediately subdued.

Pressure on my hand grounded me. Oulixeus stood beside me, squeezing my fingers with his own. The brooding shade of deep mahogany brown in his eyes bored into me. Everything stopped. The ringing subdued, and the power dispelled.

My legs buckled as I suddenly felt weak, and I fell to the couch behind me. Oulixeus brought over a shot of whiskey.

"No," Mother protested, but I took the liquor and knocked it back. Her fear dissipated and returned to pure wrath as the amber liquid soaked hints of oak into my tastebuds.

I searched Oulixeus for answers. Genuinely concerned, he wiped a strand of hair stuck to my forehead away from my face. He leaned in and whispered, "Do this for me. Please."

"No," I whispered back. His jaw muscle twitched at my disobedience.

"We anticipated your hesitation." Father placed a plain wooden box on the table between the couches and turned his gaze to the cackling fire. The flames highlighted the dark, polished box. A knot of apprehension clenched my throat like a vise, my eyes fixating on the sharp edges.

"Open it," Mother encouraged, her features stone and impenetrable.

My gut warned me not to listen, but I didn't obey. Gasping, I slammed the lid shut and dropped it, muffling my cry with a hand.

"She's in the dungeons," Oulixeus confirmed. "Alive."

"She won't be alive if you fail. Neither will her grandparents. Oulixeus informed us of the little friendship you two have formed," Mother said.

"Don't you dare." I pulled my courage from where it hid deep inside of me.

"We can go kill her right now," she continued, as I took a sharp breath.

Fuck. Fuck. Fuck.

I tilted my head back, pressing my palms into my eye sockets.

Fuck.

"How can I be certain she's still alive?" I demanded.

"You'll just have to trust us," Mother smirked menacingly. I shook my head and embraced my knees. How could I ever trust them? Oulixeus stroked my hair as disgust threatened to hurl from my stomach.

"You *promise* she's alive?" I cried through my hands.

"Yes," Oulixeus answered for them.

"Go find the Book, bring it back, and I'll release her," Father instructed.

"Fail, and she dies." Mother added.

I hid my anguish behind a stoic facade, each suppressed tear wrestling with trusting them. Did I even have a choice? What else could I do to help Cara? The Fae were just as likely to kill her. Why keep someone so rebellious alive? And if Grandmama was a witch—it was best to keep their entire family off of the Fae's radar.

Oulixeus squeezed my hand. Fuck him. Fuck him for trying to be sweet and comforting.

"Don't fucking touch me." I pushed Oulixeus off me. "Fine. I'll do it. I'll find your damned book. And when I return, she goes free." What other choice did I have?

"She goes free," Father confirmed. Unable to be around them for a second longer, I marched to the door.

"Fine," I whispered and fled.

Almost at the bottom of the stairs, a hand took hold of my wrist. A delicate, kind hand. Linnaea. Tears streamed from her sapphire eyes.

"I'm so sorry." She released me when I silently assured her I'd listen. "For my accusations last night and enduring them for all these years. I never helped you. You didn't really want to be with Oulixeus, did you? You were just trying to—"

"Survive," I said the word she struggled to find. "I'm sorry, too, Linny. If I knew they planned to ship you off..."

"Neither of us can do anything, can we?" She grasped her skeletal arm and pinched herself again, worrying me.

"I'm going to at least try," I vowed, and as I turned to leave, Linnaea took my hand, hindering me.

Sliding folded parchment into my hand, she said, "Take this, you'll need it."

And I unfolded the scratchy paper to uncover the map my parents showed me earlier. I offered a gentle smile and abruptly left her to confirm my parents' threat.

I memorised that wooden box. Its sharp edges, the orange light of the fire casting against the black wood, and what it held. Most chambermaids and servants had rough hands—fingers calloused and dirty. But Cara always cared about her hygiene and appearance. No doubt remained, as I remembered the slender, perfectly manicured finger in the box—it belonged to Cara.

CHAPTER 12

The tall Fae warrior, three times my size, struggled to maintain my swift pace rushing through the castle. Conláed bombarded me with questions as I weaved through the corridors, determined to see Cara locked away for myself and confirm my parents' threat. An image of cold chains clamped around her delicate wrists and blood staining her hands invaded my mind, and I almost threw up again.

Nobles gaped at the sight of me, not accustomed to my presence freely moving about the castle. A gaggle of ladies blocked my path to the corridor I needed, and I pushed straight through them. Their gasps echoed down the hall I turned into, inching nearer to the dungeon. I needed to navigate through a few more wings until I reached it.

"Princess." A smoky inflection drifted through the dark hall, and I spun around to see my betrothed. Beams of light filtered through the windows to my left, and the morning's gilded light emphasised the gold in Aramis' hair. I straightened my posture as he sauntered toward me.

The task my parents had thrust upon me seemed impossible. My hesitance to seduce Aramis to find the Book or kill him twisted my insides into a vortex of unease. Perhaps the solution lay in trying to free Cara and running—if she really did remain alive. It would be dangerous, but we were out of options.

"I'm busy—"

"We're leaving," Aramis interrupted as he approached.

"What? Where?" I stepped backwards, but he only crept forward.

"To the Fire Court, Stoneshalt. We leave now."

What? My brows knitted as I stared speechlessly at him. We're leaving *now?* My thoughts hurried to catch up to what my racing heart already understood.

"Don't you need to stay and have meetings with my parents? The other mortal kings? Acquaint yourself with our court—"

"I have what I came for." The green in his eyes deepened despite the light shining on his face, and they studied me, waiting for my reaction. Though no response came, as one thought remained frozen in my mind—Cara.

"An emissary will remain to handle my affairs here, and there is only one mortal king now. There are more pressing matters at the Fire Court requiring my presence, matters I'd like to deal with before our wedding on Summer Solstice." Aramis looked at Conláed. "Ready?"

"Am I ever, it's been two years since I've been home. No doubt Mistress Zoraida has missed my patronage." Conláed winked as he slipped past Aramis and me, leaving us alone.

My frozen thoughts thawed into a rushing river, flooding me with ideas on what to do next, and I evaluated each option. Refuse, run, make excuses, beg—but as Aramis guided me through the castle and to the stable yard, my thoughts abandoned me, leaving me hopeless.

Carriages, wagons, and massive horses filled the bustling stable yard. Aramis led me to a carriage near the front of the line, opening the door for me.

The cushioned seats sat empty, and the realisation of my departure from Elmswood, maybe forever, struck me. With one foot on the carriage's lowest step, and another foot still grounded, I turned to Aramis. "My belongings—" I didn't care about my things, but I searched for an excuse to stay. An excuse to get Cara and run.

"Everything in your chambers is being packed as we speak. A few of my servants have packed a small travel bag with clothing for you to wear on the trip." His explanation came across as tender, marked by patience.

"Do my parents know we're leaving?" I continued to stall.

"They'll be told." He nodded his chin toward the interior of the carriage, and his patience melted into a command. "Get inside of the carriage, Elowyn."

My skin tingled, advising me to listen, so I slipped into the coach and Aramis shut the door as I sat.

One, two, three. Inhaling... horse shit... and willing my thoughts to slow enough to figure out what to do about Cara and the Book. That I didn't have a choice now, but to participate in my parents' treason.

One, two, three. Exhaling—nothing. I felt absolute emptiness and my body jolted forward as the carriage moved. Gravel crunched beneath the wheels and the horses' hooves as I slid over to the window and peered out.

The castle's stoned walls, extending high into the sky, didn't exude their usual threatening appearance. Not when my uncertain future loomed ahead.

As the line of carriages exited the stable yard and turned onto the ward, a man dressed in black clamoured down the castle's front steps. The angle of the sun blinded my vision, but as I held up my arm and squinted, I made out Oulixeus' face.

He stopped just a breath away from the gravel, locking eyes with me. The whiskey-hued depths of his gaze deepened, his jaw tautening, and his fingers curled into fists as he fixated on the carriage driving me away from this life.

Regardless of what my future held for me, one instinct felt certain—I didn't need to be afraid of Oulixeus any longer.

CHAPTER 13

*S*o *this is freedom*, I contemplated as the setting sun cast a pale, pinkish glow behind the darkening Wyvern Mountains. Fae erected the camp in the middle of a field blanketed with wildflowers, larkspur and clover painted the green grass with purples and whites. A gentle wind blew my hair to the side, tangling the ash-blonde strands in front of my face.

The Fae addressed me as Princess. They named me their future High Queen of Niafell. They bowed and offered respect, but I was their captive. Their safety net. Maybe they believed I could be used to manipulate my father. Keep him in line. Aramis chose the wrong Princess for that. Yet, with my father wanting the Book, maybe they could manipulate him in another way.

The wind blew the sweet scent of burning hickory over to me. In the distance, the wood crackled as groups huddled around its heat, laughing at crass jokes. It brought a soft smile to my face. In some weird way, I was excited.

Being surrounded by the enemy and knowing Cara rotted in a dungeon made my stomach churn. But to be this far away from home—the excitement outweighed all logical sense.

With one last look at the mountains, I took an exaggerated breath and decided to return to the camp.

"Fuck!" I choked, walking right into a solid chest. Stumbling backward, powerful hands caught me, pressing into my waist. Veins, almost glowing red, ran between the knuckles and up to corded forearms. My gaze trailed up thick biceps hidden behind a white shirt with the sleeves rolled to his elbows.

"Sorry." Aramis' smooth voice wrapped tendrils of smoke around me. I gripped those robust forearms to steady myself. Taut defined muscles rippled beneath his golden skin. Heat enveloped me and I quickly let go, distancing myself from whatever kindled between us. He reluctantly dropped his arms to his side.

"No, I'm sorry." I straightened myself.

"You don't need to apologise. It won't happen again." Aramis smiled softly, and I studied him.

His stance was tall and proper, though relaxed. Calm. For the first time in a long time, the demons haunting me grew silent. Not daring to stand in this moment. Terrified to surface in Aramis' presence.

"What?" He released an awkward but playful laugh, running a hand through golden locks.

"The rain is coming back," I noted, pushing the foreign ease aside and making my way to the camp they erected on the edge of Ravenwood Forest. Tall flowers tickled my ankles and wrists. I carefully tiptoed around them in an effort not to crush any. Cara's Grandmama had taught me to respect all life. If we took it for granted then, one day, when it's too late to alter our ways, we wouldn't recognize our world.

"There's not a single cloud in the sky. What makes you think that?" Aramis fell into step behind me.

"I can smell it."

"Smell it? You can smell the rain?"

"Mhm," I reassured him. He stopped, and I turned to see why. His emerald gaze radiated that calmness.

"What?" My face twisted into a scowl.

"What does it smell like?"

I rolled my eyes and continued to walk. He followed. "I don't know. It's like..." I paused to consider. "It's like a sweet, pungent zing fills my nose and throat and lungs. Then a musty, earth scent follows."

A deep rumbling chuckle fell from his full lips.

"Don't laugh at me." I scolded. *He's no different from Oulixeus,* I reminded myself.

"I'm not laughing *at* you, Princess. Just impressed by your keen sense of smell," he clarified. I walked in a slow spin to see his face. Satisfied by his sincerity, I circled forward and continued, fresh spring grasses sweeping my fingertips.

He stalked me in silence until we reached the edge of the camp. Fae pitched hundreds of tents to the left, wagons filled with supplies and horses scattered between them. To the right, more tents and countless fires blazed, surrounded by Fae eating and drinking.

Conláed and Molvys sat at the closest fire pit. Conláed grinned, sipping from a wooden mug, and Molvys' attention bored into me as he ripped meat from a cooked rabbit carcass. A third guard, Ezra—who I quickly met in the morning while vomiting into a bucket before meeting my parents—sat with them.

I wandered about the clearing, unsure of what to do as Aramis conversed with his friends, and snuck glances down the aisles formed by white canvas.

Boisterous chuckles originated from the fire. I glanced over to witness Conláed slapping Molvys' back as he coughed around a piece of rabbit. The others clutched their bellies and hit their knees in an uproar. Aramis gazed over his shoulder at me, smiling.

I whipped my head to the ground and resumed meandering around until Aramis returned his focus to the group.

"Would you like to join us, Your Highness?" Two females dressed in elegant gossamer gowns paused next to me. Their invitation surprised me, and I struggled to suppress my reaction.

"We're going to play cards," the one with black hair added. They stood with their arms linked, smiling at me gently, and making me feel—welcomed. The friendly request filled my mouth with a bittersweetness, for Cara had been the sole beacon of inclusion since my ostracism. Taking me to her family's cottage, sneaking me to the tavern, and coming to my room to share the castle's latest news.

"Thank you for the invitation, but I'm tired and would like to sleep." I declined, feeling as if joining them betrayed Cara.

The ladies dipped into a quick curtsy and continued on their way. Footsteps approached from behind me and I turned around to see Aramis approaching.

"Come, I'll show you our tent."

"*Our* tent?" My brows rose, and a sly, conceited smirk formed on his face. "Excuse me?"

"You're my betrothed. I protect what's mine. Which I can't do if you're in a separate tent. Come rest, Princess. You're exhausted," he insisted, and I stopped dead in my tracks. We stood near his friends' fire again, the males and their friends eavesdropping.

"No." I forced my heart to slow and features to remain expressionless.

"I wasn't asking, Princess." Aramis cocked his head to the side, his tone stern.

"I don't understand why—"

"Do you prefer walking or being carried?" he threatened, and my left arm, still burning since Aramis first saw me, intensified.

"You wouldn't dare," I challenged. His head tilted forward and his eyes narrowed, honing in on his prey. Determined to capture what he felt entitled to. Me.

"Oh, yes, I do dare. Slinging you over my shoulder, your gorgeous ass in my grasp, carrying you to *our* bed, is immensely desirable." Aramis rolled his tongue over his bottom lip. His posture seemed to stiffen as more males and a few females gathered to watch, curious about how their king treated his prize.

I inched backwards, reminiscent of our first encounter, and Aramis lunged forward, seizing my wrist. I gasped as he did as he'd promised—slinging me over his shoulder.

"'Atta boy!" Conláed shouted. Another Fae whistled, the crowd of males laughing and jeering at the sight. Some females whispered behind palms and others left, returning to their tasks.

Pounding my fists against Aramis' solid back, he smacked a palm against my ass and firmly gripped it, claiming me. His slap elicited a shock within me so strong that I bit my lip and froze.

The males clapped and whistled as we passed them. I forced my glare upon the barbarians, angered by their cheering. Enjoying the way their high king treated his new mortal play-thing. As I continued to glower at the crowd, I spotted the two Fae I encountered in the stable yard. The ones I begged Cara to fight and help that mortal woman from being assaulted. My anger grew to a new level. Cara was locked in a dungeon, with a severed finger because of me, and these two males jeered at me.

"Put me down!"

He held onto me with one arm, and it's all the strength he required to keep my struggling body from bursting free, as he led me into a massive tent. Aramis bent from his waist to drop me onto a pile of pillows and pinned me to the bed with the weight of his body.

"I won't lock you in a tower the way your family did, but when I make a decision based on your safety, you will respect it." His voice dropped an octave, as he brought his lips close enough to brush against mine.

"Oulixeus justified his actions by claiming they were for my safety, too." A shiver rolled down my spine, but I still didn't recognise its origin.

"He's a fool, and when you're ready for him to die, I'll kill him however you wish. I'll torture him for weeks. Burn him slowly. Rip out his heart and make him watch me eat it. Whatever you want, Princess." His nostrils flared as his breath danced across my flesh.

My heart tumbled into a panic, attempting to understand the infuriating emotions brewing inside of me. But before I could interpret them, Aramis stood and sauntered over to a small desk.

He sipped from the crystal goblet, sifting through papers blanketing a table, and showing particular interest in one piece of parchment that he lifted to study.

The tent was huge. Aramis, at least six foot seven, easily stood upright without his head grazing the canvas. I sat in the middle of a miniature living area created by massive silk throw pillows, cashmere blankets, and decorative rugs resting in the middle.

Setting the goblet aside, Aramis leaned backward in the chair and allowed his head to fall backwards. The chair groaned under his brawny weight. Pinching the bridge of his nose, he massaged it and let out a soft hum of discomfort.

Arrogant, domineering, and cocky one moment. Troubled, depleted, and maybe even a little haunted the next. I watched him steal a moment to ease himself, so similar to how I'd count away my own panic.

Aramis removed his hand from his face, reaching for the wine, and our eyes met across the room. He instantly brightened, and it made me uncomfortable. This tiny glimpse wasn't enough to make me forget about the monster, so instead of allowing him a moment of peace, I stood and confronted his atrocities from his first day at Elmswood.

"Why did you burn those Spellcasters? They didn't deserve to die."

The brightness faded, leaving his mouth contorted into a strained smile. "They're an abomination. Mortals aren't meant to possess magic."

"Toivo, the God of Truth, gifted it to them—"

"That god's a traitor." Aramis tossed the paper in his hand to the table, raising to meet me. "He betrayed all the Fae and this realm when he put magic through mortals' veins."

"So, they deserved to burn to death all because you believe the God of Truth betrayed your kind? The Spellcasters didn't ask for magic, they were born with it."

"And what would you have me do, Princess? Allow them to live in a cage? People aren't pigs."

My jaw dropped, and my eyes widened. "No, they're not." I stared at Aramis, lost for words. "You could have at least shown them some mercy."

"Oh, I showed them mercy. I gave them more than they deserved in an honourable death. Fire releases the soul to the Veil. I could've just slit their throats and let them rot in the dirt." Aramis sipped his wine, grinning over the rim of his cup. Is that what the Fire Fae believed? Fire released them into the Veil? Did all the Fae believe this, or just the Fire Fae? I bit my lip, realising how ignorant I was of their culture. The years spent learning how to fight against them, but never understanding them. And the best way to defeat a foe is to understand their every move, their motives...

"Showing them a quick death and burning their bodies afterwards wouldn't have released their soul?" I glared at the monster towering over me.

"Hmm, I guess it would have." Aramis returned to his desk, studying his paper and sipping the dark red wine. A red too deep to be mortal wine. It emitted an otherworldly sweet aroma. "There's clothing for you behind that partition."

I ignored his pointed suggestion. "What about the way your scouts just sauntered into Elmswood, assaulting the first woman they lay eyes on. Did you teach them that? I hear you're quite the brutal lover. They even mentioned how you *play* with women."

"My scouts assaulted a woman?" Aramis' sharp gaze studied me the same way I surveyed others for their tells.

"Yes. And I shouldn't be surprised by the stories I hear about Fae males. You're disgusting," I whispered, my anger simmering too intensely to prolong the argument, and silently followed Aramis' gesture, spotting my clothing neatly folded on a small table. Unfortunately, only the garments Oulixeus commissioned were available, all of them low-cut and revealing. I missed my plain and modest nightgowns.

Selecting the most modest option, a navy silk shorts and chemise set, I hid behind the partition and hurriedly slid into the delicate fabric. I unbelted the sheath around my thigh and placed it on the table, tucking it under my dress, not wanting the Fae to know I carried it.

Taking a step away from the partition, it struck me—I was about to be nearly naked and without a weapon in front of Aramis. Additionally, this was our first night together. In the same bed. The sudden fear swept my anger away like a rush of water extinguishing a raging fire.

On the balls of my feet, I gathered enough courage to reveal myself. Aramis focused on his papers. Watching wine pour from the crystal goblet and into his mouth made mine water. His throat pulsed as the liquid continued to flow into him.

Spotting the bottle on the desk and an extra goblet, I walked over with tense shoulders and helped myself.

Normally, I hid my emotions well, but Aramis made me nervous. With Oulixeus, I knew exactly what to expect. Rough and direct, but as long as I listened, he wouldn't hurt me too badly. But Aramis...

He looked up from his papers and his emerald leer consumed me. Studying me more intently than the papers. I crossed one foot over the other, still on my toes, and wrapped one arm around my torso.

"You're gorgeous."

Heat rose to my cheeks, and somehow, my anger started to melt. His gaze drew from my reddening face, along my silk-covered body, and to my bare legs. Leaning back in his chair, Aramis drank from his cup, and I followed his lead.

"What is this?" I exclaimed.

Aramis laughed. "Wine—*real* wine." The liquid caressing my tongue tasted of late nights by the fire with Cara, sharing ripe plums, and laughing until the late hours of the night. The wine didn't have a flavour, it had a memory. Other fairy wine had tasted magical too, but I'd drank it when already intoxicated, and likely too numb to feel these other effects.

The effects of the wine already coursed through my bloodstream. Craving more, I tilted my head back and drained the glass to relieve myself from the unease of Aramis' stare, sending chills down my spine.

Confused by the opposing sensations, I reached for the bottle, but Aramis wrapped his hand around the neck.

"Did you enjoy riding in that coach while hung over today?" He popped an eyebrow to his forehead, evoking a glare from me.

Unwilling to verbally admit his accurate assumption, I set my glass down. "I'd like to go to sleep."

Aramis nodded and made his way over to the drapes in the corner of the elaborate tent, pulling the material back and revealing *our* bed. Luxurious fabrics and a mountain of pillows covered the mattress. Oulixeus was leagues away, but I could still feel his phantom hands slither across my body. Bumps rose on my skin, and miniscule vibrations rippled through my muscles.

I crawled into soft, cool sheets. Adjusting the pillows behind me and tossing a few to the carpeted floor, Aramis tracked my movements. Leaning against a support pole holding the tent, arms crossed over his chest and wine clasped in one hand as he looked and looked and looked.

"What?" I bit.

"Enjoying the sight of you crawling into my bed for the first time." He swallowed a sip of wine. A drop lingered on his lip, which he lapped away. I didn't know why, but I stared at where his tongue met his lip, pressure building between us.

"I'd appreciate it if you didn't." I cringed and rolled away, waiting for Aramis to crawl in next to me. For him to claim something else he felt belonged to him. My pulse thudded against my neck and my lungs worked at a quick pace. *He's just like Oulixeus,* I reminded myself. And maybe if I'd just behaved, it'd be over with quickly.

I squeezed my eyelids tight and waited for an unfamiliar touch, but heard nothing other than retreating footsteps. Confused, I sat up and saw Aramis at the tent's door, his arms holding the papers from his desk.

"I have business to discuss. Ezra will be right outside and I'll be two tents over." He gathered the papers on the desk, rolling a few into tight scrolls and folding others, tucking them all under his arm.

"You're sleeping there?" My voice squeaked, and my shoulders tensed at the slip, causing Aramis to smirk.

"Oh, no. I'll return, don't you worry," Aramis confirmed before ducking between the canvas flaps.

Instead of remaining in bed, I leapt out and grabbed the bottle of wine. "Did you enjoy riding in that coach while hung over today?" I dropped my voice low and imitated Aramis' chide. Fuck him and his judgement. Or was it caution? I didn't care, I didn't possess much self-autonomy, so I'd take advantage of his absence and do whatever I wanted.

Returning to the partition, I removed the map my parents gave me from my dress pocket, and made myself comfortable on the mound of cushions propped upon the floor. Gentle silks and satins slid against my exposed skin as I unfolded the ancient parchment and took a swig of fairy wine. Once again, it reminded me of Cara.

I didn't get a chance to fully study the map in the hidden room earlier and if I was going to find this Book quickly to save Cara, then I wanted to know exactly what my plans were before even arriving at the Blood Fortress.

Alongside the blueprint marks, unfamiliar symbols covered the edges, resembling a language I'd never encountered before, certainly not the Old Tongue. Maybe Fae? Mortals purged all Fae-language books and tomes, so I had never seen it before.

The paper, aged and stained over time, had smudged the ink, making it challenging to discern room connections and boundaries. Even if I deciphered the language, half of it had smeared away. But still, I spent at least an hour studying the paper, even the stains. I took a sip from the now nearly empty bottle, and choked on the liquid as I realised one of the stains could be a drawing.

A detail so subtle, the gentle ink strokes swirling into a rose first looked like a blot. Upon closer inspection, I saw the difference, and excitement sparked through my skin. But what did a rose have to do with the architecture of the fortress? I flipped the parchment over to confirm there were no hints on the other side—no.

As I flipped it back over, I overheard Aramis' voice approach. Eyes widening, I leapt to my feet, returned the bottle to the desk and silently crawled back into bed, tucking the map beneath the travel mattress and closing my eyes, as if I had been asleep the entire time.

Aramis blew out the remaining lit candles and approached the bed, unclasping his buckle. Curiosity overpowered me and I discreetly squinted through an eyelid as he removed his white linen shirt to expose corded muscles, large and powerful, comparable to a god. His shoulders were the width of a door frame and his abdomen... the way the muscles cut down below the line of his breeches—

"Enjoying watching *your* betrothed?" He laughed, and I whipped around, clamping my eyes shut, but the image of his muscles lingered behind my lids.

His breeches rustled to the floor, and the mattress shifted as he climbed onto it, remaining above the sheets.

"Goodnight, sweetheart," he whispered.

I steadied my breath, begging the anger to decrease. Feeling certain that Aramis' eyes had closed, I opened mine. He lay with his hands clasped behind his head, nearly naked, wearing nothing but cotton undershorts. His length was very visible. My eyes widened at the sheer size of him.

He squinted an eye open. "Yes, sweetheart?"

"Don't call me that," I ordered. A smile tugged at his lips as I rolled over to hide the flush invading my chest and face. Wanting to destroy his amusement, I added, "I know you're only using me to fulfil the treaty. I may not know why you chose me over my sister, but no matter. It doesn't hide the fact that, just like everybody else in my life, you're using me."

I felt his aura shift from light and feathery to something heavier, like a lump of lead. Aramis didn't attempt to banter or defend himself, he simply rolled over and fell asleep, leaving me to my hurried thoughts that morphed into dreams of Cara locked in a dungeon.

CHAPTER 14

An agonisingly desperate plea rolled through the tent, waking me from a restless slumber. In a rapid and abrupt motion, I searched for its origin—outside the tent. Another deep, but suppressed, groan accompanied the disturbing calls.

Aramis' spot was empty, his discarded clothing gone. Without wasting time to dress, I wrapped a soft cotton sheet around my body and sprinted outside. Two Fae males were on their knees, heads hanging low and hands manacled by iron chains. Iron—a metal that suppressed all forms of magic.

A guard holding a glowing, ice blue stake kicked a prisoner to the ground and slammed the weapon into his back. The trampled, scarlet soaked grass below muffled his cries. Wounds covered both captives' shoulders, chests, arms, and faces, black and purple splotches spread around them, blistering like... frostbite.

The males shivered as Aramis stood a few feet away, chatting with friends as if torture wasn't occurring nearby. Other Fae bustled about the camp, dismantling tents, cooking breakfast, and conversing as if chained and tortured prisoners were commonplace.

"Good morning, sweetheart." Aramis noted my presence.

"What is going on here?" I was about to launch into an argument until a captive raised his head and I instantly recognised him from the stable yard. Stunned, I whipped my head between them and Aramis. "I didn't ask you to do this."

"You didn't have to. They upset you, so they're being punished. I've also sent Ezra back to Elmswood with a large sum of coins for the woman's family," Aramis explained his actions, and my tensed muscles dropped, wilting like flowers, understanding why Aramis sent the family compensation. "I'm sorry, Elowyn."

"Thanks," I whispered, because no other words or thoughts formed between the sadness and surprise. Aramis had found the attackers I'd briefly mentioned, uncovered the woman's fate, and punished them. He just... did it. No questions asked. Aramis didn't doubt or dismiss me, only ensured the attackers faced consequences.

"As much as I love knowing you're scantily dressed under that sheet, I'm also struggling to not tear off the heads of those glancing at you. I can't kill the entire camp on day two of our travels. Go change. You'll be on horseback with me today." Aramis spoke, and I heard his words, but my mind remained on other thoughts.

If the attackers revealed what happened to the woman, then— "Did the attackers mention another woman?"

"No, they didn't. How come?"

"No reason," I mumbled, still staring at the males bleeding out, their quick healing stunted by the iron clamped around their wrists. Could Aramis help me free Cara? I didn't have to ask him to punish these males, maybe if I asked about Cara...

No. Aramis did one nice thing for me, even if it involved torturing others—a terrifying thought—but Oulixeus did nice things, too. He manipulated me into believing he cared to use me. What made Aramis any different?

I couldn't risk placing Cara on his radar.

CHAPTER 15

We broke off into a smaller group, travelling ahead of the army and attendants as they slowed us down and Aramis didn't want to be on the road for long. Our new group consisted of high-ranking generals, a small group of soldiers and attendants, and me.

The Fire Fae rode immense horses, their coats ranging from ebony to chestnut to stone, with muscles rippling along their legs and backs. The horses didn't possess magic, but surpassed any mortal-bred steed in strength and speed.

Aramis brought me to the black stallion he entered Rhyddean on—Aithon, a towering beast dwarfing Aramis' six-foot seven frame. With a firm grip on my hips, he lifted me onto Aithon's back. Nausea gripped me as the ground receded. I recalled feeling far less vulnerable atop Aithon the first time.

Securing the saddle bags, Aramis ignored my horror. Patting the stallion's long neck, he finally grinned and said, "I'll *never* let you fall, sweetheart."

"Don't call me that," I snapped. Chuckling, he lifted himself onto the massive horse with little effort. One of his powerful arms wrapped around my waist, pulling me into him, and I swallowed my gasp as he ground his pelvis against my lower back. His head hovered above mine, sending shivers down my spine.

"Fresh morning dew and ripe summer strawberries," a deep, smoky whisper caressed my ear. My left arm sizzled in response as his hand glided from my waist to my hip. Seizing my hands, he slid them across the inside of my thighs, hitching my breath. I closed my eyes, attempting to push away the disorienting tension forming in my centre. Cool leather permeated the flush conquering my complexion. My fingertips pressed into the material as Aramis steered them toward a thick, erect length, wrapping my hands around it.

"Hold the saddle horn," Aramis firmly instructed. Still queasy from the height and the nerves swirling through my belly, I gripped it tightly.

A quiet laugh rippled against my skin. "I hope you're more gentle with me."

My eyes snapped open, pulling me from the trance, and I noted the intrigued glances from the other Fae. The flush returned, rising to my cheeks as I scooted away from the arrogant male, and scoffed in disgust.

Asshole.

Three days of riding and fatigue hung over me like a pesky thundercloud. Aramis guided Aithon, but my thighs and abdomen were sore from trying to keep space between us.

"You'd be more comfortable if you moved with me, Princess." He wrapped a calloused hand around me, pulling me in snugly, but the closeness unnerved me.

"I'm perfectly fine," I lied, pushing away. Leaning into him was more comfortable, but I hated the convoluted stabs my stomach produced each time our bodies touched.

No matter how hard I tried, I dozed off and woke in his embrace. An arm curled around my body to keep me from falling, his head resting against mine to keep my neck straight, and a thumb stroked my hip. He'd gently let go whenever I regained my posture, never jesting.

Waking from another unexpected nap, I rubbed the grogginess from my eyes. Sweat pooled on my lower back, pressing into Aramis' stomach. Uncomfortable by the heat and closeness, I inched forward, as usual, and Aramis' grip loosened, cool air kissing my damp skin.

The further south we rode, the warmer the days and nights became. A heat we rarely received in Rhyddean.

Three nights had passed since we separated from the army and our group took to resting at local inns, stopping before the sun set each evening. Aramis insisted on sharing a room each time. To keep a watchful eye on his little human pet, no doubt.

He provided me privacy to wash and change into my silly little nightwear. But each night, I caught an eye spying over his papers as I tiptoed into bed. Thankfully, he didn't touch me, unlike the first night. A boundary he chose to respect.

Aramis, although clearly attracted to me, didn't make much effort to speak with me or get to know me. Though, neither did I. Our time together proceeded to be... awkward. A subtle instinct stirred within me, urging caution in his presence—a warning of concealed motives or harboured desires. His shifting demeanour reminded me of Oulixeus.

A sudden rush coursed through me, dismissing my worries. Aramis spurred Aithon forward, shouting to Molvys and Conláed, "We'll meet you at the inn later."

We fell into a canter, separating us from the group and riding toward the Wyvern Mountains.

"Where are we going?" The horse's three-beat gait thundered against the ground, forcing me to shout. I'd never ridden this fast and my hands fastened tighter around the saddle horn, but it didn't steady me enough. I jostled around too much.

"A surprise." He pressed his mouth against my temple and his forearm against my belly. Long, lean muscles flexed against my nails as I gripped him. My thighs clenched the saddle, and despite my initial resolve to maintain distance, I didn't care right then. As the horse sped through the field toward the mountains, a sense of freedom cleansed me.

"I don't like surprises!" My voice hitched as Aithon cleared a pile of rocks and landed smoothly. The terrain transformed from a field of grass to rocky hills and the mountains grew taller with each kilometre we neared, with snow-covered peaks kissing puffy clouds. The sunlight highlighting ridges, plateaus, and cirques sculpted into the mountains, perfectly shaped for a sleepy dragon. Rivers and waterfalls carved paths into the colossal stone from large flats of ice down into the trees.

I had never seen anything like it.

Wild. Unruly. A natural chaos. Excitement prickled my skin as Aithon slowed to a walk and headed toward a rushing creek, the turquoise water flowing crystal clear. Tumbled rocks of all shapes and sizes lined the creek bed and teeny tiny black tadpoles swam with the current.

"Sweetheart." My new pet name brushed against my skin, lifting the hairs along my neck. "You can let go now."

I gripped Aramis' arm after abandoning the saddle horn at some point. As I unfastened my nails from his flesh, I saw little red scrapes marring his arms. "I'm sorry."

Aramis dismounted the horse in an elegant swoop, reaching to assist me. "Give me your worst, sweetheart, and I'll make sure you enjoy every bit of it." Lustful flames danced in his irises as the corners of his lips twitched. I bit my lip and spun away from him, walking swiftly away in the opposite direction to discourage him.

Aithon wandered to the creek and drank the fresh liquid, and I followed, carefully stepping between rocks of all sizes and avoiding large, wobbly ones. Kneeling next to Aithon's long muzzle, I dipped my hands into the water.

ICE.

"Ah!" I snatched my hands out and cradled them against my chest, blowing on them. A chuckle filled the little clearing, and I snapped my head to Aramis, brows knitting.

"I'm not laughing at you, Elowyn." Aramis' wide smile softened.

"I know," I reassured. And I truly did. He just—that laugh... The way it felt lighter and more genuine with me as opposed to surrounded by his friends and subjects...

"Come." Aramis nodded toward the towering trees crowding over the hill we stood on. Pines, spruce, birch, firs, and cedars dominated the hill, climbing into the mountains.

"Where are you taking me?" Sunset approached and shadow encroached upon the clearing.

"Do you trust me?" His cheeks dimpled and the flames burning beneath his emerald eyes smouldered, catching on flecks of gold. A glimmer I first found irksome, but now stoked the curiosity within me. And the heat pulsating through my left arm encouraged me, so I decided I would trust him. For now.

"Okay." Ignoring my earlier hesitance, I took the hand he offered and allowed him to lead me into the depth of trees.

CHAPTER 16

The forest rapidly darkened, chilling the air. Aramis led the way, cutting through shrubs and branches with the swing of his sword as the sky grew darker. A ball of fire appeared in his left fist, illuminating our way, and he navigated with a purpose, following a non-existent path.

Breath pooled in my chest, refusing to refresh my lungs, and I braced myself against a tree trunk, wishing I'd jogged through the forest like Cara had suggested.

Sap stuck to my fingers, and my head fell forward.

"Are you alright?" Aramis noted my heaving chest.

"There's... easier ways... to kill me," I panted.

"Ah, but what's the fun in an easy death? I can carry you," he offered, smirking. I shook my head and proceeded forward, pushing past him.

"This way?" I moaned as my legs howled and begged for rest.

"Yes," Aramis confirmed. "A sharp right at the giant boulder and then we'll arrive."

Aramis' fire magic shone bright enough to guide me and my shadow crawled onto a dark boulder stuck between twisting roots the same thickness as Aithon. Turning to the right, I kept my gaze peeled to the forest floor as my steps disturbed ferns and tiny white spring flowers. I tried tiptoeing to avoid crushing the delicate plants, but my aching feet and calves refused.

"Wait," Aramis instructed, and I paused, lifting my head.

"Oh my gods," I gaped. The woods thinned to uncover a mossy plateau, displaying a marvellous view of the mountain range. The last few minutes of the falling sun illuminated jagged peaks stretched as far as the eye could see. Valleys dipped between them, blanketed in forests, fields, and lakes. Clear water reflecting the night sky sparkling with millions of twinkling stars and the thin strip of orange, fighting to remain lit.

"Aramis," I whispered as his heat approached.

"Do you like it?"

"I've never seen anything so spectacular." Aramis' flames penetrated me, not the fire flickering in his palm, but the ones blazing in the depths of his eyes.

His fire magic cast a warm glow to his sharp Fae features until he resembled a golden statue, carved perfectly. Each line, mark, and curve etched to display a threatening power. But a threat one may hesitate to heed because his masculine beauty insisted he'd never actually harm you.

Aramis tilted his head to the centre of the plateau and wordlessly sauntered over. He extinguished the flames he carried and sprawled onto his back.

"Stargazing," I mumbled, watching him tuck an arm behind his head. A rare activity to enjoy in gloomy Rhyddean. And even when the skies broke, they never glimmered this magnificently.

Cara would love this.

"Join me?" He patted the ground beside him. Staring open-mouthed at the sky, I stumbled my way over to him and tucked a knee behind me, sinking to the squishy moss. The damp foliage cooled my sore muscles, and I sighed in relief.

A silence rolled over us as the last light of the sun vanished, allowing the shining stars to dominate the indigo sky.

"Do you see that cluster of stars there?" Aramis pointed above me, slightly to the left.

"There are millions of stars, Aramis. Which ones?" I laughed at the impossibility of narrowing them down. He joined my laughter, engulfing my slender fingers in his massive hand, like an aching flame smothering a burning ember.

"Elowyn?"

"Mhm," my voice squeaked.

"Your hand is sticky."

"What?" I attempted to pull out of his grip, but he held firm, refusing to let me go.

"Your hand... it's sticky," he repeated.

"Oh, my gods!" I snorted, the kind only Cara successfully elicited from me. "The tree sap!"

We laughed together. Aramis' hand still holding mine, and that rush of security I experienced while riding with him returned. It seeped into me, deeper and deeper, begging to be acknowledged. But as our bodies settled, I ignored the unfamiliar surge until it became a whisper.

Aramis guided my pointer finger along the night sky, aligning it with a cluster of stars.

"Here." He traced imaginary lines between six stars, connecting them with six more closer together. "A rose. Auri's Rose, the Goddess of Light. Did you learn about the gods?"

Slightly parting my fingers, he gently curled his around mine. Another wave of heat flowed through my arm.

"A little. But I've never heard of Auri's Rose," I encouraged him to continue.

"The God of War, Iros, fell madly in love with her, but she wanted nothing to do with him. He believed displaying his power and strength would win the goddess over." As Aramis recounted the myth, I studied him, and found myself drawn closer, but didn't understand why. It was as if an irresistible magnetic force pulled me toward him. His words resonated in my mind, soothing and melodic.

As I explored his expressions, I never noticed the subtle lines at the corners of his eyes, etched there by a life filled with stories yet untold. And his touch conveyed not just physical strength, but emotional fortitude—a fortress withstanding centuries of storms.

With every heartbeat, I teetered on the precipice of inviting him closer or retreating to safety.

I retreated. Pulling my hand away from his, an unspoken tension painted an intricate tapestry that only the celestials could decipher, because I couldn't comprehend the growing inner turmoil.

"Did it?" I rolled onto my side, watching his smile lines disappear, disappointed by my escape. But it frightened me, the sensation weaving between us as delicate as the petals of a rose in a soft breeze, yet as electric as a gathering storm on the horizon. Something benign and placid, but full of potential to build into something devastatingly destructive. And just like watching a thunderstorm brewing in the distance, I almost yearned to discover how destructive this connection could become.

"No. Too violent for her. Auri possessed a graceful, gentle quality. She loved to laugh and play. But also relished in beauty, lust, and seduction." Aramis' breath swirled into the cold air.

"How did he win her over?"

"He planted a field of red roses. Her favourite flower." He rolled onto his side so we faced each other. Butterflies caught in my stomach.

"Flowers?" I cocked a brow, begging the butterflies to simmer and stop encouraging the curious sensation blooming between us.

"Yes," he inched closer. "Would a field of flowers win you over?"

"Maybe." A lock of hair falling into my eyes. "Only if they were my favourite."

"And what is your favourite flower?" Aramis relinquished his grip on my hand to tuck the unruly strand behind my ear. His touch lingered, drawing down the side of my jaw. His thumb briefly paused on my chin. My lips parted slightly as I stared into his eyes, entranced by the stars reflecting in them. "Your favourite flower?" He reminded me.

"I don't know its name," I admitted. "Sometimes I—visit this place when... the world becomes too much." My serene clearing in my imaginary forest consumed my mind. The dappled sunlight. Trickling water. Gentle grass. And flowers surrounding me. Protecting me from cruelty.

"A safe space?" Aramis pulled me from the illusion, dropping his hand and folding it between us. Not retreating too far away.

"Yeah. In my mind, you know?" I looked away, ashamed I couldn't handle everything in this world as a grown woman, evils frightening me enough to retreat into a make believe world like a child.

"I understand."

"It's childish," I muttered.

"No, Elowyn, it's not. It's survival." A protective tone weaved through his words.

Survival. Cara once said the same. But I grew tired of shutting down and retreating just to survive. Was it worth surviving if it happened over and over and over?

"Your flower is in your safe space?" Again, Aramis brought me to the present, away from the darkness.

"Yeah, I envision it each time. It appears so vividly." Air rippled through my chest as I exhaled the depressing thoughts.

"Describe it to me."

"It's white with a million delicate petals. Crowded together in the centre, ruffling outwards. Like, in a spiral direction," I explained, twirling my finger in a circle.

"Is it always white?" Aramis propped a hand under his head. The strong, vicious Fae, notorious for his monstrous ways, laying next to me discussing flowers. No mortal would believe this exchange. Not even Cara.

"In my vision, it is. In real life? Maybe it grows in other colours. Have you seen it before?" The idea of seeing one in real life, caressing its velvety petals, filled me with a gentle happiness.

"I haven't." He shook his head.

"Oh." I rolled onto my back and the moisture of the moss sent a chill through me. Aramis rolled onto his back, too, and seconds later, the moss below us warmed. Heated like a bed of smouldering coals. "Did you just—"

Aramis chuckled. "I protect what's mine, Elowyn. I meant that."

"Hmm," I offered, snuggling deeper into the warm moss as my eyes grew heavy. "Well, thank you for saving me from the big, bad cold."

The exhaustion flooding my body caught up with me, urging me to sleep. A yawn escaped me as I drifted off.

"Anything for you."

CHAPTER 17

A sharp slobbery snore rattled me from my slumber. Eyes snapping open to white linen, I realised my head lounged on an arm. A brawny arm. Strong, thick, and warm. My hands, small in comparison, rested on muscles cording through the arm, and drool puddled below my mouth.

Springing awake, I shoved my face into the heels of my palms. "I'm so sorry!"

Aramis groaned awake and the rising sun filtered through the mountains, lighting strips of the misty valley below. "For what?" Aramis yawned, stretching his arms. "Oh!" He noticed the stain of drool. I stood on wobbly legs, sore from the day before, and marched into the forest.

How did I let that happen? I'd let Aramis in, sharing things I didn't even tell Cara.

"Elowyn! It's not a big deal." Aramis followed closely as I traced the path he'd carved through the night. The dawn provided some light for my getaway, yet I moved too slowly.

Aramis gripped my elbow and spun me around. "Elowyn," he purred my name the same way he had in my chambers.

"I'm sorry." I tried to pull away, wanting to run and hide in the woods.

"Elowyn." His grip tightened, pulling me into his chest. A hand wrapped around each wrist. The predator returning.

"Aramis." My voice fluttered, toes curling. "You're frightening me."

His nostrils flared, breathing me in. My scent. A dimple pierced his cheek. "No, I'm not, sweetheart."

No.

He wasn't.

He held my wrists, restricting my movements, but it felt nothing like Oulixeus' grip. Aramis' hands didn't coil around me like venomous snakes. Instead, he held me steady. Forcing me to confront him. The drool didn't embarrass me, and I believed he knew it.

"Is there something you'd like to share with me?" He peered down. A brow lifting as strands of golden hair fell onto his face.

That I felt comfortable enough to fall asleep in the wilderness with him?

That I felt so relaxed my subconscious body curled into him?

That last night was the most free I'd ever felt?

I suppressed a knot of tension, not wanting to admit anything to him.

"Is there something *you'd* like to share with me?" I evaded. He loosened the grip on my wrists, allowing me to wrestle free, and resumed marching through the woods as the sun lifted higher.

"No." His voice carried a confused tone. "Elowyn, I know you're lying."

"And I can tell when *you're* lying." I threw a smirk over my shoulder. I studied him intently since he first arrived, and I was certain that I discovered his tell.

"Oh? Do share, sweetheart." Amused, he followed me at last.

"I can't reveal it to you."

"You don't believe it's valuable for a king to hide his bluff?" Our steps became heavy and clunky as we descended the mountain.

"I think it's more valuable for *me* to know when a king is lying." Feet snagging on my skirts, I stumbled forward and a protective arm slung around my waist, catching me before I could fall.

"Alright, don't tell me. I'll figure it out for myself. But what I *do* want you to tell me is what *you're* hiding." Aramis spun me around so my chest pressed against him, and his eyes darkened with a glint of allure. An enticing sensation skated over me and I forced a breath to simmer it down.

"What are you talking about?" I whispered, daring to confront his assessing gaze.

"The paper you hid from me the other night. What was it?" *Fuck.* "I heard you stuffing it under the mattress. Thought about taking it from you, but I'd rather hear it from your lips. What holds so much value, you hide it from your betrothed?"

How could I explain it to him? Sorry, I'm here to commit treason against you? I couldn't explain Cara. He burned six Spellcasters alive, supposedly committed a killing spree after the mortal courts surrendered, and had stalked me like a predator since the moment he arrived.

I pursed my lips, stepping out of his grip, desperate for space.

"Was it a goodbye love letter from *him*?" Aramis' tone became heavy and dark.

Wait, what? "From who?"

"Prince Oulixeus," he clarified, and I laughed. My laughter didn't stem from amusement, but from mounting frustration. Was he *jealous?*

"Are you in love with him?" Aramis stepped closer, and my frustration grew. Maybe he meant to exploit my complicated past with Oulixeus.

"What right do you have to ask me such personal questions about my past? Are you jealous of him?" I challenged, but Aramis only smiled, knowing my response indicated the nearing of my breaking point.

"Then tell me what you're hiding. What's the piece of paper you keep folded away, hidden from me?"

What could I tell him? I'd failed Cara already, and I'd die for it. Aramis would kill me on the spot, and maybe I should just accept it. I'd been trying to die for so long and without Cara and Foster to stop me... If they'd just let me die, Cara wouldn't be in this mess.

Suddenly, Aramis pulled me into him, our chests pressed against each other. Pushing the side of his head against mine, he spoke, "What is it they told you to do, Elowyn?"

"I don't know what you're talking about," I lied.

"You see, humans have a reputation for being crafty and untrustworthy, and that paper, your denial, seems to confirm my suspicions. I can only assume your parents are pulling the strings from behind the scenes—using you. Do you think my assumption is fair?"

My eyes widened, and even though he couldn't see, I knew he felt the shift in my demeanour and posture. It seemed like a fair assumption, as it mirrored what I would've concluded in his position.

"I'll take your silence as confirmation, Princess. Now, tell me. I promise nothing bad will happen to you. I've seen the way they treat you, speak to you. They're only using you as a pawn. I know that whatever it is, you'd rather not see them succeed. But if you refuse to tell me, I could always send you back. Take no wife."

My heart raced. Aramis lied about sending me back. He made it clear he desired me, for whatever reason. I didn't know why, but I held an importance to him. And I still needed to save Cara... Was there a way out of this?

"I'm looking for the Book of Toivo," I finally spilled after wrestling it over and over, the weight of helplessness pressing upon me. I had no other choice but to take a chance on Aramis. He loosened his grip and I stepped away, turning to face him, expecting to confront anger, but met curiosity.

"And your secret paper?"

"A clue to the Book's location, apparently. Trust me, I don't know much and the map is written in some sort of language I can't decipher."

"Let's look for it together." Aramis proposed, halting all trains of thought in my mind. He knows about the spell book... but how could he not know where it is?

"You don't know where the Book is?" Aramis' admission took me by surprise. Oulixeus' spies insisted the Book hid in the Blood Fortress. "My parents suspected you had it at the Blood Fortress, but their spy didn't find an exact location."

Aramis rolled his lips against each other. "I'm surprised their spies managed to gather *that* much intel... But yes, it's at the Blood Fortress, but my father never revealed its location to me. He became... paranoid as he aged."

"So paranoid that he didn't trust his heir?" Or maybe Aramis gave his father another reason not to trust him.

"Yes."

"Why do you want the Book?"

"I believe it will help me unite this realm with others. It also contains various spells possessing the potential to destroy our entire realm and dispel evil everywhere. I know others are searching for it, and no matter how secure my fortress is, I won't chance it slipping right through my fingers. Will you help me find it?"

As genuine as his motives seemed, the image of burning Spellcasters remained fresh in my mind. And a small voice wondered if my parents' motive to destroy magic held some justification. Maybe no one should hold that kind of power.

If I helped him find the Book, maybe I could use the incantation to rid the world of magic. Not the Fae, just magic. Making us all equals.

And if he could read the language on the map... I walked over to Aithon, and rummaged through my bag until I felt its delicate edges. Handing it to Aramis, I asked, "Can you read it?"

He stared at me a moment before taking in the map. Nodding his head, he said, "Yes. It's written in the Fae language. *A frozen rose that holds the key, protected by flames for eternity. Seek the light in the darkest hour, to unlock the door and gain the power.*"

"What does it mean?"

"It's just a passage from an ancient poem. However, this looks like the throne room." He pointed to the large rectangular room with eight circles drawn inside of it and the rose.

"Do you think the Book is there?"

"No, there are no books in the throne room," Aramis confirmed, but it had to have some sort of significance. "Elowyn, I'm choosing to trust you because I recognise what's in your heart, your authenticity. You know your family is corrupt. Let's help each other."

Watching his movements and body language, I studied his sincerity and didn't spot his suspected tell. Could I trust him? Did I have a choice? Taking a deep breath, I gave into my fear and decided I needed to try everything to succeed. Building a temporary alliance with him could help me take the Book and... kill him, when the time came.

"Okay, I'll help you find the Book." And the thought of my dagger piercing through his flesh pulled at my insides.

CHAPTER 18

Aithon's easy gait swayed me as we moved. Peaceful. I clenched my lip, staring into the distance at the transformed landscape. It shifted during our travels from verdant hills to a rugged terrain mixed with giant boulders, interspersed with moss.

"Lie," I announced and Aramis shook his head.

"How? How can you tell?" He scoffed in disbelief as I called his bluff for the sixth time in a row. A game he invented fifteen minutes earlier to divulge something to me, a personal detail, a fact about the Fae Court, or gossip. The objective? For me to discern if he lied or spoke true, committed to learning his tell.

"I'll never share." I lifted my chin. Aramis dug his fingers into my side, as if to tease me. I yelped and retracted my body, his other hand catching me before slipping off Aithon.

Entering a narrow glen, the rocky hills flanking us concealed the farmlands resting beyond. A stream rushed through the centre, its clear waters glistening in the sunlight. Amidst the picturesque setting, Aramis engaged in lively conversation with his friends, their boisterous jokes drowning the tranquil sounds of nature. I took a moment to immerse myself in the beauty, savouring the peaceful harmony around us.

I couldn't necessarily call it freedom, but Aramis was taunting me with bits and pieces throughout our journey, allowing me a taste of what I yearned for.

A snicker caught my attention, and I overheard General Keniris mumbling, "He'll enjoy playing with his new toy. I'm told she's not much of a rider, but seeing the way her thighs grip that saddle—"

Laughter erupted from the group surrounding him, and my face flushed. They joked about me, and I had to steady my breathing to quell the embarrassment. Despite Aramis' gestures and words, the thought of being nothing but a *new toy* for him grew more pronounced as I struggled to contain the humiliation.

Aramis wrapped his hand around my hip, startling me momentarily, and my eyes widened as I watched his face redden while he glowered at the general.

"General Keniris! What is it you wish to say?" he called, kicking his heels into Aithon's side and speeding the horse's gait.

"Nothing, Your Grace. I commented on the beautiful weather here, but those clouds to the north appear threatening." A bead of sweat formed at his temple—the general's tell. The day was sunny, but not warm enough for sweat.

"Bullshit. You were gossiping about my betrothed. Say it again," the Fae king urged.

Looking at the ground, Keniris muttered, "I merely commented on how comfortable she appears in your arms, Your Grace."

"Do you forget she will be your high queen, or are you just stupid enough to think we wouldn't overhear you?" Before Keniris could respond, Aramis leapt off Aithon with elegant grace, stalked toward the general, ripping him from the saddle. Everyone in the company turned their attention to them as Aramis pressed a knife into the general's chin.

"Say it again," Aramis snarled and Keniris' face paled. "Too much of a coward? The talented general who begged us to make peace with the mortals. Begged us not to show our strength. Spare more than just three soldiers. You used to be strong, Keniris." Aramis pushed the blade further into the general's neck, coating the shining steel in scarlet liquid.

My hand reached for my own throat. Remembering hot blood sliding down my neck as Oulixeus' mercenary slid the blade of my dagger along my throat.

"You're *weak*. Say one more thing about her and I'll slice you into pieces the same way I did to your predecessor." A sickening grin formed on Aramis' face, while Keniris looked like he would faint at any moment.

Swish. Something whizzed past my head, causing a few of my ash-blonde curls to bounce. Aithon reared. Losing my grip on the saddle horn, I reached for the reins dangling in the air and the leather brushed against my fingertips as I fell backward.

"Elowyn!" a panicked voice distantly called.

The world spun and my hair whooshed into my face, blinding me, until a *CRACK* snapped through my head and darkness took over.

CHAPTER 19

Conláed knelt over me as I rapidly blinked the darkness and confusion away. A throbbing sensation radiated from my skull as the world realigned.

"Thank Iros," Conláed huffed as I touched a warm liquid matting my hair—blood.

"What?" I blinked again, hoping to dispel the blood, but it remained on my hand. This was real.

"Stay down," Conláed ordered, and angled his shield above our heads. About to protest, Conláed shot me a dire glare that sealed my lips.

Swords swished through the air, hissing once they clashed. An arrow lay beside me while orders were shouted and groans echoed across the glen. Something or someone thudded to the ground next to us. I squeezed Conláed's arm, and my chest heaved as my hands trembled.

This was an attack.

I dared to discover the source of the thud and found a Fae soldier lying still, an arrow protruding from one eye and the other empty. I shut mine and buried my face into Conláed.

One, two, three. Inhaling serenity and calm.

One—I screamed as someone kicked Conláed, exposing me.

"Stay here, don't move!" He instructed as he stood to battle the attacker. My eyes darted across the glen, witnessing bodies scattered on the ground. Red faded into the once crystal-clear stream. A horse lay on its side, bucking and whinnying from a sword impaling its neck. Next to it—Aramis. Blood splattered across his face, blending into his dark merlot jacket. He raised a sword in one hand with flames blazing in the other as he defended our group from all who tried to attack.

Conláed instructed me to stay put, but I was so exposed here, and what could I do to defend myself? Cara insisted my defence skills were improving before I left, but I didn't want to test them out in an actual fucking battle!

Peering over my shoulder, Conláed was no longer in sight and the others in our group were scattered too far from me. I looked toward Aramis again and judged the bloodied, body-littered distance between us.

Whining through my fear, I crawled toward him, keeping low. Gripping fists full of grass and moss to force myself forward, moisture seeped through my fingers. Weaving and dodging between feet, immersed in a combative waltz, I inched closer to Aramis until a boot stomped on my hand. Fingers flattening and knuckles crushing, the aching forced me to roll over to find my assailant—a female with poker-straight hair the colour of fire. Her pointed ears were visible over the small braids keeping her hair from falling into her face.

Let me help you. The dagger strapped to my thigh spoke. I ripped it from its sheath and pointed the tip at my assailant. She laughed—a wicked laugh and kicked the dagger from my grasp, causing it to fly far from me.

I fumbled to find something else to defend myself. *Anything.* I refused to keep being the helpless princess. Another high-pitched whimper seeped through my closed lips as I impatiently searched for a weapon. Something jagged and cold fit in my palm. A rock. I gripped it and swung my arm at the cloaked figure, hitting only air.

Bending over with a short blade in hand, she gripped the neck of my dress and lifted me to her height.

I raised the stone again and struck the side of her head. Her neck wrung to the opposite side.

"Ow!" she exclaimed and threw me back to the ground, her voice sharp and bitter. "That was rude." She bent over and I lifted a foot, kicking her in the abdomen. She barely stumbled, but it allowed me enough time to grab a fallen shield next to me, blocking her swinging sword.

"Did *His Majesty* find himself a pretty little pet who can't even fight?" She laughed as she stomped on my shin and I screamed at the unexpected pain, dropping the shield as I instinctively reached for my leg.

The female knelt on top of me and pulled my hair to expose my throat, resting her short sword on my shoulder. My vein pulsated against the cold steel and mist curled into my vision.

"Damsels in distress aren't his type," she taunted. Through vibrating hands and a racing heart, I wondered what she meant. Who was this female?

She raised her sword arm high into the air, ready to strike, and a shrill, silver note pierced my ears. The blade was seconds from slicing through my neck as a torrent of vitality built within me, like it prepared me to run or fight back. Before I could process the feeling, the female flew to the ground.

"I will *kill* you," Aramis growled, and a flood of immense relief washed over me at his timely arrival.

"No, you won't." She wiped her face to reveal a blood-covered smirk. "You still love me, Aramis."

Love?

Aramis stepped toward her, bending his knees into an offensive stance. The female's mouth widened as she raised her sword, ready for his blow.

"RETREAT!" a voice called and she blew Aramis a mocking kiss before fleeing with her comrades.

The clanging of swords and shouting stopped and a metallic odour filled the narrow glen as the entire world spun.

"Are you okay?" Aramis knelt next to me, scouring my body for wounds.

"Who is she?" My brows furrowed as an unfamiliar pain struck my gut. Ignoring my question, Aramis found the gash on the back of my skull. I winced at the light pressure he applied. He took an unsettling breath, staring at the fresh blood covering his hand. *My* blood.

Conláed rushed over. "Is she—"

Aramis gripped his sword and carved its blade through a nearby Fae soldier. Blood gushed from organs and splattered across my face before the top half of his torso slid to the ground, legs following. My airways narrowed, too stunned to scream, and I slowly lifted my arms away from my body. The Fae's blood dripped from me.

Unease constricted my throat as the liquid soaked into the moss below. My skin vibrated, and I gagged as a drop of his blood mixed with the saliva I swallowed.

Aramis dropped his sword and launched himself onto Conláed, pinning him to the ground.

"If I'm not with her, *you're* with her! What part of that didn't you comprehend?" He snarled at his friend, but Conláed remained calm, as if he frequently experienced Aramis' wrath.

"Yes, Your Grace. I fucked up. It won't happen again." Conláed clearly proclaimed. They didn't move. Aramis continued to hold his friend by the collar, bearing those terrifying canines in pure rage.

"If it does, you're dead." Aramis threatened. "Sweetheart—"

The severed Fae's lifeless eyes stared at me. Horror forever painted on his dead face. Another gag rippled through my throat as my body quivered.

Aramis dropped to a knee, checking the other parts of my body. "Get the healer."

"She's dead." Molvys stepped up, drenched in blood like the rest of us.

Their mouths moved, conversing with each other, but a piercing ring cut their voices and I didn't hear them. I had never seen such bloodshed, and it brought me back to the moment at Elmswood when the fae had lit the Spellcasters aflame.

Through my dizzying vision, I took in Aramis. My betrothed.

I'm exactly the monster they claim.

I was starting to think he was right.

The biting cold wind whipped my hair into Conláed's face. After his tenth groan, he finally pushed the reins into my hands and pulled my hair back.

"What are you doing?"

He surprised me, twisting strands of my hair gently. "I'm braiding your hair. I'm sick of having half of it down my throat."

"Ew!"

"Kind of out of my control, Your Majesty." He had been in a cross mood since leaving the glen. We'd all been in a cross mood.

Aramis and a few others remained behind to secure information from a few captives and create pyres for the fallen. Conláed explained how a Fire Fae's soul was released to the Veil through flames. If the body wasn't burned, the soul would wander aimlessly in this realm for eternity, slowly going mad.

Although Aramis was furious with Conláed for losing sight of me in the ambush, he appointed Conláed to ride me to the nearest village—almost like a test. And although he and the others remained silent, I couldn't help filling Conláed's ears with questions about the ambush.

Who were they? Why did the attack happen? Why did they retreat? How come nobody saw them coming? Who was the red-haired female?

In a hushed tone, Conláed humoured me and offered small pieces of information. He did, however, confirm the attackers were Fae rebels. A group against the unification of Niafell, apparently their group never usually dared to venture so far into the mortal courts. I couldn't help but wonder what had shifted—what emboldened them in this moment?

On the subject of the red-haired female, he refused to share anything. Instead of harassing him further, I recalled what I'd witnessed at the glen while trying to calm my nerves.

"Who were you looking for?" I asked my new riding companion and his body tensed against mine.

After the battle had subsided, an attendant had offered me tea while the group discussed what action to take. I'd sipped the calming drink and watched soldiers gather bodies. Conláed had joined them, but instead of gathering bodies, he'd checked the faces of the rebels.

"What are you talking about?" his voice was laced with trepidation.

"When the others gathered the bodies, you were checking the attackers. Why?"

"To make sure they're dead," he answered through a clenched jaw.

"I doubt it. You turned them over and checked their faces. Who were you looking for?"

He leaned in close and hissed, "Aren't you clever? But if you're smart, you'll drop it." His warning pierced through me like icy daggers, and a gut-wrenching sense of caution crept over me, urging me to heed his words.

The past few weeks revealed Conláed as a carefree joker. Out of all the Fae, I felt the most relaxed around him—how quickly he'd reminded me that I was nothing but a doe being led into a lion's den.

He finished braiding my hair and tied it off with a piece of twine found in a saddlebag. Without a word, he took the reins from me and pulled me closer. I tried to create some space, but he didn't allow it. I squirmed some more and he let out a stifled moan.

"Stop that," he commanded through gritted teeth.

"Why? I'm not comfortable sitting this close to you."

"Sitting so far from me is distributing our weight awkwardly for the horse. And you wiggling your ass around is causing my cock to think for itself. Unfortunately, *it* doesn't understand *off-limits*. So if you'd prefer to *not* have my erection in your back for the rest of the day, I advise you to stop."

My face instantly heated.

"Thought so," he added when I stopped all movement and my back pressed into his chest, strong like Aramis'.

I thought about why Aramis didn't insist on sitting closer for the horse's sake and Conláed seemed to anticipate the question. "Why didn't—"

"Because he's trying to be chivalrous. You really don't recognize how difficult that is for him."

"Right, because slaughtering his own soldier and soaking me in his blood is so gentlemanly," I scoffed.

Conláed shrugged. "That soldier was in the wrong place at the wrong time. Honestly, he should've known better. It's not just Aramis who loses his temper. It's a fairly common trait amongst us Fire Fae, especially those who have seen so much bloodshed. Each death is ingrained into us—he should've known better."

I opened my mouth to continue protesting this monstrous logic, but decided against it. What was the point? Especially as conflicting emotions fought to dominate my thoughts. Despite Aramis' brutality, he actually made me feel...safe.

Mortal villagers glared at our approaching group. Some spat at the horses' hooves. Others gestured a god's warning across their chest. Wooden doors slammed shut on white-plastered buildings, shutters following suit. Children covered in filth ran up and down the streets, playing a game with a hoop and stick and their parents hurriedly shuffled them inside. The streets were littered with shit and rotting food and I covered my nose with my wool cloak as the rain worked to soak us.

Each visit to a town had been unwelcoming. The discomfort caused me to shift in the saddle and Conláed half-moaned, half-coughed as his cock slightly twitched.

"Are you serious?" The villagers who hadn't locked themselves in buildings yet gaped at my outburst.

"I'm just really... *sensitive* today," Conláed explained through a chuckle.

"And I'm ready to be alone." And I meant it, not being used to company.

"I can tell." Without seeing his face, I sensed him smirking.

A three-story building with a large wooden sign above its door came into view. Ystävä's Inn. A loaf of bread and a tankard of beer were carved into the sign, and I was eager to be indoors soon—away from these brutal Fae males and psychotic murderers.

CHAPTER 20

*H*eavy drops of rain splattered on the ground, thudding against the soil and leaving red welts on my skin. I held my skirts and ran as fast as I could, away from the heart-wrenching wailing.

Branches caught my dress, ripping away pieces of silk. One grabbed my hair, and I skidded to the muddying ground, hissing as strands ripped.

Trees grew taller and further apart and mist floated between trunks. I didn't know where I ran, but I had to run away. Stopping, I wrapped myself in my arms and started to spin. Round, round, round.

I collapsed to the ground and stretched my arm out. My fingers spread in the dirt but, as I lifted my hand, I didn't see mud. Blood. A burgundy liquid coated my palm. Tears trickled down my cheeks as something dragged across the ground toward me, whirling the leaves into a frenzy. My eyes dragged to the commotion and a *tall, hooded figure stood between the trees. A dagger in his hands—my dagger.*

"Elowyn," he stepped toward me and I sat up, pushing backwards.

"Who are you?" I demanded as fear crept through me. This wasn't right. This hadn't happened.

"You need to listen to me," the figure urged, faintly familiar.

My eyes darted about the misty forest, scouring for something safe. This wasn't part of the dream. This was too real.

A door slammed and my legs kicked out from under me. As my eyes opened, the hooded figure floated away with the dream and Aramis walked into the room from the adjoining bathing chamber.

"I woke you." Aramis padded over with nothing but a towel tied around his waist. My eyes hovered over the definition in his abdomen and the hair trailing down.

"You woke me from a nightmare, so thank you."

"Are you okay?" He sat on the mattress next to me, stretching an arm over the headboard. Leather, sandalwood, something sweet... cherries, emitted from his skin, still drying from his bath. The way his damp hair fell to his shoulders, and the steadiness of his heart formed a serene atmosphere. I looked to the cavity his arm created and recalled how I'd curled up there that night on the mountain, how warm and secure being in his arms had felt. Pushing those thoughts aside and reminding myself of who he truly was, I wiggled an inch away from him.

After a long pause, his deep smoky voice whispered, "I'm sorry that I frightened you today. There's a—darkness inside of me, Elowyn. The things I've done... the things *he* made me do..."

"Aramis."

"And to complain to you, of all people. The things that bastard did to you. The things your parents did to you. I see it in your eyes, Elowyn. Your past haunts you, and I understand why. I have no right to seek your solace. It's not fair for me to lean on you when you're battling demons of your own."

"Aramis."

"But I can't always control it. The world intensifies. Sounds, colours, movement, it all just—"

"Becomes too overwhelming," I finished for Aramis, understanding all too wholly, his description sounding so akin to my own anxious moments. "I think... there's a darkness in me, too." I rested a palm on his smooth, angular cheek, and it pulsed heat again.

I thought it impossible to find another as fucked up as me, but here he lay—in the flesh. Fire coursing through his veins. And although it simmered and warmed for me, I had an unshakable feeling that if provoked, his fire would burn the entire world to ash, with me as the sole survivor. I'd already adapted to living a life buried beneath the ashes.

Aramis pulled me into his chest and we lay in each other's comfort, though the ambush remained in my mind. He'd almost killed General Keniris, and I think he would have if the rebels didn't interrupt. And then there was the red-haired female...

"Is something else troubling you?"

I sighed, knowing only answers would still my restlessness. "Who was the female trying to hurt me?"

Aramis remained silent, almost like he wrestled with a wordless debate. I dared to reach out and place my palm over his hairless chest. A pleased grunt emerged from his throat, and he placed his own hand over mine, savouring the touch.

"You loved her once, didn't you?" I suspected from the words the female spoke while attempting to murder me.

"Yes," Aramis reluctantly admitted. After a brief silence, he continued, "Andraste. If I was a flame, then she was the whole damned world ablaze."

He drifted into memories, his face distorted between happiness and irritation. And I wanted to know more about the female he cherished, like uncovering a hidden chapter of his life, consumed by a genuine curiosity to better understand the layers of his heart. "How old were you?"

"I can't remember. Around one hundred and fifty, maybe. An arrogant, cocky adolescent." He chuckled at the recollection of his younger self as it shook me. My twenty-one years suddenly seemed like a mere blink of an eye in comparison.

"So Andraste was strong and smart."

"And insecure. Callous. Vindictive. She played the part of best friend and loving partner, but piss her off in the slightest and she became nastier than a wraith. Amusing at first, but after two centuries, the drama grew to insufferable levels. As our wedding approached," my eyes snapped to his, the thought of him marrying her churned a sharp pain in my chest, "an instinct emerged that insisted on ending it. Andraste was furious. She didn't believe me at first. Refused to move out of my apartment. So I moved. A few months later, she left. Today was the first time I've seen her in over a century."

Aramis draped the sheets over our heads like he could shelter me from the evils harassing me. A flicker in his eyes betrayed him and I realised that he wanted to pull me into his chest, part of me wanted him to, remembering how comforting his embrace felt on the mountain. But as he wished to pull, I fought to push, so instead I bit my bottom lip and he kept his hands to himself.

"Let's not speak of her again. I don't want her ruining any more of our moments," he whispered.

The fire crackled on the opposite end of the room. Lulling me into a tranquil state. As sleep started to take me, and I had no strength to fight against myself anymore, I pushed into Aramis' arms and asked, "Can you teach me how to fight?"

Brushing his lips along my forehead so gently I wondered if I imagined it, he whispered, "Of course, sweetheart."

Aramis certainly was the monster they all warned me about, but maybe only a monster had the strength to protect me from my demons.

CHAPTER 21

"We're entering the Fae Court." Aramis leaned in to share.

I scanned the bare land in front of us, appearing the same as it had for many kilometres—tall grass instead of blood-stained fields. "This is the frontline?"

"The battlefields are southeast from here." His thumb stroked the material covering my waist, a motion I ignored.

"Oh."

"You sound disappointed," Molvys, riding next to us, observed.

I expected the Fae Court to be a terrifying, insidious land with terrorising monsters instead of cattle, or ominous forests and labouring mortal slaves. Not bountiful fields and quiet farm houses. "Not disappointed, just expecting something different."

"Give it a few leagues, sweetheart," Aramis chuckled.

He passed the day with tales of his childhood. Playing with wooden swords in the grasslands, holidays and traditions observed by the Fae, and growing up with Molvys and Conláed.

Along with his childhood, he shared about the Fire Court, too. I learned their court surpassed all others in battle skills and bred the most powerful and intelligent horses. Rarely did other Fae courts challenge them because of this, respecting their power.

"There were originally seven Fae courts in Niafell. Rhyddean was part of the Mind Court," Aramis informed. "War broke out amongst them after we relinquished the eastern lands to the mortals."

"Why?" My extensive education focused on ruling and defeating the Fae. I knew iron nullified their magic, making them more vulnerable. They possessed heightened senses, making them apex predators. But I was never taught their full history, my father believed it to be inconsequential.

"The high lords refused to put the argument about the mortals to rest. Some wished to allow the mortals to live in peace with their new lands. Some insisted on re-enslaving the mortals. One suggested killing all mortals to end the debate once and for all," my betrothed continued. "Only three courts survived the Civil War. The Light Court, Earth Court, and Fire Court. All agreed to combine into one united Fae Court, and the dream of a united Niafell formed."

The ambition and pride he expressed while discussing the united world lessened my fear of their occupation over the mortal courts.

"What did—" My question vanished, and my eyes widened at the sky as my jaw dropped.

"You each owe me two silvers," Conláed said with a chuckle at the males riding behind us. "We made bets on when you'd notice the change."

The sky flaunted the lightest, palest blue with a hint of a shimmer reflecting through it. Layers of silver clouds sparkled and flowed like gentle waves washing onto the shore. Pure magic.

Our party diverted from the main road, heading for a grove of trees draped with vibrant pink blossoms. We all dismounted and soldiers conjured fire pits with their magic, attendants arranged platters of cured meats, cheeses, and fruits, and everyone gathered in their usual groups for the afternoon meal.

Aramis sat with his back against a tree, legs wide, with one bent at the knee, leaving a space just the right size for me. Yet, I searched for another place to sit, far away from him. In the corner of my eye, I noticed Aramis smirking as he watched me awkwardly survey the grassy area.

Choosing a spot opposite him, Molvys and Conláed joined us with a tray of food, plopping down exactly where I'd meant to, forcing me to sit closer to Aramis. He tapped the toe of my boot with his own, as if teasing me for my awkward resistance.

The three Fae warriors chatted as I took in the new world around me. Dark glistening lines flowed through the tree's bark, like veins carrying a life force. Leaves rustled as a few blossoms fell from the branches, gliding around me. I caught one in my palm and observed the way the petals glimmered in the sun, eliciting the same serenity I felt in my secret, imaginary forest.

"You want to learn how to fight?" A baritone voice pulled me into the present. Molvys sat across from me with a keen gaze, awaiting my response.

Gulping down the anxious knot in my throat, I admitted to them, "Yeah, I'm sick of feeling helpless."

"Good." The corners of his lips lifted into the first smile I'd seen from him.

"Have you had any sort of formal training or will we be starting from scratch?" Conláed asked, his words muffled by a mouth full of food.

"My friend taught me a few defensive techniques, and how to throw a punch."

Aramis gave my arm a squeeze, as if proud of me.

"Well, let's see them." Conláed swallowed his food and walked over to a wide clearing within the grove.

"Now?" My jaw hung loose. In front of everyone? I'd look like a fool.

"Don't be shy. We all start somewhere." Molvys extended an encouraging hand. His shift from his usual formal and distant demeanour piqued my interest, and I accepted his assistance.

"Show me what you got, Princess." Conláed bent at the hips, fists raised to his cheeks as we stepped into Conláed's impromptu training arena.

"Hit him." Aramis chuckled, arms crossed over his chest, and Molvys appeared to be just as amused.

I moved toward the tall warrior dressed in leather armour and raised my hands the way Cara taught me. *Keep your fists on your cheeks to protect yourself from an opponent's hit.*

Bending at my hips, I placed my weight onto my toes and shifted back and forth. Conláed stood nearly as tall as Aramis. How in the Veil would I reach his face to strike him? *Adapt your tactics to your opponent.* Cara's voice rang in my ear.

Without a warning, I snapped my left elbow into a ninety-degree angle, twisted from my hips, and slammed my fist into Conláed's ribs. Seconds later, as Conláed leaned over, I threw an uppercut with my right fist into the bottom of his chin.

Conláed stumbled backwards and stretched out his jaw as Aramis and Molvys clapped behind me. "Well, you're quick and you throw hard."

My heart pounded with an exhilaration I didn't recognize. From successfully executing the combo of punches without Cara coaching me, and grasping how to bring a tall Fae warrior to my level.

Large arms wrapped around my upper body, lifting me into the air. "Do you know how to escape from this hold?" Molvys' smooth words rolled next to my ear.

As my legs flailed, memories of instructions filled me. I shimmied in Molvys' tight grip until my feet hit the ground again. Pushing my elbows outwards and dropping my weight, I loosened Molvys' grip and slipped out of it. Rolling onto my back, I kicked into his stomach, causing him to stumble backwards.

"Good!"

My cheeks flushed at the praise.

Suddenly, a massive body pinned me down. Aramis straddled me and held my wrists next to my head. His nostrils flared, and a mischievous grin formed dimples. Arrogant jerk. "You're supposed to be afraid, Princess."

I bit my lip as the flush spread to my chest. But as he smirked, my determination sparked and surged into a power I hadn't felt before. Bucking my hips with force, Aramis fell forward, and I twisted my head to the side to avoid being crushed by his muscular body. I wrapped my arms around his waist to wiggle down. But I moved too slowly, and Aramis snapped his hand to my throat and I froze, eyes widening.

In seconds, I found myself back in Elmswood, laying on my mother's writing desk with Oulixeus' hands coiled around my neck. My lungs took shallow, sharp breaths as my pulse banged in my head, and a high-pitched ringing emerged, drowning out the surrounding world. My eyes closed and the vision of Oulixeus became clearer.

"Elowyn?" His venomous voice curled around me.

"Please, go away," I whimpered.

The pressure around my neck ceased.

"Elowyn, it's me, Aramis." A smoky voice curled around me with sandalwood and leather and something sweet... I'd been here before—feeling safe until the snake struck unexpectedly.

But comforting scents continued to work their way into my senses, pulling me from the dark memories. Daring to open my eyes, I saw Aramis kneeling in front of me, giving me space.

Conláed and Molvys stood nearby, concern painted through their expressions. My breaths became longer and deeper.

"Are you okay?"

I rapidly nodded my head, unable to speak yet.

"Would you like to talk about it?" Aramis' words were patient, and I knew he held no demand behind them. I covered my eyes with a forearm, wishing to disappear.

"Another time," I offered, too embarrassed to admit what had occurred.

"We know where to begin now." Molvys changed the subject.

"You have a solid foundation, Elowyn. You should be proud of yourself," Aramis added, gripping my hand.

I suppressed my shame, hiding it where I hid all of my emotions, and forced a smile as Aramis helped me. Despite the embarrassment attempting to occupy my mind, a glimmer of hope and excitement kindled. Finally, I was in control of my own life for the first time.

The stars burned intensely, radiating a reddish glow, and Aramis broke away from the group to sneak us into the capital city of Stoneshalt to avoid a long, drawn out, formal welcome. Exhausted from travelling, I was grateful for this. We moved through an unnoticeable wooden gate covered in vines and rusted hinges—an ancient, forgotten entrance.

The Blood Fortress, perched on a plateau in the city's west, featured ruby-red vines resembling life-giving veins on its sandy stone surface. Guards armed with crossbows, clad in the same silver, flame-etched armour as those who marched to Elmswood, patrolled the outer walls.

Aramis stealthily led me through the hidden entrances in the fortress and into the inner corridors, where he signalled for silence with a finger to his lips. As much as I loathed to admit it, I relished this playful side he reserved solely for me. We quietly traversed the red marble passageways until we reached imposing doors adorned with flames etched into the wood.

"Welcome home." Aramis invited me into what I assumed to be his apartment. We entered a spacious antechamber with soaring twelve-foot ceilings, adorned with slate stone flooring extending throughout. An arched doorway to my left led to an open dining hall with a round table and exotic plants lining each wall.

On the right, another archway led to a small hall housing two doors, one leading to a study and the other to a bathing chamber. However, Aramis guided me straight ahead through a door to his personal sleeping chamber.

I ambled about the room, taking in my surroundings. The far side had no wall, tall columns opening to a half-moon balcony. No windows or shutters, just open to the outside air, with sheer drapes billowing in the light, warm breeze.

"You can wear this tonight." Aramis dropped a white folded shirt on the leather sofa before disappearing into the bathing chamber. I changed into it, shedding my dirty riding dress gratefully.

A fire burned in the hearth, its grand mantle and facing matched the red marble of the corridors and antechamber walls, contrasting with the lighter, sandy walls. The design offered a comforting ambiance that was the opposite of the cold stone walls of Elmswood. A luxurious rug sat beneath my feet and scenes of lions, flames, and a bird engulfed in flames decorated it.

I tiptoed to the balcony and leaned against the thick stone railing overlooking the city. Surreal. Absolutely surreal to be at the Blood Fortress, a place I'd been taught to fear, with Aramis vulnerably naked in the other room. An involuntary laugh escaped my lips as I traced a finger along the rough stone. I felt safer here than I ever had at home.

The city below rested in tranquil darkness, with a few streets illuminated by flame lamp posts. I always imagined Stoneshalt as a place of chaos, with Fae quarrelling and humans suffering. Fire magic recklessly conjured. Yet, tonight, serenity blanketed all.

Peering over my shoulder, Aramis leaned against a column, arms crossed, one foot over the other, and full dimples.

"Gods, this is a beautiful sight." His eyes feasted upon me and my arm pulsed warmly.

"The city is beautiful." I ignored his double entendre.

"Not quite what I meant." He neared me, setting his hand beside mine, our fingers nearly touching. I fixated on the city below, where streetlamps twinkled like stars, market vendors packed up, and Fae strolled along the cobblestone streets. My effort to ignore our proximity faltered when I inadvertently stretched my fingers to his, and the warmth of his flesh struck mine.

Aramis wasn't Oulixeus or any other I'd met. He evoked a sense of safety and belonging. A feeling that...

Gold and silver sparkles darted past my face, emitting a delicate tinkling melody dancing in the moonlit air. "What the—"

Another flashed next to my ear, and I reached to swat it away. As the shimmering thing deflected my hand, it fluttered in front of me, nattering at me in an incomprehensible, soprano speech.

"Careful. You don't want to get on their bad side," Aramis warned and the tiny being curtsied mid air toward him. It rushed away on its tiny, gossamer wings and a fragrance of wildflowers and moonlight lingered in the iridescent glow of its trail. As it faded into the depths of the cypress trees lining the balcony, they looked like fireflies dancing between branches.

Aramis expanded, "They're called *keiju*. They're like sprites or... fairies. Mischievous little things."

The *keiju* moved as if in a choreographed dance, reminding me of the fireflies in Rhyddean. "Do they like rain?" Another one zoomed past me, leaving glitter in its wake.

"Some do. There are four types—fire, water, earth, and air. These are fire *keiju*. They avoid rain like the plague." And as Aramis spoke, I realised the tips of our fingers still touched.

I pulled my hand back and interrupted him. "I should get some sleep."

"Of course," Aramis replied gently, devoid of any frustration, as I walked away and slid under the luxurious cotton sheets. Aramis rested above them, hands tucked under his head and elbows out, and I took the opportunity to study him, unsure what to think. We'd agreed to work together, and he took me as his betrothed, yet I still wondered if I could trust him.

Misinterpreting my stare, he said, "If I crawl under there with you, we won't leave this room for weeks. Goodnight, sweetheart."

"Don't call me that," I teased.

CHAPTER 22

Sun poured onto his perfectly sculpted body as he breathed low and steady, the rhythm soothing. Barely shifting throughout the night, he'd remained on his back, a hand behind his head, and the other resting on his chiselled abdomen, scars marking the battles he'd fought in. His under shorts were... pitched.

Unintentionally, an influx of visuals inundated my mind, particularly all the ways he'd take me with his thick cock. Obscene images of my head tossed back, eagerly riding him as his hands explored my body overwhelmed me.

My hand trailed to my thighs and pressed against the ache the images induced, pursing my lips together to muffle any breaths daring to expose me. The shirt I wore dampened between my legs as a rush built inside of me.

I stroked my clit faster, biting my lip hard enough to break the skin, a bead of scarlet liquid rolling into my mouth. A shudder ran through me as I inhibited the breaths begging to emerge. Aramis moved.

Fuck! I snatched my hand away, depriving myself of the release, and pretended to sleep. He shifted and with a half-yawn, half-growl, I sensed his passionate gaze casting over me. "Good morning, sweetheart," he said in a raspy whisper, a soothing rumble hinting at a solid night's rest.

Pretending to blink the sleep from my eyes, I yawned. "Hi."

His eyes instantly darkened, as if he had heard me, or could smell me. Curling his hand around my chin, Aramis tilted my lips toward his. Strong and commanding, yet affectionate. We never kissed, and as the morning sun trickled over our bodies, curiosity dared me to. Just to see.

Aramis leaned in closer, our breath mingling. Golden strands mixed with ash-blonde curls. Inching closer and closer...

The chamber door slammed open, and servants filled the room. I snatched the sheets to my chin, but Aramis continued to admire me. He placed his hand between us, close to my abdomen. Close to where I'd imagined him inside of me.

"Good Iros, cover yourself, cousin!" A tall female with auburn hair stopped at the foot of the bed, averting her eyes from his groin and dramatically waving her hands in the air.

"This is my room, Fifi. If you don't like what you see, leave." He bucked his hips in the air and placed his hands behind his head again, his erection on full display for all to see.

"And this is also Princess Elowyn's apartment, who I am here to assist. So, make yourself decent." Fifi tossed a throw pillow at Aramis. She shared her cousin's strong jawline and dimples—sweet and eager.

"Get out, Fifi!" Aramis groaned, rolling to his stomach and propping himself on his elbows. He tugged on a curl trailing down my shoulder and something within me pulled, like a string.

"You, cousin, need to get ready for the council meeting. I'm going to help Princess Elowyn get ready for the day." Fifi stretched an elegant hand for me to take. Tempted to ignore her, I glanced at her hand and my stomach dropped. Perfectly manicured, like Cara's. A vision of the box resurfaced, and I silently scolded myself for the distraction.

I took her hand and rushed out of bed. Aramis snatched the air behind me and growled at my departure as Fifi dragged me to a door I didn't notice last night, opening to a nearly identical room, but decorated in lighter, softer hues.

"This is the adjoining suite. If Aramis annoys you, it's your cycle, or you need some alone time, you have your own space to retreat to!" She leaned into me and laughed with a pop of her shoulder.

As we left, Aramis shouted, "I'll just be here! Taking care of something!"

"*Males.*" Fifi rolled her eyes. And as the door shut, I caught hints of Aramis' scent infused with a musk that tensed the muscles between my thighs.

"I'm Agrafina, but call me Fifi." The female pulled me from my fantasies. I assessed the room. Crimson, chocolates, and gold accented Aramis's room. This room contained colours of dusty rose, peach, and ivory. Prepared for his wife.

"And you are..."

"Aramis' cousin. King Basilius is—was—my mother's brother." She marched me over to a full-length mirror carved into flames. Gripping the bottom of Aramis' shirt, she pulled it straight over my head, leaving me stark naked in front of several strangers.

Gasping, I covered my breasts with my arms and crossed my legs as Fifi and the other females laughed. With a flick of her wrist, a servant fetched a dress from the wardrobe, the door carved into the same firebird as the ones woven into the carpet.

"You don't have to hide yourself, dear. We may be Fae, but we have the same parts." They all snickered. "Lift your arms."

Summoning my courage, I did as she requested. A milky material cascaded along my body, thin and almost sheer. My fingers trailed along the skirt, gliding the fabric between them.

Peering into the mirror, my eyes widened. Naked. I may as well have been naked. Two panels of buttery soft fabric covered my breasts but exposed the centre of my body. Two thinly braided gold ropes kept the fabric in place. Fifi tied one under my breasts and the other on my waist, accentuating my hourglass figure. A figure barely seen under mortal gowns. The panels connected to a thick band on my hips where the skirt draped from.

I swallowed, noticing my nipples peaked through the material. Fifi cocked her head to the side, confused by my terror. I broke into a laugh. A guttural, hysterical fit. Bending at the waist, gripping my stomach.

"What's wrong, Princess?" Her brows wrinkled in confusion as I covered my mouth to end my laughter.

"Nothing. I'm—I'm—" Tears welled under my lids as I fell forward into another fit of laughter.

"Are you displeased?" She turned to the others and searched their faces for answers, all staring as if a demon from the Veil possessed me.

"Okay, now you *really* need to leave, Fifi." Aramis stalked into the room, dressed elegantly in black breeches and a white silk shirt with the first three buttons left undone. My fit halted at the intent in his gaze.

"You have a meeting to attend," his cousin protested.

"OUT!" he thundered. From anyone else, the roar would've made me jump, but from him, it reignited embers beneath the cold ashes I had adapted to.

Servants fled the room, and Fifi frowned. "Not so fast. We're not finished."

"Do not test my patience today, cousin." Aramis flashed his canines, but she held his stare, unintimidated. And surprisingly, Aramis cracked before Fifi, and he moved his attention from her to me.

"You're ravishing." He pinched the gauzy material, rubbing it between two fingers as if images of his own flooded his mind now.

Stepping out of his reach, I turned to meet him. "I feel naked." Even more so, looking directly at him, no longer shielded by the reflection of the mirror.

Kill him... The dagger reminded me. Yes, the tactic both my mother and uncle suggested. I just needed to set a firm boundary with myself. Get close to Aramis, allow him to fall for me without me falling in return. *I* had to be the manipulator this time...

"If anyone looks where they're not supposed to, I'll rip their throat out," he promised and I simpered, well aware he didn't bluff.

"I might just remain here all day," I mumbled, turning to view my reflection again. Even in the privacy of my tower, I didn't recall ever studying my body and noticing my hourglass shape.

"No, you're coming with me." Aramis gripped my hand and dragged me to the door.

"Excuse me?"

"To the council meeting. You should learn about the politics here and my plans for a united realm," Aramis clarified.

"You really want me there?"

"Of course. I don't want to rule alone." As we stepped out of the antechamber, two guards stationed at our doors followed us down the halls. I allowed Aramis to pull me through the halls as I blankly stared at the back of his head. Women didn't take part in politics in the mortal courts. And not only was I a woman, but a *mortal*.

I analysed potential benefits of attending instead of wandering on my own—primarily securing Aramis' trust. "Okay."

Aramis flashed a quick glance back at me, a pleased dimple marked his cheek. And suddenly, my convictions regarding men—and males—and their intentions with women were profoundly challenged.

CHAPTER 23

The council members assessed me. I counted seven sets of eyes, male and female, all judging silently.

"Welcome back, Your Highness," one Fae male greeted. With white hair and wrinkles carved deeply into his face, I knew he must have been ancient to show such signs of age.

Aramis helped me into the chair beside his. Unaccustomed to the sense of inclusion, a cascade of exhilaration sent delightful shivers coursing through my belly.

"Yes, let's not waste our time. Where do we stand with the east?" Aramis leaned back into his chair, a foot crossed over his knee, and watched me. The east? Did he refer to the mortal courts? He had to. Nothing lay beyond the Eternal Sea. Only myth of the entrance to the Veil.

"Well?" Aramis pressed after no one spoke. A few shifted awkwardly and others stared at their hands. "Sir Haldwin, out with it."

"We have decided it to be in the best interest of our court to not discuss such things in a mortal's presence," the ancient Fae explained. An uncontrolled snort left me, witnessing a council of wise Fae frightened of a young mortal woman.

Aramis studied my expression, his knuckles turning white from gripping the arms of his chair. "Excuse me?" He leaned toward the table, glaring at the council member who'd spoken.

"Your Grace, it is unwise to speak of such things in front of her." He nodded in my direction and continued. "We're more than happy to discuss your wedding on Summer Solstice and the coronation, of course. We'd appreciate your input, Princess. But in regards to our politics—"

Aramis rose, towering over the table. Both arms swiftly ignited. The stone table he rested his fists on began to glow from his frightening heat. "My betrothed is no spy." His voice remained eerily calm.

Sir Haldwin held firm, holding Aramis' scowl. "As your ancestors declared, there's no room for magic in politics, Your Grace."

A malicious smirk formed on Aramis' face. His flames blazed larger, wilder. The glow inched further toward the centre like molten lava seething down a volcano. "Afraid of my princess and my magic, Haldwin?"

Sweat glistened on a council member nearest the heat, sparking concern among the others. My brief sense of inclusion gave way to an unwelcome feeling. My focus narrowed on Sir Haldwin, whose eyes widened and mouth trembled as he attempted to reason with Aramis, but my ears filled with ringing, and a fog crept in at the edges of my vision. A potent surge coursed through me, the same energy that consistently shot through me in moments of panic and anxiety. Were they symptoms of that formidable, dark power within me?

"Stop." I stood, calming my tone as Aramis' flames died down. All eyes refocused on me, their lack of trust palpable. A sour scent hung in the room, and I swiftly exited to a nearby courtyard.

"Elowyn, wait." Aramis followed close behind. "They need to learn their place."

"I can't do this, Aramis." Years of emotion trailed me.

"What do you mean?" He stepped toward me, brows furrowed.

"For fourteen years, I tried to understand why my family hated me. Eight of those years I spent trying so hard to regain their favour—it nearly killed me. Multiple times. I don't want to be like that anymore. If they don't want me, then I don't want them." My gut clenched as soon as I realised how vulnerable I'd made myself.

"You're going to be High Queen of Niafell. Of the Fae *and* mortals. They need to respect you. You're more than capable of ruling by my side, Elowyn. You're educated in politics and—"

"Wait, what?" I cocked my head to the side. "How do you know about my education?"

"My father and I made it our business to learn as much as possible about each of Evander's children."

"Is that why you want to marry me? I'm just a good fit?" I craned my neck to see him, my insecurities growing.

"Among other reasons," he admitted. "Come back. I'll force them to respect you."

"You can't force respect."

"A few of them need to *retire* anyway," he jeered, as my discomfort cemented within me. I allowed myself to be vulnerable with him again, and he'd reassured me—defended me.

Changing the subject, desperate to create space, I urged him to leave. "Go talk politics. I'll be fine in our chamber."

"You're free here, sweetheart. I won't lock you in a tower like your parents did."

"It's okay for me to... wander?" I asked, moving my palms to rest on his shoulders. He stood so tall, my arms had to fully extend to reach them.

"Explore the entire fortress." He gripped my hips, mussing my dress. His head dipped low, hovering, attempting to recapture our earlier intimacy. However, I resisted the affection, anchored in reality.

"I'd rather start searching for the Book," I whispered, stepping away.

"Right. Go to the archives. The map your parents gave you seems a bit useless. Maybe you'll find a more valuable clue there," Aramis suggested and waved over a servant. "Please take the princess to the archives."

"Thank you." I smiled as one of his hands lingered near me, toying with the fabric of my skirt, as if afraid to let me escape. But with a determined resolve, I broke free from his lingering touch. "I should get going," I said, and as a servant guided me toward the archives, the fortress held its secrets, waiting to be unveiled.

Cross-legged on the floor with stacks of books towering around me, I delved into an intriguing jade-leather memoir—a stark contrast to the brown-bound volumes it hid between. The rose embossed on the cover initially convinced me to open it.

Although I didn't find the author's name, I found it fascinating to read about their life at the Fire Court during a time of peace. Even more fascinating that this Fae chose to write in the common tongue and not in the elegant Fae language. Perhaps few Fae understood the common tongue, and that was their way of encrypting their secrets?

As I dove deeper into their life, I learned this Fae held a noble title and loved to sneak about the fortress. She seemed to go about unnoticed by others, overshadowed by her older sibling's inheriting titles. By the time I reached the thirtieth page, I'd begun a list of hidden locations to search for the Book.

She spoke of hidden compartments in fireplace mantles, cubbies behind paintings, and hidden jib doors. Hopefully, Aramis could aid in locating these spots.

Reaching for the cup of coffee an attendant brought to me, I coughed on a sip halfway down my throat.

The chamber below the throne room is by far the most coveted. If Father knows I'm aware of it, he'll probably kill me. No one is to know about it, and our High Lord grows more paranoid with each passing day, much like the other Fire Fae rulers...

I reread the passage at least five times until a familiar high-pitched voice chimed through the archives.

"Your Highness!"

Fifi elegantly strode over, her dress matching the colour of pink blossoms and trailing behind her.

"Fifi, hi."

"Is the council meeting finished so soon?" She handed me a glass of gold fairy wine, its liquid shimmering with floating flakes of glitter, and my mouth watered. I had gone days without craving alcohol, forgetting about it and the solace it brought.

"Oh, do you dislike wine?" Fifi noticed my scrutiny of the liquid, and to be polite, I took a sip, melting as the alcohol filled me. Liquid sunshine. Pure molten gold, encouraging me to speak uninhibitedly.

"They kicked me out."

"Typical ancient morons." She popped open a massive ruby on her bracelet to reveal a hidden compartment filled with white powder. Holding it to her nose, she took a heavy sniff. "Seriously, it's too bad council members serve for life."

Her comment gave Aramis' *retiring* joke a whole different meaning.

Fifi stood by the book towers and began flipping through the tomes on the top stacks without bending. Her lips pursed as she asked, "What are you even doing in here?"

I couldn't reveal my quest to find and destroy an ancient spell book. Even Aramis had insisted on secrecy to avoid unwanted attention. But I'd neglected to create a cover story, an oversight.

"My tutors never taught me about the Fae courts. If I'm to be high queen, I figured it'd be good for me to understand your history, the land, and demographics," I quickly lied. Fifi nodded, but as she continued to poke around the papers, I felt like it wasn't adequate.

"You play cards, right?" She finally switched her focus away from my research.

"I do."

"Then come, let's play cards and meet new friends. This looks..." Fifi took another survey of my messy work area, "boring."

I didn't wish to leave my books yet, but declining might arouse suspicion. Roaming aimlessly with friends seemed less conspicuous than poking around alone. I rose and allowed Fifi to link her arm with mine, her smile beaming.

As the light trickled past the gauzy drapes, it highlighted the shimmering skirts and detailed jackets of noble Fae scattered throughout the room. Some sat at felt game tables while others stood in circles, gossiping and sipping wine. A few couples sprawled across the cabriole sofas, embraced in each other's arms, lips meeting. They displayed their affection so freely compared to mortals, who hid affection behind closed doors.

A glint caught my attention, and I spotted ivory betting tiles on a table where a male Fae stacked his winnings. Electricity buzzed through me, urging me to join. I could beat him. I always won.

Fifi led me to the table that I ogled. "Everyone, this is your future high queen. Princess, this is everyone."

"Please, call me Elowyn," I insisted, and we sat at the table. The male with the most tiles placed two stacks in front of me and began to deal. A couple of gold coins clinked into the centre as Fifi added them to pay for our tiles.

"I think Princess will suffice. I'm Rune," another fair-haired Fae introduced himself. His eyes, the colour of the forest, held a gentle ease.

"None of us wish for Aramis to spill our guts at the next feast for insulting his new fiancé. It's always so messy," a female with lilac hair and a youthful expression explained.

"And it kills the mood," Rune added. And despite the terrifying nature of their conversation, they both laughed it off as if the behaviour was normal.

"By the way, I'm Iris," the lilac haired female said, extending a hand across the table to shake. Catching me staring at her locks, she added, "I'm an Earth Fae, hence the hair colour. We're a lot more... colourful... than other Fae, growing up in such a lush environment. I guess we just adapted to looking like it."

Rune held the deck of cards, shuffling them with expert skill. "What have you done in the fortress since you've arrived, Princess?"

"Oh, I found her in the archives," Fifi jumped to answer for me.

"That sounds..." Iris crumpled her face.

"Boring," Fifi supplied, and Iris laughed in response.

"The archives?" Rune raised his brow as he dealt the hand, and I picked up each card gently after they slipped under my palm.

"Oh!" Fifi exclaimed as she studied her cards.

In my element, I smiled, already learning their tells.

Surrounded by my shiny winnings, I sat with my legs folded beneath me on *my* bed, in *my* airy and spacious chamber, enjoying having a space of my own that wasn't a disguised prison. I leaned over the diary I discovered in the archives earlier, rereading the intriguing passage over and over.

The chamber below the throne room is by far the most coveted. If Father knows I'm aware of it, he'll probably kill me. No one is to know about it, and our High Lord grows more paranoid with each passing day, much like the other Fire Fae rulers...

My gut sparked, urging me that this was a clue to the spell book's location. It *had* to be. The spark in my gut seemed to spread to my thigh, my calf, my foot... wait. My leg went numb. The coins and jewels clinked as I shifted to rest on my hip.

"What do we have here?" Aramis broke my concentration, standing in the door frame joining our two chambers.

Instinctively, I tucked the diary beneath my hip. Coins chimed against the stone as they slid from the bed. "Fuck," I muttered as I made a mess of my space, remembering I worked *with* Aramis now. He chuckled, arms crossed over one another and an eyebrow curled high with amusement, and I joined his laughter.

I almost *wanted* to share this information with him, somewhat excited to have someone else included. Like a team.

No, don't be stupid. Stick to the plan. Which plan? Seduce Aramis and kill him. How would I even do it? As

I watched him approach me with his stealthy saunter, I played the multiple possibilities through my mind.

Poison was out of the question. He'd smell it. Fighting was just stupid, even if they trained me. No, the best way would be through manipulation and stealth. To get close to him, make him feel so comfortable and when he let down his guard, I could slide the blade along his throat and watch him choke on his own blood.

But my gut chastised me, not liking any of those ideas.

"Look at this." Standing on the mattress, I leapt onto the cold stone to show him the diary entry and some of my winnings spilled onto the floor. I pointed at the passage I refused to let go. "I'm not too sure who's diary this is. But they note many secret locations within the fortress. This one, in particular, stands out to me." I passed the book to Aramis and left him to read it as I retrieved the ancient map my parents had given me. "They mention a secret chamber under the throne room. So secret that your lords killed to keep it hidden. And you said earlier that this room on the map looks like the throne room, right?"

Aramis slowly nodded his head as his gaze switched from the diary to the map I held up to him.

"I know you said that there are no books or storage in the throne room, but this passage confirms something's hidden there. Something important. I think we've found our location."

He handed the diary back to me as he took the map, studying it with squinted eyes.

"Well? What do you think?" I urged him, waiting for his opinion. He eventually dropped his arms by his side and grinned.

"I think you're absolutely correct."

And I beamed at his praise.

CHAPTER 24

*H*eavy drops of rain splattered on the ground, thudding against the soil and leaving red welts on my skin. I held my skirts and ran as fast as I could. Away from the heart-wrenching wailing.

Branches caught my dress, ripping away pieces of silk. One grabbed my hair, and I skidded to the muddying ground, hissing as strands ripped.

Trees grew taller and further apart and mist floated between trunks. I didn't know where I ran, but I had to run away. Stopping, I wrapped myself in my arms and started to spin. Round, round, round.

I collapsed to the ground and stretched my arms out, my fingers spread in the dirt. But as I lifted my hand, I didn't see mud. Blood. A burgundy liquid coated my palm. Tears trickled down my cheeks as something dragged across the ground toward me, whirling the leaves into a frenzy. My eyes dragged to the commotion and a *tall, hooded figure stood amongst the trees. A dagger in his hands—my dagger.*

Raising my elbows, I pushed myself away from the stranger, but he stalked forward. "There's no need to fear me, Elowyn."

"You—" My eyes widened as I finally recognised his voice. It matched the cloaked figure from the tavern, the one who'd lost his dagger to me.

He stepped closer, and I scrambled to keep the distance between us. Noting my reaction, he paused as my interrogation started. "Who are you? How do you know me?"

"My name is Seth, and I'm not here to harm you."

I shook my head, unable to believe this. "This isn't real. I'm dreaming. This is a dream."

"You're right. It is a dream, but it's still real, Elowyn," Seth confirmed with a patient tone.

"Stop it! Get out of my head!" I clamped my eyes shut and pictured laying in bed next to Aramis.

"Don't shut me out, Elowyn. This is important."

A trick. A demon or darkness trying to find a way to possess me. None of this was real.

"Elowyn," the hooded man warned.

Waking, my body thrust forward and toppled over my legs. I held my hand to my chest and my lungs felt tight, as if I had been holding my breath.

The fire in the hearth had burnt out, and the purple light of the dawn slowly crept its way in from the balcony and cascaded across the stone floor. The wind blew stronger and colder than before, chilling my flesh and flapping the drapes vigorously. I pulled the sheets to my chest and noticed Aramis had already prepared for a busy day on his side of the apartment.

Am I going mad? Or did someone actually attempt to communicate with me through my dreams? Was he truly the hooded man from the tavern who lost his dagger in the card game?

"You're up," Aramis noticed, leaning against the doorframe, an annoyingly attractive pose, defining his muscles and height.

Tucking my knees into my chest, I rested my cheek on them and admired the light trickling into the room. There were so many subtle differences in the Fae Court, but the way light shimmered and glinted was the most drastic.

"Is something wrong?"

Yes, I'm going mad. And you're becoming less repulsive with each passing day.

"I'm just nervous about training," I lied, and he responded with a forced smile.

Yesterday, he'd arranged for Conláed and Molvys to train me every morning before researching the Book's location. Our next step—sifting through millennia of blueprints.

Aramis, as high king, lacked the time to train me and find the Book, so he delegated training to his friends. The

Book held greater significance for both of us, and we preferred to keep our endeavour discreet.

"You'll do great. You truly have the basics down. Practice and building strength will get you there. And your trigger..." Aramis' words trailed off.

"My trigger?"

"When I clamped my hand around your throat, it clearly triggered something. We need to work past it because it's a common tactic," he warned. I bit my lip, fully aware of how men favoured it.

"Is it something I'll ever get past?" I asked, more to myself than to him.

"Absolutely. You're so strong, you can get past anything." Aramis' gentle and smooth tone wrapped around me like comforting flames. And for once, I believed the encouragement I received.

I'd get past the trauma Oulixeus inflicted upon me, not because I had to, but because I *wanted* to.

CHAPTER 25

As the morning sun lifted higher into the sky, I jabbed the point of the wooden dagger into the left side of Conláed's torso. But right before the tip met flesh, Conláed gripped my wrist and slammed his wooden shield into my forearm. A sting vibrated through my muscles and my hand reflexively opened, dropping my dagger to the ground.

I cursed through gritted teeth as the massive Fae warrior bent my arm, twisting my entire body. Conláed chuckled as my back pressed against his bare chest, and he wrapped his arms around my body.

Other Fae training in the arena stopped their practice to watch.

Wiggling my body, I attempted to slide downwards and slip out of his grip the way Cara taught me. But Conláed held me too closely. I shifted some more until something solid pushed against my back. I paused before my cheeks coloured.

"Seriously?"

"What? It's the morning," Conláed grunted as he squeezed me tighter. Rolling my eyes, I flared my elbows apart and pushed with all of my strength until I felt a tiny slip in his grip. Within seconds, I had rolled out of Conláed's grasp, onto my back and reclaimed my wooden dagger.

"Good," Molvys called from the sideline, holding his chin between his fingers. My chest pulsed with my quick breaths as I fully relaxed into the ground beneath me. Dried dirt stuck to my tacky skin, and I stretched an arm out to my side. The familiar position instantly reminded me of my recurring dream, and I sprung upwards before the image of blood coating my hands emerged.

The other Fae clapped at my minor success and returned to their own training. It amazed me to see both males and females training together in the ring. In Rhyddean, they taught only men how to fight.

Despite the cool breeze, sweat drenched the training clothing Conláed found for me. I pinched the fabric to unstick it from my skin and waved it to create a makeshift breeze beneath my attire.

"You did well. You're a quick learner, and I think your friend was correct—with consistent training, the more this will become second nature to you, you'll freeze less and less." Molvys took the wooden dagger, roughly the same weight and size of my own back in my room, and returned it to the weapons rack.

Conláed brushed the dirt from my back, but I swatted his hand away as another set of clapping hands approached us—Aramis.

"You're incredible. You'll be a Fae warrior in no time," he praised, and I blushed, imagining myself as skillful as a Fae. Being independent and courageous finally became an attainable goal.

"Thanks—" I began before Aramis' face soured toward Conláed. I searched the space between them to understand the sudden change.

"Go find something to fuck," Aramis growled at his friend, who sheepishly grinned, and my eyes unintentionally darted to his groin as he readjusted his pitched pants. He coughed a few times before walking off, Aramis' glower following him all the way into the shadows of the hall.

"Hungry?" He turned his attention back to me.

"Starving," I confirmed.

"What are you looking for?" Aramis asked, setting a crinkling map on his lap. Though he'd intended to take me to lunch in a courtyard, our excitement to begin researching prevailed. Aramis needed to return to meetings soon, so we opted to combine our meal and search.

Maps, blueprints, and tomes adorned our polished wooden table, the diary resting nearby amidst scattered platters of food and our growing stacks.

I reached for the porcelain bowl full of dark cherries and popped one into my mouth. Aramis watched me intently, focusing on my lips, and elusive flutters erupted in the pit of my stomach.

"So, you're telling me that my best spy's tell is his voice raising?" Aramis returned to our conversation about my gambling experience the other day.

"It's not obvious, though. It's the tiniest shift that took me a few rounds to notice." I felt the need to reassure him and not be responsible for someone's dismissal. "I have unnatural hearing. That's what my mother called it before boxing my ears." I pretended to show more interest in the book in front of me, not wanting to discuss it more.

Aramis frowned at my story. "No one will ever touch you again." And he held a dark gaze over me, like a promise to use his wrath to avenge me. His intensity was overwhelming, and I discarded my book for a blueprint, avoiding his words.

"Is it normal to have so many council meetings?" I changed the subject.

"No. The council has reported more pressing issues than I expected."

"Is it about the east? What's over there, anyway?" I buttered a slice of bread, careful not to drop any crumbs onto the ancient tomes around me. The crust crunched in my mouth and the soft centre melted, exactly like Grandmama's.

"The east?"

"Before they kicked me out of the council meeting—"

"Before you chose to leave," Aramis corrected with a playful grin.

"You mentioned the east. Do you mean the mortal courts? Or the Veil?" I reached for another cherry. He watched me swallow the fruit and pull the stone from my mouth before indulging me.

"A realm hides behind the Veil. I want to find it," Aramis shared without hesitation. He plucked a cherry from the bowl, holding its stem, and handed it to me. I accepted, but twirled it between my fingers.

"Why?" I slowly pushed it between my lips, forming a round opening, knowing full well I teased him. He liked me, and he didn't hide it.

"I don't just want to unite this realm, Elowyn. I want to unite all the realms," he growled, watching me intently before offering another cherry.

I ignored his silent, sensuous request and studied his face and mannerisms. "All realms?"

"Yes." Recognising my boundaries, Aramis returned the cherry to the bowl.

"How do you know about this realm?" I asked, thankful for his surrender.

Aramis shifted through the stacks of books on the table, searching for something. "My pyromancer saw it."

"Pyromancer?"

He chuckled, as if understanding how foreign everything sounded to me. "They can see things in flames. The future, the past, prophecies, hidden objects or people. She discovered the land, and the book required to get there."

"The Book of Toivo?"

"Yes." Aramis grabbed a book from the bottom of a stack and the pile fell to the floor, their impact echoing through the room. "Here it is." He quickly flipped through the book, the edges of parchment scratching against his calloused fingers, before handing it to me. "We don't know how many realms there truly are, but this lists a few of them."

As I took the cracked leather-bound book from Aramis, my arms fell to my lap with the book's weight. Aramis quickly reached out and helped me position it on the table.

"Heavier than it looked," I muttered under my breath, my arms feeling sore from my morning training session.

I fell into a trance reading about the three realms described in the book. The Realm of the Gods nicknamed The Garden. The Realm of the Dead, or the Veil, as we called it. And the Shadow Realm. All three existed on different plains than our own, something I didn't fully understand, but my engrossment in reading prevented me from asking.

The ancient parchment felt rough against my skin as I hovered a finger over the text.

Those with a connection to shadow can walk its plain, though only feminine beings may travel freely.

"Who has a connection to shadow?" I asked Aramis without looking away from the page.

"Shadow Fae, demons from the Veil, some claim female mortals with the Gift can travel there, too. The scholars who wrote that book believed demons escaped the Veil through the Shadow Realm."

Don't wander the Shadow Realm without purpose, or the shadows will seek your mind and choose one for you.

My brows furrowed, wondering what purpose one would have in a realm described as containing only shadow and mist. "Is this the realm your pyromancer told you about?"

Aramis stood and leaned over my shoulder to view the page I read. "No. Only the Book of Toivo describes the land she discovered and holds the key to travel there."

"How can you be so sure?" I asked, surprised by his willingness to share so much. Yet, we both recognised how our cooperation hastened our path to the Book.

"A few of those ancient, fearful council members aren't completely useless yet. They may not know the Book's location, but a few have seen it and read its contents." The edge of his shoulder nudged mine and I cleared my throat.

"And you trust them?" I asked, ignoring the sensation of his shoulder lightly grazing mine and the ripple it sent through me.

"Not a single one of them." His breath danced along the flesh of my neck, daring to break my concentration.

Focus on the Book... focus... "Then why do you think they speak the truth about the Book?"

"I have to start somewhere, Elowyn. Why not start there?" Aramis stood and returned to his seat and the book he studied.

Grateful for the space, I felt my mind clear. "And you're certain there's not a door or cupboard or hidden switch in the throne room?"

"Elowyn, I spent my entire childhood running around and exploring the throne room, playing knights and bandits with my friends. If obvious, we would have found something by now. The entrance is either extremely well hidden, protected by magic, or it's been built over. That's why we're going through these architect notes. Someone had to have recorded something..."

Aramis stared blankly at the pages in front of him and, with an exhausted groan, he snapped it shut, tossing it to the table.

I reached my hand over to comfort him, but stopped right before my fingers met his flesh, instead offering him uplifting words. "We'll find it."

"I know. I should get back to the council, though. You'll be fine here?"

"I'll be fine here."

Gentle lips lingered near my ear, and warm breath caressed my skin, coaxing excited shivers along the back of my neck. My eyes fluttered open to see Aramis leaning over me, a hand rubbing my back, as I awoke surrounded by peaks of parchment.

"You fell asleep," his gentle voice whispered.

"Sorry, I didn't realise how tired I was."

"It's been a long trip from Rhyddean, and a busy first two days here in Stoneshalt. I hoped to have some time to ourselves to relax, but it'll have to come after the wedding."

That woke me up.

The idea of marrying Aramis still didn't feel real. Although fear remained, my feelings were inconsequential, as rescuing Cara was my only priority.

I faked a smile and rose from the table. "It's late, isn't it?"

"Midnight."

"Let's go to bed," I suggested and gathered a few of the papers with potential to take back to our apartments. Aramis held out his arms to take them from me, and I handed them to him. Reaching for the diary, my fingernails clacked against the polished wood. My eyes darted to the location, and I halted. No diary. It wasn't there.

Frantically, I scoured the table, pushing parchment to the side, books thumping on the floor.

"No, no, no, no, no," I muttered throughout my search.

"What's wrong?"

"The diary with the entry is gone. How is it *gone*?" I didn't halt my search and Aramis placed the stack of papers I gave to him to the side as he began to poke around to help me.

"It has to be somewhere, Elowyn."

"I left it right *here!*" I snapped at him, pointing at the only empty spot on the table.

"Maybe you left it in our chambers," he offered. But my frantic frustration shut him out.

"No. I swear I left it right *here*, and now it's *gone*. Would someone have taken it? Who would've taken it?" I thought aloud, every possible reason and outcome flooding into my brain simultaneously. "You said others could be looking for the Book too, right?"

"Yes, but it's highly unlikely, Elowyn. Let's go to our chambers and look there. I'm sure this is all just a misunderstanding." Aramis confirmed. I reluctantly nodded, but proceeded to follow him as he gathered my other papers and left the archives.

But it wasn't there. Neither was the map. The wooden box where we'd hid them, on the top shelf of the firebird wardrobe, was gone. Though the rest of our chamber remained undisturbed.

"Aramis, they're not here," I whispered, staring at the empty shelf. My mouth hung open, unable to comprehend the fact that someone stole my clues.

"They're not here," I spoke louder, turning to face him and his expression mirrored my thoughts. Someone else in the fortress sought the Book, just as Aramis had predicted.

CHAPTER 26

My heart frantically pounded against my rib cage as sweat beaded along my hairline and dribbled down my skin, skirting along my neck. The air felt thin as my lungs heaved, avidly attempting to soak it in. My body's reaction matched the frenzied state of my mind. All week I scoured my shared apartment with Aramis and the archives for the clues we lost, afraid to fully admit they were stolen. Yet with each passing day, my panic and distress rose, knowing someone watched me. But who?

I didn't care about the thief's motives. My sole focus revolved around finding and securing it before them, because losing the Book meant losing any hope of saving Cara.

Fuck. Fuck. Fuck!

A jab landed on the side of my ribs and I keeled over into the dirt, raising dust on either side of me.

"No! Elowyn, where in the Veil are you today?" Molvys shouted from the sidelines as Conláed grinned at the blow he threw. I didn't bother to hurry off of the ground, laying down and attempting to huff away my worries instead. But they refused to abandon me.

On top of racing some mysterious thief for the Book, I'd endured seven days of gruelling morning training. My muscles ached as Molvys, instead of easing up, intensified my workouts with extra laps, added weight exercises, and forced me to stay thirty minutes longer compared to our initial sessions.

He wanted to kill me. I remained certain of it.

The lack of sleep didn't help, either, worsening my battle with the relentless demon haunting my dreams. To thwart his intrusions, I resorted to brief naps, never truly sleeping to prevent Seth from fully entering my unconscious mind.

Conláed offered a hand and I reluctantly took it, rising from the dry dirt and back to my feet.

"You should've seen that one coming, Elowyn. We've been practising it all week," Conláed agreed with Molvys and, instead of taking the criticism, I balled my hand into a fist and struck his jaw. His head shot to the side and a wide grin appeared as I lowered my fist, glaring at him.

"There's our feisty girl!" he exclaimed, and even Molvys let down his guard and cracked a miniscule smirk. "Now, where has *she* been all week?"

"Preoccupied," I mumbled, walking over to grab the waterskin I strategically placed in a shady spot.

"Hey, are you okay?" Conláed followed me. He quickly became a friend, regardless of its unexpected nature and my determination to fight it. He was kind, encouraging, and funny.

"I'm fine." I sighed and forced a smile.

Conláed smirked at my weak attempt to lie, something I rarely failed at, and draping his arm over my shoulders, he suggested, "Let's do something fun today."

"Like?" Training and research occupied my days at the Fae Court.

"We'll go into town. I'll show the market, we'll stop at the river for the best fried fish you'll ever taste, and—"

"No," Molvys' baritone voice startled us both.

"Come on—"

"*No.*" Molvys refused to relent, folding his arms over his chest to stand his ground.

"What's the harm?" Conláed unleashed me, his words snapping at Molvys and I backed up, not wanting to be caught in the middle of them.

Molvys stepped into Conláed's space, and the extra inch he had on Conláed became two extra feet. "You know exactly what, and Aramis—"

"Isn't here."

"Conláed—" Molvys paused and noticed my wide gaze. A tightly wound ball of frayed nerves reminded me not to piss him off. The serious Fae directed his friend to the far side of the arena to debate privately and I spied from a distance as their arms flew around in gestures, the grunting of the other sparring soldiers hindering my ability to hear.

Pacing around the arena, my thoughts proceeded to drift back to the dream and the hooded figure. Did he produce my gruesome visions and troubled mind? If he'd caused it all, why did he only appear in my dreams now? And what did he want from me?

A wind rushed through the training arena and stray hairs from my braid blew across my face. As the wind settled, it left a distant, high-pitched ring.

No. I recognised this now. Whenever fear threatened to control me, a darkness swept in, attempting to protect me. It urged me to follow through with my violent visions, to fight back.

My stomach dropped, and I felt like hurling. Refusing to allow the building darkness to seize my sanity, I marched toward Molvys and Conláed.

"I want to go to the market." Straightening my spine, I stared into Molvys' austere amber irises.

"See—" Conláed waved at me as if I'd proved his point.

"I'd like to acquaint myself with it if it's to be my home." *Lie. I wanted to distract myself from whatever darkness haunted me, and take my mind off whoever else hunted the Book.*

Molvys crossed his arms, and we fell into a staring match. Both of us were stubborn and unwilling to quit.

Whatever his fears for allowing me into the city, my own fears held greater sway, and I wouldn't relent.

Just as his round eyes twitched, Conláed grabbed my arm and pulled. "We're going."

The breath I held on to escaped as a yelp, and I tumbled into Conláed's arms. Quickly restoring my balance, I chortled as we headed for the door.

"*Fine.* But I'm joining you." Frustration rolled through Molvys' words.

"Are you concerned about me?" I joked, batting my lashes as Molvys fell into step beside us.

"No. Someone needs to keep him out of trouble." He tilted his chin toward Conláed, who donned a roguish smirk as he led us out of the training arena and towards the city.

Navigating through a rainbow of colour, Conláed held my hand to ensure he didn't lose me in the sea of brightly-dressed Fae. Molvys stalked close behind, glaring at those who got too close, which was everyone.

Fae crowded the market and bodies jostled off one another, pushing and squishing through the throng. Chatter and shouts filtered into the desiccated air that formed beads of sweat along my hairline and parched my throat. Vivid pyramids of spices, sizzling meats, and fruits filled the market with exotic scents and my stomach rumbled as we passed a stall with meat rotating on a spit, grease dripping into the coals below, and aromatic spices melding into the steam.

Conláed stopped at a cart displaying jewels glinting beneath the shimmering blue sky. Plucking a tiara set with a yellow jewel resembling the sun, he positioned it on my head and squinted an eye as if evaluating its suitability. Laughing, I removed it and placed it back on the cart, the vendor already reducing the price. I shook my hands in a declining motion as Conláed readjusted the gossamer hood I wore.

Wanting to fit in, Fifi had assisted me in choosing an outfit and we'd settled on a loose fitting silk dress. She'd tied more gold ropes around my waist to display my figure, and the sweeping neckline and short, ruffled sleeves helped to keep me from overheating. The mauve material wasn't as sheer as other dresses in my armoire, allowing me to feel more comfortable pushed up against strangers.

Leaving the fortress, Fifi had fluffed my curls and draped matching material over my head. Not a single Fae spared me a second glance the entire time we wandered through the market.

"I never want to wear a Fae jewel ever again!" I pushed Conláed along, and although I shouted, not even the Fae closest to us heard me over the market's raucous.

A stall across the way interested me, and I suddenly shifted directions, losing Molvys and Conláed. Instead of a colourful awning like the rest, a dark purple, almost black, linen fabric shielded the heat of the relentless sun.

Streams of light still poked through the tattered holes here and there and herbs, ointments, tinctures, and gemstones lined the shelves in the back, with additional items scattered on the tables. I dragged my finger along the edge of the table covered with a rough wool sheet. The nail I broke during training caught on a loose thread, creating a tear, and a female popped up from behind the table. Her large, green gaze snapped to the rip I made.

"Shit, I'm sorry. I'll buy you a new one. Conláed—" I turned around to ask for some coins as Conláed had insisted I'd be pickpocketed within seconds, but he remained nowhere in sight.

"It's fine." The young female seemed to tremble as she added ingredients to a mortar, grinding them to a powder. As she ignored me, I resumed surveying her items. I recognized items necessary for herbalism—sieves, grinders, scales, vials and jars, droppers, herbs, and oils.

"Do you sell tools and ingredients, or just finished product?"

"Mostly ready-to-go remedies, but the odd healer comes to me for ingredients. Are you a healer?" Her focus remained on her work.

"No, but I have recipes for my own tinctures and salves and whatnot. I'd like to make them." I missed creating concoctions with Grandmama and having them to use. An emptiness swept through me as I thought about Cara's family and the time I spent with them. Maybe resuming herbalism would fill the depressed feeling?

"I can put together an apothecary chest for you," she offered, drizzling a golden oil into her finely ground powder.

"Really?" My voice popped higher than I wished.

"What would you like?" She ducked back under the table and returned seconds later with an empty cedar apothecary chest with embellished brass latches. As she unfolded it, I grinned and listed the items I wished to purchase.

Within minutes, the chest resembled Grandmama's kitchen, pinching my heart with a bit of homesickness. And all of her recipes I had memorised came forth in my mind. I'd have to write them out before time swept them away.

Lost in nostalgia, a rough cough brought me back to the present, to the vendor hacking into her fist and bracing herself against the table. A little stone tablet with an interesting mark tied to a string swayed from her neck. The symbol formed the shape of an *N*, but more primitive and jagged.

"Are you okay?"

A couple more hacks and she straightened, brushing her hair behind an ear. A rounded ear. My jaw slacked from not seeing or interacting with another mortal since we left Aberevin. The *woman* frowned at my reaction.

"I wondered when I'd see another mor—"

"You can't run off like that." An arm snatched my bicep and an angry Fae snarled in my ear. The vendor

255

across from me dropped her frown, tucking the necklace back beneath her dress. Her eyes widened, and she quickly covered her ears with thick, jet-black hair.

"I'm fine." I shrugged out of Molvys' grip. A puffing Conláed flanked my other side.

"Fun's over, we're leaving now."

"Oh, come on, Molvys. She wants to get to know the city, the people," Conláed attempted to defend me as I held the vendor's stare. She'd hid her race from them, but why?

The woman swallowed as if silently begging me not to reveal her secret. Aramis led me to believe mortals were safe and even welcomed here. However, mortals with the Gift...

"We can go home, but first I need to pay this female for my purchase." Her shoulders slackened with my word choice.

Conláed shifted on his feet, reaching for the bag of coins he strapped to his belt. "What did you purchase?"

"An apothecary chest." The vendor snapped it shut and passed it over to me. Wanting to leave swiftly before Conláed or Molvys discovered what I had, I paid the vendor and marched back into the crowd.

As the crowd thinned, we stumbled upon a group of entertainers using fire magic to enhance their performance. Molvys refused to let us stop, but I watched as we passed.

A thin female danced on her toes, turning in tight circles, arms waving in the air, and completely engulfed in flames. Though she didn't burn. The magic didn't harm her, it didn't redden her skin and force her flesh to blister. Not like... the Spellcasters.

My head whipped around to the market, the witch's stall barely visible. And I understood why she didn't want to be discovered. I couldn't help myself but smile at her audacity to hide in plain sight. That was clever, and I liked clever people.

CHAPTER 27

I entered the archives, not expecting to find my betrothed hidden behind stacks of tomes, rummaging through text after text. Tiptoeing in, not wanting to disturb him, I came around the towers and evaluated everything we had already searched through, piled on the far side of the table.

Picking up an ancient tome, the spine snapped as I opened it, ripping it in two. "Fuck!"

Aramis' head snapped up at my curse and his eyes widened like a little boy's on the morning of Winter Solstice. "I've found something very, very useful!"

Rushing over, I took a seat next to him, discarding the book I destroyed, and he produced a list of names and years. "This is a list of all the architects who have worked on the fortress over the centuries. Wings were added here and there, towers built and torn down, room plans modified, and this—"

His fingers traced the delicate script and I couldn't help but admire the intensity with which he approached every discovery, each word that might hold the key to unlocking the secrets we sought. Pointing to a passage next to one of the names—

Ammar al-Nazir - throne room modification autumn of the Gods' Year 7204.

"Okay—" I stared at the passage and name, attempting to find the significance that Aramis saw. Many rooms underwent alterations throughout the centuries. Why would this entry matter?

`As I leaned closer to the tome, our shoulders brushed, and a warmth spread through me from the accidental touch. I quickly pulled away, sending an apologetic smile his way, yet Aramis' affectionate smile met mine and his eyes softened.

"Elowyn, it's the first passage referencing any change to the throne room. It's the only untouched room since the fortress's initial construction."

"Oh!" Of course. I hadn't come across any reference to the throne room either, since we focused our research on blueprints.

"So, then, I decided to do what you would do, and research the architect." His mention of doing what *I* would do softened my heart. No one ever attempted to be like me.

He produced a folio filled with sketches and notes, all written by the architect Ammar Al-Nazir. As he fumbled through the pages, my thigh brushed against his knee, and before I could pull away, Aramis pushed his knee further into me. A blush crawled from my chest to my cheeks.

"Nazir was renowned for crafting elaborate keys for his buildings and rooms. Many hired him for designing and constructing secret passages and treasuries."

"So, we need to find a key and the location of where to use it" I deduced, and Aramis grinned from ear to ear, our legs still pressed into each other.

"I found it."

"What?"

Flipping through the folio, Aramis handed me a piece of parchment with various drawings. Amulets. He pointed at one in particular, moulded into flames with a unique open shape in the centre.

"You think it's this one?"

"I *know* it's that one. This is the amulet that every Fire Court ruler inherited. I went to the hall where all the rulers' busts are on display and the first ruler to be depicted wearing it is Lyrius, the one who commissioned Nazir." He flicked the page in his triumphant deduction skills, and I honestly found myself impressed with him.

"Where is it now? You're not wearing it," I noted.

"I never wanted to. It reminded me of my father. So instead, I buried it in my room. When we get back, I'll grab it and keep it on. Ensure our little thief doesn't get their hands on it!" With Aramis' reminder, I folded the page with the amulet sketches and tucked it into the pocket of Aramis' jacket. We didn't want to leave clues lying around.

"So, we just need to find the keyhole, then." Everything fell into place. We'd possess the Book in no time.

"Yes."

"Is Nazir still alive? Can we just ask him?"

Aramis shook his head. "That's the other thing making me certain about this. He died shortly after the modifications were completed, and Fire Fae rulers are notorious for growing paranoid as they age."

I studied the papers he gathered and undoubtedly agreed with his significant findings. We'd lost our first two clues, but they confirmed the location of the hidden entrance. This clue actually showed us how to get *into* the hidden entrance. Our last step was to actually find the mechanism to use the amulet on.

Butterflies fluttered in my stomach and a wide grin formed on my face as I pictured returning to Rhyddean with the Book, presenting it to my father and rushing to free Cara. Once I freed her, I'd take her and her family away. I didn't know where we'd go, and we'd have to go slowly, but we'd leave. I wouldn't be afraid of Oulixeus or my parents anymore.

And then Aramis' knee pushed further into mine, and my excitement diminished, leaving behind a tangle of emotions I couldn't unravel. A sensation that defied logic and reason, and a connection that I dared not acknowledge.

CHAPTER 28

Leaves whirled into a frenzy as I dug my nails into the moist soil, slowly transforming into mud. The blood, I knew it'd be blood this time, squished out of the dirt and slid down my fingers. I lifted my palm to see the dirt and blood mix into a deep maroon. Instead of panicking, I rubbed my fingers together, enjoying the velvety texture of the two substances conjoining. Pieces dropped onto my face and into my tangled hair.

"Elowyn." I knew he'd speak before any words sounded.

This demon refused to leave, determined to haunt my dreams.

"If you're here to claim my soul, just take it already," I dryly spoke as I continued to analyse the blood coating my hand. I didn't want to die or give up, but the torment this creature put me through every night drove me mad. For years, I suppressed the darkness through harmful ways, but I'd succeeded. Now, as I strived for change, it tried to capture me at my weakest.

"I'm not here to take anything from you."

I laughed and sat up to meet Seth's face, still hidden in shadow. "Then why do you haunt me?"

"To show you the truth." He spoke as dryly as I did. Almost like he mocked me.

"I know my truth, demon." Lie. I didn't know the truth about anything. Only recalling bits and pieces of fragmented memories scattered throughout my childhood.

He scoffed, as if reading my mind.

"You're courageous, Elowyn. More than you know. And I can help you find your courage, to tap into it and hold it." He took a step forward, his fist clenched, but not angry or in a threatening way. He tensed his hand out of... excitement.

"Leave me alone. Allow me some peace and quiet without disturbing my sleep," I requested, laying my body back onto the ground, now wetter.

"You won't listen to me yet, will you?" Disappointment emanated from him.

The rain poured on me, cleansing me, as if the rain wanted to wash away my fear to clear room for this courage Seth spoke of. "No," I said flatly.

"Fine."

A sudden burst of energy hit my core and permeated my body. The air I held onto expelled from my lungs, and

I gasped in fright as a transcendental force flowed into me, awakening a crackling presence. My heart raced with an uncontainable excitement as my veins thrummed with a power I recognised from somewhere before. A power laying dormant for too long.

A tingle began at my fingertips, an electric current spreading up my arms and throughout my entire body. My senses in this dream forest seemed to heighten. Every touch, sound, and smell amplified, as if the world had been injected with a vivid intensity. Colours within the forest became richer and more vibrant, and an ethereal light peeked through the fog, dancing around me like a playful sprite.

But the transformation encompassed far more than just the physical. Something awakened emotions deep within me, ones I yearned for my entire life but kept hidden and suppressed, afraid of their potential.

A surge of euphoria flooded me, coursing through my veins like liquid fire. The intoxicating high overwhelmed me, becoming a heady rush, making me feel simultaneously invincible and vulnerable and... dangerous.

Joy clashed with fear, curiosity intertwined with caution. I teetered on the precipice between control and surrender, my heart thirsting to embrace this limitless power that beckoned me, while my mind recalled whispers from the past.

This was magic, and it pulsed through me like a raging storm threatening to engulf me completely. It demanded to be released, to be harnessed, and I battled to keep it contained, because the familiar senses reminded me of something terrible, though I couldn't quite place it.

It felt as though my very essence was being stretched and moulded, blending and bending into someone—something—indistinguishable...

With a final jolt of power, I met Seth's eyes and, this time, he pushed me out.

Flinching awake, my eyes focused on the soft billowing of the curtains as I evaluated myself. My heart beat strongly, but I didn't panic as my lungs expanded and detracted at a calming pace. My nerves didn't shutter and the remnants of energy tingling through my body felt relaxing, like stretching muscles I'd forgot existed.

And although my physical body relaxed peacefully, my mind raced with horrifying images of a young girl traumatised by blood curdling wails, angry pounding against wood, and the sizzle of burning flesh.

Seth tried to awaken the darkness that loomed over me my entire life. Why else would he visit my dreams? Why else did he show me this energy?

The questions surfacing pushed my body into the same panicked state as my mind. But through the panic, I missed something... the euphoric sensation of the energy he gave me. It was more powerful than anything I'd experienced before, more than alcohol, gambling, or sex. And I wanted more. I wanted to chase that high.

With the moon rising high outside, I knew exactly where I could find it.

CHAPTER 29

With a coupe glass in hand, I whirled around the room, adding to the blur the fairy wine provided as musicians assembled in the corner of the parlour and plucked away at violins, cellos, and a harp playing cheerful, exuberant songs. Halos circled around tiny flames on the golden sconces, luxurious fabrics flowed together, and bodies pressed into one another.

Iris gripped my hips, spinning me to the middle of the floor, and I wrapped my arms around her neck with a drink still in hand. We laughed and twirled to the beat of Fifi's clapping, and wine from our glasses sloshed onto the floor.

The others dancing near us laughed hysterically, not bothering to move out of the way as our slippers began sliding on the wet stone. Rune rushed over to steady us and refill our glasses with a bright pink liquid. As the first sip coated my tongue, I widened my eyes and Rune grinned, swigging from the bottle before joining our dance.

Sugary raspberries bubbled on my taste buds along with a rush of ecstasy gushing through me, but I instantly frowned. The alcohol wasn't nearly as titillating or satisfying as the energy my demon had pulsed through me earlier.

The music crescendoed and a noble Fae took my arm, spinning me on tiptoes. As my skirt flared, flecks of gold in the fabric sparkled in the dim light. The room merged furniture, people, and walls into a frantic blur.

My head rushed, everything moving too quickly and everything in my stomach unsettling. I halted, tumbling into Iris, who fell into Fifi, and resulted in Rune catching both females. All three of them burst into tipsy laughter, but I grasped my stomach to steady myself, urging the alcohol to quiet.

"Oh, you poor thing, sit." Fifi regained her balance and guided me through the maze of card tables to a quiet corner across the room.

I needed to experience the indescribable high again. I wanted it so badly that my mouth salivated, searching for the euphoric ecstasy. But my usual vices weren't enough.

Fifi rested her palm on my knee and I glimpsed the giant ring she wore on her slender finger. The ring she popped open and snorted a powdery substance from before. I lifted her hand and popped the secret compartment open. The first time I watched her do this, the powder looked white, but now I could see it shimmered of all the colours of the rainbow so brightly that it only looked white.

Bowing my head, Fifi laughed. "Hold on there, Princess!"

I stopped and glared at her for interrupting me.

"Have you done this before?" Her brow quirked, like she already knew the answer. I shook my head in a silent *no*. "Okay, then. Not so much. Here."

Fifi leaned over the sofa arm and plucked a book from a nearby shelf. Opening it, she tore out a page and ripped it in half, setting one page on the coffee table in front of us and rolling the other into a tiny tube. Tapping a little powder onto the flat page, she pushed it into a thin, straight line.

"Okay, hold this piece up to your nose, close the other nostril with your finger," I did as she instructed, "yes, just like that. Now snort up the powder with as much gusto as you can!"

I leaned over and did exactly as she instructed. The dry powder attacked my nostril, burning the skin from where it first made contact, all the way up between my eyes and into my head.

"Fuck!" I leaned backwards and shook my head when suddenly a rush hit me, an instant flood of happiness overwhelming my senses, freezing me in awe.

"Welcome to the *real* party now, Princess," Fifi laughed in her high-pitched tone and popped her shoulder as she always did when excited. I clasped her hands in mine and leaned into her while giggling like a little child.

I felt unstoppable, like every worry and concern in my world melted away. I couldn't even recall what troubled me.

The high hit me instantly, but it was still nothing as euphoric as whatever type of energy the demon had shared. The drinking and gambling didn't compare, either. But Seth's magic... it made me feel whole and like I belonged.

I wanted it again.

Fifi caught the disappointment in my gaze.

"Is everything okay? Is it Aramis? Is he okay?" I attempted to answer her, but Fifi continued rambling faster than ever. "You two have been spending a lot of time in the archives. And I see the way he looks at you while your nose is buried in those dusty, old books!"

"Fifi, no—" The world spun as I held my hands up to deny Fifi's suspicions of *anything* going on between Aramis and I.

"Please! Your first morning here, when we met in his chamber..." Her voice trailed on with more questions and speculations, but I stopped listening to her, my attention drawn to another sitting at a table near the tall windows.

The female radiated a sensual confidence I had never witnessed before, silky red hair, the colour of flames flowing to the ground. As others around her gossiped, flailing their hands in front of them, and laughing obnoxiously, spilling their drinks, the female sat casually, her elbow thrown over the back of the chair. There her shoulders and stance relaxed, her elongated neck stretched to the ceiling, chin held high.

Where other females dressed in revealing dresses, the red-haired female wore an indigo short-sleeved tunic, gold thread embellishing the collar, and tied at the waist by a thick leather belt. Black elbow-length gloves added an additional layer of elegance to her stature.

And despite the radiating confidence she exuded, she displayed no hint of arrogance or superiority. No. She gently smiled at the others' jokes and comments, listening intently to them all and taking the time to acknowledge each individual sitting at her table.

"Elowyn?" A voice pulled me from my trance and I looked to Fifi.

"Hi." I smiled at her, a bit lost in my fuzzy mind.

Amusement painted crinkles around her eyes as she watched the drug affect me. "You okay?"

"Who is that?" I nodded toward the beguiling female, sipping on whiskey.

"Aramis' sister, Kenna."

"His sister?"

"He has two sisters. Certainly he mentioned them?" I shook my head. Aside from his father's paranoia, Aramis didn't mention his family. And needing to complete my mission, I never asked myself. Fifi looked amused as she finished her explanation. "Well, that's his sister, Kenna. They have a young twelve-year-old sister, Aideen, too."

"How come I haven't met them yet?" I wondered aloud. I lived in the fortress for over a week and never crossed paths with them.

"They've been visiting their aunt, the High Lady of the Earth Court, for quite some time. I think their aunt reminds them of their mother, Ellaria. She died a few years ago." Fifi held a wealth of information. Information I knew I should leverage to my advantage.

"Aramis' mother was from the Earth Court?" I didn't know much about the other Fae courts, only that they no longer ruled independently.

"Yes, but none of them have any Earth magic. Aideen might. She's still young. But Aramis and Kenna are pure fire. Come, let me introduce you!"

Kenna's attention immediately focused on us as we approached. A couple of Fae stood and left the table, making room for us to sit.

"Cousin, you haven't met your future sister-in-law. Elowyn, this is Kenna." Fifi made the introductions and Kenna adjusted herself to stand, but I quickly gestured for her to remain still and sat next to her instead. The female paused and surveyed me before falling back into her relaxed posture.

"It's a pleasure to meet you, sister." She even spoke eloquently. So eloquently, I almost missed the humbled feelings soaring through me as she named me *sister.*

"You as well, Kenna." I surveyed the table and noticed Rune sitting amongst us. He leaned over, placing a glass in front of me.

"I hear you and my brother have been spending quite a bit of time together. So much so that the council is annoyed with you stealing his attention away from them."

"Oh? I... he made it sound like he finishes all of his work before joining me."

"Nevermind them. The council would occupy him twenty-four seven if they could. A bunch of greedy old bastards." The group laughed with Kenna, as if the council held no respect. The thought of Fae serving the council for life seemed so... flawed.

"She's definitely been preoccupying him. They spend *hours* in the archives together," Iris joined our table, adding her two cents to the bit of the conversation she overheard.

"Does everyone know where we spend our time?" I quietly asked, about to look at my fingers resting in my lap to shrink away, but held my chin high instead.

"Oh, she's the court gossip. She makes it her business to know everyone's whereabouts and secrets," Fifi assured me, but concern gnawed at me. Both Fifi and Iris noted our time spent researching. Could they have something to do with my missing clues?

Smiling, trying to ignore the concern, I noticed Kenna's eyes barely widened, a motion I doubt anyone caught but me. And her head tilted ever so slightly to the side, as if curious about our whereabouts too.

Rune pushed the wine glass closer to me, noticing I didn't drink. I sent him a kind smile, but pushed it back. The alcohol wouldn't simulate the high I sought. And I felt like drinking more would only lead to further disappointment.

"What are you doing in there, anyway?" Iris asked as the rest of the table remained silent, though I picked up on their cues of silent curiosity.

"My mortal tutors never taught about the Fae courts and I want to learn as much as possible since I'm to be high queen." I smiled lightly, sticking to my lie. But Kenna's eyes slightly shifted again, this time into an extremely minor squint as if doubting me.

"Are you sure you don't want more wine, Princess?" Rune asked, and I sent him a look of confusion for pushing the wine on me.

"No, I'm fine, thank you. I should really get back to bed. I couldn't sleep earlier, but now I'm tired," I excused myself and left the now-awkward setting.

Not only did I fail at replicating the high, but a gnawing suspicion crawled upon me, as if being stalked by a hungry lion.

CHAPTER 30

Groaning at the blinding light pouring in through the walls made of windows, I staggered behind Aramis, attempting to keep up with his eager pace to find the entrance to the hidden chamber in the throne room. All clues pointed to the long vaulted room lined by massive columns.

To say I wasn't eager would've been a lie. But fuck, I wished I didn't drink so much and snort whatever powder Fifi hid in her ring the night before. I should've been more prepared for this, because once we found the Book, I'd have to step into action and decide how in the Veil I'd take it from Aramis before running back to Rhyddean. Or kill him, and I wasn't sure if I *wanted* to.

The room sat empty aside from eight statues and a massive ornate chair with golden spires twisting from the back, climbing like a blazing inferno—a throne. Instantly, I pictured Aramis sitting upon it and the room filled with his Fae subjects, scattered about the black marbled floors.

His sharp Fae features and confident stance would look powerful sitting on his throne of fire. He'd look like a ruler no one would ever dare to oppose.

My soft slippers swept against the marble as I hurried to catch up to Aramis. He walked down the centre of the room in the middle of the statues, marching straight for the throne.

Four statues stood to Aramis' left, the other four to the right, standing maybe ten feet into the air, towering above us both. Each grey-ish white statue represented one of the gods, accompanied by symbols depicting each one.

I slowed down again, abandoning my attempts to catch up to Aramis as I surveyed the wheat weaved through Akka's hair, the Goddess of Earth and the Feminine, with a cornucopia laying at her feet and scythe in her hand. Her husband, King of Gods, stood tall and menacing next to her.

Awaldir. A raven perched on his burly shoulder, and mushrooms of all shapes and sizes grew around his sandaled feet. Roots of an oak tree bursting from the ground crawled up his legs to a skull resting in his open hands.

Backing away, I moved to the other side of the hall toward Auri, Goddess of the Sun and one of the goddesses of fate. Bees hovered amid the drapery of her dress and carved bunches of grapes poured from woven baskets at the base. Bottles of wine littered the space. Offerings, perhaps?

And roses caught in her hair.

Roses.

I bit my lip as thoughts in my head began to connect and looked at the god two statues over—Iros. Massive. Formidable. Stern. Everything one imagined the God of Violence and War to embody. Protecting his muscular body with a round shield and a sword boasting a lion's head pommel. With his sword lifted above his head, ready to strike, the sculptor carved him into an offensive position with a horse rearing next to him and flames surrounded their feet.

The god who gifted the Fire Fae. He shared a similar, sharp jawline to Aramis, and his hair waved down to his shoulders, too. Dripping blood was carved into the stone as if he stood on a battlefield, the way I imagined Aramis on the front lines.

I reached for an out-of-place rose. One of Auri's symbols, not Iros'. My fingertips grazed the surface of the cold stone and...

"Aramis," I called out to him, my voice echoing in the long hall.

"Did you find something?" He exuded an ambitious avidity as he approached me.

"A rose. Roses, they just seem to be a continuing theme. A rose drawn on the map, another one on the diary cover, and the riddle on the map—*A frozen rose that holds the key, protected by flames for eternity. Seek the light in the darkest hour, to unlock the door and gain the power.*"

"I said before, it's just an excerpt from a longer poem—"

"No. My gut is telling me it's all connected. This symbol keeps popping up. That can't be a coincidence. And even the riddle says, *a frozen rose that holds the key*. This rose *is* frozen, Aramis. It's frozen in time because it's made of stone. And *protected by flames*. Iros *is* fire. He's protecting the rose with his flames. Can I see the amulet?"

Aramis lifted the chain over his head and passed it to me. He started wearing it ever since we discovered it could be the key. I held the golden flames in my palm and lined it up with the rose.

A perfect fit.

We gazed at each other, both smiling impishly. This was it. We were going to discover the door to the hidden chamber and finally obtain the Book. I'd finally be able to save Cara!

I attempted to turn the amulet, but it wouldn't budge. I tried pushing the stone rose down. Nothing.

Aramis offered a gentle hand, and I stepped out of his way. He performed the same motions I did, but again, nothing happened.

"Ugh!" I buried my fingertips into the crown of my head and bent over, either out of frustration or from my hangover. Maybe both.

"How can this *not* be it?" I waved at the supposed key.

"Maybe we're missing something. Maybe there's a spell, an incantation, or something's warding it. We'll figure it out, Elowyn." Aramis remained surprisingly calm, despite his eagerness to acquire the Book and begin his dream of uniting the realms.

"We've been searching for weeks! And what if the others already found it?" My head spun with a million possibilities. What would I do if the spy already stole the Book? Would Aramis help me rescue Cara? Could I trust him? I stopped to evaluate him and his body language.

Without hesitation, he gripped my shoulders firmly, providing a comforting, slight squeeze, creating an instant reassurance, making me feel like everything would be okay. An accomplishment he made with one simple motion. Stepping out of his embrace, I marched from the throne room, determined to find more information, and push aside the conflicting emotions confusing the Veil out of me.

I glared at the city below me on the balcony. It hadn't done anything wrong, but I needed something to bear the brunt of my anger. My frustration emitted out toward the world. Even the nosey *keiju* stayed unseen, afraid of me. Weeks spent researching, piecing together every little thing, and actually *finding* the key to the hidden entrance, and it still didn't open. What did we miss?

I reanalysed every single clue we came across in my mind over and over, going as far as to grab more texts from the archives related to the architect we discovered and ward magic. Aramis finally forced me to put it all away and step outside for a breath of fresh air. He could tell my frustration rose, an emotion I felt but didn't display often, and I think it made him wary.

Joining me, Aramis tugged on a strand of my hair hanging next to my ear. And I hated the thrill it gave me. I pushed those thoughts aside.

"You're like the moon," Aramis finally spoke, securing the strand behind my ear. My brows crinkled, not understanding him. "Remember how I spoke of that darkness inside of me? Well, just like how the moon is the only light shining tonight, you're the only thing shining through my darkness. You bring me hope and inspiration, Elowyn."

Guilt shuttered through me. He'd started falling for me, or had he already fallen? If I killed him, I wouldn't be killing my enemy. It'd be someone who loved me.

"My light in the darkness," Aramis repeated, whispering into my ear.

My light in the darkness.

The only light shining tonight.

Light in the dark...

I snapped away from Aramis, spinning around to face him, and gripped his forearms.

"Oh, my gods!"

"What?"

"The key didn't work because we were there in daylight. *Seek the light in the darkest hour, to unlock the door and gain the power.* Let's go." I grabbed Aramis' arm, ensuring he wore the amulet, and led him straight for the throne room.

Racing down the marbled floors, we halted in front of the statue of Iros. Silver moonlight cast directly on the lone stone rose we'd attempted to open earlier.

Without exchanging words, Aramis pulled the amulet from his neck and placed it on top of the rose, the flames surrounding it, and turned it to the right. With a single *click*, the amulet locked into its new position.

The floor gently rumbled below my feet, pulsing through my legs and into my chest where it met my excited heart. A louder groan came from behind the statue and we cautiously walked over to see the floor lowering to create a stairwell descending to a black stone door.

I found it.

CHAPTER 31

My throat tightened as the walls closed in suffocatingly narrow, snuffing out any chance of light.

Darkness flourished here.

"Well, let's go find it." Aramis stepped into the chamber, igniting a fist of flame, and I drew from Iros' courage to follow. So many interconnected tunnels created an eerily muted maze, where even my slippered steps resonated, rebounding off the black stone.

"You didn't know this existed?" I asked, peering down a new hall. It seemed odd that something crafted so elaborately could be a grand secret.

"Not at all. My father was paranoid and distrusted everyone. Including me. If he knew this place existed, he would've kept it to himself. But I'm surprised none of the council members knew."

I bit my lip, wondering if I should share my suspicions about the council. About everyone in this court. Even the friends I made. Things felt... off. "Maybe some do, Aramis. Maybe they don't trust you either. It seems everyone in this court plays their own little game."

"Honestly, Elowyn... it's crossed my mind, too." He turned left, but I gripped his elbow.

Find me. Find me. Find me.

The same ominous voice I'd heard in the Vault at Rhyddean coaxed me now, and I knew it was no coincidence.

"This way." I guided us past two other tunnels, finally turning right and making an immediate left. We passed at least seven more tunnels before turning left again. My instinct led us through the maze to a massive stairwell swirling into a menacing abyss with no bottom in sight.

"Keep your hand against the wall," Aramis directed, and I heeded his advice, leaning against the cold stone and cautiously following the steps into the darkness, folding my fingers into the back of Aramis' shirt.

Too apprehensive to speak, I counted each step as we descended in silence instead of doing my usual breath exercise. The counting kept me from losing the thin thread of courage I held on to.

Aramis' flames flickered and their strength reduced as the temperature dropped. "Sweetheart, it's too cold. I need to conserve my strength." And as Aramis extinguished his magic, we fell back into pure obscurity.

Expecting step one hundred and five or one hundred and fifteen, we stumbled when we reached the bottom and found level ground. Aramis steadied me as I remained clutching the wall as my lifeline, the stone slick and frosted this deep into the earth.

I pursed my lips to muffle an anxious whine.

One, two, three. Inhaling.

One, two, three. Exhaling.

"Hey, are you okay?" Aramis asked when he noticed I no longer walked by his side.

"Yup," I squeaked, quelling the ember of anxiety. As I practised my breathing exercise, warmth enveloped my hand. Aramis interlocked our fingers, squeezing as if transferring his own fortitude into me, and I sighed in relief, realising I never stood alone as long as Aramis was with me.

Ignoring the thought, we continued through the dark until a gentle reddish-orange glow emerged, outlining an ample curved arch. It led to a monolithic cavern, walls and ceiling made of raw natural stone, not polished like the corridors above, and reddish-orange orbs illuminated the space.

"How did you not know this existed?"

"You're not the only one with a fucked up family, sweetheart." Aramis' voice reverberated across the chamber, his wide-eyed awe tinged with a glint of hunger.

My eyes roamed the vast, sparsely furnished chamber, fixating on nine towering doors. Grandiose doors of pristine white material, adorned with intricate golden hinges and handles, featuring distinctive carvings of unique symbols.

"Stay here. I'm going to try the doors. If I tell you to run or you sense any sort of distress, you go. Run as fast as you can and find Molvys, okay?" Concern coated Aramis' order. I wanted to take the time to decipher his tone, but the fear within me focused on the unknown dangers. When I didn't respond, Aramis repeated, "Promise me, Elowyn."

"I promise."

Satisfied, he stalked forward, inspecting the first door on the left as another noise distracted me. A low rumble to my right revealed another tunnel. Its allure defied explanation, seducing me like it promised answers to the mysteries plaguing me, whispering desires I hadn't dared dream.

I faced the dark tunnel with unwavering resolve, unafraid as the dark reintroduced itself, driven by determination to uncover the promised answers and desires.

After instinctual turns in pitch blackness, I entered a square corridor. Its rough, stone walls replaced the natural rock and three iron doors lined the left, with another at the hall's end. The air thickened with centuries of dust, dirt, and a potent, untamed, ancient power, each door tempting me with promises. Yet, the fifth door at the corridor's end concealed the greatest treasure.

As I approached the first door, a woman on the other side screeched. A familiar guttural wail falling into mewls. I pressed my back against the opposite wall, needing to distance myself from the lugubrious soul.

So mournful, a depth of sorrow born of devastating loss, but laced with vengeance and malice, craving retribution, and striving to inflict suffering on whoever hurt it.

Biting my lip, I leapt away from the door, and the wailing hastily ended, though the second door convulsed against its frame. The soul trapped on the other side wanted free. My pumping blood urged me to run and hide as a thundering groan vibrated the door. My arms flew over my head as I cowered against the opposing wall.

It seethed with fury at me. Iron hinges loosened as the door thrashed and thumped, savaged by the outraged force preparing to maul me to death.

It's okay, the third iron door assured me, saving me from my paralysis. Daring to look, I peeked through the space between my shielding forearms.

I'll protect you. Believing it, I crawled forward on my hands and knees, afraid the rabid entity would stalk me. But once out of its vicinity, the door ceased, and the bellowing went.

Thankful, I scrambled to my feet, ready to thank the third soul free of anger and vengeance, willing to protect me, but then it spoke...

Good girl.

I squeezed my eyelids shut, tears seeping through the slits. I bit my lip hard enough for metallic liquid to stream between my tastebuds.

"Go away. Go away," I chanted, and the entity remained quiet, playing games and bringing forth a haunting past. One I wished to leave behind, for good.

"Fuck you," I spat at the iron and moved to the last door. An inexplicable underground wind insisted I confront my ghosts, carrying the scent of wildflowers from my childhood meadow, trying to remind me of what I suppressed.

I did something terrible that day. More and more, I believed myself to be responsible for the scarlet blood splattered across Linnaea's face. Withholding a shattered cry, I dared to open the fourth door, gliding open as if recently maintained.

The room, small and circular, featured a domed stone masonry ceiling, though no taller than eight feet.

A tapestry hung across from me. Rich, ominous black fabric absorbed the light from the torches on either side of the door, threatening to suffocate the fire completely.

A thin, fragile gold border framed an intricate design of lavish, ambitious golden greenery and florals. A dull, ashen grey speckled throughout the tapestry as if a wind threatened to blow it away.

A remarkable weave. Elegant. Ethereal. But the bottom right corner remained unfinished. The ends remained unincorporated into the piece, or roughly tied off. Instead, they appeared carelessly cut and left dangling—unfinished.

I reached my fingertips toward the tapestry, and as I touched the creamy fabric, a jolt of promising passion and agony accelerated through me. Images accompanied the electrical sensation. But the premonition blurred too fast to make anything out, like the haze of smoke surrounded it all. I gasped.

"Elowyn! Are you okay?" Aramis rushed through the door behind me, breathing heavily.

"I'm fine, why?"

"I heard you screaming—"

"The captives, behind those doors, screamed at me like they wanted me to release them... or kill me."

"Those doors?" Aramis pointed behind himself, into the darkness beyond. "The iron doors?"

"Yeah—"

"That's impossible." His eyes widened, and he brushed a hand through his hair.

"Why is it impossible? How do you know what's behind them?"

"My father once told me of his three trophies. Powerful demons he captured and hid deep within the fortress. I always thought he meant within the dungeon, but I felt the blood magic sealing those doors. I'm certain it's them, and you shouldn't be that—"

A low growl rumbled in the distance cut him off as it grew louder and louder as the sound echoed in the large chamber and reverberated in the tunnel behind us.

Aramis cocked his head as the growl strengthened, sending vibrations through the floor beneath our feet. "Sounds like we're not alone."

"What is that?"

"I don't know, but we're leaving." He gripped my hand with a protective force I was still growing accustomed to, a grip holding no anger or control, and led me back into the corridor of howling demons. Pausing at the door frame, I hesitated, and without allowing me time to summon my courage, he pressed forward.

Returning to the main chamber, Aramis surveyed the area, searching for the potential threat, but it remained as empty as before. Aramis' shoulders relaxed as we moved to leave, but as we approached the archway, a giant mass stepped out from the shadows to block our path.

I gasped as I absorbed the sight of the monster standing in front of us.

Standing twice as high as Aramis, with a width three times his size, the monster stood erect, with muscles bulging all over its decaying body. Strips of flesh hung from the creature's arms and chest, white and yellow fluids oozing from the wounds.

A gag nestled in my throat as the putrefying stench wafted over, but my body fell into a state of shock, holding the gag in.

Despite its disintegrating form, the monster held firmly to a shield and sword, ready for battle, and its face—an almost human face, but unusually lengthened and thick like a snout. Two thick horns jutted out from either side of its head, curving upward like the horns of a bull. The lower side of its right jaw exposed its sharp teeth, and despite half of its face missing, it formed a distinct expression of wrath.

It wanted us dead.

Leaping into action, Aramis pushed me behind a boulder and unsheathed his sword, ready to brave the beast before him. The monster lifted its sword into the air and brought it crashing down to where Aramis stood, but he tucked and rolled out of the way.

Aramis smirked and raised his left hand, igniting the fire magic he'd conserved on our descent. My chest lightened, believing this fight wouldn't last long given the potency of Aramis' magic.

He threw a blast of flames at the beast, engulfing it from head to toe. Sitting a few feet away, I crawled to the other side of the boulder to avoid the scorching heat Aramis' magic produced, my exposed flesh brightening. I leaned against the cold rock, thankful for the impending demise of this beast. We just needed to grab the Book and leave this labyrinth behind.

But as my nerves settled, the rumbling growl returned, vibrating through the ground and into my bones, causing my heart to take a new beat. I peeked over the rock and the horned monster's chest and abdomen thrummed, pulsing up and down as if... *laughing.* Its sword and shield hanging by its sides, completely unthreatened, and Aramis gaped, backing away.

As the monster finished laughing, it dropped its shield, crashing to the ground and disrupting centuries of settled dirt as its hand erupted into flame.

Fuck.

Aramis leapt behind another boulder as the creature sent a ball of fire flying towards him. I shuddered as the ball collided with the boulder and the flames whooshed around. Fire couldn't burn Aramis, but if this monster possessed fire magic, then Aramis' magic suddenly became just as useless. Within seconds, the clashing of swords rang through the chamber, accompanied by grunts.

And what the fuck could I do? Aramis would win. The realm described him as the most powerful Fae in centuries—comparable to Iros himself.

Peeking over the boulder, Aramis sent another blast into the monster, sending it across the room. As it crashed into the ground, Aramis' quick strides and powerful legs pushed him into the air, ready to bring his sword down onto the monster, but it deflected Aramis' strike with its own sword.

Aramis jumped backwards, readying himself to conjure another ball of fire. But as the flames ignited, they flickered out. I ducked back behind the boulder, anxiety pounding through me as a thought crossed my mind—he's going to die.

And I should use that to my advantage. Find the Book and grab it while the bull-like beast occupied Aramis. Entomb him here, as I hastily flee back to Rhyddean. It was the perfect opportunity.

But I couldn't. Aramis had begun breaking down the walls I had erected a long time ago, and instead of being repulsed by what I revealed, he embraced it. All of it. All of *me*. My twisted visions of violence. Transforming my weaknesses into strengths. Believing in me when I didn't have the strength to believe in myself. He... brought me back to life, and I didn't even realise it. I couldn't leave him here to die. I didn't *want* to. But I was too useless to help.

No, you're not. My dagger warmed against my thigh and a cold sweat broke out across my skin as I remembered all the times Oulixeus held me down, and I just took it, like a *good girl*. Or in the stableyard, I asked Cara to defend the woman for me, because I was useless, and she'd paid the price for being my friend.

No, you're not weak.

A gruesome cry carried through the chamber, and without having to look, I recognized it as Aramis'. Before I could allow myself to argue with the dagger, I forced myself into a sprint and ran toward the duel.

The monster stood over Aramis, laughing at the slice he cut through Aramis' chest. With my gathered momentum, I leapt onto another rock, bringing me high enough to stab the creature on its left side, the area Molvys had taught me to strike my opponents. It may not have the same organs as Fae and mortals, and in its rotting state, it may not affect it, but I needed to try.

Unsheathing my dagger, I struck.

The beast howled and swung its arm at me, sharp claws digging into my flesh and throwing me across the chamber. I landed with a hard thud and screamed. Black venom coated my arm, burning my skin. It marched toward me, ready to finish me off.

But before it reached me, a sword slammed through its abdomen—Aramis. The beast howled and fell to its knees. While incapacitated, Aramis grabbed my hand and pulled me from the chamber, and we raced up the stairs.

"Can you make it?" Aramis asked as the beast roared loudly and the entire stairwell shook.

"I think so."

Leaping up the giant staircase, we reached the black stone labyrinth. But it was... different. The corridors switched locations, as if moving on their own.

"Did we make a wrong turn?" Aramis pulled me, attempting to navigate the route again. And in front of us a wall materialised out of thin air.

"It's changing." Dread filled me from head to toe upon realising what this meant. Memorising our route served no purpose, it would inevitably shift. Whatever ventured down here was meant to remain trapped. The ground trembled as the beast drew near.

We fled aimlessly, desperate to distance ourselves from the roaring beast. But exhaustion crept in, my legs weakening as the venom coursed through my bloodstream.

This way. My dagger spoke again. I gripped Aramis' arm and dragged him along.

"No, the beast is there."

"Trust me, please." He nodded and followed me as I twisted and turned, listening to the dagger.

As we made our last right turn, the black studded door appeared in front of us, and the beast caught up to us.

We broke into a full on sprint, but what if the door couldn't keep the beast out and we unleashed it upon the entire fortress? Families lived here...

Trust me. The dagger insisted, so I did, and we sprinted.

The creature's breath huffed against my back, and I let out a scream as we neared the door.

Bursting through, Aramis slammed it shut, and the creature bellowed behind it, but didn't follow.

I fell to the floor, huffing and puffing. Relief washed over me, but it was fleeting as Aramis growled and a low, but feminine voice rolled over us.

"Hello, lover."

CHAPTER 32

I recognised that voice... Andraste.

"You've kept your little pet, I see." Disgust dripped from her words as I took in the gorgeous red-haired female in form fitting leather armour, her mocking pout fueling my frustration. I'd spent years being *helpless.* Years of never knowing how to defend myself, but things had changed. I just took on a fucking fire magic monster and helped Aramis. I wasn't the same girl who left Rhyddean. She perished, giving rise to someone more courageous.

I scowled at Andraste as I rose and lunged at her with my dagger aimed for her torso. She gracefully stepped out of the way and my exhausted body slumped forward.

"Oh, feisty. Aramis may make something of you yet." She laughed, turning away from me as if I posed no threat.

"What are you doing here, Andraste? *How* did you get here?" Aramis raised his sword, preparing himself to attack his former lover with no hesitation in his eyes.

"You never were as clever as you thought." Her hips swayed back and forth effortlessly as she approached Aramis.

"Fine, don't tell me. I'll kill you, regardless."

"See what I mean, Aramis? A clever ruler would want to capture me and torture the truth from me."

As Andraste continued to taunt Aramis with belittling words, it fell into place in my mind. The missing clues. My suspicions about the Fae who had been getting close to me. Andraste's unrequited love.

"She's here for the Book," I said, raising to my feet again.

Andraste quickly whipped around, her hair bouncing with the movement. "She's clever, at least."

"Andraste has someone working for her. Someone who stole the map and the diary. Someone who's been getting close to me..." I watched her face and body language for any sign of a tell. But I didn't need to learn it because she confirmed everything with her words.

"This will be a much more entertaining game with a player like you!" A slight bounce came to her movement, like a giddy little child excited to receive a treat.

"This isn't a fucking game, Andraste! What do you want with the Book?" Aramis tightened his grip around his sword, clearly struggling to withhold his wrath.

"I don't really care about the Book. But the rebels do."

"The rebels—but you supported our goal of uniting Niafell."

"Yes, but the rebels made an offer I couldn't refuse." We stood silently, waiting for her to finish her sentence, but she waited, like she wanted Aramis to guess. When he didn't, she continued, "They promised me revenge."

She dragged the pad of her finger along the blade of her small sword, laughing as though it held an inside joke.

At that, Aramis lost his temper and raged toward Andraste, sword aimed for her heart. It didn't phase her. She continued to laugh and the moment Aramis pulled his arm back to strike it through her; she vanished in a cloud of black smoke.

CHAPTER 33

The Book hid right below the fortress. Nestled surreptitiously beneath layers of resplendent marble, amidst oblivious nobility, and below a cornucopia of showcased riches, heavily guarded. As I gazed out at the city's luminous lamps, their flickering mimicking the graceful dance of fireflies, I contemplated seizing the opportunity. With Aramis occupied with his impromptu council meeting, strategising ways to fortify the fortress against rare and ancient magic, I could do it. He even entrusted me with the amulet. He did so because he... trusted me.

Aramis *trusted* me. A trust I'd meant to manipulate him into—the only way for me to successfully kill him. But somewhere along the way, I'd started to trust him too, blurring the lines between us.

My left arm pulsed with the veracity flowing through my veins. A truth I unabatedly ignored and denied. My muscles twitched as if reprimanding me for my indecisiveness. But if I admitted my enigmatic secret, everything would change and make my task impossible.

Lost in thought, a comforting smokiness swirled around me, mixing with the essence of leather and sandalwood. The scents seeped into my confliction, soothing me and pulling me away from those troubles.

"Elowyn?" Aramis' voice rumbled, carrying a deep timbre that wrapped around my senses like a silky cloak. He stood between two columns, head cocked, and an assuasive smile shining. "Are you okay?"

A question as unfathomable as the Veil itself. My heart desired two paths, each incredibly different from the other. And no matter which route I chose, I betrayed someone—a weighty shadow tainted my every choice.

Refusing to sit with discomfort, I bluntly asked Aramis, "Why me?"

Two tiny *keiju* flitted from a cypress and pranced around Aramis' head. He swatted the fairies away as his expression distorted into a frown. "What do you mean?"

"I wasn't the only eligible mortal princess, Aramis. My father has three daughters old enough to marry. The King in Penre has a daughter the same age as Orla. So why me?" I couldn't move on until I learned his motives. The fairies perched on the railing next to me, whispering secrets in each other's ears.

My left arm fired again. A delicate, fiery arrow of warmth surging through my veins as if they whispered secrets of sensation. I grew accustomed to it, but the escalating intensity made me tenderly massage it.

"Because of that right there." Aramis' dimples appeared as he threaded a hand through golden locks. The fairies' squeaky tittering amplified, as if mocking me. "You never complained about it, never asked about it, either."

"Your magic?" By the time I trusted him enough to ask, I didn't notice it anymore. The fairies burst into frantic giggles. Exasperated, I rolled my eyes and waved the *keiju* away. "Get!"

As the tiny beings fluttered away on delicate wings, Aramis closed the gap between us, weaving his fingers through mine. When our left palms met, a syncopated rhythm emerged, as if our heartbeats synchronised into a single, unified pulse.

"It's not my magic, sweetheart." The gold flecks immersed in his emerald irises blazed with an eager anticipation.

"If it's not your magic, then what is it?"

"You feel that?" The rhythm heightened, and Aramis pressed against me, eliminating the remaining space. "We're Fated."

His words baffled me. *Fated?* Yet, a part of me whispered that explanations were unnecessary, for being with Aramis bestowed a profound sense of belonging and security. I felt like *his* and he felt like *mine*.

"It's extremely rare. The goddesses of fate, Auri and Mielikki, sometimes weave two tapestries together, leaving each individual unwhole and incomplete until they meet. They're equals."

Equals. The word gently embraced my very existence, offering me solace.

"I chose you that night as my betrothed, because the moment I saw you in the woods, I felt the tug. I understood its meaning. You were mine, and I was yours. Then. Now. And always." Aramis displayed no signs of lying. And he didn't just speak truthfully, he spoke from the heart, expressing a yearning I'd questioned for a while now.

"You didn't say—"

"I didn't want to frighten you. In the woods, it didn't matter to me if you were a princess or a peasant. I didn't let you escape because to lose you would be torture. Being expected to solidify the alliance through marriage and you being one of the three eligible daughters was fate, bringing us together at long last. There was no choice to make, Elowyn. It was always you. It *will* always be you." Aramis cupped my cheek in his palm, the magical heat coursing through his body burned raw and fervent.

"I love you, Elowyn. I loved you the moment I felt your presence in the woods. Your gentleness." He brushed his lips along my jaw.

"Your strength." His breath caressed my ear.

"Your chaos." And his lips dipped lower, leaving a wet trail along my collarbone.

"All of you. From the moment your voice rang through my ears in that clearing, until the moment I die, my body burned, I will love you. I will continue loving you as I fade into the Veil, wandering until I find your soul."

I broke.

Dismissing the choices and questions plaguing me. Discarding every previous vow and responsibility. The walls I built crumbled. Crumbled for Aramis.

All hesitation vanished as I pressed my lips against his, the rhythmic pulse of the bond returning. Uniting us.

Desperate to be closer, Aramis' hands twined into the ash-blonde curls trailing down the nape of my neck. Answering him, I parted my lips and allowed his tongue to dive into my mouth, starved for me. He tasted of fire. The scorching, fiery kiss of flames left my tongue ember-kissed and tingling with the essence of pure sensual heat.

He elicited a heat that curled through my body, rippling through my veins, vibrating my muscles, and thrumming at the apex between my thighs. With his Fae strength and elegance, he lifted me with ease, cradling me as he led our aching bodies to the bed in my chamber.

Falling into the soft cotton sheets, Aramis moaned into my ear, sending blissful shivers down the length of my neck. His lips trailed the shivers to my chest and stopped to nip the silky fabric shielding my erect nipples, desiring more.

"This needs to go." Aramis ripped the chemise in a single pull, individual threads shearing apart from the intrusion. As the fabric fluttered away, he eagerly took a breast into his mouth, flicking his tongue over my nipple and evoking whimpers from me.

Switching breasts, he began the sensual act all over again. I ran my hands through his lustrous hair, searching for a way to stay grounded as he built my lust. Teeth grazed my taut nipple before Aramis moved on to my stomach, wrapping his large hands around my waist, attempting to keep me from wiggling.

Aramis explored all parts of my torso with his kisses, noting my reaction to each location—which coaxed a lustful plea and which forced a giggle. Each touch drove me mad with anticipation, until he finally dipped a finger under the material of my silk shorts, grazing alongside my centre, feeling the dampness.

"Is this how wet you were for me that first morning?" He groaned and my body shuddered.

"Yes," I admitted with a breathy moan, and Aramis grinned mischievously.

"Sweetheart, you're dripping. The silk is soaked through," he teased more, and I liked it, the way my nerves pulsed at his words.

"I soaked through your shirt too," I confessed, recalling our first morning in Stoneshalt.

"I know. I held it, inhaling your scent while rubbing myself raw that afternoon." He pressed his nose against my swollen clit, inhaling deeply. "Fresh morning dew and sweet summer strawberries. I wonder if you *taste* like plump juicy berries too." Desperate for more, I went to pull off my shorts, but Aramis halted me. "Don't open my gift. I've been excruciatingly impatient to unwrap you and I want to savour this moment."

His fingers slid along the damp centre of the silk, stoking flames within me. As he reached my clit, my hips bucked, and he did it a second time, enjoying my reaction.

I whimpered helplessly again, and Aramis finally gave in, pulling the delicate fabric off of me and discarding the nightwear onto the marbled floor. As I opened my legs for him to see me bare for the first time, he moaned. A rich primal moan that claimed me forever as his.

"You're exquisite," Aramis whispered before plunging his face between my thighs. He faltered for a split second after nipping my flesh and I leaned onto my elbows to question the hesitation when his tongue delved into me, and I melted into the pile of silk and velvet behind me, dismissing the concern.

Aramis feasted on me. Lapping every last drop of my wet desire, his tongue devouring me, studying my sounds and reactions. As he made my body twist with intoxicating yearning, playing me like a skilled musician did their harp, I slipped into an unknown existence. An exhilarating descent into a whirlwind of emotions, where control was a distant memory, and the heart danced to the whims of magic—edging me closer and closer to the release I craved since I first saw him.

Flicking his tongue faster and steadily, a predator feasting on his prey, I realised it wasn't just him who felt the bond in the woods that day. I did too, fighting it with every ounce of strength within me. But no more.

Gripping the sheets tightly, at a last thrust of his fingers, I unravelled, frozen in a moment of ecstasy. Aramis licked his lips and slipped his fingers into his mouth. Pulling out the digits, he grinned. "Plump. Juicy. Strawberries."

He prowled over my body and kissed me with savage power, our tongues meeting with an explosion of a sweet, fresh flavour.

"Strawberries," I whispered as he pulled away, peering deep into my eyes as if he discovered a secret amongst my ashen depths, an ancient grove where love would take root and flourish into a connection as timeless as the earth itself.

With the link joining us, we both recognised what we wanted—to be one. And without waiting another second, Aramis pushed my thighs wide and guided himself inside of me. The pressure he caused evoked me to moan for more. Obliging me, he pressed further. Slow, deep, and hard.

My core spread for each inch of his solid length and girth, filling me with a sense of completeness I'd unknowingly craved my entire life.

"Breathe, sweetheart," he panted. Not realising, I held my breath as I savoured the experience of him entering me—completing me—for the first time. I let the breath go and it produced a low, lascivious purr cascading from my lips.

Ravenous for more, and unable to hold back, Aramis braced an arm against the headboard, and held my hip down with the other before thrusting into me with a satisfying power. Each plunge unwound me, and euphoria washed away the final pieces of my guard.

Approving my animalistic sounds, Aramis took my hands into his, winding our fingers together above my head. The tether tightened and pulled us closer, my body arching into his.

Unable to last any longer, my centre dripping for him, I clenched his waist with my thighs and allowed the burst of my orgasm to ripple pleasure through me. Aramis came undone with me, groaning as his come filled me so fully, the excess pushed past his cock and slid down my thighs, saturating the linens.

Neither of us dared to move. Wrapped in a tight embrace, still inside of me, we inhaled each other's essence. Memorising his alluring, dusky scent, and how he felt inside of me, my thighs tightened. I would never let go.

I loved him.

He loved me.

We were fated.

CHAPTER 34

The burning sensation in my left arm had extinguished, but not without evidence. The morning after we first made love, I awoke with markings on my arm. Swirls shaping into flames twisted from my hand, along my wrist, and most of my forearm. They morphed into whirls resembling smoke near my elbow and climbed to my bicep. Aramis lay beside me as I studied the shapes breaking off into flecks of what looked like ash.

Identical markings tattooed his left arm. In the past, it may have shocked me, but it felt *right*. Whole. It fit. He smiled and took my hand, tickling me as he traced the marks.

"I think the tattoo formed since we've both accepted the bond," he explained. "All will know we belong to each other, but we should keep this hidden for some time. Until things settle down."

"Why?" The entire realm was already aware of our betrothal. What difference did the fated bond make? I scooted into him as he wrapped his arms around me, keeping me safe.

"I'm afraid of enemies using this against us, taking you from me." A cold edged Aramis' words as if making a promise to all of his current and future enemies, like they heard him despite us being alone.

Almost a week passed, and we refused to leave our chambers. A poor older Fae servant walked in to find us propped on throw pillows in the middle of Aramis' room, both on our knees as Aramis pumped into me from behind, tugging on my nipples and sucking my neck as I gripped his golden hair.

The platter of pastries clanged against the marble floor right as Aramis pressed into me, becoming one, and climaxing simultaneously. Other servants tumbled into her and quickly retreated as Aramis' command boomed, ordering no more disturbances until told. Servants had left food and wine in the antechamber since then.

Aramis even dismissed the council until further notice. We became completely enthralled with one another, and nothing in all the realms had the strength to pull us away from exploring our connection.

On the third day of our incessant lovemaking, Fifi banged on the door while I sat on Aramis' leather sofa, legs spread apart as he feasted.

"Everyone is irritated with you two. Especially you, Aramis!" The door muffled Fifi's shouts. Ignoring her, Aramis delved his tongue further into me and lightly massaged my bundle of nerves with skilled fingers. My hands clutched the back of the couch as I rolled my head back in pure ecstasy. He summoned an exquisite delirium that birthed vivid, ethereal hues, whisking me away to a realm saturated with euphoria.

The door opened, and I met Fifi's sparkling chestnut eyes. I chortled as Aramis forced my eager hips to remain still, and I mouthed *I'm sorry* to my new friend.

"There's a lot to deal with, Aramis. You two can have your fuck-fest after you're married," Fifi scolded with crossed arms.

Aramis pulled himself away from my centre, but not without a caress on my sensitive clit first. He sauntered to Fifi, stark naked, wiping my glistening sex from his mouth, and scowled. "Cousin, I love you, but I swear to Iros, I will rip your head from your shoulders if you enter this chamber again before I'm finished."

"But—" Fifi stopped her counter as Aramis gripped her throat, his hand still slick with my wetness.

"Ugh, pig!" She marched out the door, slamming it behind her.

Aramis placed me in positions I'd never experienced before, each more pleasurable than the last. We fucked on every surface between our adjoining rooms—beds, sofas, dressers, chairs, and the floor. We worshipped each other.

The worshipping spilled onto the balcony by the fifth day, taking me over the stone rail. Leaning over me, he tugged my ash-blonde curls and whispered with a thirst, "This is all ours."

"Stoneshalt. The Fire Court. All of Niafell. And soon, the whole. Fucking. World." He plunged into me with each word, building my excitement and desire to hold his dreams with mine.

"My high queen," he said in a promise-laden hush, gliding his thumb along my chin, filling me with his climax. As he finished, I glimpsed firefly-like specks dancing in the air—the *keiju*. The playful fairies, with wings like gossamer threads, flitted about like mischievous sparks in the growing night. Their gossiping laughter, like tinkling bells, reached my ears and my cheeks flushed a shade of pink, not realising they'd watched our salacious exchange.

Our fanatic fucking eventually digressed into snuggles and the exchange of secrets. I shared things I'd refused to admit aloud to anyone before. Visions of harming my mother, feeling... *something*... for Oulixeus, attempts to fade into the Veil, and the looming threat stalking me. Aramis validated and accepted everything, and I felt my self-acceptance sprouting at last.

On the sixth day, we decided to emerge from the lustful trance that had been consuming us for nearly a week. I rested on the bed enjoying a breakfast of fruit, cured meats and, my favourite, sourdough bread that exuded a warm, earthy aroma. Its tangy, chewy crust held a plethora of rustic flavours, evoking nostalgic memories of days spent at Cara's and Grandmama cooking for us. Reaching for a cherry to refresh my mouth, Aramis growled as the scarlet fruit touched my lips.

He pulled off the silk shirt he had just slipped into and threw it to the floor. And in a few long strides, Aramis reached my side, propping my hips on a pillow. He glided his hands along my spine, stopping on my lower back where his thumbs rubbed the indents laying there.

"I spotted these delectable dimples on our very first night together. As you crawled into bed, your chemise lifted just enough for me to catch a glimpse," he growled, taking hold of his erection and caressing the tip along the marks. My centre pulsated with anticipation, silently begging for him to enter. My fingers curled around the silky sheets and pressed my forehead into the mattress, my body begging for more.

"So eager." He teased me by gradually gliding the tip of his cock along my centre. "Will your pussy ever get enough of my cock spilling inside of you?"

"No," I admitted, pushing my hips back into him.

"Patience, sweetheart." Aramis caught me and finally sank in, slowly but so forcefully that my entire body shuddered. Muscles clenching and a cascade of irresistible bursts firing inside of me, pulling a heavy, savage groan from me.

Inching into me, I naturally spread for his girth, and once fully inside, Aramis gave one forceful thrust, turning my low groan into a high-pitched shriek of bliss. Recognising neither of us would last long, he fell into a rough rhythm, satisfying both of our impatience for release. My inner walls tightened around him as he coaxed my orgasm.

Aramis' thrusts quickened as the velvety pillow stroked my belly and thighs, increasing the delectability. Our tattooed hands entwined, bringing each other closer, blurring my vision. As I moaned, the swirling flames and smoke spiralled, the physical manifestation of our bond. A bond and tether that seemed to grow stronger the longer our bodies remained joined.

With ecstasy about to sweep me away, I pushed my hips back into his and Aramis roared, his convulsing cock pumping come into me. Finished, we collapsed into each other, bodies entangled and Aramis played with my hair as we caught our breath. "I'm never, and I mean *never,* going to get enough of you."

Despite the elation created from the past week, a thought dawned on me, my melancholy never fully retreating. "How old are you?"

"Five hundred and thirty-four," he announced, staring at the ceiling. My breath hitched, and I quickly swallowed to hide my shock. "You're twenty-one, right?"

"Yeah," I muttered, the gloom usurping my joy.

Laying a light kiss on my head, Aramis asked, "What's wrong?"

"I'm not immortal," I whispered, tracing the lines of his defined chest.

"Neither am I," he stated. "I'm Fae, but we eventually die."

My finger stopped, not being comforted by his words. "I'll die a lot sooner than you."

"No. You won't." He squeezed me tight before wiggling out from under me, disappearing into his chamber. What could he do to prevent the inevitable?

Aramis returned with pants and plucked his discarded shirt from the floor. "Fuck me," he groaned, viewing my body stretched upon the pale mauve sheets. I stretched my arms above me, one leg bent with the other stretched out, and forced the depressed thoughts away.

"Okay." I laughed and purposefully added a slight arch to my back.

"Tonight. Tonight, I want you in this position—this *exact* position. And I'm going to kiss you, starting with your toes and slide my tongue along your calves to your thighs, and then—" he paused and growled again as I reached to touch my already wet centre.

"Mhm?"

"Fuck." He bit his lip as I opened my legs, allowing him a better view. Bucking my hips with a jolt of ecstasy, my fingers slipped inside of me.

"And then what, Aramis?" I gasped, moving to my clit.

"And then I'm going to come so hard I won't be able to walk for weeks." He joined me on the bed and inserted two fingers inside of me, gently massaging that tender spot deep within. He ravenously studied my expression as I came, his fingers pressing firmly on the pleasurable spot, unmoving as my muscles vibrated.

When I finished, he stood and buttoned his shirt. "Seriously though, I need to do some work."

"Fine," I whined and reached for my clothing. I actually missed Fifi and wanted to spend some time with her and the others. As I stepped into a pair of lace panties, Aramis coughed, catching my attention. He stared at the *O* branded into my flesh.

"Did *he* do that to you?" Aramis nodded his chin at my leg.

I'd felt grateful for Aramis ignoring the mark all week, but I still didn't wish to speak of it, so I mumbled my dismissal as I dressed quickly. "Yup."

"Our healers will remove it." Aramis leaned against the edge of the vanity, arms crossed as if attempting to read my mind, but misunderstanding me.

"No. It serves as a reminder." My voice grew bitter as I padded to the phoenix-carved armoire and retrieved a blue-sleeved dress, modest compared to the dresses Fifi chose.

"A reminder of what?" Aramis' tone matched mine, even more protective of me after the week we shared.

"Men use women. We're their pawns in their political games." The armoire rocked from slamming the door. "You noticed it before. Why didn't you say anything?"

"Because I didn't want *him* ruining our moment," Aramis clarified, eyes darkening.

"Go work. I'm going to find my... friends." The foreign word fumbled on my tongue. Cara and Foster were my friends, but I regarded them more as family.

"Elowyn." I ignored him, searching for complimentary slippers on a shelf. "Elowyn, look at me." His tone grew stern. I spotted a pair of copper velvet slippers to complement the dress.

"What?" I snapped and turned to him, not meaning to sound so angry. He pushed off the vanity and strode to rescue my dimming mood, holding my soured face between his palms.

"I love you. You are my *equal*. You will soon be my high queen. We're *Fated*. The next time I see Prince Oulixeus, I will slice my blade straight through the centre of his skull, as I should have the night of our betrothal," he vowed, but again, the words he meant to be comforting only pinched my gut, because he didn't understand.

"No," I whispered. His brow arched. "Only a stab to the heart can kill a dragon."

CHAPTER 35

Falling into old routines, I headed for the kitchen as Aramis caught up on politics—agreeing that we'd start researching ways to kill the bull monster soon. Servants with empty trays led me to the kitchen, where I planned to subtly ask for a contraceptive tea. I didn't purchase any from the suspected witch vendor because I certainly didn't expect to be having sex with anyone here.

Bleached cabinets and wood-block countertops lined three walls and floor-to-ceiling windows covered the fourth. Steam from pots and pans swirled through the light pouring into the kitchen. The savoury aroma of roasted game birds floated through the room, rich and tantalising, as they sizzled on the open flame. Drying herbs, onions, and garlic lined the walls beneath the cabinets.

Servants bustled about, weaving between each other with knives and hot dishes in a risky waltz. Some joined the dance from a back door, incorporating crates of wine and fresh produce. The head chef stood out, marching around in a crisp white apron, choreographing the dance.

Smiling, I raised my chin to greet her, "Hi."

"What do you want?" She barked as she stopped to chop fresh sage with a large cleaver.

"Umm, yes, I need tea." Taken aback by her tone, my words faltered as the other kitchen staff stopped to watch our exchange.

"Tea? You're interrupting my staff for tea? Have your servant bring you tea," she scolded. "Get back to work!" Instantly, the eavesdroppers returned to their duties.

"Of course, but we asked them to avoid our chambers for a while." I bit my lip, nervous of being chided again. "And it's a... special kind of tea." Rhyddean outlawed contraceptive teas and tonics, considering them too close to magic. Unaware of Fae laws, I chose discretion.

The head chef stopped and narrowed her brows, taking me in, head to foot and back, resting a fist on her hip. Analysing me. She stood short, but her presence towered over me.

"Oh, thank the gods! You're free!" Fifi ran into the kitchen, embracing me. "Rune, Iris, and I have missed you. Well, maybe not Rune. He wasn't impressed with losing."

The chef pointed her knife at my stomach. "Your cousin's bride wishes to rid herself of a baby."

"Why, in Iros' name, would you wish to do such a thing?" Fifi gaped at the chef's proclamation, taking me by surprise.

As I mustered the courage to defend myself, the chef interrupted with a grumble, "Take your dramatics elsewhere."

Fifi led me to the nearest courtyard, taking hold of my shoulders and forcing me to sit on a cool stone bench. "Okay, but Princess, you have the honour of bearing the first heir to a *united* nation. Isn't that incredible?"

"One day, yes. Maybe. Fifi, I want my tea," I said firmly, my crinkled expression revealing my reluctance to engage in the conversation. The Fae appeared to openly embrace sexuality unlike the mortal court, and they probably used contraceptives, whether legal or not, as there were few children present.

"It's not your decision to make anymore." Fifi's words carried a casual tone as she plucked a lilac from the blooming shrub behind us. A heady cloud of floral sweetness burst forth, a stark contrast to the anger welling up within me.

"It's *my* body!" I countered, and unable to contain my frustration any longer, I snapped at her. "Fifi, what the fuck! I can't believe we're even discussing this."

"You know how difficult it is to have children. If you don't want a child, you should have waited until Light Bearer's cycle finished before laying with Aramis." Fifi finished her argument with a curt nod, a firm hold on her beliefs, but my head cocked to the side as I absorbed her strange explanation.

"Wait, what?" I paused, counting my inhales and exhales to calm the frustration. "Fifi, we've misinterpreted each other."

"How?" She frowned as I placed my hand on top of her freckled arm. The amber hue of her sheer panelled dress flattered her glowing olive skin.

"I'm thinking Fae females and human women have different cycles," I speculated. Fifi's features widened before she fell into a loud yet elegant laugh. "What is the Light Bearer's cycle?"

Fifi held her manicured nails to cover her mouth as she finished laughing and explained the Light Bearer. A comet that orbited the skies for four months at unpredictable intervals. Females ovulated during its orbit and menstruated for four weeks once the comet left, and even then, fertility rates remained low.

"Healers and priestesses believe it's nature's way to balance a race with such a long lifespan," she added.

"Well, mortal women ovulate every month," I informed, recalling all Grandmama taught me about a woman's body. Fifi gawked at the new information. "Most do. My period comes once a year, so I might not ovulate as frequently."

Shaking her head, and laughing again, Fifi pulled me from the bench. "Okay, let's brew your tea. I'm so sorry, Princess."

As we returned to the kitchen, I forced Fifi to pause and squared our shoulders. "Elle. I don't care what Aramis insisted. *I* insist you and Rune and Iris call me Elle or Elowyn."

My new friend beamed as she ordered a servant to brew the tea. The head chef scolded us for returning, so we hurried out the moment the brew reached my hands and the chef shook her giant knife in our direction. Full of glee, we compared the differences of female Fae and mortal women all the way to the gaming parlour.

Sipping the bitter tea, Fifi divulged court gossip as we covertly observed others visiting the parlour—the conniving social climbers to avoid, who was engaged and married to who, the countless Fae embroiled in scandal, and the secretive liaisons among them, including her own past lovers. Keeping up was a formidable task.

Iris waltzed in, wearing a plum purple dress matching her lilac hair, framing her delicate face with draping curls. Her cheeks had a faint, rosy stain, and upon spotting us on the sofa, she joined our company.

"Thank the gods, *normal* people. I am so sick of this court—" Iris paused, her eyes locking onto the teacup in my lap. Her nose twitched, as if catching hints of the ingredients in my cup, and she gasped. "I know what *that* means. Tell me, what's he like? I've heard so many rumours!"

"Iris!" Fifi smacked our friend's shoulder.

"Ow!" Iris swatted away Fifi's hand. "Well, how can I *not* be curious? He's very handsome. And ruthless." Fifi continued to frown at the purple-haired Fae. "Oh, leave the judgement to the prudish, ancient grannies. I know you love a domineering lover."

A myriad of thoughts emerged as I stared at the shiny white floor. Fifi rested a comforting hand on me. "She's just a gossipy twit, Elle."

Fifi presumed me angry or jealous, but as I met their gazes, I burst into laughter, originating deep in my belly, contracting my abdomen until the muscles grew sore. The two watched me quizzically.

"I'm sorry. This is just... just..." Bizarre! Ridiculous! I felt like I'd stumbled into Orla's world. "Fascinating."

"The mortal court must be quite dreary," Iris mumbled, tucking a perfectly curled hair strand behind a pierced ear.

Suddenly, my shoulders twitched as the parlour door banged open and Fifi and Iris swivelled their heads in my direction. "Are you alright?" they asked in unison.

Faking a smile, I nodded. "Yeah." My attention shifted to the Fae servant approaching us, a young female carrying a silver platter. She gracefully bent at the waist, aligning the platter with my line of sight.

"Your Highness," she mumbled, avoiding eye contact.

A parchment letter, roughly folded as if in a rush, lay upon the glinting plate. I swallowed and reached for the letter, a bad feeling curling in my gut.

"Thank you," I dismissed the servant, staring at the note in my trembling hand.

"Oh! Can you bring us some sweets? Whatever the kitchen has!" Iris shouted after the young female, leaving to attend to other tasks.

As Fifi and Iris bickered about the courts and weather, the parchment before me seemed to mock my apprehension. Could it be a message from Oulixeus, already aware of Aramis and me finding solace in each other's company? Or perhaps from my father, growing impatient? Though, the wax seal bore neither of their distinctive marks. My father boasted a regal, dark green hue adorned with the royal bear crest, while Oulixeus favoured a glistening golden wax bearing a shield emblem. Unless they sought to remain inconspicuous...

One, two, three. Inhaling.

One, two, three. Exhaling, I swallowed the anxiety forming in my throat and broke the seal, a delicate crackling like autumn leaves beneath my fingers heralding the secrets concealed within the parchment.

No, neither my father nor Oulixeus had sent this. The hastily scrawled writing held an undeniable sense of urgency. Three lines of tangled script dominated the centre of the page:

I'm safe for now. I haven't figured it out yet, but something isn't right. Be careful who you trust, Elowyn. - C

I studied the page, unable to look away. *C?* I brought the page closer, as if it could reveal its secrets through proximity as I scrutinised each letter's slant, the curve of every *g*, and the spacing between words. Finally, I recognised the messy penmanship as Cara's.

Cara's safe? Cara *wrote* me a letter! She had to be safe enough to have the time to write something. A dozen questions flooded my mind. How did she escape? Did Foster help her? And what of Grandmama and Grandpapi—were they unharmed?

I wanted to leap from the sofa and ask Aramis to permit me to find Cara and confirm her well-being, ensuring the authenticity of this letter and ruling out any possible trap.

But the warning, *be careful who you trust*—if someone had forged her handwriting, why would they warn me of this? I flipped the paper over, searching for more clues or a location. Even just a *hint!* But I found nothing more.

"Elowyn?" Fifi frowned.

I abruptly folded the letter to hide its contents, having forgotten others surrounded me. "What?"

"Is everything alright?" she asked as both she and Iris once again stared at me curiously. Could either of them have stolen the clues?

"It's fine," I snapped. An elegant brow popped up at my rare shortness. "I'm sorry. It's nothing. You have fire magic, right?"

Fifi observed me for a moment longer, her curiosity fading away. Her shoulders eased as she smoothed the front of her dress. "A little. Nothing like Aramis and his friends."

"Can you start a flame? Just a small one. Enough to light this on fire?" I asked, crumpling the letter. Wordlessly, Fifi snapped her fingers and a tall, thin flame ignited—elegant, like her.

I positioned the paper above it, and the flame flickered beneath the parchment. Black smoke enveloped the crumpled ball until the page caught, transforming it into wisps of thin smoke.

Be careful who you trust.

CHAPTER 36

Thrown for a loop, I'd left the parlour shortly after Fifi destroyed the note, unable to feign amusement. Happiness and worry competed for my attention. Cara wrote to me, she truly had escaped. How, I didn't know, but did it matter? She was free. But worry refused to let happiness take full control of my emotions as Cara's rough scribble burned into my mind.

I haven't figured it out yet.

Figured out *what?* Oulixeus' plan to obtain the Book? Betraying Aramis could be necessary to ensure Cara's safety and even aid her in uncovering the secrets of my parents' court.

Be careful who you trust.

Cara knew I'd be cautious. Her reminder tugged a smile on my lips, always looking out for me, yet I couldn't return the favour in whatever she'd involved herself in.

Striding with purpose through the airy corridors of the fortress, the light fabric of my blue dress fluttered behind me. A tug guided me, as if my soul knew who I wanted to speak to before my mind even realised it. Without question, I followed the intuition to a courtyard.

Spring florals shimmered in the sun, and I ducked to avoid colliding with an extended tree branch and halted. Hiding behind the wide trunk, I peeked out to discover Aramis. The intuitive bond had led me straight to him, but he wasn't alone. Molvys hid in the shadows next to him, both sharing serious expressions.`

"Have you told her yet?" Molvys held his dimpled chin in his hand, contemplating their conversation.

Upset about something, Aramis shook his head, staring at the ground between them. "No, I don't want to burden her. Not yet."

"She's not a child, Aramis. She can handle more than you give her credit for," Molvys scolded, leaving me curious about the subject of their discussion. A prickling along the base of my skull questioned if it concerned me. But why whisper about me so secretively after everything we'd been through? But then those rough scribbles Cara had sent returned to the forefront of my mind.

"I don't doubt her!" Aramis' teeth gritted together, hands balling into fists. "She's so strong. So powerful. But to throw this at her might be too much right now."

Strong and powerful. No, they didn't speak of me.

"Whispering in the shadows? Whatever could you be hiding?" A smooth voice joked. Kenna. She strode over to them so stealthily, I didn't hear the crunch of gravel beneath her boots. She wore attire fit for hand-to-hand combat, moving as gracefully as a single flame, dancing higher than the rest of the fire.

"Nothing." Aramis ran a hand through his hair and looked around the courtyard. I dipped further into the foliage to avoid his gaze.

"If it's so secretive, maybe you should speak behind closed doors, brother," the graceful flame lectured Aramis, eliciting an irritated frown from him.

"Mind your own business," Molvys grumbled in his deep baritone voice, but it only made Kenna grin, as if his response confirmed whatever suspicions floated through her mind.

Provoking them, Kenna pressed further, "I hear the council isn't impressed about your ex-girlfriend breaking into the fortress. How'd you let that happen?"

"Back off, Kenna," Aramis snapped, taking a step toward her and Kenna faltered ever so slightly that I didn't think even Aramis or Molvys noticed it. But I did. Something about Aramis frightened her.

I shifted to see better, and my head grazed the bottom of a branch. The leaves swished and Kenna's head whipped in my direction as I ducked behind the bushes in front of me. *Fuck.*

Swiftly reclaiming her composure, Kenna donned a fake smile. "Keep your secrets." As she strode out of the courtyard, Kenna cast a knowing glance over her shoulder, piercing through the shrouded darkness where I concealed myself amongst the shrubs.

Be careful who you trust. Those words repeated over and over as an unshakeable mantra. The image of Kenna shrinking from her brother, my Fated Mate, remained etched in my mind, an unsettling tableau.

I trusted Aramis wholeheartedly, he'd offered me countless reasons to trust him. So why did my instincts persist in urging me to keep Cara a secret?

Be careful who you trust.

The weight of overwhelm threatened to engulf me as I navigated the fortress's corridors, fleeing from the clandestine gathering I'd inadvertently witnessed. Turning a corner, I stumbled upon Conláed jesting with two well-dressed companions. All three exuded an air of courtly elegance. Conláed leaned casually against the stone wall, exuding a regal charm in his rich clothing.

"What's wrong?" he asked the moment his eyes fell upon me, the others bowing in deference.

Looping my arm around Conláed's, I steered us away. "Please excuse us."

"Are you alright?" His arm tensed under mine, confused by my spontaneous action.

"I'm sorry to steal you away from your friends." I ignored his question, leading him aimlessly.

"They're not my friends. Besides, you're better company." He winked, attempting to diffuse the tension with humour. "But seriously, what's going on?"

"Find me some of that fucking fairy wine," I ordered, seeking solace in its familiar numbness, the way I used to, and he grinned.

As the high king's best friends, Aramis had gifted Conláed and Molvys beautiful apartments within the fortress. Conláed's apartment profusely expressed one thing—*I am a single male and loving it.*

Weapons decorated the living room walls, an array of swords, maces, knives, bows, lances, and axes. Above the fireplace, the grandest piece, a longsword, gleamed. Its polished blade bore intricate carvings, the pommel fashioned into a golden lion's head—exactly like the stone sword carved into Iros' hands in the throne room.

Conláed poured himself a second whiskey while I cradled my untouched fairy wine, swirling its contents in the delicate crystal, carrying a fragrance of silvered dreams and star-kissed blossoms.

I shrugged into the oversized leather chair by the fire, tracing the chair's brass embellishments. Conláed settled into a matching chair beside me.

Noting my interest in the sword, he boasted, "Forged by the Water Fae themselves. They're master forgers. Fire Fae are excellent too, but the Water Fae developed unique techniques with their water magic, crafting impossibly strong metals. One of the few left in the world."

"How did their magic make the metals so strong?" I mused, contemplating a sip of wine to quell my nerves.

Conláed stared at the magnificent weapon, a longing developing behind those playful eyes. "They found a way for their weapons to enhance Fae magic. During the foraging process, a Fae possessing a specific elemental magic needed to be present to bind their power to the weapon."

"So, your sword enhances fire magic?" I concluded, and a sly smirk crept onto his face.

"You're too clever for your own good." The ice in his glass clinked as he took a sip, evaluating me, as if I kept secrets worth sharing.

"Why?"

"Most believe my sword is a plain weapon forged by the Water Fae. They aren't aware that my great-great-grandfather commissioned it. They don't know his power runs through the blade and enhances fire magic. It'll enhance any Fire Fae's magic, but enhance mine the most. My power would match Aramis'." A curious grin played on his lips, but the muscles along his jaw twitched, trying to suppress it.

"Why?" I pressed.

"Because I'm a direct descendant of the magic inside of the sword. I could be a great threat if I wanted to be." Conláed ran his tongue over his teeth, as if savouring the prospect. Suddenly, I realised, whenever Conláed indulged in alcohol, some kind of malign weaved its way through him, a merciless side of him lurking beneath his jovial exterior. I mistook it as drunken confidence, but now to see the look on his face...

Leaning forward, I placed my untouched wine glass on the nearby table. The liquid flowed as brilliantly as a full moon on a dark winter's night. Alcohol had always been my refuge, a means to drown out the anxiety and disturbing imaginations within. But it possessed a dual nature, for it perpetually hindered my ability to face and control the burgeoning darkness. Perhaps it's why I'd struggled to become stronger, to assert my will, always relying on others for protection.

Seeking distraction, I asked, "What happened to them?"

"The Fae courts unanimously deemed the weapons too powerful and hid them, since their magic made them impossible to destroy," Conláed shared and his eyes glazed over, as if overtaken by an unsettling cynicism.

"I meant the Fae. What happened to the Water Fae? Are there any here, at Stoneshalt?" I interrogated, finding the Fae courts confused the Veil out of me.

"No." His voice dripped with bitterness.

"So, what happened?" Leather squeaked as I leaned over the chair's arm.

"They're all dead." He downed his whiskey, rising to pour another. Sensing to drop the topic, I stood, ready to confront Aramis. Attempting to stand, my legs twisted, and I toppled over. I guess my clumsiness had never stemmed from drinking too much.

Shedding his seriousness and bursting into laughter, Conláed reached me in two long strides, catching my waist before I could land on the floor. Helping me regain my footing, he glimpsed the hand he caught and his eyes widened. I had deliberately concealed my hands beneath draping sleeves to evade prying questions or disdain for a mortal being Fated to a Fae high king.

"What?" I didn't need to ask. I knew why he starred.

"I had a feeling you two shared a Fated connection," Conláed traced the lines of my new tattoo.

"How?"

"He loved someone a long, long time ago—"

"Andraste," I interrupted, already aware of her.

"Yes. Aramis lost interest, and she left the court. Told me he was too young to commit, claiming another waited for him. He couldn't explain it, but knew another existed. I know he loves you because the way he treats you and acts around you is different compared to Andraste. And that mark, right there," Conláed said, pointing to my tattoo, "proves he sensed you." I said nothing and he didn't seem to mind. "No wine, Wyn?" He noted the abandoned glass.

"Wyn?" I raised a brow, avoiding answering his question.

"It suits you."

"And how does it suit me?" I laughed at my silly friend.

"Because you're a winner." He winked, and I rolled my eyes. How in the Veil could I be a winner? I grabbed the little pillow from the chair and playfully smacked him across the jaw. Laughing, he wrestled the pillow from my hand and swatted my hip before tossing it back to the chair.

As our laughing subsided, I whispered, "Do you know what it means to have a Fated Mate?"

"The goddesses wove together your fates." Conláed cocked a brow, confused by my sudden question.

"But does it mean... Can... can *I*..."

"Trust him?" Conláed grasped where my words led.

"Yes." I sought confirmation, grateful for his understanding.

"If I'm being honest, Wyn, there's no magic stopping him from being deceitful. But I know Aramis. I really *know* him. He's fiercely loyal and when he loves, it's with unwavering depth. You have nothing to fear. Aramis is head over heels for you. No one has ever kept him away from killing something for longer than a few hours, let alone a whole week." And although he jested, I recognised the seriousness within it.

"He truly is a killer, isn't he?" I peered at Conláed, who rubbed his teeth with his tongue again, unable to deny my worst fears.

CHAPTER 37

The gritty mud coated my hand as usual while drops of rain splattered across my bare skin, soaking my dress. Wailing continued in the distance, melding with a child's cries. This time, a man's bellowing roar joined them. It still ate away at my insides, because I increasingly believed the demon hadn't hurt my sister.

"I thought you abandoned me," I said as the familiar swish of his cloak approached, and the petrichor mingling with the subtle essence of the woods, washed over me. He hadn't visited my recurring nightmare for weeks. Not since he pushed his power into me, spreading a delicious pulse through my body, and creating a high like no other. I yearned for it. The sensual sweetness still coated my tastebuds, but I didn't seek it out, afraid of another addiction consuming me.

"No, I would never abandon you. Others required my attention."

I leaned up on my elbows. The wind shifted and blew the edges of his hood, though I still didn't see his face.

"Are you a demon trying to possess me? Make me addicted to your power, use it to control me, and influence me to do your bidding?" I finally felt the courage to speak up more freely. To fight back. The cloaked figure laughed.

"I am certainly no demon, Elowyn. And it certainly wasn't my power you felt." He stepped closer, and I felt the surge through me again. Just like the first time, it rushed through me, creating an intoxicating dizziness.

"Then whose power—"

The entire room shook. The bedframe below me rocked back and forth as glass, mirrors, and decorations rattled. A deafening blast resounded from beyond the balcony. Within seconds, Aramis' solid body covered mine, and a burst of air hit us, knocking us to the floor.

"What the—"

"We're under attack. Stay here," Aramis ordered as he rushed to slip into his battle armour placed on a bust in his chamber.

Hurrying to the balcony, I witnessed a devastating scene unfolding. A massive funnel of swirling air unleashed a furious might upon the unyielding protective wall around Stoneshalt. A deafening roar shattered the skies, scattering debris and colliding with the poorest districts of the city in a tumultuous crescendo. Dots of ruby and amber flickered throughout the pastures, swiftly encroaching upon the city.

I sensed it wasn't my father or any mortal court, as they were too weakened to engage so soon, and Father wanted the Book before taking action. No, this assault was the work of the Fae rebels.

Bells rang throughout the city and even from this distance, the sharp clanging of armour and weapons rang clear.

"I'm not staying here. I can help." Returning to our apartments, I hastily dressed in my training clothes.

"No!" The order rolled out like a growl, but it didn't phase me like it would've when we first met in Rhyddean.

"I'm not the same little girl all those weeks ago, Aramis. I've come a long way. Even Molvys and Conláed say I'm a great fighter. Their sharpest student."

"Exactly, *student.* I know you've grown, Elowyn. But you're not ready for an attack of this calibre and you fighting out there will distract me. If you're here in the fortress, then I *know* you're safe and I can focus on what needs to be done." He gripped my arms firmly, but still gently. I bit my lip, empathising with thoughts. Distracting Aramis could also mean putting him in danger.

Regardless of understanding, I wanted to be helpful. "I can't just sit up here and watch."

"In attacks like this, the fortress residents gather in a chamber with an emergency exit, just in case we're breached. Find Fifi. She'll be assisting with ensuring everyone is safe and you can help her." Aramis rubbed my arm, and I smiled at the compromise. We quickly departed and ran our respective ways.

CHAPTER 38

Guards scrambled through the corridors, rushing for the gates as those who couldn't fight held small bags and children, scurrying to the emergency chamber. I dodged the soldiers in their clattering armour and followed the others, keeping an eye out for Fifi.

Turning a corner, a slender body shoved into my shoulder, and continued to hurry on in the opposite direction from the crowd. I spun to see a cloaked figure striding away, a wisp of red hair peeking from her hood.

Kenna?

My curiosity drove me to follow at a discreet distance. Initially, I suspected she'd snuck off to join the battle, perhaps barred by Aramis, too. But her path led to the throne room.

What business did Kenna have in the throne room in a time like this? She slipped behind one of the many columns lining the entrance to the grand room. I ducked behind the one closest to me, wishing to remain hidden for a little while longer.

"We need more soldiers at the gate!" A stern voice called from the other side, and the twelve guards assigned to the room bolted out, abandoning their post and leaving the Book's entrance unattended. As they departed, Kenna strode toward the statue of Iros.

No. Could Kenna be Andraste's spy? I recalled how Kenna had spied on Aramis and Molvys in the garden. How she flinched as her brother snarled at her...

Touching the base of the stone, as if reciting a silent prayer, Kenna looked up to meet Iros' face. Mustering my courage, I stepped out from the shadows to confront her.

"You're definitely more brave than I gave you credit for." The voice rolling from her lips didn't belong to Kenna, but Andraste herself.

Ignoring my surprise, I stepped closer. "How did you get in here?"

"Everyone's too distracted to spot a commoner," she said, lowering her hood. A strategy I recognised, mirroring what Cara and I had used to sneak into Elmswood Castle.

Before I had a moment to think, Andraste kicked her heel into my chest, knocking me to the floor. The smack of my head on stone echoed through the hall as a harsh sting radiated on the back of my skull.

Let me help you, the dagger sheathed on my thigh spoke. I swiftly armed myself and pointed the tip of the blade at my assailant. She laughed wickedly and attempted to kick the dagger from my grasp, but my training with Molvys and Conláed had paid off.

I dodged her foot, rolling to the side and using the momentum to leap onto my feet, ready to slam the hilt of my dagger into the side of her head. As the metal met Andraste's skull, her head snapped to the side and blood trickled along her temple, the scarlet liquid painting my hand.

"I really hate you." She quickly swept her leg under mine, bringing me to the ground for a second time. But with Molvys and Conláed's training, I didn't wait a beat to kick my foot into her abdomen. She barely stumbled, but it allowed me enough time to jump to my feet and regain my stance to fight.

Andraste glared at me, her eyes squinting and brows knitting, hating my resilience. The strength I'd lacked for so long finally showed through—the potential Cara had known I possessed.

Taking one step toward me, her blade ready to strike, I dipped downward to avoid the blow. She stumbled forward as I threw a powerful uppercut into the side of her ribs.

A frustrated grunt fell from her lips as her hand snatched out to me and clenched my throat. Within an instant, my confidence disappeared and fear consumed me as I remembered a different time, a different hand. I gripped her forearm with both of my hands as hers squeezed tighter, cutting off my airflow. Debilitating memories drowning my ability to think.

No. No. No.

Her strength was evident as she effortlessly lifted me from the ground with one arm, conjuring fire in the other.

Heat from her flames pierced into me and rippled through my skin, more powerful than I expected. Sweat quickly dribbled from my forehead and the back of my neck, joining tears I didn't give permission to fall.

Kicking my legs out from under me, I attempted to strike her again, a last ditch effort to escape her. Her grin returned, so malicious, exactly as Aramis described her.

"I'm going to burn you alive, you filthy little pest," she whispered, as if making a sacred oath. The last bit of air within me released as a whimper. "Oh, don't worry. I won't touch your pretty little face. I want Aramis to know for certain it's you who's dead." Andraste pushed her flaming arm toward me, ready to burn my abdomen. Closing my eyes shut, I prepared for the excruciating pain of being burned by her flames.

I'd always imagined my death as a result of Oulixeus— hitting me too hard or squeezing my neck for too long. I knew it would be agonising and painful, however I died, but I never expected to be burned alive.

The pain never came. Instead, I fell to the ground as a shrill scream came from Andraste. Daring to look, I witnessed another Fae slashing her blade across

Andraste's shoulder. Blood sprayed from the impact, speckling all three of us.

My saviour and my attacker fell into a graceful battle with each other. Swords clashing, legs sweeping out, hair spinning as they twirled and dodged each other's blows. One would lunge and the other would parry, always expecting the forthcoming move, as if they had once trained together. They probably had—because they once expected to become sisters-in-law.

Kenna had arrived just in time to save me and now I watched her fight Andraste, both evenly matched, and a swell of gratitude and hope welled up within me. I didn't have nearly as much experience as these graceful warriors, but I'd proved myself good enough. I believed it now, and I possessed the ability to offer Kenna an advantage.

Leaping to my feet, I joined Kenna in sparring with Andraste. Together we pushed her further and further down the throne room, closer to the fire spired throne itself. When Kenna struck Andraste, I attacked wherever Andraste left herself open, causing her to stumble further. I quickly learned that she often failed to keep her elbows tucked into her body to protect herself and my dagger sliced her ribs, eventually carving through her leathers and nicking her flesh, the metallic tinge of her life force encouraging my aggressive offence.

Andraste stumbled onto the steps leading up to the throne. She crawled backwards, away from us for a moment, eyes wide, when I saw it—the amulet.

"How did you get that?" I pointed at her neck with the tip of my dagger. She grinned in her malicious way, which soured my stomach.

"You're so fucking clueless. You all are." And before we could force any more information from her, she vanished in a plume of smoke.

"No! How did she—" Aramis had the fortress warded to block the ancient magic.

"Someone must have released the wards when the battle started. They still have a spy within the fortress," Kenna answered, her typically serene features marred by furrowed brows and a troubled countenance. "The Book is located here, isn't it?" Kenna turned to me, her chest rising and falling, catching her breath from the attack.

"The Book?"

Be careful who you trust.

"Don't pretend like you don't know what I'm talking about—I know about the Book of Toivo. I know Aramis is after it, and I know the rebels want it, too. Father grew paranoid about Aramis. Believed he'd take things too far and destroy this realm and the others. So he told me about the Book and asked me to keep it away from him," Kenna spoke so bluntly, so honestly, it took me aback.

Cara's warning simmered within me. Aramis' father mistrusted him, but was Kenna's claim accurate? Conláed even confessed this in his chambers and Aramis' actions unmistakably pointed towards danger. Could I trust him solely based on our Fated connection?

CHAPTER 39

Aramis' forces pushed the rebels out of the city, but not without extensive damage to the outer walls and neighbourhoods and my heart ached with a profound sorrow as I stood looking out at the aftermath. Crowds of the less fortunate gathered their remaining possessions as their neighbourhood lay in ruins, the charred remains of homes serving as grim monuments to the lives lost. Broken stone bore witness to the fierce battle where the blood of Aramis' people—*my* people—mingled with the dirt, turning it to a macabre shade of crimson.

I gazed upon the wreckage, unable to fully fathom the rebels' motivations, a subject most withheld from me. Aramis had divulged the rebels' desire to return to the system of individual courts, something he and the council dismissed as inefficient and outdated. But the pain and suffering of my people remained undeniable, the wailing and cries of children shattering the streets.

In the midst of the anguish, I found myself curious to understand the desperate hearts of those who sought to overthrow our united court, even as it crumbled before my eyes. Why did they protest a united realm so intensely? What information had eluded me?

Dragging me from my thoughts, a young girl knelt in the ash, covered in soot, and pushed burnt debris around. Blonde hair tangled down her tattered dress, tears welled, and she wiped a palm across her brown eyes, painting her face in grey and black. A girl around the age of seven or eight—no, twelve. There wouldn't be any children born after the last cycle of Light Bearer. She appeared exceptionally small for her age.

I walked over and knelt in the debris. "What are you searching for?"

Her pouting face took me in, ready to burst into tears. "My... my lion."

A toy or stuffed animal, most likely. Wordlessly, I joined the little girl's hunt for her lion, falling to my knees and allowing the soot to stain my azure-blue dress. Sifting through the rubble disturbed the ash, and it floated like sorrowful drifters from the heavenly realm, their grey whispers coating the world in a shroud of melancholy. It felt as though nature itself had crumbled into a ghostly powder, a spectral residue adhering to all, obscuring the vibrant tapestry of life. And despite my efforts to shake off the growing unease, it felt undeniably like a warning. For what, I didn't know, but a warning, unquestionably.

Heavy steps trudged toward us, halting on the edge of what used to be the house's outer wall. The essence of sandalwood and sweet cherries attempted to dispel the acrid bitterness of charred wood. "Elowyn—"

"I'm helping this girl find her lion," I said without looking at Aramis. If I looked at him, I'd join the girl's silent crying.

"Sweetheart—" his voice softened to the gentle caress of silk on flesh.

"If I don't keep busy, I'm going to be sick," I explained, trying to keep strong, but the crack in my throat betrayed me.

A second set of boots clanked next to Aramis. Conláed spoke lighter than Aramis. "Elowyn, there are many ways you can help. Fifi can assist you in organising a relief effort, tend to the wounded—"

"And if I want to do more?" I threw a piece of charred timber into the wreckage, swirling the smoky remains as it thudded into soot. "I want to know *why* the rebels attacked innocent Fae. To plan a counterattack, put my education to use. Learn how Andraste got back into the Blood Fortress. I *need* to do more."

"I can assist with that." Rune approached dressed in dark leathers, a stark contrast to the courtier clothes I normally saw him in.

I tossed another piece of rubble away, and it crumbled to ash. "What did you find?"

"The spy." Rune grinned, proud of himself, but a sense of dread washed over me as I recalled who'd taken the time to get close to me since I'd arrived. The likelihood that either of my new friends, Fifi or Iris, could be the spy was alarmingly high.

Steeling myself for the truth, I asked what I feared. "It's not Fifi or Iris, is it?"

"Sweetheart—" Aramis' face contorted with confusion.

"What?" "Conláed stared at me, unable to believe my concern.

But Rune shook his head, and a weight lifted off my chest. "No. The spy isn't Fifi or Iris."

Aramis sighed deeply, his armour clanking as he squatted to my level. "Come," he said, his voice tender. "Let me take you somewhere to clear your head, sweetheart."

The little girl crawled on her hands and knees, digging into the rubble, desperate to find her lion friend, and Conláed joined her. "Can I help you?" he asked, already sifting through the ash with his metal clad hands. The girl nodded without looking at him.

Grief and anxiety overcame me, so I allowed Aramis to lead me away from the desolation, clinging to his strength. He became a beacon of light, guiding us through the abyss that lay ahead.

CHAPTER 40

Aithon bolted into a gallop seconds after we settled into the saddle, my dress fluttering in the wind and merging seamlessly with the boundless expanse of the sky. An excited shriek escaped my lungs and Aramis held me tight, my sorrow already fading. We raced past fields of wheat, horses grazing in meadows, and tiny farmhouses spread across the land.

Aramis guided Aithon toward the reddish-brown mountains rising in the distance. The Scarstone Mountains, he told me, dividing the Fire Court from the Earth Court.

Slowing down to a trot, we approached a towering sandy-coloured rock face shimmering in the beams of light breaking through clouds. Dismounting Aithon, I brushed my fingers along the rough stone, shiny dust covering them.

"If the rock fascinates you, I look forward to your reaction to what we're truly here to see. Aramis chuckled as he tied Aithon's reins to a tree. I rolled my eyes as the strange flow of the cliff dazzled me.

"I'm still not accustomed to the illumination of the Fae realm," I admitted.

Aramis leaned flat against the rock and shimmied his muscular body through a hidden, narrow crevice. "Come on."

With my mood quickly improving, I followed him, sparkles of dust falling onto my skin. The secret path broadened, and we strolled beside each other, our fingers playfully reaching and withdrawing. Our teasing evoked a lightness in my heart, carrying away my concerns.

An ethereal glow winding through the sandy crevice of burnt siennas and golden yellows emphasised the dimples growing on Aramis' face as our game ended with my hand resting in his.

Reaching a dead end and seeing no other passages or subtle crevices to squeeze through, I turned in confusion to Aramis.

"Here." He pointed to a dark hole hiding behind a large sandy boulder, barely large enough for a body to fall through. My eyes widened with concern.

"Trust me." He flashed a playful grin before he leapt into the hole and was swallowed by its darkness. An excited shout reverberated through the shadows and into the light I stood in. A few more seconds passed and his thrillful calls ended with a splash.

As the water rippled into silence, my heart raced, unable to see where he fell to or how he landed.

One, two, three. Breathing in.

One...

"Elowyn! Come on! Don't be a chicken!" His shout bounced back to me.

"Gods," I muttered to myself and called back. "I can't swim!" Cara and I skinny dipped, but never waded further than our shoulders.

"Trust me, I'll catch you!" he coaxed.

Trust me...

The concerns implanted by Cara's note and Kenna's words tried to re-emerge, but I didn't want to confront them. Not yet. So I bit my lip and jumped.

Devoured by the narrow tunnel, my cries of fright reshaped into gleeful shrieks as I plummeted, untouched by rocks, plants, or the monsters my mind irrationally invented. In complete darkness, I entered a vast chamber bathed in a shallow light. And before I could take it all in, warm velvety sapphire water engulfed me.

Fully submerged in the dark liquid, I opened my eyes to bubbles swirling around me and Aramis' legs slightly kicking above. Despite being unable to swim and unsure of what to do, the dark water calmed me.

I'd developed a love-hate relationship with darkness. The way it attempted to take over and isolate me terrified me. Yet, in moments like this, it felt soothing as brooding tendrils wrapped around me in solace.

Aramis dove into the water to retrieve me. "I knew you'd like it." Water dripped from Aramis's face and golden hair as we surfaced. I inhaled fresh air, the chamber carrying scents of delicate florals and mosses.

"I've got you. Kick your legs like this." Aramis demonstrated his legs moving in gentle circles. I imitated him and my body became more buoyant. "Perfect."

We swam in the centre of a grotto. Soft light filtered in through various holes and cracks in the roof. A large natural stone platform jetted from an opening into the pool. Waterfalls trickled down parts of the stone walls. Vines decorated with glowing pink flowers covered the walls between the waterfalls. I marvelled at the scene.

"Does everything glow here?" Though my question carried a serious undertone, I couldn't help but snicker at how ridiculous it must've sounded to him. He laughed with me.

Becoming more comfortable treading the water, I let go of Aramis and waved my arms back and forth, the way he did. To my surprise, I floated on my own.

"It's the magic," he explained.

"Magic is making me float?"

"No." A deep chuckle fell from him. "Magic is why nature glows here. Rhyddean used to glow too. All of Niafell did. The gods gifted magic to the Fae. It's why we each have a different type of magic—it's based on which region our ancestors lived in. Iros gifted Fae within his land, the Fire Court, with fire magic. Toivo bestowed mind magic upon the Fae living in the Mind Court, which is now Rhyddean. And so forth. A Fae's magic comes from within. When we use the magic, the earth absorbs it and can give off its own magic."

"So there's no magic in Rhyddean because mortals banned the Fae after the First Mortal War?" I pieced together, and Aramis nodded his confirmation. "Oh."

Gaining confidence, I kicked my legs and hands to move around the grotto. The water felt freeing.

Freedom.

Playing with my new skill, I tested my comfort, leaning backward and allowing the water to hold me. Slightly sinking into the sapphire pool, I caught myself and laughed.

A melodic call sang through the grotto, distracting me from floating. Large birds swept into the chamber, singing to each other. They soared gracefully, long red wings and tail feathers flowing behind them like flames in the wind. Counting nine, they perched in separate nesting spots throughout. Their flaming red feathers extinguished as they sat.

"Wait, are they on fire?" I gaped at Aramis.

"Yes. They're phoenixes. Native to the Fire Court." He swam over, noticing I struggled to keep my chin above the water as my dress weighed me down. Aramis placed his hands on my hips and propped his knee, resting it between my thighs.

"Will magic return to the mortal courts with the return of the Fae?" I asked, desperate to distract myself from where his leg touched me. He meant to keep me afloat, but it stoked something more.

"We hope so, but only time will tell," he added, pulling our bodies closer.

"I hope it does," I whispered, falling in love with the world of magic. "What is this place?"

Aramis pressed his face into the crook of my neck. "This is my secret place."

"Nobody else knows about it?" The muscles along my neck fluttered as Aramis' breath coated my flesh.

"No." He attempted to remove the space between our lips again.

"Not even Conláed and Molvys?" I refused to allow him to kiss me, teasing him.

"Not even them." He impatiently leaned closer, but I turned away to survey the space again. Spectacular. Magical. Sighing, he rested his forehead on my temple. "You're cold."

I hadn't noticed my chattering teeth and the goosebumps speckling my shoulders until he assisted me to the rock platform, helping me ascend the natural steps forming along one side. Gathering a handful of weathered logs, Aramis stacked them skillfully and set them ablaze with his magic.

We sat in hushed tranquility as the flames danced away, their warmth and crackling tongues chasing away the chill of the water. Aramis nuzzled his face into the curve of my neck, and my palm rose, fingertips grazing his cheek, savouring the exquisite moment.

"Together, we'll be the best versions of ourselves. Unstoppable." His whisper stoked a passion within me. "I'll always be here for you, Elowyn. To catch you when you fall, fight next to you, and bring you back from the darkness. I don't deserve you and your patience. But if you'll let me, I'll keep you forever."

A month ago, I'd yearned for freedom so feverishly. Desperate to run away from a man who wished to keep me, locked me away in a tower, promising brief hints of freedom if I behaved. Now I lay in the arms of a powerful Fae high king, willing to submit to him. Because I knew keeping me didn't mean locking me away.

The crackling fire, the gentle scent of cedar burning, and the thought itself lulled me into a state so relaxing my eyes fell. For the first time in a long while, I drifted to sleep easily.

CHAPTER 41

*S*urrounded by bright yellow and white mum flowers, I watched the blooms sway back and forth in the gentle summer breeze. It kissed the top of my exposed shoulders, highlighted by the rare sun.

My sisters giggled and ran around the field. My last moment of peace with my family—before something awful had happened. The memories pieced together slowly as I watched my sisters play.

And then I saw him.

The cloaked demon haunting my dreams, the dark entity that dwelled within my mind. Was this the moment he possessed me?

Leaving my sisters to play, I walked to Ravenwood Forest to confront the man who ruined my life. He waited patiently for me, standing perfectly still beneath his black cloak, hands folded in front of him.

"I don't want your dark magic, demon. You tried to use my weaknesses to trick me into falling for whatever plan you have. But I finally understand. I finally *get it*. The drinking, the gambling, the risk-taking, I abused it all to avoid finding what I truly wanted. Love. Not freedom. I wanted love. Real, unconditional, treasured love. And I've found it. Your magic may have given me the greatest high of my life, demon, but I don't want it."

He remained stoic as I made my speech, and when I finished, he nodded in silent acknowledgement, signifying his belief in every word I shared.

"Good. You deserve love, Elowyn. You deserve to live a life you're not fearful of. A life you aren't constantly trying to run away from. To live safely and happily will allow you to develop your power and full potential."

I scrutinised the demon carefully. Even though his face remained obscured, I sensed his genuineness, piquing my curiosity.

"I didn't give you my magic, Elowyn. And I'm no demon," he continued. He'd insisted many times before that he wasn't a demon.

"Then what are you? What was that power?" A lump caught in my throat, warning me that I may not like his response. I swallowed it down anyway.

"I'm Fae, Elowyn. And so are you."

My body froze. Paralysed by his words. Fae? Me? My jaw slacked open to deny it until he continued.

"You sensed your *magic* the other night. You just didn't know how to tap into it. I've been visiting you in your dreams, trying to explain this, to teach you how to use your *magic, but you kept pushing me out. Your pervasive fear of... everything... led you to instantly assume the worst of me, and you repeatedly expelled me night after night, leaving no room for me to explain. I didn't wish to influence your magic prematurely, but I became desperate, believing it was the sole means to get through to you."*

I bent over at the hips as a laugh expelled from deep in my belly, resting my hands on my knees. The entire notion seemed utterly absurd. Me, a Fae? No. This demon continued to manipulate me, and my patience wore thin.

"Demon, you are no Fae and neither am I. I will find a way to banish you and your darkness. Now leave. Me. Alone!"

Lifting my hands, I shoved them forward and watched the demon slam back into a tree trunk, his bones cracking with the force I used. I didn't know how, but I absorbed the energy I had sensed previously. And it felt comfortable. It felt... right.

The demon stood, and I knew he smirked at me beneath his hood. "You'll be back," he insisted as I severed our connection.

Waking, I watched Aramis struggle to stand on the opposite end of the grotto platform. The fire, once fierce and dazzling, abruptly extinguished, leaving behind nothing but a swirling plume of acerbic smoke and a delicate dusting of ash, reminiscent of the remains of the dream I'd fled.

Aramis rested a palm on his knee, pulling himself up. I had never seen him struggle physically before, even in battle he stayed fiercely strong. And his eyes...

They locked onto mine, sending an electric jolt of fear coursing through me. They held a whirlwind of emotions, a turbulent sea of fear, shock, and yet a glimmer of astonishment, like a wild storm simultaneously terrifying and enthralling.

The wall behind him cracked, displaying a prominent fissure at its core. From there, a network of cracks spider webbed outward, interspersed with silver specks.

"What happened?" I asked, unable to move. "How did you get over there?"

"I went to add more wood to the fire and... and..." he faltered, his stare fixed on me, a bewildered and emotionally tangled expression on his face.

"And *what?*"

"Fuck." He ran a hand through golden locks. "I knew you'd be powerful but *this.* Fuck, I didn't expect this."

Aramis finally stood, bracing himself against the cracked wall. I tilted my head and replayed what he just said.

I knew you'd be powerful, but this...

"What do you mean?" My question remained firm, even as the gears in my mind whirled incessantly. He ignored me, beginning to pace back and forth like a trapped lion. "Aramis, you said you knew I'd be powerful. What do you mean?"

He avoided eye contact. Pausing and shaking his head, he pinched the bridge of his nose, as if formulating an excuse—a lie.

"Aramis?" I edged, yet he still refused to face me. Anxiety clawed at me. No, not anxiety, but an encroaching darkness. The telltale signs, the initial symptoms, manifested—high-pitched ringing, a haze clouding my vision. But was it the darkness itself, or perhaps... the demon?

"*Aramis!*" I screamed at the top of my lungs, done with his stalling. Not allowing him the time to create another lie. My throat burned from aggressively pushing air through my voice box.

"I'm sorry." He finally dared to confront me, and the darkness took a step back, offering him a chance. "I didn't know when to tell you. Didn't know if I *should* tell you. You've been through so much." He spoke gently.

"Tell me *what?*" I slowly stalked toward him, recalling his conversation with Molvys in the courtyard. One small step at a time. Like if I got too close to his explanation, it would burn me worse than any flame he conjured.

"Elowyn." He completed the distance between us and took my hands, his thumb stroking the flaming swirls tattooed on my wrist. Emerald golden-flaked irises met forgotten ashen ones, boring straight into the depths of my soul as if begging to decipher his honesty and guilt. A kind smile graced his face, but the dimples I admired didn't form. Aramis revealed, "You're Fae."

I ripped my hands from his and backed away. "No," I whispered, but my tone grew wild. "What game are you playing?"

First the demon and now Aramis too?

No.

Impossible.

"Sweetheart—"

"Look at me! Aramis, look. At. Me! I'm not Fae. My parents are human. Mortal."

"Think about it, Elowyn. *Really think* about it. It's so clear once you see it," my betrothed—what a stupid notion—insisted. I couldn't help but comply. The darkness within urged me to consider it.

And memories. So many memories flashed through my mind, reliving it all.

All the times Mother boxed my ears because I heard too well.

My wounds and bruises healing fast, and I rarely became ill.

My appearance. *Your beauty is more exquisite, elegant, ethereal compared to what these mortals are used to,* Aramis had said upon our first meeting.

The outbursts. The darkness.

And Oulixeus. *You have no idea just how unique you are.*

My stomach knotted. Ready to hurl. "No." I shook my head, trying to expel the memories. "I don't even look Fae."

"You do. You have high cheekbones like us." He placed his palm on my cheek, running his thumb along the bone carved more angular than my sisters.

"Your jaw is sharp." His hand slid to my jaw and fingers glided along it.

"Your eyes have a dimension no mortals can possess. They're not just grey. There are pieces of silver floating within your irises, and your pupils are a magnificent abyss. And then there are your ears." He tucked a curl behind one.

"What?" I snapped a hand to one of them.

"They're slightly pointed, Elowyn." He smiled. My fingers explored the tips of my ears and, sure enough, a subtle point where a bone jutted out. Instantly, I recalled Mother adjusting my hair at the welcome feast, hiding my ears. I perceived it as a maternal gesture, but she'd only meant to hide a Fae trait.

"Speculation. You're speculating." I started my own round of pacing. The proclamation felt preposterous. *Lies.* But to what end?

Expecting to be bombarded with high-pitched ringing and fog and a racing pulse, I paused. None of the symptoms showed. Anxiety didn't taunt me. I paused. "How?"

"Sévérine, your mother, must've conceived you with a Fae. She's your mother. I saw her once. A young maiden of sixteen, belly swelled with you, her first pregnancy. She accompanied Evander and his father, Alastair, to a meeting between realms. My father urged Alastair to strike a treaty, but your grandfather refused. Such a stubborn, righteous bastard. I hated that man." Noticing my impatience, Aramis pinched the bridge of his nose. "I don't know how, Elowyn. That's the extent of my knowledge regarding your conception and birth," he admitted.

Question after question flooded my mind, unable to keep up. Magic. Not outbursts or a haunting darkness, but magic had surged through my veins this whole time.

My magic.

What did I do with my magic to cause my outcast? Caused my entire family, except Oulixeus, to despise me? Fear me? Father must've known what I was. Why did he let me live? He hated the Fae.

Regarding fathers, who truly was mine? What type of Fae magic did he possess? Who else knew? How did—

"Aramis." My racing mind halted on one question. A query I needed answered now.

"Yes, sweetheart?" His brows rose.

"How do *you* know I'm Fae?" I held his gaze the way he held mine earlier. He claimed he didn't know *when* or if he *should* tell me. How did he learn this in the first place?

"Rumours and when I saw you—" The vein along his neck shuddered, indicating a slight shift in his heartbeat.

"Lie."

"What?"

"Your tell, Aramis. The one you teased me to reveal. It took me a few days to notice it, and over the past month, I've confirmed it." I shook my head, angry with myself for not heeding the warning my gut screamed for so long.

"So?"

"Your heart can't lie to me. The beat slightly shifts whenever you try to lie. I can hear it and I can see the vein in your neck ever so slightly twitch," I finally revealed. "Don't lie to me. I deserve the truth."

"You really are more clever than they give you credit for." He sighed before continuing. "Spies. Your uncle, well, step-uncle, Oulixeus, has had spies in our court for years. We infiltrated one of them, and she'd reveal to Oulixeus whatever I told her to. She'd remain in Rhyddean for a while, snoop around, eavesdrop, gather intel, and watch and listen. Roughly four, five years ago, she formed quite the alliance with a chatty tavern owner," Aramis confessed.

My heart felt as if someone squished it. Squeezing every last ounce of blood from the muscle.

"He bragged about the strangely beautiful girl who'd come to his establishment and drink his wine cellar dry. Who dressed like a peasant but had skin too supple to have worked a day in her life."

I pressed my back against the stonewall of the cave, leaning into it and allowing it to give me strength to stand as it felt like Aramis reached into my chest and clutched my heart.

"After watching for a while, she realised what you were. We agreed." And now my heart fully ripped from my chest.

"It's why you chose me," I whispered.

"What?" Aramis took a step closer. He paused as I recoiled. From the moment he announced his intention to take me as his wife in the great hall, I'd known it.

"You didn't choose me because of the Fated bond. You chose me because of my power," I confronted, and pushed down the hurt, my warmth freezing into abhorrence.

"No. I mean... Elowyn, no." He stumbled.

"*Don't* lie to me," I warned.

"At first, yes. Okay. Is that what you want to hear? That before we came to Rhyddean, I schemed to bring home the half-Fae princess by any means possible. Whether accomplished through an arranged marriage, or kidnapping, or force. We couldn't risk having a Fae as powerful as you, with such raw potential, in the hands of the mortals." He gritted his teeth in frustration. He hated this. And I hated him.

"I'm such a fool. This isn't a fucking bond. You tricked me. You used me. This is a brand. You *branded* me just like *he* did!" I accused him. A whirlwind of emotions swept through me, and I felt like the very ground beneath my feet was giving way. As if my trust had been a delicate tapestry, painstakingly woven, and he callously tore it apart. A relentless ache in my chest emerged, and the world around me blurred as I struggled to hold back tears, grappling with the raw, overwhelming hurt of it all.

"No! Elowyn, no." He sank to his knees in front of the hearth. "No, the bond is true."

"So it was just a fortunate coincidence that the half-Fae princess you needed to steal also happened to be Fated to you?" I laughed at the notion.

"Yes. The goddesses of fate wanted us to be together. They weaved our tapestry in a really fucked up way, Elowyn. But nonetheless, we are meant to be—fated," Aramis pleaded. "Sweetheart—"

"*Don't.* You're every bit the monster they claimed," I confirmed with a quivering voice mixed with my pain and that gnawing fear deep within me. Aramis took two steps toward me and I backed two steps away. His eyes widened and jaw fell at my reaction, at my fear resurfacing and taking hold. Did I ever truly know him at all?

"I fucked up. I'm so sorry." He took two steps away from me. "If I could go back, if I could do all of this over again, I'd tell you everything the moment we met in the clearing by the waterfall. I'd confess everything, even if you presumed me mad. I love you, Elowyn. Please, you make me a better person. You've given me hope! Something I've never experienced before. Elowyn, I—"

I needed to get away from him. Far, far away from Aramis and the Fae and everything. I wanted to be alone. *Needed* to be alone. I couldn't trust anyone.

Be careful who you trust.

A tear stung my eye as I thought of Cara and her warning. Was this what she'd meant? To my left, a large opening loomed, and without looking backward, I sprinted away.

CHAPTER 42

The dark forest spanned for miles. As I wandered deeper into the sombre wood, shadows wrapped themselves around me like cold fingers of a vengeful spirit. My heart, heavy with the revelation of my half-Fae heritage, thudded in my chest. Anger simmered beneath my skin, a tempestuous storm of resentment toward Aramis for keeping such a life-altering secret from me.

Half-Fae. The cloaked male in my dreams had unveiled the dark secret, and Aramis confirmed it. I believed it. It made sense once everything pieced together. But what bothered me was Aramis' lies.

The frigid air cut through my nasal passages with an edge that caught me off guard. Typically, the nights in the Fire Court didn't get cold. I rubbed my pink nose, debating what to make of Aramis.

He lied. He *lied.* Even though I noticed his tell here and there, each untruth pierced my heart with a searing pain. I couldn't find solace in his misguided attempt to supposedly protect me from the daunting Fae world. It was nothing but cruel betrayal after everything we shared. The safety and acceptance he provided me had vanished in mere moments, leaving me exposed. My stomach twisted into a knot, the ghost of his touch haunting me, as I yearned to cast him and his feelings for me into the darkest abyss of the Veil.

Deeper into the forest, darkness enveloped me, suffocating the starlight. Sinister tree canopies cloaked the night with their fresh spring leaves, murmuring secrets to one another. The once balmy breeze turned icy, prickling my exposed skin like a thousand needles.

As I ventured further, branches rustled and my steps reverberated, crushing the dirt's fragile grains and piercing my slippers with unforgiving stones. Fog crept between gnarled tree trunks, and the temperature plummeted ominously. Why had it grown so bitterly cold? I clutched myself, rubbing my arms for warmth, but the chill mocked my feeble attempts.

Snap. My shoulders tensed, and I scrutinised the looming trunks, only to find lurking shadows amidst the fog, tree trunks, and bushes. Yet, my heart pounded a baleful warning.

One, two, three. Inhale, eyes closed.

One, two, three. Exhale, my eyes. The moisture from my breath coalesced into a frosty cloud. My rational mind struggled to dismiss these tricks of the dark.

SNAP.

Louder. Clearer. *Closer.* The air behind my neck prickled, sending shivers down my spine. I glanced over my shoulder, scanning the dark woods to my left and right, finding nothing. A relieved sigh escaped my lips, and I resumed my walk, ready to return to the city.

Just two steps later, I halted. An elongated, bleached object peeked from behind a tree trunk, its details obscured by the fog. My throat tightened as I tried to rationalise it—a Fae forest charm, perhaps, or a sculpture, maybe even some form of white tree bark, resembling birch in its smoothness. Yes, it had to be birch bark.

Chuckling to myself, I dismissed my momentary lapse into fear. "Idiot," I muttered, laughing softly.

But then it moved. My laughter died in my throat as the tingling sensation returned, spreading like wildfire from my spine to my limbs. My heart raced, screaming at me to flee. *Run, run, run.*

The elongated, bleached object swivelled toward me, and two more emerged from behind trees. Shifting fog unveiled repulsive markings on these objects—hollow sockets and cavities where eyes and noses should have been. I took a step back, and all three crept around the trunks.

What I had mistaken for tree branches were, in fact, long, sharp antlers, resembling those of an elk but far more nightmarish, with six points of bone that forked into a chaotic pattern, each ending in a menacing tip. Strands of moss hung from them as though they had sprouted from the earth.

Taking another step back, I watched in horror as they inched closer, revealing their massive gangly bodies. They moved anomalously. Unsettled, disjointed, and slow, their heads swivelling as if conferring silently with one another, as if seeking to decipher what I was.

The adrenaline coursing through my veins urged me to flee, but I stood paralysed. The creatures' bones protruded through their blanched white skin, their limbs and torsos elongated and fragile, grotesquely unnatural.

My body tensed, blood rushed through my veins, preparing me for escape, but my mind refused to engage.

A thunderous crack rattled the sky, rumbling above the dense canopy blanketing the forest. My body felt it, yet remained frozen. A flash of lightning in the distance briefly illuminated the figures, their taut skin highlighting every bone in their spindly bodies, brightening their bleached skulls, and emphasising their formidable antlers. It also revealed the glinting length of their talons—talons as long as their entire bodies.

Talons so sharp, they dragged them through the dirt and moss.

Talons that promised swift, merciless death.

Finally, my mind caught up with my body, and I sprinted toward where I believed the city lay, the echoes of those grim creatures' pursuit filling the forest. The world around me blurred as my legs carried me away from the impending horrors, guided only by the rhythm of their eerie pursuit.

Suddenly, one of them leapt out, its momentum carrying it past me as it fumbled to regain its balance. I banked left, into the increasingly dense trees, using their shelter to obscure my presence. Despite their lanky frames, the monsters struggled to navigate the tight confines, their antlers forcing them to slow. The swooshing of their gait grew fainter as I lost them.

Thank the fucking gods.

I spotted a fallen tree with its uprooted trunk and dove behind it, taking refuge in the shadowy embrace of the gnarled roots. The musty scent of decay concealed my own fear. My hand rested over my racing heart, providing my terrified insides a grounding comfort.

Talons scraped the forest floor as the three creatures roamed in no particular pattern, hunting me. I willed my lungs to steady, embracing silence as my saviour. Within seconds, the scraping receded, their interest in the hunt waning. My lungs dared a full intake of air, greedily absorbing oxygen in my moment of respite.

Then it happened. A bleached, elongated skull discovered me, leaning over the upturned tree. Panic surged, and I scrambled forward, nails gouging dirt and moss, and worms squished beneath my panicked retreat. Almost standing straight, ready to flee, my feet caught on my dress, and I tumbled to my knees, my sleeve ripping as I skidded on my forearm. With a whimper, I rolled onto my back, desperate to evade the creeping terror.

It descended upon me, assessing its prey with hollow eye sockets and a predatory grace, its elongated form now fully over me. I froze in terror as it leaned in, ready to strike with a deadly talon. I wanted to close my eyes, to avoid seeing my own blood spatter on the decaying skull, but my muscles refused.

"Come," a casual order barked from behind me. The creature shifted away, and two more emerged from the foggy darkness to join it.

Heavy panting ruptured through me as death walked away. I rolled onto my belly and strained my neck back. Each muscle ached.

The beasts retreated, falling in line behind a dark figure approaching me. They flanked her like loyal servants. Another flash from the encroaching storm illuminated her fire-red hair drifting in the wind.

"Andraste," I rasped as I struggled to pull myself upright.

"We just keep running into each other." She laughed, her voice a seductive huskiness tinged with playful giggles.

"What are you doing here?" I questioned, my voice quivering.

"Do you know why he likes you?" She continued to prowl, her hips swaying with a sensuality I couldn't invoke. "You're perceptive. But don't be too clever, though. He doesn't appreciate being outwitted."

As she approached, she squatted down about six feet away, her almond-shaped hazel eyes locking onto mine. I studied her in return, taking in her elegant face. A galaxy of emotions and history swirled between shades of brown, honey, green, and grey irises. Detailing a dark, lonely childhood, isolated and feared. Like mine. But moving towards a softer, warmer life. Full of laughter, security, and love. And finally rippling into envy and cold vengeance.

"What do you want with the Book?" I cautiously asked.

"The question is, what do *you* want with the Book? Your friend escaped your father's dungeon. Why in all of the realms do you still want it? Do you share Aramis' masochism?" She smirked as my eyes widened.

"How do you know about any of that?" I faltered, my thoughts racing to whether Aramis knew as well.

"Aramis and Prince Oulixeus have their spies. We have ours," she said, holding my gaze. Afraid to look away first. Afraid to show me a glimpse of her insecurity.

We continued evaluating each other silently. Like other Fae, her cheekbones were high and angular, but hollow in the crease below, as if pain carved through them like limestone. Her slim lips helped to keep her domineering features balanced, but they twitched with a miniscule hint of unease.

"You're pretty," she muttered, the sneer in her voice making it clear it wasn't a compliment. "Pretty ones always did distract him. Has Conláed tried stealing your attention yet?" She laughed to herself. My jaw tightened. Conláed and I had grown to be close friends and I knew it bothered Aramis, regardless of our feelings being purely platonic.

"He *has*. Oh, this is too good," Andraste cooed, mistaking the sudden softness in my expression. She moved closer, unsheathing a dagger at her waist. Her *pets* remained in the distance, growling and shifting. "You're stupid," she taunted. "Pretty, but stupid. You've walked into quite a mess."

Her laughter grew borderline hysterical, and I frowned, my brows knitting together, both from the need to escape and my growing realisation of my own naivety. How little I knew of this court and the dynamics between Aramis and his friends.

But her chortle slowed into huffs, as she shook her head. Suddenly, her amusement turned to cold dismay. She grabbed my left arm, her grip iron-tight, and her eyes widened in horror as she studied my flesh beneath the ripped sleeve.

"What is this?" she demanded. "How did you get this?"

My arm nearly tore from the socket as she wrenched it closer.

"Let go of me!" I cried, tears welling up as I struggled against her grip. The repugnant monsters began to pace, sensing the rising tension.

"Did someone tattoo this on you?" Andraste's voice rose to a shrill pitch. Furious saliva sprayed on my face. "*Answer me!*"

She pinned me to the ground, one hand pulling my hair, the other propping her dagger beneath a fingernail. Her grip and position were strong enough to keep me still, unable to attempt the defensive moves I had learned. Without warning, she popped off the nail on my left index finger and I screamed, the miniscule action producing a torturous pain.

"Where did you get this tattoo?" Andraste pressed her forehead into my temple, baring her teeth. She meant to break me, to torment the truth from me. Squeezing my eyes tightly, I wanted to remain strong, but she increased the ferocity of her torture, digging the tip of her dagger into the base of my jaw. And the night my throat was slit flooded back to me, the excruciating pain, and I gave in, never wanting to feel my neck sliced open again.

"It just appeared!" I howled as she tugged my hair again. "It just appeared!"

Her grip slacked for a moment, and I gasped for air, tears streaming down my face. "No," she whispered, her voice shaking. She straightened her torso, straddling me. I dared to look at her, tears blurring my vision as Andraste surveyed the dark forest, searching for answers. Wanting to confirm the truth in my claim. And she found her answer.

"You cunt." Pushing my face with her palm, she spat insults and curses, her nails digging into my skin like claws, blood seeping from the wounds and trickling into my mouth. I groaned as she buried a knee into my left elbow, keeping me trapped and unable to move. My eyes strained to discover what she planned next.

Another flash of lightning illuminated her dagger high in the air, aimed for my arm. A thunderous crack followed as she slashed the flesh just below my shoulder, severing my bicep muscle.

The excruciating pain elicited a scream from me. My pulse rushed to the attacked location, pumping blood into it in a hurry to heal me. But Andraste lifted her blade again and cut deeper, clashing with bone as my entire body jerked at the horrifying sensation.

"St-o-p!" I cried through beseeching breaths.

"You stupid whore!" The female ripped my head backwards and pressed her forehead into my face again. "You're a fucking slut."

Pushing my face with her palm again, salty tears mixed with blood cast across my face and I choked on the salty, metallic mixture as it filled my nostrils.

Another raise of her arm, and Andraste cut down a third time, hitting a tendon in my shoulder. Determined to remove the tattoo—my whole fucking arm. To sever the Fated bond I shared with Aramis. The bond she craved.

My mouth opened, but no sound came this time. I was going to die here, bleeding out on the forest floor all because of her envy. My body wanted to shut down, the way it did months ago when those men attacked Cara and me.

An unexpected heat rushed over me, and Andraste flew off of me, slamming into a distant tree. Opening my eyes, I saw flames catching on the material of my dress. Searing pain from my arm and shoulder hindered me, but I managed to sit up and pat the flames burning the material.

A burly figure fell to my side and assisted me in snuffing out the flames. "I'm sorry," he muttered a throaty apology. I whimpered with relief as I discovered an ever-so-serious Molvys scouring me for injuries, his features twisted with concern. "Good Iros, what did she—"

"Andraste!" Aramis prowled through the dark toward his ex-fiancé, clad in his golden armour. Conláed fought in the distance, daring to brave the creatures on his own with fire magic.

"What?" Andraste steadied herself against the tree she smacked into, blood was splattered across her face and upper body—my blood.

"I made you a promise, and I intend to keep it," Aramis grimly reminded her, his voice laced with determination. A torrent of flames erupted in his grasp, casting eerie, dancing shadows in the darkened forest. With a swift, deliberate motion, he hurled the searing fireball toward Andraste, who deflected it by conjuring a blazing shield with her own fire magic.

"Good. I still have my wedding gown," she jeered sarcastically as she unleashed a fiery projectile aimed at Aramis. He agilely sidestepped the impending inferno, his body moving with a warrior's grace, his purpose unwavering as he continued his relentless advance.

"No, Andraste. My pledge to kill you." He tilted his head, readying to charge her. Conláed valiantly clashed with the dreadful creatures in the distance, their blood-curdling shrieks carried through the forest. Molvys dribbled a potent elixir onto my grievous wounds, the concoction sizzling malevolently upon contact with my blood and I longed to scream in agony but anchored my focus on Aramis.

A shroud of smoky darkness enveloped Aramis, halting his advance and replacing his resolute, murderous stare with bewildered confusion. As the smoke dispersed, it unveiled the presence of a female.

She stood as night and stealth in the flesh, cloaked in the inky garb of a phantom assassin, a black hood obscuring most of her visage, leaving only chilling moon-white irises exposed. Her body bristled with an arsenal of deadly weapons, poised for swift and merciless death-dealing.

Aramis didn't hesitate, striking first, his clenched fist driving mercilessly into her abdomen, causing her form to buckle inward. Hope fluttered through me as he seized the opportunity and delivered a punishing knee strike to her face, crimson blood spurting from her battered nose. Drawing his gleaming sword with lethal intent, Aramis poised to deliver the final blow, but she skillfully dropped to her knees and executed a swift leg sweep, sending

Aramis tumbling off balance. And it felt as though I fell with him.

"Shit," Molvys snarled, his attention riveted on the dire situation unfolding before us as Conláed was beset by the ravenous creatures, his magical flames flickering in exhaustion.

"Help him," I begged Molvys, pushing him toward our friend. A deep helplessness whirled within me, my injuries preventing me from joining them in battle. My heart ached to help Aramis and Conláed along with ripples of pain shuddering through my body. Molvys scrutinised my wounds, torn between helping his friends and my safety. "Go!" I urged, and he dashed to assist Conláed.

Aramis no longer stood tall, but knelt with a blade perilously close to his throat, ensnared within unyielding iron cuffs. Emerald eyes, brimming with both power and pain, bore into my very soul, and my trembling lip betrayed my torment. "Aramis!"

A searing agony erupted within my gut, causing me to crumple to the ground. Andraste, her cruel laughter reverberating through the darkened forest, cruelly kicked my vulnerable stomach, her fingers entangling in my hair as she yanked me upward. "Oh, shut up!"

"Andraste, leave the girl," the shadowy female commanded with authority.

"*What?*" Andraste shouted through clenched teeth.

"We came for the Book and Aramis. I have one. We need to leave, *now.*" She pressed the dagger into my mate, just enough to draw a bead of blood.

"I want to kill her, Vey," Andraste snarled.

"Get over it," the other female urged, compelling Andraste to relent.

Andraste cast one final, malevolent glare my way. "Don't sleep too soundly. I'm going to kill you one day soon." She walked toward the female named Vey, who held Aramis captive. He growled beneath the blade, never breaking eye contact with me. My heart urgently pounded as I watched Aramis, my Mate, being mercilessly taken hostage.

Aramis struggled in his chains, and Vey rammed the butt of her sword into his temple, the blow sending shockwaves through me as he slumped further to the ground. A relentless tide of panic flooded my senses.

My injuries rendered me helpless to intervene, as I longed to shield him from harm. The intensity of our bond surged, a visceral instinct to protect him, to shield him from their brutality, overwhelming me. Every second felt like an eternity as I grappled with the emotional tempest raging within, my world unravelling before my helpless eyes—again.

Leaning heavily on my one good arm, I pushed myself onto wobbling feet. Despite my vision swimming from the loss of blood, I was determined to save him, as he came to save me.

Andraste reached Vey and taunted me, "You're a fool."

With a sinister flourish, they vanished into the wisping smoke, leaving me to shout helplessly into their absence.

"Run!" Conláed's urgent bellow reached my ears, and I heeded his desperate plea. But my weakened body instantly collapsed and within seconds, the putrid slobber of one of the creatures drenched my back and the dead weight of my limp arm sent me tumbling to the ground. Rolling over, the monstrous beast snapped at my kicking feet before bringing its fetid jaws to my face. Desperation overtook me, and in a frantic bid for survival, I raised my trembling hands, pushing with all my might toward its bleached, skeletal face. A brilliant ash-grey light erupted from my palms, searing into the creature's exposed ribcage, propelling it skyward before it collided with a tree, emitting a chilling, otherworldly cry.

The second beast surged toward me with unrelenting ferocity, and without a moment's hesitation, I expelled a panicked breath. Miraculously, the second creature began to slow, disintegrating bit by bit, like wind eroding ash from a long-dead fire.

My final nightmarish foe reached me, its talons ready to tear me apart. And my vision blurred as it raised its razor-sharp appendages, slashing at me. My neck twisted violently, and the creatures mimicked my movement, its skeletal head snapping to the side with an audible crack, its lifeless body slumped to the ground.

Conláed and Molvys, rushing to my aid, approached with expressions of awe mingled with trepidation. "Wyn, your eyes. They're... they're black and silver." Conláed dared to reach out and dropped to his knees in front of me. "And your veins."

My fingers and hands shrouded in inky darkness, and the veins in my wrists and forearms turned obsidian, gradually fading back to their normal bluish-green hue. I opened my mouth to speak but found it impossible, a lump constricting my throat.

Struggling for air, I attempted to cough, producing only a gurgling sound. A burst of hot, coppery liquid burst from my mouth in a horrifying display. Frantically, I tried to breathe but couldn't. Trembling fingers reached up to wipe the blood that poured from my lips.

"Wyn," Conláed summoned a single flame to see better, his features contorted with fear. "No."

As my body convulsed and obsidian veins faded back to blue, Molvys pressed his palm firmly against my throat. My vision plunged into inky blackness, and darkness swallowed me whole.

CHAPTER 43

Giggles and squeals filled the wildflower field. Yellow and ivory cosmos cheerfully bloomed all around. Moist, cool dirt squished between my bare toes. The blonde girl ducked between the velvety petals. Golden hair blending in. Searching, I looked left to right and didn't see her. Another girl, with almost black hair, held her arms straight out and spun. Round, round, round. She wobbled and tumbled into the sea of flowers. Giggles ruffled from the blooms.

Combing the field for the blonde girl, I tried deciphering petals from strands of hair. A rustle next to me. I halted, my heart thudding as I tiptoed forward... forward... "RAWR!" The blonde girl leapt from the field, forming bear claws. She tapped me with a paw. "You're it!" And ran away.

"Not fair!" I whined as she scampered away to hide again. They both hid now. I held my arms out and let the soft petals caress my fingers. The susurrous flowers hid them, so I quit trying to tag them. They didn't play fairly and always ganged up on me.

I lay down in the field instead. Flowers squished under me as other blooms towered over, threatening storm clouds swirling in the sky above.

A song hummed far away. I sat up and surveyed the sea of yellow and ivory. Something sang to me. My eyes fell upon the forest. Ravenwood Forest. We weren't allowed in there. Monsters haunted it. But the singing came from there, growing louder and louder until...

Heavy drops of rain splattered on the ground, pounding against the soil and leaving red welts on my skin. I held my skirts and ran as fast as I could. Away from the heart-wrenching wailing.

Branches caught my dress, ripping away pieces of silk. One grabbed my hair, and I skidded to the muddying ground. I hissed as strands ripped.

Trees grew taller and further apart. Mist floated between trunks. I didn't know where I ran, but I had to run away. Stopping, I wrapped myself in my arms and started to spin. Round, round, round.

I collapsed to the ground and stretched my arm out. My fingers spread in the dirt, transforming into mud. Lifting my hand, I didn't see mud. Slick, gelatinous tendrils wrapped around my skin, leaving a chilling residue of dread. Its metallic scent lingered, a sinister bouquet of iron and fear, staining the air with a nefarious aura. The crimson stain, a haunting masterpiece, gleamed *malevolently against the stark contrast of my pale, trembling hand.*

Blood.

Thick burgundy liquid coated my palm. Tears trickled down my cheeks as a swishing approached. The brushing of a long cloak dragging along the dirt...

My body jolted upright. My mouth dropped into an inaudible shriek. Thrashing between sheets, my hands formed claws, and I swiped at all who dared to near me. A large male contained my assault with large blood-splattered arms and fatigue encouraged me to comply.

"You're safe, Wyn. You're safe." The massive body wrapped around me cooed. Strong steel and a hint of sensual, yet playful, cinnamon. Conláed. I recognised his scent before his voice. Another Fae trait I'd never noticed until now.

Molvys stood at the foot of the bed, arms crossed and face stern. Blood crusted over him as well. Dusty-pink and blush accented the room. My new Fae chamber.

I opened my mouth to speak, but no sound. Pushing from my lungs up my burning throat, the air stopped. The muscles used to produce my voice remained slack. I pounded my fist on the mattress.

"A *hiisi* sliced open your throat," Molvys described with his stern expression. I felt a bandage around my throat. A second one covered the left side of my jaw, with a third covering my right collarbone. A final bandage, the largest, curled around my left shoulder and arm, forming a sling.

Flickers of memories rendered. A red-haired woman straddling me. A hacking dagger. Billowing black smoke. A dark, foggy forest. Swooshing. A bright, ashen-grey light. And, finally, three terrifyingly grotesque creatures.

I attempted to speak again.

"Don't you dare! You're going to be scarred as is." A female dressed in ivory robes entered the room carrying fresh linens, a selenite bowl full of crystals, and jars. "I told your friends you'd be fine, but they wouldn't stop fretting. Especially this one." Her eyes darted to Conláed, who remained at my side.

Setting her supplies on a nearby table, she folded back the bandages to examine my wounds. "The bleeding has stopped. Just as I predicted. Good thing Molvys had my healing tincture on him, otherwise you may have lost all use of your arm."

She sifted through her bowl of crystals, stone tumbling against each other, finding one she approved of. A palm-sized tumbled amethyst. She placed it inside a knitted chain like a cage and looped it around my neck. "Your Fae blood allows you to heal rapidly, but this will assist against the mortal blood holding it back."

I shot Molvys and Conláed a scowl. They'd hid my heritage from me, too. How long did they know?

"We had to tell her. She needed to be aware of *what* she was dealing with," Molvys defended dryly. As my scowl darkened on Molvys, the female reached to spread a cream on my wound. I pulled away.

"She's a healer, Wyn," Conláed encouraged. I shook my head and pointed at my apothecary's chest.

"If only the king didn't eradicate all the Mind Fae," the healer mumbled. Conláed retrieved the chest for me as I inspected the female, contemplating what lay between her words.

"She's bold because she's the best in the court," Conláed whispered and winked at me.

I scoured the drawers, glass clinking on wood, gathering the ingredients needed for Grandmama's healing ointment. It would take time to create, but it would be helpful. The healer inspected the ingredients I gathered and with a nod of approval and slight surprise, she noted, "You're right, those ingredients can make a stronger healing agent. I'll make it, but for now, mine is better than nothing."

The healer removed all of my bandages and dressed the wounds.

"They're a lot better. When we fetched Meryl, they'd sliced your throat to the bone. Same with your arm. The tincture Molvys used clotted the blood temporarily," Conláed shared, gliding tender fingers along my shoulders. Molvys glared at the gesture.

"That's why you can't speak. But you will, in a few hours." Meryl displayed gentleness, along with thoroughness, in her work. "Whatever type of Fae you are, it's a strong bloodline. I've lost many patients to those demonic pests. You should be dead, but when I saw how well your injuries responded to my healing, I knew you'd be fine."

Meryl re-wrapped my bandages in fresh linens and pressed me into a mound of pillows. "Rest," she ordered, and left the room.

But how could I rest? I began to remember everything. Andraste taking Aramis in a cloud of smoke, disappearing the same way she did the other two times in the fortress using the ancient magic.

He kept so much hidden from me. Things I *should* have known so long ago. My family lied and Aramis did, too. But despite the lies and scheming, I had already forgiven him, because I trusted his misguided actions aimed at keeping me safe and at ease. He loved me and I loved him.

The moment the blade appeared at his throat and those cuffs around his wrists, the instinct to protect manifested. It quashed all emotions of ire and hate.

"Listen to the healer. Rest," Molvys commanded. His scowl lingered on Conláed for another split second before he left.

My body thrashed awake again. This time from Fifi shaking me. Her perky voice scolded Conláed laying next to me. I sighed at her frenzy.

"Elowyn, come quick!" She rushed to the fireplace as I rubbed dried sleep away. My body ached a little less. The shoulder Fifi shook loosened and mobility returned.

"What is it?" I asked groggily. "Wait, what?"

"Your voice is back!" Conláed grinned, the worried lines on his forehead softening.

"Thank fuck. Now I can yell at you." My voice cracked like rust. I punched Conláed's shoulder. I'd already decided to forgive Aramis, but my frustration with everyone else remained. "How long have you known about me being half-Fae?"

"What?" Fifi stopped mid step and gaped at me. Her eyes darted between me and Conláed, who rubbed his shoulder where I struck him.

"Well, at least the entire court didn't know." I threw my arms in the air and shifted my attention to Molvys. "And you. If one of you knows something, the other one does, too."

The two males made eye contact, silently debating on what information to feed me.

"No, tell me the truth. Don't pick and choose which truths to share." No one would lie to me anymore.

Conláed sighed and caved into my demands. "We've known the entire time. Since Aramis figured it out."

I fell back to the bed, rubbing my throat, hoarse from yelling. I think I already knew what he'd confessed to, but I needed to hear it from him. We were friends. Molvys, too—caring and encouraging in his own stern way.

As I sat silently, with all eyes on me, I contemplated everything. Aramis and his friends lied to me, choosing me because of being half-Fae, and wondering *why* they wanted me. To make sure the mortals didn't have a Fae on their side? They hated and feared me. I doubted they plotted to use my magic. But... Oulixeus. *You're more powerful than you even know.* He'd clearly had a plan before I left Rhyddean, one most likely involving me.

As if reading my mind, Molvys spoke. "Elowyn, it doesn't matter what we knew and how long we knew it for. Was it wrong for Aramis to keep it hidden for so long? Yes, I believe so. But I also believe he kept it hidden from you because he cares for your wellbeing. We all see that you're struggling to battle your demons, and he feared pushing you over the edge. But I understand why you're Fated. You allow him to be who he's meant to be. And he brings you the courage and strength you need to battle what haunts you. If... When you both work past it all, you'll be unstoppable. You'll be the change this realm— this entire world needs." Molvys' amber eyes glowed as if envisioning what the realm could be, sharing the same passion Aramis held for it.

I didn't recognize how Aramis and I fit together. Didn't understand the bond. Not like that. Aramis became the fire, igniting the strength of my darkness. And I tamed the violence flaming within him. Together we smouldered like an ember veiled in ash.

"I actually do have something important to show you all," Fifi spoke up, and we all glanced her way, momentarily forgetting her presence in the room, a rare occurrence. Guiding me to the hearth, a Fae I didn't notice before crouched in front of the flames. Dressed in dark red robes lined with golden lace. She turned to me, revealing a fully tattooed neck. Geometric shapes, triangles within triangles. Her eyes clouded in white. No trace of a pupil or iris.

Refocusing on the flames, she watched them intently. Her head whipped back and forth, up and down with each spark and flame. Ultimately concentrating on the centre of the inferno.

"She's a Priestess of Iros and a pyromancer," Conláed whispered, as I studied my friends.

Fifi observed the fire as if it may speak to her first. Her full lips, resembling Aramis', slightly parted. At first glance, I'd think the priestess's talent wowed her. But she constantly rubbed her hands. Her thumbs pressing into the opposite palm, like enough pressure on the nerves possessed the power to rescue her cousin.

Conláed refused to let me go, his hand fused to the small of my back. I imagined Aramis swiftly removing Conláed's hand from his body. Our friendship made Aramis nervous, and Andraste suggested Conláed would try something. As I stared at Conláed, he leaned toward the fire, and the corners of his lips lifted. Hopefulness. No, he'd never betray Aramis' trust—he just felt protective of me.

Molvys proved the most challenging to decipher, given his impassive expression, yet everyone possesses a tell. With his arms crossed, one hand continuously squeezed his bicep. A minor movement most wouldn't catch. Additionally, the dark, swollen marks under his heavy eyes disclosed his restless nights. Molvys worried.

Ashes sparked. Conláed stomped a large ember which landed on the carpet. Fifi flinched while Molvys held still. The heavier logs split to expose a forbidding, chasmal core. From within, an abyss of swirling shadows and ominous darkness clawed its way into existence, as if I had peered into the gateway of another realm, where secrets and terrors awaited, hidden within the heat of the inferno.

"He no longer walks this realm," the pyromancer illuminated in a low, lyrically eerie voice.

"Is he... *dead?*" Molvys implored. I held my breath. He couldn't be dead. My anger burned too intensely. He needed to be alive for me to unleash my fury, to confront his broken promises. He needed to witness the pain he'd inflicted, and above all, he needed to be alive so I could forgive him. For all of it—for running away, for the chaos I'd caused.

"He lives," she assured and relief washed over me.

"Where is he?" Molvys pressed.

"He's in the Shadow Realm," the priestess announced. She turned to face us and the cloud over her eyes dispersed, allowing glimmering blue irises to shine. Taking my tattooed hand, she said, "Fate."

"It's not a brand?"

"Oh no! No, this is no brand." Her eyes widened. "This is definitely the Fated bond. The tattoo shows his magic. Fire. And morphs into yours. Though I haven't seen these symbols before."

We both frowned. What type of magic did I possess? The pyromancer priestess continued, "If he dies, you'll feel it. It will feel as if you have died too. That's how strong the bond is. Rarely do Fated live without the other. If he dies, you probably will too."

I swallowed a lump of fear as she bowed and left the room. Falling onto the sofa, I leaned over my knees, letting my head hang between them. My blood rushed, and the room spun. "Well, do we know anyone who can take us there?" I asked dryly.

"You know about the Shadow Realm?" Molvys cocked a brow, seemingly impressed.

Staring at the ceiling, I sighed. "Yup, I learned about it while researching in the archives. Do you think they have a Shadow Fae working for them?"

Conláed shrugged his shoulders. "We haven't seen or heard from the Shadow Fae in centuries. It's possible they're working with the rebels."

Molvys leaned against the mantle. "Yes, it is," he agreed after mulling it over.

"How are we going to find a Fae with shadow magic to help us?" My brow arched.

"You mean how do Molvys and I find someone? You're still healing and staying in bed," Conláed interjected.

But I objected firmly, determined to bring Aramis home. Conláed sought support from Molvys, yet the brooding Fae simply left the room, leaving Conláed to mutter, "Helpful."

As I grappled to piece together our limited options, frustration set in. We possessed no leads to rescue Aramis, no information about the Shadow Realm, and no one to consult among the rebels. But a sudden realisation struck me. "What!" My voice strained through my tender throat as I recalled a small stroke of luck locked within the fortress. "Rune caught a spy."

Conláed spun around, strands of his sandy-hair falling in front of his face, and our shared thought shone through his cinnamon-brown eyes. "I'll go question them immediately."

"I'm going with you." My words carried the unwavering resolve of my desperate determination to rescue Aramis. I was prepared to journey to the furthest corners of this realm and beyond to reclaim my Fated Mate. However, a surprisingly firm hand seized my wrist, grounding me in the face of my relentlessness.

Fifi admonished me, emphasising the need to rest and heal. About to roll my eyes, her uncharacteristic seriousness halted my initial resistance. "Being fully healed and prepared to fight is more valuable to Aramis than remaining weak because you refuse to rest." And unable to dispute her logic, I allowed her to guide me back to bed as Conláed departed.

Molvys shortly returned with a stack of ancient tomes. He handed a book to each of us and instructed us to research. To analyse each word and read between the lines for any hint of the Shadow Realm.

"Are these from the archives?" I opened the book Molvys shoved in my hands.

"No. The library," he grunted.

My face scrunched, recalling the absence of a library. "There's a library?"

"Yes." He sat on the sofa and propped his weatherworn boots on my coffee table.

"Where?" Ignoring his boots dirtying my furniture, I examined the tome written in a foreign language. I didn't recognize the letters or shapes.

"It's not available for public use, same as the archives." Fifi interjected, crawling into the bed next to me. She lifted the blanket and made herself comfortable.

"Why not?" I recognized the mortal language written in her tome. I closed my book and held it out to her as she allowed me to silently steal hers.

"Oh, you know how it is. Give everyone a book and suddenly they all know what's best for the realm," she laughed.

We researched for two days. Molvys filled my room with stacks of ancient books accompanied by their musty, stale odour. Combing through hundreds of books, a way into the Shadow Realm remained hidden.

I sighed, flipping the fragile parchment. The edges scratched my thumb as they quickly fluttered. Briefly, a large square caught my attention. My thumb halted the pages, and I flipped back a couple of pages. There. A square drawn over two pages, filled with little lines. A maze with multiple large openings. As I studied it, the intricate lines in the middle changed, routes never remaining consistent.

"Go to sleep. I'll continue searching in the library," Molvys instructed.

My eyes fell to the orange-ombre sky darkening, souring my stomach. Another day without progress. What did the rebels want with him, anyway? Did they coerce him into negotiations?

"We'll find him." Fifi shared a gentle smile and squeezed my arm. I closed the book. No title on the spine or cover. I tucked it under a pillow to revisit.

Without warning, an intense pain soared through the centre of my body. My back arched and spasmed as I howled.

"Oh my gods, Elowyn!" Fifi's tome thudded on the stone. She gripped my body, attempting to lessen the spasms.

A pain so cold that it burned, exploded from the space between my breasts. As suddenly as it came, the pain dissipated. I drooped over Fifi's lap.

"What happened?" Fifi asked. The frigid burn returned to the side of my torso. I shrieked again. Clutching my side, I fell to the floor.

"Oh, gods!" Fifi joined my screaming, waving her hands in the air and hyperventilating. The pain worked its way deeper and deeper into me, like ice sliced open my entire side.

A door banged against a wall in the distance. "Find Meryl!" Molvys knelt next to me as Fifi darted for help. He lifted me with ease and returned me to bed, checking the area I clutched beneath my nightgown.

The pain receded. I panted and gawked at my side. Nothing. No marks. No redness. We shared a confused expression.

Fifi returned with Meryl and the priestess. The healer checked my vitals as I explained what I felt. Before I finished, another jolt of pain pierced my cheek. This time feeling as if a sharp point impaled my flesh straight into one cheek, through my tongue, and out the other side. I screeched and squeezed my face with my hands. Legs frantically kicking before it subsided.

"He's being tortured. You're feeling his pain. It's the Fated bond," the priestess concluded. Tortured? The rebels were torturing Aramis? My anger exploded.

"I need to find him," I growled at Molvys.

"We need to find a way *there*," Molvys reminded me. A hint of compassion glimmered in his dark eyes. We had one thing in common. He refused to quit and so did I.

CHAPTER 44

The air hung heavy with the acrid scent of smouldering embers, and torchlight cast grotesque, flickering shadows on the rough-hewn stone walls as the male swung back and forth, the chains groaning with each rock. Ominous etchings marked the stone behind him, as if others desperately attempted to claw their way out.

He appeared so plain. Almost deliberately common, as if he'd made an art of blending into the crowd. With a face of classic handsomeness, he had perfectly symmetrical features and high cheekbones—like most Fae—and a straight nose. His hair flowed like a billowing, dark cloud, caught in an invisible breeze surrounding his face in a captivating vortex of rich brown strands.

Each step I took on the uneven, blood-red flagstone floor echoed with a sinister resonance, as if the very stones whispered secrets of suffering. As I neared the spy, the air was thick and oppressive, suffocating hope with every breath, but not my hope—*his*. The occasional drip of blood from the slices across his torso reminded me of Aramis' suffering and fed the anger within me.

He held my gaze with eyes, a shade of a pale grey storm, holding a depth of magic he yearned to use, but the iron constricted. "Hey," the prisoner spoke with a voice like a gentle breeze, soothing and measured. It was the first moment he spoke directly to me. For hours, I stood in the corner observing him as Conláed and Rune questioned him about the rebels and the Shadow Realm.

His expressions revealed little. To the casual observer, he would appear entirely ordinary, innocent. But his enigmatic demeanour suggested he held hidden knowledge, setting him apart from the rest. Though I *still* couldn't spot his tell. The entire time, he shared the truth—he knew nothing of Aramis' whereabouts—or he lied better than me.

My jaw tightened as I fixed a piercing gaze on the spy. Conláed's patience had already worn thin, and with his continuous pacing of the crimson-stained floors, I knew it wouldn't be long before he exploded. Yet, while Conláed's agitation grew more palpable with each passing stride, Rune, seated at the corner of the dimly lit chamber, remained an epitome of calm and composure, his steady gaze never wavering from the unfolding confrontation.

"Is Aramis in the Shadow Realm?" I demanded, urgency and frustration simmering beneath my controlled tone. With Conláed's growing irritation, and Rune's extremely passive exterior, I'd find a balance between the two.

The spy leaned his head back, chains rattling as he fit his head between his suspended arms, a sardonic smile playing on his lips. "Oh, dear Aramis... You've been searching for him tirelessly, haven't you?" His eyes darted to the magical ink peeking beneath my sleeve. The material hid most of it, but a few marks swirled onto my hand, and this spy had noticed them. My fingernails dug into my palm as a spark flared within me.

Keep control, I reminded myself. Each passing day, my magic stirred within me, a volatile force that I feared might ignite at the most inopportune moment. "Quit the theatrics," I breathed fiercely, my voice struggling to maintain composure.

Conláed's patience snapped as he slammed a fist into the stone wall, causing it to crack. "We've had enough of your insolence! Tell us how to get to him!"

My shoulders tensed at the sudden motion and I dared to de-escalate the situation with a hand on his back as he made his way over to the hanging prisoner. "Conláed—"

The spy's eyes glittered with mocking amusement. "And what if I don't?"

A cold knot of frustration twisted inside of me. My heart pounded, and a rush of heat flushed my cheeks, though I wasn't sure if it was the spy's responses, Conláed's growing wrath, or my magic.

Conláed leaned in, his eyes blazing with anger, and grabbed the nape of the spy's neck. "You'll regret it. Now, tell us how to get to the Shadow Realm."

A shiver of dread coursed through me as an unsettling storm brewed within my friend's eyes. I gripped the back of Conláed's shirt as a silent plea for him to back off, but his body temperature rapidly rose, making my skin prickle at the looming fire storm. My own magic churned within me, a turbulent current warning of the impending deluge.

The spy's grin dropped as he spoke clearer than a winter's night. "I don't know."

And he spoke true. I knew it. But before I could intervene, fire erupted from Conláed's arms and quickly caught the skin of the prisoner. The magic rushed so fast, I still held on to the male and my hand, still gripping his shirt, burned.

A chair tumbled in the distance as the prisoner wailed and Rune wrapped his arms around me, pulling me away from the blazing hurricane growing in the dark dungeon. "Conláed, stop!" I ordered as his magic grew to an unbearable force and Rune's strength continued to pull me away. "He's telling the truth. Stop it!"

"He can't hear you," Rune grunted, thrusting me from the cell. And Rune was right, Conláed didn't hear me, and within seconds the prisoner—our one informant to find Aramis—was dead.

CHAPTER 45

My footsteps echoed through the dimly lit corridors—the fortress seemingly darker since Aramis' capture—as I fled from the cruel reality behind me. For the first time since my forced betrothal, the fortress felt like a prison, the weight of Conláed's careless mistake pressing down upon me like the very walls themselves. My heart pounded in my chest, a frenzied drumbeat matching the storm raging within.

The anger seethed within me, bubbling over in a molten fury. Conláed incinerated our last hope. My vision swam with tears of frustration and I needed an escape, a way to dull the agonising edge of my emotions and the magic I felt growing within me at an alarming rate. So similar to the night in the woods.

The spiral staircase leading to the cellar was treacherous. I had ordered the blunt head chef to point out its location, and upon seeing me—the sleep deprivation from phantom pains, the agony of losing Aramis ripping at me, and now this—she had withheld all of her smart remarks and steered me true. I clung to the rough stone railing as I descended, my fingers trembling with tension. Ancient wood and dampness made the air musty and thick, a sinister veil that embraced me like a shroud, promising quick solace.

I stumbled into the underground chamber and studied the rows of dusty wine barrels, some ancient and cracked, lining the damp, uneven walls. The rich, earthy aroma of wine filled the air, and the soft sound of liquid sloshing in the wooden confine of the barrel I leaned on whispered temptation into my ears.

Wine would help me, as it always did before. It would numb the darkness I didn't know how to control. The darkness I learned was my magic, a part of me, not a curse.

My thoughts were shrouded in shadows, haunted by the allure of that liquid escape. The dark, twisted tendrils of desire coiled around my consciousness, promising numbness, forgetting, and a respite from the relentless storm of life. With wine, the world would cease to exist. It was only me and the relentless whisper of temptation that coursed through my veins.

I rested my hand on a dark green bottle, the glass cool to the touch. My inner struggle played out in silence, a bitter battle waged within my mind. Each moment of resistance was a tortured symphony of longing, a dark aria of cravings and regrets. The room remained still, my nails clicking on the glass was the only sound, but within me, a hurricane raged, threatening to devour the fragile threads of my resolve.

I yearned for the comfort of the bottle, the illusion of control it provided. I had been a slave to its call for far too long, and the gnawing need clawed at my insides. But as each nail clinked, I recalled how the alcohol never really saved me from the turmoil in my heart, nor from the unpredictable and wild magic that surged within me.

Resting my full palm on the chilled bottle, fingers trembling on the glass, I recognised that no one, or nothing, would save me. Not that spy. Not my new friends. Not my Mate. And certainly not this liquid. As my heart warred against my own poisoned instincts, I grabbed the bottle and hauled it across the room. It shattered against the stone floor, sending a dark liquid splattering across the cellar like a gruesome omen. My anger violently pulsed through me, and my magic joined it.

The room quivered as invisible forces tore at the cellar walls. Barrels toppled and cracked, their contents spilling onto the ground, staining everything a deep crimson. And as my senses filled with chaos, dust and shards of wood dancing in the air, I grabbed bottles, smashing them into stone and wood. My body, and the room, trembled, trapped between my fury and the unpredictable energy that coursed through my veins.

Slowing my breath to ragged gasps, I stared at the wreckage around me, a manifestation of my inner turmoil. My magic reigned itself in, recognising my exhaustion.

One bottle remained untouched. Clear, filled with a lavender liquid. I picked it up and removed the cork with a pop. Its aroma replicated delicate wildflowers and radiant sunrises. A threatening tear bubbled in the corner of my eye as I imagined lying next to Aramis on the mountain, the sunrise warming our sleeping figures.

I hurled it to the floor and my sanity shattered with the glass as I bared my teeth with a guttural scream. Cursing the wickedness of my life and challenging the rebels to break us, to break me and the darkness I had no choice but to confront.

CHAPTER 46

A *boot kicked the side of my ribs. Not roughly, just a gentle nudge forcing me to wake. I knew where I lay before opening my eyes as the scent of rain and mud swirled around me. I needed to stop waking in Ravenwood Forest. The wailing and shrieking tormented me, and I just wanted to bury it far, far away.*

"What do you want?" I groaned, pushing myself up. Even in my nightmare, I felt like shit.

"What are you doing?" A disappointment that cut into me like a sharp blade edged the cloaked figure's question.

"Surviving. Like I always have." I leaned my elbows on my knees and pushed a heel into the muddy earth I sat on.

"You're stronger than this. And if you didn't push me away for so long, you may have learned how to use your magic instead of suppressing it and saved Aramis instead of allowing him to be taken."

"Allowed?" My glare dug into him. "This isn't my fault!"

"Isn't it? You had months to work with me, but you kept denying the truth you knew deep down."

"Fuck you," I spat.

"What are you going to do, Elowyn? Drink yourself to death?"

"No. I didn't touch a drop." I had come too far to revert back.

"Then what—"

"I don't know!" I didn't have the patience for this and so I closed my eyes to push him away again.

But he recognised my attempt and pushed back. I felt his energy. No. His magic. And it's like it possessed an imprint close to mine. Wild. Chaotic. Edged with a ruthless darkness.

"I'm going to steal the Book, and take it to Rhyddean. Make sure Cara's actually safe before I die." I'd thought about it for a while now. As each day passed without any further knowledge into the Shadow Realm, I thought more and more about Cara.

Did she truly write and send the note?

Did someone try to manipulate me?

I wanted to continue with my task, just to be certain. And with Aramis gone, it'd be easier.

"But you'll die," the cloaked figure whispered.

"Yes, thank you for pointing out the obvious. I've been told what this Fated bond means." I held up my tattooed arm as I spoke. "Don't patronise me, demon!"

"I think you know by now that I'm not a demon, Elowyn."

"Shut up." I didn't care about him anymore, he kept annoying me, and I didn't want to accept anymore truths.

"You will not die. Go save your mate and live."

"What if my fate is to meet death? Whatever happened back there—" I gestured toward the wildflower field and the desperate cries. "Maybe I meant to die there. Or locked in my tower without Oulixeus' interference. How many times do I have to keep surviving to accept the inevitable?"

"If fate wished you an early death, you'd be dead. You're destined for so much more. Use your perceptiveness. Use your magic. And find a way to save your mate."

"Why do you want him alive?"

"I don't. I want you alive."

"I don't know how to use my magic. You're the one who pushed it into me."

"No, I didn't. I simply reminded your spirit of what it felt like, so that you'll recognise it and know how to channel it. In the forest when Andraste attacked you, that's exactly how you used your magic. Your fear grew so strong that your magic instinctively came forth, ready to defend *you. This time, your body understood not to fear it. So you used it. Use it again, Elowyn. And save yourself."*

"Why do you care so much about whether I live or die?"

"Succeed in this, Elowyn, and I'll reveal everything. There's just no time now."

As the rain soaked my hair and washed away the soreness plaguing me, I thought of the cryptic messages he fed me over the past month. And now he offered me a chance to learn everything. Uncertainty chewed at me, but the lure of answers, the promise of understanding the enigma that had tormented me for so long, was too tantalising to resist.

My heart was a drumbeat of exhaustion, the darkness that had pervaded my life seemed insurmountable, and all hope had nearly slipped through my fingers like sand. But in that rain-soaked moment, hope slowly returned. Hope to finally learn my full truth and to save Aramis. If the demon believed there was a chance, then there must be.

Feeling a glimmer of hope and control, I nodded my head and silently accepted the challenge.

CHAPTER 47

I glowered at the eggs I stabbed over and over, imagining the fork as a thick trident piercing through Andraste's body. She needed to die. She'd attempted to kill me multiple times, came close to slaying Kenna, had an unknown co-conspirator within the fortress, and now she stole Aramis from me all because of her vindictiveness.

An ethereal glow from the morning sun illuminated the dining room of my apartment, highlighting the floating specks of dust like falling stars shimmering out of place. The gentle breeze presented the promise of a mild day, uplifting florals mixing with the essence of fresh rushing water from the river below, encouraging a positive outlook. But none of it penetrated through my wrathful shell.

"Elle, please *eat* your breakfast," Fifi pleaded, but I scowled at the plate before me. My mood soured the grand meal, coating my tongue with a wave of acrid bitterness, like a sinister reminder of my life, leaving an unsettling aftertaste clinging to my senses, casting a shadow over my palate.

I dropped my fork and pushed my plate away as silver clanged on porcelain. After the demon's speech, a week before, I dove head-first into the archives and library, scouring texts for clues and answers. It made Fifi distraught, claiming I had lost too much weight, not eating or sleeping enough. Not that I got much rest with the torture I felt through the bond, anyway. But I became almost as thin as Linnaea, the definition in my cheeks growing hollow, my bone protruding and skin stretching in an attempt to keep me whole. The linen nightgown I wore for three days straight now drowned me.

Fifi brought Kenna and Aideen, Aramis' youngest sister, in hopes I'd eat something and put my books away if not for myself, then at least to be polite.

Both daughters shared fiery red hair. A trait inherited from their mother's side, Aideen informed me. Chatty for a child of twelve, conceived during the last orbit of Light Bearer.

"Mamma is an Earth Fae and the Earth Fae have all sorts of hair colours," she elaborated in her darling raspy voice. "Just like flowers."

Kenna leaned over and whispered, "Eggs don't replicate the feel of flesh. Stab the ham." She flashed a devilish grin before popping a piece of ham into her mouth and sliding my plate back towards me. For how regal Kenna portrayed herself, a ferocious warrior lay beneath her exterior, one to be cautious of.

She didn't wear her warrior clothing at breakfast. She dressed in billowing silk pants and a crop top displaying a pierced navel. The dark royal blue allowed her vibrant red hair to shine and complimented the emerald in her eyes. The same colour as Aramis', though instead of golden flecks, stripes of chartreuse rippled through them. Her irises didn't flicker like wild flames either. The shades of emerald and chartreuse waved like leaves floating in the wind.

"Seriously?" Fifi flashed Kenna a look of disappointment, which only made Kenna's smile grow. I never spent time with my sisters, but I imagined this to be the typical way a family interacted, bringing a sad smile to my face.

"What?" Kenna shrugged a shoulder and neatly cut a piece of ham, shoving it into her mouth and chewing it slowly, using the smacking of her lips to make a show of it to Fifi. Aideen giggled and sipped on her glass of fragrant elderflower juice.

"Are Molvys and Conláed guarding my doors again? Just like old times?" I scoffed at everyone's overprotectiveness. It slightly reminded me of being trapped in Elmswood Castle, but I knew their observations stemmed from genuine care. Not fear and hatred.

"No. That's what the three of us are doing here. One of us will be with you at all times. Molvys and Conláed are at the council meeting, I think."

I stopped stabbing and stared at Fifi. She continued to eat her eggs and avocado, not even realising the shift in my demeanour.

"The council is meeting? To discuss Aramis' rescue?"

"Oh, I don't know. I don't really pay attention to—"

"No. They're not discussing Aramis' rescue. They've been focusing on fortifying the city for another attack," Kenna interrupted, but speaking without a hint of concern for her brother.

"And this doesn't bother anyone?"

"Of course it does, but we can't do anything about it," Fifi spoke calmly, still focused on her breakfast. My shoulders slumped over the table and my head fell between my arms, defeated yet again.

"Elowyn, you say he's in the Shadow Realm. I don't think there's much the council can do, anyway." Kenna reached for the steaming, buttery potatoes, her attitude suggesting complete indifference for losing her brother.

My lips parted in shock at her statement. "That's ridiculous, Kenna." Her features proved difficult to decipher, but the subtle undulations of her irises conveyed an instinctual sense that she harboured secrets. "Old and ancient Fae sit on the council. Supposed intelligent minds, specialising in certain areas. How can they not pull their resources together and help?"

Fifi reached a supportive hand toward me. "It's best to leave it be—"

"No!" My chair toppled to the ground behind me with my force. "I refuse to accept that." A harsh pinch formed on my lower back, and my muscles spasmed in agony. I collapsed, grinding my teeth to suppress a scream forging in my lungs.

"Elowyn!" Kenna and Fifi jumped to my aid. The acute pain dissipated, and I sat tall. Kenna's thin brows furrowed. "Shit, Elowyn. What happened?"

Molvys insisted we keep our torture theory quiet. He made Meryl, the priestess, Fifi, and I vow secrecy, going as far as forcing the priestess to cast a binding spell. If anyone broke the vow, our tongues would dissolve into a liquid. Molvys stated that revealing Aramis' torture possibly weakened his position, and spreading knowledge about our connection might endanger both of us.

"Phantom pains from the other night," I lied, and Fifi squeezed her fingers together. Kenna's wrinkled forehead conveyed her skepticism of my excuse, but she didn't press for the truth, either.

Fifi shooed the fiery sisters from my apartment as I squeezed my arm, attempting to focus on something other than the piercing slice along my torso. I bit my lip to keep from screaming and the skin burst, sending trickles of coppery liquid into my mouth.

"Oh, my gods!" Fifi rushed back into the dining room and pushed a handkerchief against my cut. And just as the other times, the pain vanished within seconds. Regaining my composure, I ordered Fifi to stay behind while I shared a piece of my mind with the council.

CHAPTER 48

Marching through the marbled corridors and lush courtyards at my quick pace heightened my fury. My anger simmered like a turbulent sea, and with each step, it grew more palpable. I swelled with a determination to confront the council, to make them feel the weight of their inaction with every accusing word hurrying to escape my lips.

Towering doors stood at the end of the final hallway, veins of charcoal crawling across the pristine white marble like deception slowly invading altruistic rule. I clenched my fists, straining the muscles in my wrists. The immense columns lining the hall loomed over me, warning me to back down—reminding me I didn't belong. But fuck that. I belonged in this court, and I refused to tolerate this rejection any longer.

Despite my weakened and starved body, I pushed open the dense doors with a wrathful force and they groaned through the movement. The chatter amongst the council members ceased and all seven scowled at my interruption. I saw neither Molvys nor Conláed, as Fifi had assumed earlier.

"Guards. Escort the Princess to her chamber," Sir Haldwin ordered, without hesitation, not even a single glance at me, and two soldiers stationed by the doors seized my arms.

"Get your hands off of me," I shouted, struggling in their grip. Haldwin's face eased at his easy victory. I didn't know what to do. I didn't possess the physical strength to fight. My magic stayed stagnant. It didn't spark the way the demon described in moments of need.

"Release her, you morons," Conláed scolded the guards holding me. Instantly, they obeyed. And despite his recent fuck up, I was grateful for his help. "Are you okay?"

"Yeah." I turned to see Conláed, Molvys, and Kenna striding in.

"She isn't a member of the council, nor is she welcome here. She needs to leave," Haldwin announced to the newcomers.

"Not until I've said what I need to say." I straightened my posture and lifted my chin. I looked ridiculous in my dirty nightgown, surrounded by elegantly dressed Fae. But they no longer intimidated me. Not anymore. Aramis needed me to be strong. To have courage.

Exasperated, Sir Haldwin raised his hand. "Fine, speak mortal." I suppressed a grin. The council remained unaware of my secret. Good.

With a strong posture, I stood at the head of the table. Molvys and Conláed flanked me like personal bodyguards. I braced my hands on the table and inspected each council member. The icy touch of the smooth stone beneath my fingertips sent a shiver down my spine as I evaluated them. Absorbing their judgement. Allowing their disdain to fuel me.

Seven. Seven council members and not an ally within a single one.

"I've been led to believe you are not searching for your high king," I summoned a superior tone.

"He is lost. The rebels are barbarous. He's most likely dead. What we *can* do is repair the city, build our defences, and prep our next ruler," Sir Haldwin curtly shared. All eyes turned to Kenna leaning against the door frame, shoulders relaxed, one foot crossed over the other. Did she want to be high queen? Was that why she'd encouraged me to accept her brother's fate?

I watched the council of Fae, convened in all their grandeur, their ethereal beauty marred by the darkness of their intentions. Multiple voices spoke. Beginning as a discordant murmur of dissent quickly escalated into a cacophonous symphony of anger, wild-eyed, and voices lashing out like whips.

Some shouted vehemently, their words like barbed arrows seeking the hearts of their adversaries. Molvys stepped into Sir Haldwin's space, using his debating skills to threaten the male, while Conláed pushed a guard into the wall, unsheathing his sword.

The council chamber, a space meant to be a sanctuary of wisdom and unity, had transformed into a battlefield of chaos and distrust. I clenched my fists, my anger deepening. From the moment they'd first dismissed me, I sensed they masqueraded as nothing more than a facade of power and authority, and they had finally laid their true nature bare for all to see.

All the while, Kenna leaned against the door frame and observed me.

He is lost. The council refused to help. Refused to rescue their sovereign. No loyalty whatsoever. My father, or I guess stepfather Evander, commanded greater loyalty than this. Shit, Oulixeus' hired spies and mercenaries showed his diabolical ass more allegiance.

"Quiet," I said to the room. No one heard me. They continued to shout and argue. A familiar fog rolled into my vision. A high-pitched ringing pierced through the room's frenzy. "Shut up!"

Silence took the room. I slowly swivelled to Sir Haldwin. "You're the high king's advisor, correct? That's the role you play?"

"Yes," he cocked a brow.

"And you currently don't have a high king to advise," I noted. He frowned.

"We are preparing for the next ruler!" he objected. I threw him a contemptuous smirk.

"So, whenever your high king disappears, you abandon him and move to the next heir? Is that not treason? I believe treason calls for resignation."

"Excuse me? You, a mortal, will not enter this chamber, accuse me of treason, and demand my resignation! Members of the council do not resign. We serve for life!"

"Thank you for the reminder." Allowing my intimidating smirk to fester within, my anger built, being mortared stone by stone into something strong and fortified. And then it happened. That spark, tiny yet brilliant, ignited deep within my core. Threads of magic, iridescent and unyielding, weaved through my veins. My fingertips tingled, yearning to touch the elusive threads of fate.

The demon told me the magic would instinctively come forth. I just needed to be open to receive it. And this time, I tugged at those threads, coaxing it forward.

A gust of icy wind rushed through the windows, knocking over a planter resting on the windowsill, shattering clay across the marbled floor. Menacing clouds blanketed the sky as the surrounding room blurred, my focus turning inward, drawn to the incandescent current flowing through me. Fear and anger acted as the catalysts, but I needed to comprehend, to control, my newfound power. I closed my eyes, willing the emerging storm's fury to mirror the tempest within. A bolt of lightning streaked across the heavens. I felt a resonance, a shared heartbeat.

With a surge of determination, I stretched out my hand, fingers trembling, and relished in the tingling sensation flowing through me. The air crackled with energy, a charged atmosphere seemingly drawing the brewing storm nearer.

My heart raced in synchrony with the storm's tumultuous rhythm. I tasted the power on my tongue, a heady mix of anticipation and trepidation. However, the moment to shed my fear had arrived.

I still didn't know *how* to use the magic or *what* I could do with it, so I mimicked the motions from the night Andraste and her monsters attacked me. Puckering my lips into the shape of an *O*, I gently blew air toward him and the energy understood my intention. A bright, ashen-grey light flowed through my veins, amplifying my blood. My pulse. My existence.

Sir Haldwin's brows remained furrowed, uncertain of my actions. The other council members realised before he did. Gasps circled the table as others saw pieces of Sir Haldwin breaking off into ash and floating away.

The ancient Fae advisor noticed the other's reaction, confused, until his hands began to flake away. He cast his shock and horror at me as realisation dawned on him.

"Impossible," he whispered before I blew harder and the rest of him drifted away.

The room remained speechless, an unnatural silence hanging in the air. "On behalf of our high king, I assign his closest and most trusted friend to replace Sir Haldwin.

Molvys, please take your seat," I announced. The council glared at me. Molvys strode to where Sir Haldwin's ashes lay and brushed them to the floor before sitting.

My teachings from Rhyddean suggested the necessity of constructing a well-rounded council to guarantee equality for everyone's needs. But I required individuals I trusted, and doubting Molvys' loyalty to Aramis proved to be an impossibility. He'd make a valuable ally within the council.

"You can't do this! You are not married to Aramis, you are not the high queen," a light-haired female on the opposite end of the table shouted. She wore a silver gauzy dress cinched at the waist with a metal corset, a warrior.

"Yet," I muttered, the promise of a darker fate hanging in the hushed silence.

"Never!" She rose and slammed a fist on the stone with a fury that shook the stone beneath her hand. I climbed atop my chair and strode along the plank of ominous black stone, casting an intimidating shadow over the council members. They cowered in their seats, their once-proud postures now slumping, and their arrogant facades crumbling under the intensity of my gaze. I fixated on the defiant woman, her earlier bravado now reduced to a mere ember, her body shrinking into the chair as if seeking refuge within its cushioned sanctuary. Her eyes, once ablaze with defiance, had dimmed, her lips tightly pressed together in a desperate attempt to maintain composure. But the fragile threads of her resolve were unravelling, and I could see the vulnerability beneath the cracks of her expression.

Midway across the table, another burst of frigid pain hit me, coursing along the length of my right leg. I halted, refusing to yield to the agony threatening to engulf me. The pause, however, held greater impact than any words, sending shivers down their spines.

"Please," the defiant female stammered, her courage faltering. I allowed a triumphant smirk to creep across my face even as I pressed on, my barefoot prowl tainted by a slight limp. My right foot turned slightly inward, a testament to the wrenching pain surging through my calf.

I would become a reminder. A symbol. I possessed no legal claim to their court, no royal bloodline, nor great riches, nor feared armies. But I had power, and in this realm, power surpassed all.

Squatting before her, I rested my elbows on my linen-covered knees, my lips puckering into the sinister *O* shape. She flinched and shielded herself behind her forearms. Laughter bubbled from within me, taunting her fear.

After a tense moment, she dared to peek, her shoulders sagging in relief as she realised her form remained intact. Her defiant gaze met mine, and within her upturned eyes, a challenge sparkled.

With her challenge, I cocked my head to the left.

SNAP.

A sickening crack of bone reverberated, instantly killing her. Her once-powerful, muscular form slumped lifelessly in the chair. Gasps followed. Rising to my feet, I surveyed the council, daring them to question further. Waiting to see who else wanted to... retire. Yet they remained quiet.

The pain tormenting me vanished, replaced by an air of undeniable confidence as I gradually retraced my steps to the far end of the table. "What was her position?"

"Iniga was the Lead War General," Molvys announced.

"Conláed, you've been promoted. You're now the Lead War General." His eyes widened as he helped me descend from the table. I hadn't fully forgiven him for killing the spy, but I couldn't deny his loyalty to Aramis and me. "Your high king is *not* dead. Here is your proof."

And against Molvys' guidance, I pulled back the sleeve of my nightgown to reveal the Fated Bond marking my left arm. Various members gaped at the revelation, while others made the holy mark across their chest.

"You're Fae," a white-haired male whispered. But I continued without acknowledging him.

"Your top priority is to find Aramis. If I discover more plotting to overthrow him, I will *retire* more members."

Kenna remained leaning against the doorframe, a knavish grin painted across her lips. At that moment, I didn't know what to make of her. She was Aramis' sister, but did her allegiance entirely align with his? While the council prepared to crown her high queen, she appeared indifferent. Not encouraging, nor discouraging. With a curt nod of her chin—almost like I'd impressed her—she turned and sauntered from the room.

CHAPTER 49

A hushed flutter of parchment hummed as Molvys thumbed through an ancient text, his dirty boots propped on my coffee table. We resumed our research in my chambers with extra guards as a security measure. The stoic Fae believed my *stunt*—as he referred to it—may provoke a council member or two to send an assassin. So Fifi periodically left to retrieve more books to study, bringing back obscure texts, frustrating Molvys.

"Fifi, seriously, none of these are helpful!" He scoffed and tossed a giant tome onto the table with a loud thud. I understood his increasing frustration, but none of us knew what to search for.

"That's not nice, Molvys. Let me see." I gathered a few of the new books, but Fifi ripped them from my grasp, insisting I don't strain myself. The torture I felt through the bond intensified to the point of exhaustion. How did Aramis fare?

The aged, cracked paper covetously absorbed the oils from my skin, desperate for hydration. Flipping through the pages, I recognised it as the book about witchcraft I studied in the archives. Exuding a musty, haunting aroma, withholding secrets from centuries past, it seemed to whisper ancient incantations beneath my fingers, beginning to tremble with an eerie chill imbued into the air.

Familiar symbols and passages leapt from the parchment, each attempting to persuade me to study further, but I ignored them all. An intuition insisted the answer lay deeper in these pages, and refused to accept any other distraction. As the pages rippled against my thumb, a sharp jolt shocked me. There. Pausing on the page, I stared at the symbol calling to me, insisting we've met before.

Witch's mark.

I stroked the script back and forth, wondering. Where had I seen this mark before? And just as sudden as the jolt which shocked me, I recalled the stone tied around the mortal-in-hiding in the market. She wore this mark carved onto her necklace, confirming my suspicions of her magical gifts.

For the first time since Aramis showed me his secret place, I felt light. A dread that oppressed me for weeks faltered, breaking way to hope. The authors of this text believed witches possessed the power to travel to the Shadow Realm, and I had access to one.

An uncontrollable glee rushed through me, and I parted my lips, ready to share my discovery and suspicions with my friends, but hesitated. Aramis—and the others, for all I knew—desired to kill all Gifted mortals. Was saving Aramis worth endangering this woman? I needed to get Aramis back, but I didn't want to betray someone to do it, no matter how little I knew of her.

Fuck.

I swallowed the acidic bile rising in my throat and closed the text. Making my decision, I brewed a strong concoction Grandmama taught me. A brew that gifted stealthy escapes.

CHAPTER 50

Midnight approached. Fifi sprawled on my bed next to me in a sound sleep, a thin line of drool spilling from the corner of her mouth as her nose created a soft rumble of snores. Molvys had passed out on the sofa. His neck was kinked uncomfortably, and I felt guilty for the soreness he'd feel in the morning. But I had to do this.

Pulling a light, silky cloak over me and my training clothes, I gently opened the apartment door, leaving my sedated friends behind. The guards standing watch were slumped on the floor, sharing Grandmama's potent brew with them, too.

Within the moonlit tapestry of night, I slipped through the corridors I had grown familiar with, treading softly, the soles of my shoes caressing cool marble. I darted through the shadows, a phantom navigating the lines of the known and uncharted. The portraits of bygone rulers gazed down at me, their painted eyes bearing witness to my transgression.

A flicker of candlelight spilled from a partially ajar door ahead, right in the direction I travelled. Two guards shared stories and laughter, their armour glinting like a silent warning. Receding into an alcove, the lacework of shadows became my sanctuary. They passed by, the echo of their footsteps fading into silence.

I emerged, a whisper against the tapestried walls. The corridor yawned before me, its end concealed by a veil of uncertainty. I could almost hear the collective breath of the fortress, its ancient stones holding secrets that dared not speak.

As I tiptoed forward, approaching my exit, the air cooled. The moon lent its luminescence to my path, painting ethereal patterns on the marbled floors. A guard patrolled ahead, his footsteps rhythmic and steady. I retreated, seeking solace within a niche carved into the wall, my breath suspended in the space between heartbeats. His gaze swept over the shadows I allowed to conceal me, and then moved on, oblivious to his future high queen.

The fortress came alive with murmurs, the night a symphony of secrets. I descended a winding staircase, its steps worn by the passage of time. The grand gallery opened before me, its windows like portals to the night sky. Bathed in starlight, I stood amidst the whispers of forgotten generations, my reflection cast upon the polished marble floor.

A distant clock chimed, a solemn reminder that time was my enemy, and slipped into the corridor leading to the kitchen. My heart swelled with a mixture of exhilaration and trepidation, gaining a thrill from the rebellious action. It's why I risked so much with Cara. But the fear of being caught formed an uncomfortable pit in my stomach.

At last, I reached the kitchen, concealed in the far corner of the fortress. Beams of light cascaded over the eerily quiet room, melding with the remaining aromas of savoury meats contrasting with sweet fruit pastries, its waltz from the day finished. In a few hours, the kitchen staff would resume their work, so I marched toward the back door, ready to save Aramis.

CHAPTER 51

Beneath the canopy of a starlit night, I weaved through the cobblestone stress of Stoneshalt. My entire body shivered as I attempted to retrace my steps to the market, following the mental map I'd made from all those nights admiring the city from the balcony. The air was alive with whispers of enchantment, as if the very fabric of reality had been stitched with threads of magic and intrigue. Like finally accepting the magic within me had helped me sense it in the world.

My steps were hushed, my breath held, for I moved as a mere shadow myself, not wanting the shivers plaguing me to show through. The rebels tortured Aramis again. Using some kind of weapon or magic to make him freezing cold. In my short time here, I'd learned it was near impossible to make a Fire Fae cold, and the ice shooting through my veins made me nervous about Aramis' fate. *Our* fate.

The streets paraded as a masquerade, painted with the vibrant hues of euphoric dreams. Taverns spilled their mirth onto cobblestone streets, their warm light flickering like fireflies trapped in jars. Laughter cascaded like a symphony, rising and falling with the rhythm of life thriving in this mystical realm.

A body pushed into me, driving me into a stone wall. A jagged brick tore into my cloak and scraped my skin. Such a small cut, but agonising with the pain I shared with Aramis. Catching my stumbling body, I came up to the gambling houses beckoning with promise of fortune and folly, their doors opening to reveal the heartbeats of risk takers and fate chasers.

Fae crowded around tables, shouting and cheering, tossing coins and tiles onto sticky wooden tables. One male in particular caught my attention. The way the pot in the centre of the table dazzled him and made him lick his lips sent a sudden jolt of ignominy through me. Was I like him? So transfixed by the win that I ignored everything happening around me, the way this male ignored the female massaging his shoulders and the brawl forming behind him.

While I always paid attention to my surroundings, I became so distracted that I failed to recognize how Oulixeus had exploited me and concealed information.

Yet, amidst the revelry, my gaze remained steadfast, my heart a compass pointing toward a single goal—the witch holding the power to travel to the Shadow Realm.

A shout rang out on the far side of the street, closer to the fortress. Guards held torches high into the sky. I counted five, prowling like wolves, their eyes glinting with suspicion.

Fuck.

Conláed's voice rang out into the crowd commanding orders to his squad, most likely having discovered the sedated guards and our friends in my chambers. As a friend, Conláed had grown protective of me. So my disappearance with the rebels breaking into the fortress so frequently had probably sent him into a state of panic. As much as I wanted to comfort him and tell him I was fine, I couldn't. So I conspired with the very essence of the night to remain unseen, to sway with the breeze and meld into the rambunctious crowd.

I sculpted myself as a ghost, flitting between pockets of light and shadow, guided only by the glow of my purpose. The music seemed to know my secret, its melody concealing my footfalls as I traversed alleyways lined with whimsical shops and mesmerising displays of enchantments. Dancers moved in a fusion of grace and wildness, their laughter an echo of ancient melodies showing off their magic. Some twirled in gardens of moonflowers, others spun in savage flames, and one female even glowed as bright as the sun, cascading light onto the street like a prism.

Turning a corner, I recognised the market square. Dark and abandoned, locked in the embrace of night, the canopies of the empty stalls flapped in the gentle breeze, blowing the remnants of sweet and spicy treats away. Not a single being occupied the moon-kissed courtyard, holding a polar opposition to my first visit.

I stalked toward the witch's stall. Its dark, raggedy canopy stood out against the brighter vendors. The shelves lay bare, an herby residue infused the wood, and nothing sat on the table. I ran my finger across the rip I'd created on my first visit. A hopeful part of me believed the market might be open to the crowds partying in the streets. I sighed, leaning over the table in search of clues to where she may live.

Nothing.

Leaning against the counter, I pulled the cloak closer to my skin, the phantom freeze stabbing into me. As I stood, unsure of my next move, a lone figure, tall and broad, emerged from the embrace of shadows. Darkness followed him, almost like the phantom tendrils were a part of him.

He stopped in the centre of the square, partially cloaked in shadow. The bustle of the city became a whisper, a backdrop to the unspoken conversation unfolding between us. Sensing the male meant no harm, I dared to approach him.

"It isn't wise for a young woman to be wandering in the dark," he said gruffly, taking me in from head to toe, as if evaluating me. I mimicked his review, analysing his appearance. He packed on a bit more extra flesh compared to the other Fae I've met. Dark, almost black hair, but the moon illuminated streaks of silver throughout the unkempt mane.

"How do you know I'm mortal?" He referred to me as a *young woman*, words chosen deliberately.

"Lucky guess." He shifted on his feet, grinning to reveal a missing canine tooth. His teeth didn't rot, nor present a yellowing stain.

Liar.

Conláed's voice echoed through the narrow streets, tipped with anxiety. I didn't have time for games. "I'm searching for someone who I think can help me. She tends to this stand during the day."

"Beatrix. If they catch you with her," his eyes darted to the city behind me, "she'll burn."

"I know. That's why I need to hurry." The gleaming of the moon revealed the sincerity within him, a gentle soul wrapped in a rugged body.

With a knowing nod, he gestured for me to follow, leading me through a labyrinth of stalls. His steps were ragged, incongruous with the city's pulse, like he didn't belong there. But I followed, trusting the currents of fate bringing us together.

As we navigated the serpentine alleys of the city, stories and whispers brushed against my senses like a cautious breeze. Warning me to keep my guard up, to safeguard my perceptiveness.

"The name's Dühghall," the gruff man announced, turning down a dark street. With each step, we walked further and further from the city's core, closer to the poorer communities near the walls. Near the site of the rebel attack. The streets became narrower, darker, and putrid. Rats scurried across our path as the less fortunate huddled under tattered material pressed against any available alcove.

Though some of the more affluent Fae wandered through these streets too, clinking coins into the hands of scantily dressed females. One repeatedly kicked a sleeping homeless Fae, laughing as the poor male vomited. Dühghall gripped my wrist and pulled me forward, like he'd felt my imminent intervention.

Walls between worlds seemed to thin, revealing an execrable connection binding the city's inhabitants in an intricate dance. If I asked Aramis to clean up these neighbourhoods and assist in ridding the city of poverty, would he have the support of the council and nobles?

Finally, as the last note of the city's symphony drifted away, the male stopped before a black door veiled in starlight. Here, under the cover of night and within the embrace of the witch's secrets, I'd find my way to Aramis. Dühghall turned to me, his eyes reflecting the magic surrounding us, and in his gaze, I saw a person with a path of conviction. Our destinies had intertwined in this dance of shadows and moonbeams, and as the first tendrils of dawn painted the horizon, I knew we'd meet again.

With a curt nod, Düghall left me to visit the witch alone, melding seamlessly into the shadows. For a fleeting moment, he truly appeared to be one with the shadows, but I quickly dismissed the notion.

Knocking on the wooden door, the young witch, Beatrix, opened the door. I held out my hand to greet her. "Hi, I'm—"

"Don't. I recognise you. The less we know about each other, the easier it is to stay hidden." She coughed and nodded her head, gesturing to come in.

"How did you know I'm mortal?" I stepped into her miniscule apartment, filled with fetid mildew and mould crawling across the ceiling. No windows to ventilate the space.

She tucked a strand of her straight ebony hair behind a rounded ear and poured two cups of tea. I nodded a *thank you* as she pushed one of the clay cups into my hands.

"You look very Fae, but I caught your ear shape behind your hood at the market." Her voice rasped, probably from the mould. A slight smile crossed my lips. I admired fellow perceptive people, like we developed a sixth sense in the name of survival.

The earthy tea spilled over my tongue, its warmth attempting to counteract the shivers, but to no end. I stared at the steaming liquid, swirling it. "I need your help to get to the Shadow Realm."

"You don't want to go there," she warned.

"I need to go there."

"There's dark magic within you. I can sense it. Something untamed and... erratic. The Shadow Realm may feed on that. Use it against you to consume you. It's a relentless land." Her dark eyes bored into me, expressing a dire graveness, and I didn't take her lightly, but I *needed* to go there. Recognising my tenacity, she sighed and moved to a wooden bench with threadbare pillows pressed against a wall.

Pulling a black tin box from underneath the bench, she knelt on the rough floorboards and sifted through the insides. A deck of bent and scuffed cards, crystals of all shapes, sizes and colours. Some tumbled and some raw. Bones, rune tiles, incense sticks, and jars of salt made up the rest of the box's contents.

She poured coarse grains of white salt in front of her.

"What are you doing?" I tiptoed closer, not wanting to disturb her but curious.

"Creating a door to the Shadow Realm. Witches cannot travel there the same way Shadow Fae can. They use their magic to teleport. Witches have to harness their magic," she elaborated, less afraid, as if magic soothed her.

The salt created the shape of a star, and she placed various crystals at each point. "Clear quartz for opening the doorway. Selenite to keep the shadows at bay. Hematite for grounding and strengthening the connection between spirit and body. Angelite for positive vibrations and connecting with your guardians. And finally, black tourmaline for protection."

As she placed the black tourmaline at the top of the star, she scurried back to her box and grabbed a jar of black salt. "Obsidian salt," she described, and poured the salt in a circle around the star. "It is used as a compass."

"A compass?"

"To guide you out of the Shadow Realm." Plugging the jar with cork, she placed it to the side and sat cross-legged in front of the portal. She gestured toward me. "Step into the centre of the star."

I lifted the hem of my oversized pants, to not disturb the salt, and sat cross-legged where she instructed. All hesitation vanished within me as a powerful tenacity rushed over all logic and reason.

Pulling a cage out from under the bench, she released a long, slithering black snake. A body too thick to wrap a hand around. A black tongue jetted in and out of its mouth. Milky white eyes evaluated its surroundings, searching for prey or predators. The creature made me think of Oulixeus. Sly, lying, bastard.

She recited an ancient language I didn't recognize as she chanted the spell, her body rocking back and forth. The snake in her hands spasmed. Bringing it closer to her chest, she rocked faster. Bit by bit, the snake faded into dust, the same way I obliterated my enemies into ash.

A high-pitched ringing filled my ears, and my vision clouded over. My throat scratched and ash filled my lungs. The witch kept chanting, but I suffocated. Like Oulixeus coiled his hands around my neck again. The witch's voice faded.

Real hands gripped me, the fog cleared to Oulixeus bent over me. Maliciously smiling. I gripped his forearms with my hands and tried pushing him away. My back arched as he choked the air from me.

Shoving a leg into him, he stumbled away, dissipating into smoke. Gasping, I stood and surveyed my surroundings. The world around me unfolded and writhed in an eerie, ashen ballet, like the restless spectre of a lost soul.

Beneath my feet, more shadow. Afraid to step and fall into nothingness, I cautiously pressed a foot down. Solid. I took another cautious step. Solid. Gaining confidence, I searched for Aramis. For anything in this shadow world.

Snap.

My shoulders hiked. *Not again, not again.* I grasped the hilt of my dagger and whipped around. Shadow. My peripherals caught the shape of antlers. I whipped around. Nothing. The shadows playing tricks on me.

I walked for minutes, maybe hours. How did beings live here? In a dark world. No sky, water, ground. I pushed my palms into my eyes and sighed.

Laughter. My head perked, and I slowed my heart to listen. It was the same cackle from the forest. Andraste's laugh. My steps quickened and in the distance, a light diffused by the swirling shadows emerged.

A sconce bolted to a stone wall protected a single flame the size of my thumb. It illuminated an archway with stairs leading downward and Andraste's cackle bounced off the walls.

One, two, three. I inhaled courage.

One, two, three. I exhaled all the anxiety and fear.

Descending the stairs, the dungeon's air clung to my skin like damp cobwebs, carrying with it a palpable sense of foreboding. Torches cast flickering shadows that danced in macabre harmony, painting the stone walls with eerie silhouettes. I pressed forward, my steps soft against the unforgiving ground, every fibre of my being attuned to the rhythm of danger echoing through the corridor.

My heart raced like a wild stallion, galloping against the reins of fears as I rounded the corner, coming face to face with two guards. They were formidable, their armour gleaming in the torchlight, their eyes sharp and vigilant. My hands tightened around the hilt of my concealed dagger, determination and desperation forging a steely resolve within me.

With a fluid motion, I propelled myself forward, my dagger singing through the air in a graceful arc, not allowing them time to conjure their magic. The dagger found its mark, meeting flesh with a whisper of steel, and silenced the guard's startled gasp as his body crumpled to the ground. My heart thudded like a war drum, the moment demanding all my focus.

The second guard spun toward his fallen comrade, his eyes wide with shock and alarm, not expecting an attack in their concealed location. Exploiting his distraction, my body became a blur of controlled urgency as I lunged forward, delivering a swift and precise kick to his knee. I clamped a hand over his mouth, muffling his cry of pain.

A fierce but brief struggle ensued as his attempts to break free were met with the unyielding force of my determination. With a swift swipe of my blade across his neck, his body went limp. I lowered him to the ground, my breath uneven, my senses still heightened with adrenaline. The corridor bore witness to our silent battle, the shadows themselves seeming to applaud my triumph. But then Andraste's voice rang toward me, reminding me that worse approached.

A light at the end of the corridor displayed two shadows. A lean female and a broad, thick male hanging from a chain, his arms stretched above his head. I peeked around the corner and swallowed a gasp.

The skin on Aramis' chest appeared black and blistered, a shade more menacing than onyx lightened to indigo and maroon. Another section of marred flesh ran from his ribs to hip bone on his right side caused by a dreadful slice. Blood slowly dripped from the wound and splattered to the floor below, a palm-sized puddle already forming.

I experienced his pain when he'd received those wounds. So brutal and cold. Fire didn't cause the black and blistering. Flames and heat couldn't burn a Fire Fae—those came from frostbite.

Recalling the excruciating pain of an invisible force piercing through my cheeks and tongue, I dared to inspect his drooping head. Blood crusted along his cheeks and square jawline. A puncture wound through each one.

"I know it's in the hidden chamber, Aramis. And the amulet is used to open the door." Andraste lifted the amulet lying around her neck. "But I also know that something prevented you from retrieving it yourself. Tell them what to be prepared for and I'll help you escape. We'll run away. Like we always dreamed." Holding his wounded cheeks in her hands, she forced him to look at her. "We can be together. Just us."

A weak, deformed smile formed between the puncture wounds. Andraste faced away from me, but the muscles in her shoulders relaxed at his reassurance. She brushed a strand of red-stained hair from his face.

"To that tropical island we found once when sailing?" Aramis gleamed.

"Yes, yes exactly. It can be just us. We'll feast on tropical fruits and buttery shellfish. Swim naked in the ocean. Make love on the beach, under the stars," Andraste purred, sliding a finger down to a frostbitten pec.

"It sounds nice."

"It does, doesn't it?" She stepped closer to him.

"Alone and isolated," Aramis added.

"Just us."

"Where no one can stop me from ripping your heart from your chest and squeezing it in front of you," his voice transformed into a monstrous snarl. She stepped away as he lunged forward like a feral beast, the clanking chains stopping him.

"You'll be begging me to rescue you. Give it time." Andraste walked over to a table displaying various weapons and instruments. She inspected the selection, choosing a long, sleek pick. It glowed white like ice with a metal handle, the same weapon used against those Fae Aramis had arrested for harming the woman in the stable yard.

Returning to Aramis, she drove the pick straight through the left side of his torso, under the ribs.

He groaned in pain and my body folded over. I glued my lips shut and inhaled sharply, trying to not give away my position. My side burned with a frigid cold right where Andraste stabbed Aramis. Clutching my flesh, my knees buckled and smacked against the floor. The pain suddenly ceased.

For a brief moment, there were no words, no movement. Aramis and Andraste stared at me, and I winced back at them. The only path to defeat Andraste lay in having surprise on my side, and I'd let it slip away.

"Interesting," Andraste whispered.

Aramis rattled the chains over his head and growled, "Elowyn, run!"

Ignoring his plea, I marched toward Andraste, readying the dagger in my hand. She quickly sliced the ice pick across Aramis' abdomen, blood running from the new scratch. He growled, and I brought a hand to the same spot on my stomach. A weak, brief pain sliced through me.

Andraste rose a perfectly shaped brow, this time stabbing the pike straight through Aramis' gut. I hunched over, groaning in pain as Aramis howled.

"Andraste, stop this," Aramis shouted through his pain.

"I wonder if it works the other way around, too. Want to find out?" She laughed at Aramis and removed the ice pick, dropping it.

She unsheathed a dagger on her hip and I readied myself. I bent my knees and moved my weight to the tips of my toes.

"Aw, how cute? Your little pet wants to play," she jeered.

"Let her go!" Aramis struggled with his bindings.

Andraste threw her dagger at my face. Unexpectedly, I managed to slip out of the way and lunged for her side. I aimed the dagger, ready to thrust it through her waist and into a kidney, but she anticipated my move. Grabbing my wrist, she twisted my arm and my dagger clanged to the floor.

She persisted until I fell, my arm burning where she held me. Smoke floated between her fingers as my wrist burned red and my flesh sizzled. Although fire and heat couldn't harm Aramis, he felt it fine through me. He gritted his teeth, attempting to be strong.

"Go away, you interrupted us." She dropped me and kicked my body away and as I rolled on the floor, the stone swirled back into shadows and Andraste and Aramis disappeared.

CHAPTER 52

Sitting on my ass, I searched the darkness.

"Fuck!" I stomped on the nightmarish obsidian floor.

Suddenly, a small girl with blonde hair pranced past me and bright white and yellow mums bloomed from the shadowed floor, creating a field I recognised, that produced a haunting perfume carrying the essence of long-forgotten secrets. The girl weaved through the flowers, giggling.

"Orla?" I whispered and followed her. She weaved back and forth through the wildflower field. With a joyful giggle, she ducked under the blooms and I tip-toed to where she hid.

"Rawr!" I shouted and crouched to her, but no child stood between the flower stems. A little hand tapped my shoulder and my head whipped around to witness her running away.

"You're it!" she squealed.

"Not fair!" I whined. She hid again, and this felt eerily familiar, as if this had *happened*.

As I searched for Orla, Linnaea's dark hair rippled through the flowers. I reached my arms out and let the soft petals caress my fingers. Every so often, a rustle and a few giggles caught my attention. I chose not to chase them and laid down. Flowers squished under me. The other blooms towered over, and I glimpsed the shadows swirling above like clouds on a sunny day. A set of short legs stopped at my head.

I leaned up on my elbows. The little girl had Orla's blonde hair, but not her round face. My brows scrunched. "Where's Orla?"

The little girl pointed to the side and I followed her finger to see Mother and Father on a picnic blanket with a pudgy-faced toddler. *Orla.* I returned my attention to the other blonde girl. "Who are you?"

Linnaea ran over and stood next to her. Identical. Linnaea and the girl were identical apart from their contrasting hair colour. Twins.

A memory tugged deep within my mind. "Rosalind?" I whispered. Both girls giggled and scampered away. I urgently followed them.

"No, Rosalind! Come back!" A faint recollection of a memory tugged at me, a looming darkness emerging that I struggled to recall amidst my frantic search through the wildflower field.

"Rosalind!" I cried in a panic and ran my fingers through my hair. A cloaked figure stood on the edge of Ravenwood Forest.

"No," I whispered and searched faster. The mysterious figure would hurt her.

"Rosalind! Linnaea!" The edges of my vision fogged over, morphing with the shadow walls around me and I screamed. It echoed through the shadow and the flowers at my feet all faced me. Petals stretched out. Black holes forming in their centre, mimicking my screams, their leaves and velvety petals aggressively vibrating.

My chest pounded and tears streamed down my face. "Leave them alone!" I screeched at the shrieking blooms and shadowed figure. My vocal cords burned.

I spun in a circle. Spinning faster and faster. A squeal. "Rosalind!" I ran in her direction. Finally, I caught up to her. She ran an arm's length in front of me. "Rosalind, stop!" Her brilliant shining hair bounced amongst the flowers.

"I said stop!" I shouted with frustration.

She giggled, making a sharp left.

"Rosalind!" I tripped. At the moment she halted, turning to face me, a burst of energy surged from me. A bright, ashen-grey light exploded from every pore on my skin. I held myself closely. Knees tucked in, head between my elbows. The burst rang like a cymbal, vibrating my ear drum and pushing its way into the base of my skull.

My mother shrieked. The light subsided, and the ringing stopped. Unwinding from my protective ball, I found the wildflowers surrounding me gone. Only ash remained. Rosalind lay limp on the ground ahead of me. Ash and crimson spread across her porcelain skin. Eyes open and lifeless. Staring at me.

Little Linnaea stood on the edge of the ash circle. An expression of shock carved into her face, stained with our sister's blood. Mother flung her body over Rosalind as she pointed a finger at me. "YOU! YOU DID THIS!" Letting go of Rosalind, she dug sharp, pointed nails into my shoulders. Shaking me, she wailed in a deep, hoarse, mournful way.

"Mommy, stop!" I pleaded.

"YOU DID THIS!" she repeated over and over, her face mere inches from mine. I stifled my cries. Ripping myself from her grip, I ran toward the woods, but they vanished. So did my mother and sisters.

I tripped over a wooden toy horse. Falling onto a plush carpet, I evaluated my new surroundings. My room at Elmswood Castle. Not the room in the tower, but the room I'd lived in before becoming an outcast.

The door rattled with force and I ran to a corner and crouched between pink wallpapered walls and a white stained dresser. I drew my knees into my chest. Wrapped tightly, I rocked back and forth, ash and blood covering my clothing.

The door continued to rattle as I bawled. *"I'm sorry! I'm sorry!"* But a furious grunting joined the convulsing door. My father. He emerged into the room and stomped toward me, lifted a large hand, and struck my face.

I squeezed my eyelids as his hand connected the piercing pain radiating through my head. Expecting a second strike, I opened my eyes.

A navy blue canopy hung over me and, suddenly, I was back on my bed in my tower. Oulixeus knelt in front of the fire, younger than when I'd last seen him. He kept his hair longer in his twenties—so handsome. The only one who visited me, defended me, and still treated me as Rhyddean's future queen after my exile.

He rose to his feet, holding an iron rod. The tip, shaped like an *O*, glowed orange. I crawled backward on the bed with no place to run. He protected me and loved me... he wanted to *own* me.

"It won't hurt for long," he cooed. Tears threatened to fall as the bed shifted and he knelt on the edge, pushing my legs open. Holding my left thigh, he plunged the burning iron into my flesh. I bit my lip, refusing to show any sort of weakness. "Good girl," he said, whispering his approval for the first time, as the charred acridity of my skin filled the room.

I wanted the pain to stop. I wanted this all to be over. The pain, the trauma, life. I finally allowed myself to scream when the burning became unbearable. I fell into a fetal position and rocked myself. Sobbing and whimpering.

"Rosalind. It was my fault!" I sobbed, recalling my forgotten sister. The horrendous tragedy my family refused to speak of, including her name. Blood pounded through my heart, forcing it to pound against my ribcage. My lungs expanded and collapsed at a vigorous rate, making it impossible to absorb the oxygen. A dizziness exploded in my head and spun the room and tingles crawled up my jaw into my cheeks.

A snickering burst through my panic attack. "Don't like what the shadows showed you?" Andraste's knee-high boots filled my vision. I was sprawled against the stone floor again. Beatrix had warned me of this, of the Shadow Realm feeding on my magic, finding ways to consume me.

Andraste crouched and rested her elbows on her knees.

I didn't care about her anymore. I killed my sister as a child. Linnaea's twin. I killed her with my magic.

My nose ran as my lungs slowed and Andraste took a fistful of my hair and pulled. I let her. Too stunned to care. Too focused on the traumas my conscious hid from me.

CRACK!

Aramis exclaimed something in the distance, and my head throbbed.

The stone floor cracked the side of my skull and Andraste lifted my head, smashing it into the stone a second time. My hearing ceased, blood gushed from my ears, and as the vengeful female cracked my skull a third and fourth time, sound completely muffled.

I was going to die.

Aramis was going to die.

All because I was useless, weak.

The banging ended as Andraste dropped and released my crushed head.

Renouncing the world, I waited for the Veil to claim me. To die here with my Mate—his emerald eyes, blazing with intense depth, being the last thing I see. I was ready for this. Death. As I mentioned to the demon—no, the Fae—in my dreams, I think I was meant to die a long time ago. The Veil stalked me, whispering encouraging notes of death ever since that day in the meadow. Teasing me and taunting me with moments bringing me closer and closer to its dark realm with the beatings, heavy drinking, and those nights on the roof at Elmswood, staring at the solid ground below. I was tired, and I was done fighting it.

Although I prepared to give up, Aramis refused to surrender. As darkness started to warp the Shadow Realm around me, a smoky voice billowed around me. Soothing words of confidence, encouragement, and love. I felt safe.

Safe.

A feeling still foreign to me. And naturally, my instincts told me to not believe the voice. *Lies, lies, lies.* Everyone just hurts you eventually. They use you until you're no longer valuable.

My parents used me, grandly accepted me as their heir, the shining pride and joy of Rhyddean, until they locked me in a tower after deciding I was a dangerous monster.

Oulixeus had used me, too. For his enjoyment, but he'd also groomed me to love and obey him, hoping I'd follow his lead without question once I knew the truth and extent of my powers. But he fucked up.

Cara never used you. Another voice inside of me said.

No. Cara and her family never used me. They treated me as a part of their family. Feeding me, teaching me, *caring* about me.

The smoky tendrils of the voice embraced me like a lover, and I pushed away the dying instinct. I wanted to believe this one didn't use me either.

Just open your eyes.

Open your eyes and you can do anything.

The dagger lay in my view. Its chaotic quillon branched off in all directions, each tine holding a new possible outcome, all dependent on the choice I made now. The lacklustre blade projected a plain weakness, nothing like the power and importance of Conláed's mounted sword, but beneath its disguise lay the most formidable weapon in the realm, because it enhanced *my* magic.

Andraste had continuously proved her skill as a warrior, as adept as the male warriors I'd come to know as friends and my Mate, but she didn't possess my unique magic, nor a weapon to enhance it. I could beat her and save Aramis. I *had* to. Despite the countless possibilities the tines teased, I knew her death would be the ultimate fate.

Grabbing my dagger, the room swirling around me, I gripped it tight and fell into the defensive position Cara had taught me and Molvys helped me to perfect. My weight was light on my toes and my arms were up, ready for any blow.

Andraste heard my movements and rolled her eyes. "Ugh, she's annoying, isn't she?" Snapping around, she flung a dagger at me, which skated across my cheek as I dipped out of its path.

Too close. Molvys and Conláed had trained me better than that, yet the room persisted in its disorienting twirls while my head throbbed from Andraste's relentless assault on the stone floor. Fuck, it felt more dreadful than indulging in fairy wine.

She stood at the table full of weapons and relentlessly threw knife after knife at me. I dodged them all, only tiny scratches marking me. The entire time I attempted conjuring my magic to turn them to ash, just as I did with the *hiisi* and Sir Haldwin, but my headache overwhelmed me, making it difficult to focus.

Come on!

Andraste smirked, knowing I struggled to regain my balance and strength. Choosing the largest knife, the same length and width of her forearm, she bent her wrist backwards and whipped it at me.

The tip of the blade aimed straight for the centre of my chest cavity, flying with a force so powerful it would pierce right through me. Inheriting Fae healing wouldn't save me from a wound like that.

It's as if time slowed down. I witnessed the panic form on Aramis' face and Andraste's smirk grow as she predicted her winning moment. She no longer cared if she killed Aramis along with me. Her insanity overtook any concerned thought of him. Or maybe she wanted him to die, knowing he'd never break and return to her.

As the blade inched closer and closer, the magical energy sparked within me. Cascading like a severe storm bolting through my veins and thundering from my physical body, pushing everything away from me. The giant knife clattered against a wall, chains violently rattled, and Andraste screeched as her back hit stone. Aramis gripped the chains above his head, as if expecting the impact, and his massive body rocked as the force hit him.

Aramis had bore witness to my magic in the lagoon when I threw him against the wall, but he hadn't seen everything else I'd done since then. A spark of pride mixed with curiosity rippled through his widened eyes.

"How?" Andraste rose to her feet, unsheathing the sword tied to her hip, and stalked toward me.

Ready to decapitate me in one strike, Andraste swiped her blade at my neck and I ducked just in time to dodge it.

"Are you Gifted? A witch?" She spat at the word *witch*. "Aramis, how could you sleep with one of them? Defend one of them?"

She struck again and I tucked tightly into my body, somersaulting out of the way. Attempting to call forth my magic again, it failed. I felt a faint flicker, but it refused to ignite. I didn't know how to use it. My physical strength and fighting skills may have improved, but magic remained unfamiliar to me. My defence and attacks occurred out of sheer luck and instinct.

Andraste continued to pursue me as I ducked and jumped and slid to avoid her strikes, attempting to strike her when I could. As I dipped, I'd thrust my dagger forwards to puncture her torso, but she always expected it. When I'd roll to the ground, I swiped at her ankles and shins to bring her down. But she moved quicker. I found myself in over my head—I shouldn't have come alone.

As she finally cornered me, she clasped her hand around my throat and conjured her flames. I screamed at the heat's intensity as it quickly reddened my skin, and the unforgettable scent of burning flesh reached my senses. In a last ditch effort, I raised my dagger to stab her throat but she grabbed my wrist with her free hand and twisted my arm until I dropped it.

"I'm going to burn you alive," she leaned close to me and whispered against my ear.

"Kill me, and you kill him," I rasped.

Laughing, she met my gaze and I saw everything she felt in those irises. The pain, disappointment, hurt, and all of the hope she'd once held swirled together. "If I can't have him, no one will."

Her fingers pressed into the flesh of my neck so tightly, they began to hurt more than the flames themselves. I felt my skin blistering and my airways constrict. Even though her arm blazed with threatening fire, I wrapped my hands around her, desperate to be released. But she squeezed harder, just like Oulixeus had.

I always suspected I'd be strangled to death, but by his hands. Not the hands of a female Fae warrior.

And as I felt my grip fall, my esophagus collapse, my skin melt, my mind began to fall away, to search for someplace safe. Someplace like... my forest clearing. Not the one where I met my demon in my nightmares. No. The one I went to when Oulixeus hurt me. I could die there and be at peace.

Just as the faint trickle of the creek materialised, the leaves rustled, and the flowers swelled with a peaceful fragrance, another spark—ever so tiny—emerged instead and forced me back to consciousness.

Kill her.

A zap escaped me and bolted into Andraste. Her body jerked and she fell backwards.

"You fucking witches," she sneered. And as she stalked towards me, she stopped, held back by massive arms.

"She's not a witch, Andraste. She's Fae." Aramis grinned against her ear, holding her arms taut behind her back. His shackles hung from the ceiling, one link broken, and the cuffs lay next to a hacksaw on the floor. Andraste's eyes widened in disbelief at his declaration.

"That's impossible," she whispered, extinguishing her flames, useless against Aramis.

"Kill her," Aramis ordered me.

When it came to saving him, when it concerned self-preservation, I stood prepared to end her life. To thrust a blade into her, employ my magic against her, anything necessary. Yet at this moment, why did the necessity to kill her arise? In her present state, she posed no challenge against Aramis, even with his tortured condition.

"Shouldn't we take her back for interrogation?" I didn't quite understand why I protested. Andraste had attempted to kill me multiple times, she obsessed over Aramis, and she worked with the rebels. But something about killing her didn't sit right with me.

And with that emotion brewing, I suddenly felt a pang in my gut about Sir Haldwin and Iñgir. I'd killed them in the moment without thinking. Without understanding anything about where their true allegiances laid, or if others relied on them, their usefulness to the realm. I rarely reacted like that... I always thought of everything before acting. Was I losing a piece of my humanity in the process of discovering and trying to embrace being half-Fae?

"Elowyn, all she's ever done is evil. She can't live."

"But what if she has valuable intel?"

"Elowyn, this is our only chance. Take your dagger and end this!" Andraste thrashed in his arms, and Aramis gripped her tighter, forcing her to be still. "She'll never stop coming after us."

I shook my head. No. I couldn't do this. I'd already crossed a line that I couldn't come back from, I couldn't keep going further. I couldn't lose myself right when I'd started to find myself.

"Listen to me. Think of how everyone has treated you. They feared you so much that they treated you like a monster, beating you into submission, hiding you away. Reclaim your power, Elowyn. Show everyone how strong and in control you are."

With my eyes welling up with tears, I choked out, "But Aramis, I don't want to become like them. Like Oulixeus, so filled with hatred and darkness. I've finally started to overcome that pain and now..."

"She's a fucking coward, Aramis. You chose a real winner here—" Aramis clamped a hand around Andraste's mouth to keep her quiet.

Aramis' voice filled with urgency as he continued to encourage me. "Elowyn, this isn't about becoming like them. You will *never* be anything like them. This is about surviving." My eyes darted to his. *Survival.* I understood survival. "Andraste wants to kill us, to destroy everything we're working towards. Think about all the innocent lives at stake. Fae *and* mortal. If we don't kill her now, what consequences will there be?"

My limbs trembled as his words rattled through me, considering the validity of what he spoke. She possessed the skills and power to greatly aid the rebels. If not, they wouldn't have kept using her to get into the fortress and capture Aramis. Andraste provided the rebels with advantageous knowledge of the Fire Fae and the fortress. Eliminating her would remove the upper hand they had gained.

Noticing my hesitation, Aramis dropped his voice and softly said, "Sweetheart, I know you're scared. But sometimes, in the face of darkness, we have to make difficult choices. You're so strong and courageous, rising above the cruelty you've endured. Don't let your past define you. You're fearless and can overcome every obstacle thrown your way. This is just another challenge. I *know* you can succeed."

I took a deep breath to steady myself, choosing to trust Aramis, and not let my past define me. I wouldn't let everything my parents and Oulixeus had put me through determine every action I take. Andraste needed to be eliminated. She'd never stop and I needed to kill her. Not for me and not for Aramis, but for the good of the entire realm.

Meeting Aramis' intense gaze, I nodded my understanding, and he grinned. "That's my girl."

Bending to retrieve my dagger at our feet, I took a step toward them and raised it high, ready to strike Andraste and end this threat. As the blade descended, closing in on her heart, my mixed emotions spurred the energy hiding within me, and the need to protect overrode all hesitation.

As the dagger's cold steel breached her delicate flesh, my magic entwined with it, an emotional force coursing through her form, crawling along her veins. The lifeblood oozing from the fresh incision dissolved into desolate ash, drifting to the floor. Her once-vivid eyes, marred by creeping shadows, shifted to a haunting grey, until the ashen hue consumed her irises entirely. Andraste's warriors-frame surrendered, an eerie stillness replacing the vindictive glint in her hazel gaze. With immense effort, I reined in the unruly tendrils of my magic, and Aramis relinquished his grip on her lifeless form, allowing her to fall upon the unforgiving stone floor with an ominous thud.

My hands trembled and Aramis took them into his, bringing them up to his lips to press a deep, caring kiss to them. As he pulled his face away, a predatorial, prideful smile lifted on his face, ready to help me embrace the Fae within me.

CHAPTER 53

Pride and awe buzzed between Aramis and me, charging the room like a bolt of lightning arcing through a sea of menacing thunder clouds. It escalated the various emotions flowing through us. Each battling for supremacy—which would ignite first?

Aramis' grin dropped and his face tensed, a matching severe tone coated his words. "You never should've come after me. Where's Molvys or Conláed? Fuck, Kenna could've come."

He scolded me. Scolded me for saving him. A bitter tang coated my mouth with reminiscing notes of anger and shame. His fury originated from a place of concern, but for a second time, he took me for a feeble little girl, just as he did by keeping my heritage a secret.

Throughout our time together, my time at the Fae Court, I became stronger—both physically and mentally. I wasn't the same girl he'd met in Rhyddean. Did he not notice? The shame within me shattered my perceptions.

The night of the bond, Aramis had insisted upon our equality. Hadn't I proven its veracity? Again, my shame rippled through me like a pebble—no—a giant fucking stone thrown into the centre of a black pond, eliciting a giant splash and waves to push outward. And abruptly, my anger pushed my shame and reason aside and I glared at him.

"I save your ass and you're reprimanding me?" The words I shouted hit Aramis like the giant fucking stone sinking in my imaginary pond. His forehead crinkled as his brows hiked high and eyes widened in surprise, but the shock lasted seconds, evening out to a grin of curiosity. "Besides, I didn't just save you. I saved *us*. Did you know the bond connected us like that? We feel each other's physical pain and if one of us dies, so does the other. It would've been a nice heads up!" Dagger still in hand, I waved it back and forth as my arms flailed with a frustrated wrath. The chamber crisped to an icy cold, the walls flowing into a smooth liquid, as if the shadows refused to hold the shape of the dungeon for much longer. We needed to leave.

"I didn't know. Fated Bonds are so rare, Elowyn. I imagine we're going to learn a lot of forgotten knowledge." His voice remained so calm, it infuriated me. How could he stand in his ex-fiancé's blood in the Shadow Realm and still have the composure to berate me?

"Then write a damned book for the next lucky couple in a thousand years. I'm so furious with you!" I spun to leave the chamber, the cold piercing into my flesh, and the raw astringency of the blood making me nauseous. We needed to leave. But I slipped on the scarlet liquid staining the illusionary floor, the momentum of my determined body hurling me down when Aramis caught me.

"I get that—"

"Do you?" I shrugged him off, straightening my posture, readying for my turn to scold him. "Because right now you're doing the same thing you've done from the moment we met."

Aramis' head tilted to the side, as if ensuring he heard me correctly, and the curiosity vanished from his expression.

"You withheld my heritage from me because you believed I was too mentally unstable to handle it. Now, you scold me for rescuing you because I might have gotten hurt. You continue to treat me like some powerless fool. But guess what? If what just occurred here didn't tip you off, I'm really fucking powerful and I can handle my own."

And as rapidly as a rolling storm, the shadows appeared to darken around Aramis, adding a threatening aura I didn't expect. "She could've *killed* you!" His words cracked like thunder and a bright ruby-red flushed across his complexion, his hands balling into fists as if to keep his rage from escaping.

Words spewed so forcefully would've caused me to shrink in the past, but never again.

"I'd be dead if they killed you, anyway! Aramis, I don't need your constant protection. I can fight and hold my own. I will fight *by* your side, not hidden away. No one will ever hide me away again."

His chest heaved stronger now than after a battle, eyes darting across the room, being gradually reclaimed by the shadows, as if processing it all. "I-I know, but seeing you pressed against the wall... The thought... the *possibility* of losing you..." Aramis clenched his teeth hard enough to tense the muscles in his neck. I pressed an assuasive palm against him, a physical touch to remind him I still stood next to him and I wasn't going anywhere.

"Aramis," I whispered, wanting to comfort him. But his gaze snapped to me, frantic and hungry. Fisting my hair, he forced my head back and kissed me hard. My skull throbbed from where Andraste smashed it into the stone, but I didn't care. I wanted it to hurt. Aramis pressed his tongue into my mouth, ravaging me, claiming me more fiercely than ever before. Almost as if he needed to confirm I truly stood in front of him in the flesh—alive.

"I will *never* lose you. Do you understand? And you will *never* lose me again. I'll do whatever is necessary to ensure we're together until the end of time, Elowyn. The mountains will crumble to dust, oceans will consume the land, realms will collapse upon each other, and we will still be together. You and me," he growled, his breath rolling across my ear as a steadfast vow.

"Then you need to *trust* me," I whispered back, forbidding myself to accept his oath until he made the promise I needed.

"I trust you." Aramis pulled away, showing me the conviction darkening his irises from their usual emeralds to a shade that haunted forests. "You are powerful. Brilliant. I trust you with every fibre of my life."

The rap of my heart pumped an invigorating strength through me, a secure faith that Aramis spoke true. "Then I'll stay with you even after all the realms collapse upon each other."

We pressed into each other with an eager force, sliding on blood and falling into the crimson puddle still expanding from the blood draining out of Andraste's wounds. The viscous gore didn't hinder us, and we continued to devour each other.

Our mouths and hands rediscovered each other's bodies and the new wounds marring them, tongues reacquainted with our taste, nails breaking flesh, and strained limbs tangling into an insatiable rapacity. We needed this to feel whole again after being deprived and craving one another for weeks. I now understood, neither of us would feel whole without the other again.

Wiggling out of my pants, I reached for Aramis' laces to tug his erect length free, hungrily groaning at its presence. He lifted me into the air and sat me on his lap, melting seamlessly into me.

Simultaneously, we moaned, staring into each other's eyes to witness each other's ecstasy. With my mouth open, he gripped my bottom with one hand and pressed his fingers into my mouth with the other. Blood coated them and I closed my mouth around his fingers and sucked, caught in the euphoria. The subtle metallic tang, reminiscent of the brisk bite of a winter's frost spread across my tastebuds, thrilled me instead of repulsing.

Aramis guided my hips with his free hand, leaning his head back and groaning as I rode his pelvis harder and harder, slowly reaching my climax. My hands ran along his torso and suddenly Aramis grimaced and pulled his fingers from my mouth, gripping my hips.

"Fuck!" Looking down, I realised I'd pushed a thumb into one wound on his torso, pulling me from our lustfully induced moment.

"Just finish." Aramis bit his lip and attempted to keep me seated on him.

"No!" I struggled to resist his strength, but he finally lost the energy to keep me in place. "This was stupid. We need to leave and get you to the healer."

"I'm already healing."

"Not fast enough. And look. The shadows are consuming the dungeon." I scrambled to my feet, slipping on the blood-coated floor, and held my hands out to assist Aramis. Amused, he rolled his eyes the way I always did to him, and pretended to use my arms to get up.

Retying my pants and grabbing my dagger, I took one last look at Andraste. Once a vivacious, ambitious female completely destroyed by the rejection of love. For a split second, I felt bad for her, but I decided not to let my thoughts linger with her.

Marching for the exit, Aramis gripped my hand. "I'm sorry. For everything."

Sighing, I told him, "I know your intentions were to protect me, but I need you to trust in me and my abilities. We're a team, and I'm improving. We can overcome any obstacle. I just want us to face challenges side by side, as equals, like you promised."

"You're right. I want that, too, and I'm sorry for treating you like you're defenceless. You keep proving yourself time and again. I should've recognised that."

Like a weight being lifted off of my shoulder, I gratefully wrapped my arms around him, gently this time. "Thank you, Aramis."

"Together, we'll face whatever comes our way. We're going to rule this entire fucking world." Embracing me in his arms, he squeezed me as if trying to ensure I took his promise seriously.

And I did.

But, inexplicably, my gut didn't rest easy.

CHAPTER 54

Never underestimate intuition. Beatrix had instructed me to trust myself and open my consciousness to find my way back to the obsidian salt circle. As I navigated through the shadows, pain seared through my body and Aramis wrapped a burly arm around my waist, insisting on keeping me close to his side—perhaps afraid to lose me. Our injuries were considerable, and even Aramis limped despite his quick healing abilities, knitting his wounds back together.

Aramis turned to me, his voice ragged with exhaustion. "Elowyn, how much farther do you think?"

An empty hollow rang through the dark realm, its dry icy air stabbing my skin. I closed my eyes briefly, reaching out with my senses, relying on my intuition. "Not far," I whispered, my voice strained but resolute.

We stumbled forward, our steps heavy with fatigue. The oppressive atmosphere of the Shadow Realm weighed down on us, a constant reminder that we might not be safe yet. And then, I saw it.

A faint, otherworldly glow in the distance, shimmering like a beacon of salvation. The obsidian salt circle, our portal back to Niafell. But worry accompanied my relief. Worry for Beatrix and Aramis' reaction to her existence in his court.

Aramis found a new determination, quickening our pace, drawing nearer to our ticket out of this nightmarish place. As he guided us toward the crystal white light, I crafted a speech. One to convince Aramis to leave Beatrix alone. To allow her to live her quiet life in Stoneshalt and continue operating her market stand. He owed it to her, because without her Gifted abilities, we both might be dead.

Stumbling into the circle, a rush of power surged through us as the witch's magic embraced us, tearing us away from the Shadow Realm and hurtling us back home.

As we materialised on the other side, only the salt circle and crystals opening the portal and putrid air remained. Beatrix and her belongings were gone. My worry vanished, she'd snuck out of the city safely.

Aramis took in the rundown apartment, spying the magical tools on the scratched wooden floor, but before he could ask questions, I pulled him outside and he followed without protesting. "Let's go home."

Shouts and loud thumping reverberated through the streets, streaked with the soft purples of dawn. Guards jogged down the cobblestone, their armour clanging with each stride, and pounded authoritarian fists against doors as they searched for us.

"Wyn? Aramis?" Conláed stood in the distance, ready to search another minuscule shanty. He rushed to our side, his face a mix of relief and concern.

"I found him." I stuck my tongue out at Conláed, the same way I used to with Cara.

"You drugged us!" His concerned face contorted into anger with the skin between his brows scrunching and jaw tensing.

"She's certainly full of surprises," Aramis chuckled and raised a brow at me.

"You killed the spy." I threw Conláed's mistake in his face.

His shoulders slumped as he shook his head at me, focusing on his high king instead. "Aramis, are you okay?"

"I'll give you and Molvys a full report back at the fortress, and you're going to tell me about this spy."

Conláed nodded and led us through the silent streets—an eerie contrast from earlier—back to the safety of the fortress. Our injuries were healing, and with the support of our friends, we would recover fully. But my thoughts lingered on the revelations I'd encountered in the Shadow Realm. I looked up at Aramis, stretching my neck to meet his gaze, but the emerald flames didn't flicker. And I wondered if the shadows had shown him nightmares, too.

Lightly snoring and chest rising and falling in a deep, steady rhythm, I stared at my soon-to-be-husband—only days away from Summer Solstice, and our wedding day. His wounds had healed so quickly they now appeared as minor scratches caused by a cat instead of the fatal gouges Andraste created two days ago. I followed a long, thin scab from his temple to his pronounced jawline with the tip of my finger, caressing his rough skin and stubble with minimal pressure.

Feeling me move, Aramis tightened his grip around my waist. Meryl had attempted to keep us in separate beds but even in sleep, Aramis refused to leave my side.

I cupped his chin with my hand, running my thumb along the plump skin of his bottom lip. A smile tugged at my lips, crinkling the corners of my eyes, at peace wrapped in his sandalwood scent. And grateful. Grateful that he slept next to me alive, healing, and safe, *home.*

As Aramis' arms tugged me closer to him, I winced at the pressure against my bruised and exhausted body. Meryl insisted my Fae magic was healing me, just at a much slower pace due to the amount I'd used to end Andraste. Killing the *hiisi* and council members within such a short amount of time didn't help. But Aramis and my friends assured me that my magic would strengthen over time, building it like a muscle.

Aramis' grip loosened the moment he felt me sink into him. I played with his curls and watched his body fall into a calm relaxation. We were safe.

CHAPTER 55

My forest clearing emerged, the one I'd visit when wanting to escape this world. I hadn't been here for so long, finally feeling at peace and happy in the real world. The stream trickled and the dapple light warmed me. Dainty flowers of all kinds swayed in the breeze and I rolled onto my back and drew in the rich, dewy essence of the woodland, its earthy aroma filling my senses.

"Elowyn," my demon said. I really needed to stop calling him a demon. He'd admitted to being a Fae, and I trusted that he spoke the truth.

"What are you doing here?" We always met in Ravenwood Forest, where I ran to after I'd killed Rosalind. Something I still struggled to accept, so I tried not to think about it. It felt safer to ignore, for now.

"I appear wherever your dream takes us."

Rolling onto my side, I faced the cloaked male. But this time, he pulled the hood of his cloak back to uncover a *young, handsome face. Ash-blonde hair curled around his face and reached the top of his shoulders. Arched ears pointed between strands. Thick brows framed almond-shaped grey eyes. No, not grey—ash, silver threading through them.*

He knelt in front of me, and I rose, bringing a palm to his high cheekbones. I dragged my hand across his stubbly face and studied his clear-cut jawline. He beamed.

"You're my father, aren't you?" I didn't really need to ask. I had suspected for a while. His magic held an imprint familiar to mine, and seeing his face removed all the doubt within me. This male who haunted my nightmares, begged me to listen, and guided me when I'd finally allowed him to, was my real father.

He bobbed his head and pursed his lips in acknowledgement.

"And you were there that day," I concluded, recalling the black-cloaked figure in the forest when I'd killed my half-sister.

"Yes. But I shouldn't have been. All the pain and suffering you've endured is my fault." We sat cross-legged, facing each other. I still studied his features, unable to look away from how similar we appeared. Odd but comforting.

"How?"

"Your mother, Sévérine—" I inhaled sharply at the mention of her name. Noticing my cringe, his face softened into disappointment. "She wasn't always so cruel. You actually remind me of her. The way she used to be."

"Don't defend her." I tore blades of grass out of the ground. Their sharp, sweet juice released in my hands as I tossed the blades away from me.

"I'm not. Sévérine begged me to stay away and, because I loved her so much, I obeyed her wishes. But you never left my thoughts, and I had to return to see you.

It took four days of watching the castle before I finally saw you running and playing in the meadow with your sisters. Seeing you laughing, living a safe and happy mortal life, allowed me to feel peace."

"But I'm not mortal. You didn't think they'd fear me, eventually?"

"No, because your magic should never have manifested. Not in this realm. But I didn't consider the dagger and how it amplifies our magic. It felt your presence and called to you."

"The one you lost to me?" I tried piecing it all together, to fit it together like a million-piece puzzle. All the answers I'd sought my entire life were finally being laid out in front of me, and they were nothing like what I expected.

"Do you really think I lost that game, Elowyn?" He smirked. "It's not an ordinary dagger."

"The Water Fae forged your magic into it." I'd realised it after Conláed taught me about the Water Fae and their superior forging techniques, and how the magic sparked effortlessly in the dagger's presence. He tilted his chin upward and gleamed pridefully at me, a look neither of my mortal parents had shared with me for many, many years.

"Yes. And the mere second it took for the dagger to recognize you, it evoked the magic lying dormant inside."

"And I killed my sister." Staring at my favourite flower, I recalled how powerful my magic pulsed through me each time I used it. Erratic, uncontrolled, wild. It's amazing I hadn't killed Linnaea too. I plucked the bloom from its stem and twirled it between my fingers.

"You're not to blame, Elowyn." He leaned over and brushed a curl out of my face. His fingers accidentally touched the gash healing on my temple, eliciting a shrill ache, causing me to wince. "That looks bad."

"I'm used to it." I shrugged my shoulders, afraid to meet his frown.

"The day your magic came forth, I panicked and fled. Not a day goes by where I don't regret my cowardly decision. I should have taken you and raised you myself. Taught you to use your magic." His compassion twisted into bitterness, ashamed of his past choices. "I will kill every last one of them for what they did to you."

Admiring the flower, I considered his words, the missing parts of my childhood slowly returning to me, and the vow he made. So similar to Aramis'. They both wished to protect me and dish out my revenge, but I refused to let either steal it from me.

"No. You're not going to kill anyone for me." My true father's face darkened at my statement, wanting to dole out his justice, but I needed to fight my own battles. "Because I am."

I closed my fist around the flower, squeezing the velvety petals until they flaked into ash, my first attempt at controlling the intensity of my magic. Shifting my gaze upward, my father grinned, more pride flowing through his features.

"You're certainly my child. There's no doubt about it."

"Why did it take you so long to return? You mentioned we're not from this realm. Which realm do you mean? And why give me the dagger now?" Question after question flooded from me, so much yet to learn and understand.

"The Realm of Chaos is our home, Elowyn, and we need to discuss it. The portal between this realm and ours opens once every seven years, when the celestials align a certain way."

It had been fourteen years since the dagger sparked my magic, since he'd fled and left me to the wolves. "Why didn't you come for me seven years ago, then?"

Guilt warped his grin into a grimace. "A goddess, not a king or queen, rules my realm. She hasn't abandoned us like the gods here. It's why our magic remains so strong and raw, but she's weakened because of it. She required my services the last time the portal opened. I protected her. Our realm is now stable enough for them to spare me."

"Our magic—"

"Chaos magic. We can manipulate it in ways other Fae only dream of. Nearly anything you wish to be, you can create, influence, or destroy."

"So why not tell me this at the tavern all those months ago? Why not take me back to your home?"

"Would you really have believed me, then?" His brow rose, and I bit my bottom lip, knowing the truth. I would've written him off as a drunk lunatic and laughed about it later with Cara. "I also need a favour from you..."

This time, I raised my brow. A favour? What in the darkest depths of the Veil could I do for him? Seeing my confusion, he continued, "Your Mate threatens the Realm of Chaos."

That had to be the realm Aramis wanted to unite with and create an undefeatable power against any sort of threat.

"He doesn't threaten your home. He wants to unite us," I explained, my father misunderstood.

"Unification is a ploy, Elowyn. He craves power and control. His ambitions lie in conquering. He won't stop until he threatens the gods themselves, and then what? We'll all die in his quest to become a god himself."

"No. He's nothing like—"

"Fae magic is delicate, Elowyn. We can easily... snap. And when Fire Fae snap, they grow paranoid and even masochistic. Developing a... bloodlust." As he explained, I recalled the diary I'd read and the father of the writer becoming more and more paranoid. Even Aramis had

noted how many Fae died so kings could keep their passages and chambers secret. "Aramis is already showing signs—"

"You're wrong. You don't know him like I do. He's different." My heart sped, pounding within my sore rib cage. I refused to believe Aramis shared those qualities with his ancestors, but an anxiousness threatened to take hold of me. In the depths of my concern, panic was a bitter elixir on my tongue, a noxious brew crafted from the ashes of my fears, each sip searing my taste buds with the acrid tang of desperation.

I'd finally found someone worth loving and who encouraged my genuine self. I believed in him. But the concern clung to my palate, leaving a sinister aftertaste of dread that I couldn't swallow, a venomous nectar from the abyss.

Sighing, my birth father softened his face. "Elowyn, he's your Mate. I'm not asking you to part from him or hurt him, but he cannot enter the Realm of Chaos. Please, help me protect our people." He leaned in and rested a hand on my shoulder, grounding me and easing my racing concerns.

"Your queen, I mean goddess, doesn't want Aramis' allegiance?" I asked, and he shook his head.

If they didn't want or need an alliance, why should we force one upon them? Isn't that just as bad as an invasion? Nodding my head, I realised I could make a difference. "How can I help?"

"Retrieve the Book and hide it. It can't be destroyed, so you need to send it far away from him and keep it somewhere no one will find it. Not even me. I'd take it myself, but the portal is closing and I'm running out of time."

"How much time do you have left? I know where it is and with your help, I'm sure we can—"

"No, Elowyn, the portal is closing now. I've been trying to get through to you, but you've become very good at blocking others from entering your mind. A useful skill... but the portal is closing now, and I need to know you can do this for me. For our realm."

The clearing dimmed and, and shadows slowly invaded. Our connection was breaking, and I was beginning to wake.

"Will you come back?" I choked, not understanding why my emotions overwhelmed me.

"Yes, I promise." And with his vow, shadows swirled around us, swallowing my father and forcing me to wake.

CHAPTER 56

The city awoke beyond our balcony. Excitable bartering between vendors and customers resounded from the market square, bells jingled from dancers unable to contain their elation, horns squeaked and string instruments strummed to find their tune, and comforting cinnamon and cardamom followed the morning breeze into our chambers.

They prepared for our wedding today.

Aramis buried his head between my breasts as my arms cradled him, admiring the coral and honey sparkling sunrise shimmering through the flowing drapes. Birds chirped early morning melodies as *keiju* fluttered around the balcony, peeking into the windows, jubilant over the upcoming festivities.

I stared at the crystal vase displaying a single velvety flower. Its delicate petals like layers of satin, their purity radiating a soft, ethereal luminescence, as if inviting my fingers to trace the cool contours of its blooms. A ranunculus, I recently learned, was the name of the flower I continuously held in my dreams. The one Aramis gifted to me last night.

This felt right.

Despite his misguided prejudice of Gifted mortals, and Seth's warning, I loved Aramis. The goddesses chose us as equals, intertwining our fates to hold a rare grandeur.

Shuffling feet and the clang of a metal tray echoed from the antechamber. The servants were still too nervous to enter our rooms since the week our bond solidified. Scents of savoury eggs, buttery potatoes, and fresh dill alerted my nostrils to my hunger, my stomach suddenly grumbling. I shifted to stand, eager to fill my mouth with those tender spring potatoes, when Aramis wrapped his arms around me tighter, forcing me to remain still.

I grappled with the undeniable fate binding us, truly comprehending it. Neither he nor I were perfect, but our flaws provided me with solace.

Kissing Aramis' forehead, he nuzzled deeper into me, his golden locks ticking my skin and coaxing a soft laugh from me. I would never let go. He belonged to me and I belonged to him. We were entwined and harmonious with each other. Fated.

I lifted the bedsheet and tucked ourselves under its silky fabric, trapping us in this moment. The golden morning sun cascaded an ethereal glow over us, highlighting the fire magic flowing through Aramis' veins. *This* was freedom. Not the kind I expected to find or what

I chased, but the type of freedom I needed. A freedom complimented by safety, love, and patience.

We'd be together forever, and that belief beamed with more power than the magic flourishing within me.

Aramis dragged his nose up the length of my neck with a slow, smooth inhale, like he meant to soak in all I had to offer. "Sweetheart?" he whispered.

"Mhm." Eyes peacefully closed, I allowed the warmth of the rising sun and Aramis' magic to seep into me, melting the icy walls I kept erected for so long. *Keiju* giggled and whispered on the balcony, their wings flitting as one shrieked at a bee buzzing too closely.

I loved this realm and couldn't wait for magic to return to the mortal courts.

"Something's been on my mind." His lips glided across my skin, gentle and full of promise.

A lust slowly crept through me, a kind only he elicited and I would never get enough of. "Yes?" I shifted to press my centre against him, to show him my increased desire. Aramis groaned, pleased with my motives, and dug his fingertips into my flesh.

"How did you steal the Book?" He asked casually. I froze. Aramis pulled away, allowing space to study my response. Searching my eyes, exploring the twitches of my muscles and the steadiness of my heart. He'd learned a thing or two about tells, and now he searched for mine.

Fuck.

Acknowledgements

Brandon—There are no words in any language to fully describe how thankful I am for you. You're the only man I know who will stand by his partner's delusional aspirations and not just tolerate them, but encourage them. When I fly so high into the sky that I'm about to break through the atmosphere and into space, you don't pull me back down to where the pessimists live. You simply remind me that there's earth below me that I may want to visit from time to time. Thank you for not simply accepting my ridiculous weirdness, but loving me for it. I appreciate all of your hard work to keep us going in the darkest timeline, feeding me when I forget to eat, stocking the forbidden candy drawer with my favourite chocolates, walking the dogs when you see my office door closed, and doing your own laundry to save my clothing. I don't deserve you. And one day I'll write a male lead to show the world just how incredible you are.

Shanna—You're always first on this list, girl, because without you constantly listening to my wild ideas, reading everything I send your way, and your continuous encouragement, I wouldn't have written any of these books. You repeatedly amaze me with not only your kindness and friendship, but with your strength to be there for your loved ones in their tough times while going through your own shit. Please don't ever leave me!!! I'm so proud of you.

Sheena—You're my biggest fan and cheerleader, and I would've become one with my mattress and lost in my duvet by now if it weren't for you. I love how we dream big together, not afraid to take on the world and create the life that we desire—not what society expects of us. If it weren't for you, I don't think I would've had the guts to keep defying the norm. You're my girl boss friend, and you inspire me to live up to my full potential instead of allowing it to scare me. I'm so proud of the life you've created for yourself and how far you've come since we first met in that coffee shop and you bawled your eyes out in front of a group of entrepreneurial women. From the first tear that you shed, I knew I wanted to be best friends with you, because it takes a brave woman to show that kind of vulnerability in a public room full of strangers. I admire you so, so much—seriously, ask Brandon, I talk about you ALL the time! You're incredible and you deserve the world.

Mom, Dad, & Brother—None of you were surprised when I announced I was writing a full-length novel. I've been writing for as long as I can recall, and you all remember the awards I won for poetry and how I excelled in Language Arts/English. Actually, I was the one who was surprised by how easily the three of you accepted my sudden new career choice with little to no hesitation. I expected lectures on how difficult it will be to make a living and support myself. Every time I drove out to the countryside, I expected to walk into an intervention with everyone reading letters on how stupid I am to quit my exploding photography business for an industry where only 1% succeed. But none of that came, and I think that helped reaffirm just how right this choice was for me. The three of you encourage me in your own little ways—some that drive me crazy—but without your support, this entire process would have been ten times more difficult and I appreciate and love you so, so much for it.

Meghann, Sheena, Shawntel, & Sadie—My absolutely incredible beta readers, you're the real MVPs with A Curse of Flame and Ash! I knew I wasn't hitting the mark on various aspects of my story, but after months of reading and rereading and revising, I couldn't pinpoint them. And all four of you detected exactly what was lacking, confusing, missing, and what worked great. I'm so lucky to have ended up with such an incredible beta team and I really hope to work with you all again in the future. And Sadie, thank you for stepping in *again* to proofread this sucker!

Nicole & Janna—OMG, you two! I absolutely LOVE working with the two of you. How many shoots have we done together now? Nicole, I love how when I asked for an author's portrait unlike any other; you fucking delivered! And Janna, I will forever be grateful for touching up my hair and makeup throughout the entire shoot and creating epic wind and smoke moments to make me look like a damn supermodel! I already can't wait for my next shoot with you two, because there will definitely be more to come.

Readers—Lastly, but certainly not least, my readers. I know this is my debut novel, but so many of you have been with me since the release of my free short-story, which turned into a novella series because you all demanded more. Your demands gave me the confidence I needed to fully believe I can be a writer. It's not just a delusional dream, its actual reality! And to all my readers who have loved A Curse of Flame and Ash since I first started talking about it on TikTok and Instagram, thank you! Truly, your encouragement is what gave me the confidence to hit publish on Amazon. I hope you love Elowyn and Aramis' fucked up story and everything that's yet to come. The characters that are yet to be introduced, the plot twists coming, and the endless drama that's ready to unfold. Thank you for joining me on this incredible journey.

About the Author

Kaitlyn lives in Edmonton, Alberta with her patient and encouraging husband, Brandon, and their two dogs—Hades and Molly—bred from the darkest, wildest depths of Chaos itself. She received a History and Classics Bachelor of Arts degree from the University of Alberta—focusing her studies on women's history and ancient Greek life. After years of stumbling from desk job to desk job in libraries and archives, Kaitlyn realised the chances of discovering a magical, ancient text made to transport her to a fantasy world were slim and evaluated her life. In doing so, Kaitlyn remembered her oldest and biggest dream—becoming a fiction author. Stumbling into the world of dark romance stories, she decided to put her traumas and past challenging and embarrassing experiences to good use. Kaitlyn is grateful to all who purchase her books and wants all to remember to never give up on your biggest, most daunting dreams—they do come true.

www.kaitlynlhill.ca
Instagram and TikTok @kaitlyn.l.hill